Women, Kids
&
Huckleberry Wine

Women, Kids & Huckleberry Wine

ANNE CAMERON

HARBOUR PUBLISHING

Harbour Publishing Co. Ltd.
P.O. Box 219
Madeira Park, BC
Canada V0N 2H0

Cover art by Paul Montpellier
Cover design by Alex Baggio, Creative Graphics

The author gratefully acknowledges the assistance of the Canada
Council in the completion of this book.

CANADIAN CATALOGUING IN PUBLICATION DATA

   Cameron, Anne, 1938 –
      Women, kids & huckleberry wine

      ISBN 0-920080-68-5

      I. Title.
   PS8555.A44W6 1988   C813'.54   C88-091383-5
   PR9199.3.C34W6 1988

Printed and bound in Canada

CONTENTS

Nan's Frog   1

Not Playing with a Full Deck   23

Here Kitty, Here Kitty . . .   61

The Turkey Catcher   80

The Common Name for Digitalis is Foxglove   173

Emma Jonstone, the Pie-Faced Church   209

Did'ja Ever Hear of a Goolieguy?   231

"So long as we regard a tree as an obvious thing, naturally and reasonably created for a giraffe to eat, we cannot properly wonder at it. It is when we consider it as a prodigious wave of the living soil sprawling up to the skies for no reason in particular that we take off our hats, to the astonishment of the park-keeper."

G.K. Chesterton
A Defence of Nonsense

"Conrad, in a text unworthy of Conrad, said that he did not write fantastic tales because writing them would be denying that life itself is fantastic. But that is not so. On the contrary, a truly good fantastic story will echo that which escapes explanation in life; it will *prove*, in fact, that life is fantastic. It will point to that which lies beyond our dreams and fears and delights; it will deal with the invisible, with the unspoken; it will not shirk from the uncanny, the absurd, the impossible; in short, it has the courage of total freedom."

Alberto Manguel
Black Water

PREFACE

We are all profoundly influenced and shaped by our geography, and nowhere is this more evident than in British Columbia. Even those souls so unfortunate as to have not been born here, are who they are because of where they lived, and, should they move to the coast, and should they be able to pass the severe tests the coast imposes on those who would seek sanctuary here, they begin to change, to adapt themselves to the climate, to adapt their political outlooks and reactions, to become less and less what they once were, more and more what the coast has insisted we will be.

There are some who say the entire North American continent is formed on a decided tilt, resulting in all the nuts rolling to the west. We have never denied this. It is possibly why we had the foresight to erect the Rocky Mountains; the nuts hit the barrier and ricochet, like pool balls, back to source. And only the stout of heart and stalwart continue on to Eden.

And yet Eden, which influences and shapes her accepted children, is, herself, influenced and altered by their very presence. A town is not streets and sidewalks, buildings and roads, sewer systems and industry; a town is made by the people who live in it, people who are formed by the power of their geography, people who adapt to or alter their surroundings, are adapted or altered by them. What can ever be said of a town without focusing on the people who live in it? Without people, towns sit abandoned, are taken over by mice and bats, are destroyed by weather and die of broken hearts. Deprived of people, towns vanish; denied of a town, people on the coast will build one. Then, if they decide they don't like where the town sits . . . they will gallantly move it several miles in any direction, to a site more pleasing. After all, "take away the people and what have you got but some rocks, trees, beaches, and the ocean."

A.C.

NAN'S FROG

There was nothing particularly propitious about the circumstances of her birth. No stars burning in the heavens, no comets streaking across the skies, no mysterious travellers on exotic animals, and the celebration was, at best, considered minor. She wasn't the first child in the family, certainly not the first grandchild, and she was no better and no worse than any other kid in Bright's Crossing. In fact, for the first year of her life there wasn't much about Nan Carson to set her apart from the rest of the world. Nan loved music, but most babies do, so even that wasn't extraordinary. Nan thought music came from the radio, so she loved the radio, even when it wasn't making music, even when strange voices issued from it, talking about things Nan didn't understand in the slightest.

Nan's mother sang to her, as all mothers sing to their children, and she loved that. Nan's father whistled, and she loved that, but neither of her parents played an instrument, so Nan was more than a year old before she found out music did not originate in the radio. It was a story the entire family treasured, probably because most of them were present at the time. Nan's aunt Dianne made her living playing the piano with a small dance band and giving music lessons from the living room of her small apartment on a street overlooking the bay. On her mother's birthday, Dianne had a party which the entire family attended. Including Nan. All the aunts, uncles, cousins, brothers and sisters arrived first, and were gathered in the living room when Grandpa arrived with Grandma. As Grandma stepped into the apartment, Dianne began to play the piano and everyone began to sing ''Happy Birthday to you, Happy Birthday to you, Happy Birthday

1

dear Mom, Happy Birthday to you.'' The song ended, there was a happy, laughing flurry of kisses, hugs and best wishes, and then it was Grandma spotted Nan, staring round-eyed and shaking with joy, her attention focused expectantly on the piano, the biggest radio Nan had ever seen in her entire life.

Grandma moved quickly, scooped up the ecstatic child, sat down at the piano stool with Nan on her lap, and with one finger plunked out the beginning notes of ''My Bonny Lies Over the Ocean, My Bonny Lies Over the Sea.'' Nan was so delighted that tears slipped down her face. Having exhausted her own repertoire, Grandma handed Nan to Aunt Dianne, who slid onto the stool and positioned Nan carefully and safely on her own blue-jeaned lap. Then Aunt Dianne, showing off a bit in honour of the occasion, ripped into as fine a rendition of honky-tonk as she had ever managed—honky-tonk being Grandma's favourite kind of music and the occasion being, after all, Grandma's birthday. The effect on Nan was electric. She clasped her hands together, pressed them to her chest and gawked in amazement as Aunt Dianne's two strong hands positively demanded music from the radio, which Nan was beginning to suspect was not a radio at all.

When the music stopped, Nan looked trustingly up at Aunt Dianne and waited for her to command the big thing to make more music. Instead, Aunt Dianne took Nan's own hand, her own very little hand, and placed it on the keys. Then she pressed Nan's thumb and the thing made a sound. ''C,'' said Aunt Dianne. Then she pressed the next finger, the pointer, ''D,'' and then the middle one, ''E.'' Nan quivered with excitement and almost disproved the stories about how thoroughly she had been potty- trained. Aunt Dianne repositioned Nan's hand, again pressed her thumb, ''F,'' and so Nan learned that her fingers could make more than one sound come out of the thing.

Of course Aunt Dianne did not spend the entire party trying to teach scales to a one-year-old. A safe chair was brought from the kitchen, the first two books of the *Encyclopaedia Brittanica* were set on the chair, then a cushion and finally Nan, around whose waist was cinched her father's belt, holding her to the back of the chair so she would not tumble to the floor in the throes of joy. Nan pecked at the keys, one finger at a time, making separate and distinct notes, as happy as a clam in deep cool water, for almost an hour. And then her face crumpled, her lip quivered and she began to weep. They lifted her from the chair, fussed over her, asked repeatedly ''What's wrong, dear?'' and other things that really made no sense at all in view of the fact Nan could not yet talk. But Nan could communicate. She went to Aunt Dianne, grabbed her hand and pressed her own very tiny pale palm against her aunt's, large, strong, trained and tanned one. She looked into Aunt Dianne's face with the most pathetic expression imaginable. There was a long pause and then Aunt Dianne said, very gently, ''Nan, I promise you, one day your hand will be as big as mine and you'll be able to play chords.''

Whether or not Nan really understood what Aunt Dianne said was a subject of much friendly discussion among family members for years. But Nan stopped crying, sat on her Grandma's knee and ate an egg salad sandwich, had a piece of birthday cake and some strawberry ice cream, then fell asleep. As soon as the family began to sing around the piano, Nan was wide awake and laughing. She stood to one side, where she could watch everything, and jiggled up and down on her baby legs, hands clasped once again, pressing against her thudding heart. Even if it wasn't much of a dance, the look on her face dampened every eye at the party.

Aunt Dianne got Nan a little toy xylophone that was nowhere near in tune but was at least small enough for a baby to have some chance of playing. And then other little instruments: kazoos, mouth harps, mouth organs, flutophones, recorders. But Nan yearned for the piano. When she was three and a half, Aunt Dianne started regular lessons. There wasn't much real music happening until Nan was almost six, but in the meantime both she and Aunt Dianne enjoyed the lessons and the daily practising visits, Nan's mother enjoyed the break and a bit of time to herself, and everyone in the family started saving up for the piano they planned to buy as soon as there was enough money.

Nan was in every other way quite unremarkable. She had dark blonde hair, like every other kid in the family; blue-grey eyes, like most of the other kids in the family; a sturdy, somewhat long-legged body, again like most of the other kids; but her little round face was undoubtedly her own. Nan's Grandma insisted Nan actually had two faces: the very serious one she wore most of the time and the other one, the one that made you feel happy just looking at her, the face she wore when she smiled. Nan's smiles did not flash. Nan's smiles took so long to happen that sometimes the person at whom they were aimed had already started to look away before the smile was in place. Once in place, the smile was dazzling, so much so that those who had seen it once tried many and various things to see it again. One uncle did coin tricks, another pulled funny faces, some of the cousins stood on their heads or hung upside down from tree branches by their knees, and Nan's brothers developed stand-up comedy routines so polished and hilarious that they spent most of Christmas holidays performing at one concert after another.

The smile flashed its widest and broadest at a time when none of those vying to see it were there to get even so much as a glimpse. Less than ten minutes' bike ride from the back steps, Haslam Creek ran sparkling in the sunlight, and Nan loved to go there, sprawl her body across a rock and listen to the music hidden in the sound of the water. On weekends, when the weather allowed, she would take a lunch with her, sometimes even a book, and spend as long as she liked by the creek. She was lying on her belly on a sun-warmed rock, listening to the creek and watching a column of ants exploring her apple core, when out of the creek, literally out of the blue, a large blur of green and white flipped, and a positively *enormous* frog landed right next to her. Nan stared at the frog. The frog stared at Nan. The frog blinked. Nan began her slow, incredible smile. The frog stared. The frog blinked. The smile grew. The frog sat for long moments in the radiance of Nan's smile and then blinked again, the long, curled-up, sticky tongue unfolded and—zip'plurp—there were fewer ants investigating the apple core. Nan laughed, the tongue unrolled—zip'plurp—and the number of ants was again diminished.

High over the frog's head, a triangular green bug with yellow spots on its back was sunning itself and chewing holes in the alder leaf that was its perch. Nan reached up, plucked the leaf, set it on the rock near the apple core and—zip'plop—the bug was gone from the leaf and the frog was blinking at Nan. She looked around for another and within seconds a June bug had disappeared forever. All afternoon Nan listened to the music from the creek and found bugs for the frog to eat. When Nan left for home, the frog plopped itself back into the water and disappeared.

Nan said nothing to anybody about her frog. She continued to live her life as usual, going to school, practising piano, riding her bike and helping with the dishes. But she began collecting bugs and flies, keeping them in a Mason jar with little holes in the lid. Nobody noticed, or if they did notice, they didn't pay attention; kids are notorious for catching and keeping the most godawful things. Every night, rain or shine, as soon as supper was over, Nan took her jar of bugs to the creek.

At first the frog wasn't regular in her visits. At first, more times than not, Nan had to dump her bugs onto the surface of the water, knowing that some of them would be eaten by fish and others would simply drown. A few, she hoped, would be found by her frog. But after a week or two the frog caught on, and no more would Nan settle herself on the rock than, ker-thunk, the frog would hop from the creek to settle beside her.

You will have some idea of the size of this frog when I tell you that the rock was a good eight feet above the surface of Haslam Creek. The frog that began to make friends with Nan was not one of those fifty-cent-piece-sized green tree-climbers, or even a mandarin-orange-sized ditch-croaker. This frog was a true wonder of a frog and, Nan decided, could only have lived this long and grown this big by being extraordinarily smart. Or lucky. Or both. It also occurred to Nan that to feed a bulk of that size required an incredible number of bugs every day, and the frog had probably often gone to sleep hungry. If, in fact, frogs sleep. So Nan redoubled her efforts to find bugs and began ripping open half-rotted logs and scooping out entire jars full of termites, carpenter ants, woodbugs, pillbugs and other sorts of grubs.

Eventually somebody noticed. It was Mother. "Nan," she said, "what in heaven's name are you doing with a jar full of termites?"

There was the usual pause while Nan's smile appeared and settled into place, then Nan said clearly, "I'm catching them for my frog."

"Oh," said Nan's mother, who had already lived through Jake the Snake, Agnes the Toad, Harry the Rat and any number of kittens, chicks, caterpillars and one puppy who grew into a very quiet Labrador-cross bitch. "A frog, huh?"

"Yes," Nan said, "a great big huge one." Nan's mother knew that anything bigger than the palm of a child's hand is gi- normous, and so for a long time she had no idea how big Nan's frog really was. All spring and summer and most of the autumn, Nan raided termite logs and ants' nests, scooped flies off windowsills and tabletops, and diligently went through the potato patch, catching every potato bug she saw. By this time Nan was becoming an expert; she could spot a bug from an amazing distance.

Mid-autumn and the days shortened. It was getting dark before supper was over and the dishes done. Nan began to worry. Bugs were in shorter supply too. One night Nan's frog did not show up on the rock. Nan waited until she had overstayed and then she went home, expecting to get Told Off for Being Late.

"All right," said her mother sternly, "all right, Nan, what's your excuse? It had better be a good one, you're nearly an hour late." Nan just stood, accepting her Telling Off. "Come on," said her mother, "you know you aren't allowed out after dark, you know all about strange men and weird people and how much I worry. And do I really have to go into the one about how would you like to be lying in a ditch with your head split open and nobody even worrying because everyone is used to you coming in at any old hour at all?"

"My frog," Nan gulped, "she didn't show up tonight." She looked up at her mother with such a sad little face that her mother wished heartily she hadn't been quite so quick to go into the Telling Off.

"Ah, don't cry," her big brother Sam said casually, "it's too cold for a frog to wait around for you to visit her. She's probably found herself a nice patch of mud and she's buried up to her eyes and her nose holes, sound asleep for the winter." Sam knew about Nan's frog, although he had never seen it either.

Not really consoled, Nan allowed herself to be fussed over a bit. She had her bath, got ready for bed, then went to sleep with only a few worried tears. But on the weekend, when there was no sign of the frog, not even in broad daylight, Nan cried for over an hour before she gave up and went home. For weeks she was not herself, although nobody could say for sure who she was. Nan concentrated hard on what Sam had told her, and pinned her hopes on the springtime.

Through the winter she immersed herself in her piano practice and played in public for the first time at the Christmas Concert. Everyone thought she had done very well, and Aunt Dianne swelled with pride and got six new music students because of Nan's performance. "Stellar," they said. "A credit to her family and her music teacher." "Got a future," they said. "Just like Dianne, must run in the family." "Some people," they said, "are like that, just got a natural bent for it," as if all the hours and hours of practice had either never happened at all, or had nothing to do with anything.

After Christmas the days got longer and longer until it was springtime, and it wasn't even officially springtime when Nan heard a little ditch-croaker warming up her throat tubes and rejoicing in the pale sunlight. Nan raced to Haslam Creek and waited expectantly. No frog. Same thing the next afternoon after school, and the one after that. Then on Saturday, as Nan approached the big rock, there was her frog, blinking welcome. Nan was so glad to see her she ran forward and tried to lift her friend. She couldn't, however, so she sat down on the damp rock, patted her lap, and the frog hopped over and sat between Nan's legs, close enough that Nan could encircle her with her scrawny arms and hug her. Nan didn't have any bugs with her, not having really expected to see the frog, but the frog didn't seem to mind. They just visited for a while, then the frog hopped to the side of the rock and launched herself into the water. Nan went home, happy.

She announced the return of her frog at supper and everyone smiled, thinking that one frog looks like another and a little kid would never know the difference.

"You sure it's the same frog?" her big brother George teased gently.

"Oh, yes," Nan said, "I know my frog when I see her, she's the biggest one I ever saw."

"How big?" asked George, still gentle, still teasing.

"Well," said Nan, thinking hard, "I can get my arms around her, but I can't lift her."

Everyone stared.

"How big?" asked Sam.

"Real big," Nan repeated, and made a circle with her arms to show them. Nan had a reputation for being a truthful child—as truthful as a child can be in a world where all the rules have been designed to pester her.

"Would you mind," asked George, "if I went with you tomorrow to see her?"

"Me, too," said Sam.

"Sure," answered Nan, "why not?"

She headed outside to try to find some bugs. The only ones out were the little white fly things in the old stumps, mostly wing and whisker, and Nan was feeling more than a bit pressured, but then George and Sam came out with a couple of shovels, unearthed a few worms which they generously contributed, and the next day all three of them went to Haslam Creek to see Nan's frog.

Again the frog was waiting. When she saw George and Sam she moved closer to the edge of the rock, having already had several years' experience in what happens when boy meets frog. But Sam and George were Nan's brothers, quite the nicest boys Nan knew, and they just stared.

"Hoooo-lee," said George.

"Geeeeee-z," said Sam. "Honest to heaven, Nan, I will never again doubt anything you say. That is the most gi-normous son-of-a-gun of a frog I have ever seen in my life!''

''I told you.'' Nan said, ''Didn't I tell you?''

She spread the worms on the rock and the frog peered at them. ''They helped me,'' Nan explained, ''because there aren't many bugs around right now.'' The frog looked at Sam and George, then blinked and—zip'plurp—one of the worms was gone. The boys hunkered next to Nan and watched as the frog, with what positively had to be her very best manners, dispatched the worms, one at a time, until every one was gone. Then she sat in the warm sun, blinking with satisfaction.

''Never saw anything like that in all my entire life,'' said twelve-year-old George.

''Me neither,'' said ten-year-old Sam.

''Better not tell the others,'' George advised, ''they'd come to chuck rocks at it.''

''*Her*,'' said Nan, ''she's a *her*.''

''How do you know?'' both boys asked. ''He's so big he must be a guy.''

''No,'' Nan said, ''she's a girl. I know. I just do. And whose frog is it, I'd like to know?''

''Easy, easy,'' they said. ''If you say it's a girl, it's a girl, nobody is arguing, it's your frog, for sure.''

Nobody had *dis*believed Nan, but when both Sam and George said how big the frog was, everybody wanted to see it. They all helped collect an entire Mason jar full of worms, grubs and even the occasional early fly, and went down to Haslam Creek to see Nan's frog. Frog heard the tramping of a family-ful of feet and plopped back into the creek, proving right then and there that Nan's estimation of her intelligence had not been very far off the mark. ''Come on, frog,'' Nan said, scattering a few worms on the surface of the creek. The worms disappeared. The frog stayed disappeared too. A few more worms, and a few more, and finally the frog showed herself. But she did not come up on her usual big rock, she appeared on the other side of Haslam Creek, on the sand bar.

''My goodness,'' said Nan's mother.

''Holy spit,'' said Nan's father.

''Where's the camera?'' they all said, and they got several very good pictures of Nan's frog.

It's hard to keep any kind of a secret in a small town, especially a secret you really want to keep, and soon other people knew there was a humungous great lilypad leaper up Haslam Creek. Try as they might, they could not get the frog to show herself. And try as they might, they could not get Nan to go up and coax the frog out of the water. Nan was getting quite heartily sick and tired of all the noise and accompanying ballyhoo; she couldn't even hear the music in the creek for all the, "Hey, where is it," "I can't see anything," "Are you sure there's a big one in there," and Nan was convinced the frog was as fed up with the noise as she was. "Hey, Nan, give you a quarter if you call your frog," they offered, but Nan just glared.

After a while, the nay-sayers and negaspeakers decided it was all a spoof. "No frog in that creek any bigger'n any other," they scoffed. "Just a little kid with a big story," they sneered. "Buncha BeeEss," they mumbled. "I never believed it, not for one minute," they declared. "I only went up to prove it was a lie." They called Nan a liar. Worse, they said her entire family were liars and the pictures were fake. After all, there was nothing there to show any relative size, it was probably just a close-up of an ordinary, baseball-sized frog, and the whole family was paddling upstream with only one paddle and no bailer.

Nan cared what they said and didn't want anybody calling her family a pack of liars, but she wouldn't summon the frog because if the frog didn't trust all these people, then the frog knew best; you don't get to be that big in a vicious world by being stupid.

Some people who neither believed nor disbelieved began to hide in the bushes, hoping to catch sight of Nan's frog. And a few of them were rewarded, enough of them to keep alive the tale of the huge green frog with the white belly and slowly blinking wise eyes. The naysayers would have liked to call these people liars too, but you think twice about that when one of the people calmly insisting the phenomenon exists is the Anglican canon or the Roman Catholic monseigneur.

The polarization grew. And Nan suffered. She had hardly any time at all to herself any more. Even if she didn't *see* anybody up the creek, she could feel their eyes peering at her from the salal and Oregon grape, the fir and cedar, the maple and alder. The staring eyes so distracted her she began to lose the music in the water.

There is always a certain element in any population, fortunately no more than two or three or maybe four percent, who lean toward drastic measures. And Nan's community was no exception. The fanatic fringe started off discussing the possibilities of the monster frog, then arguing, from that to fistfighting and finally to Let's Find Out. They headed up Haslam Creek with several sticks of dynamite and several jugs of hooch, determined, if necessary, to blast every square foot of the creek bed until they either proved the frog existed or proved the frog a figment of over-active imaginations. And they did not care one fat rat's ass how many trout went sky-high in the process; there is no limit to scientific curiosity in the minds and hearts of man.

The fanatic fringe heaved the first stick of dynamite some half a mile below Nan's usual meeting place. There is no telling how many trout of various ages, sizes and species perished when their air sacs exploded with the concussion, no telling how many smaller frogs, toads, lizards, newts, salamanders and other harmless miracles went to their rewards. What is known is that Nan's frog again proved her supreme wit and wisdom. She left the water and headed off through the bush, following the track Nan's little feet had made over a period of time.

Nan, as soon as she heard the exploding dynamite, was up and out of her school desk, bolting down the hall, screaming with fear, pain, rage, sorrow, frustration and redhot fury. Followed by at least half the student body, including her brothers, sisters, cousins, shirt-tail cousins and two teachers with until then impeccable work records.

Halfway to Haslam Creek they encountered the frog bounding toward them. Most of them stopped dead in their tracks and gawked. One of the teachers rubbed his eyes and began to recite the only prayer he knew, ''Good food good meat good God let's eat.'' Nan, George, Sam and the Sister Superior of St. Beatrice's Academy continued down the path. Nan collapsed in a grateful heap, hugging her frog. The frog puffed, panted, swelled its pouch throat and croaked a deep bass ''B'' of relief. George and Sam took off their shirts, laid one on top of the other for supposed strength, and the frog hopped on. They managed to lift her clear of the path, and the triumphant procession turned and headed back toward Nan's house, the bigger boys taking turns carrying the frog on the shirts.

Nan's mother was on her way to the creek too. She had been forced to wait a minute or two after the first explosion until she could do things like move the kettle off the stove, pull the cake from the oven and never mind if it did go flat and get ruined, and then she was free to go and do whatever she could to keep her kid's heart from being broken. When she saw the triumphant procession she turned and headed back, hoping she could think of something to save the cake, now that the frog was saved. Maybe turn it into a pudding or cover it with custard and invent a fancy name for it.

They got the round galvanized washtub, filled it with water from the garden hose and put the frog in the water.

"Great God," said Sister Superior, "there's hardly enough room in there for her."

"Now *that* is a frog," Nan's homeroom teacher announced, awed and quite deeply grateful his prayer had worked.

"I hear the p'lice," said Sam. They all sighed with relief as three RCMP squad cars raced past on their way to Haslam Creek to stop the fanatic dynamiting fringe.

The furor died down, as furors have a habit of doing if you allow them to follow their own courses. The fanatic fringe was duly arrested, arraigned, denied their constitutional rights, found guilty, fined and suitably chastened, and after they had all had a chance to see a galvanized washtub full of blinking frog, they stopped being naysayers and joined the believers.

A creek does not recover overnight from being dynamited, polluted or trashed around, and while the healing was taking place the frog lived in the back yard. At first she seemed happy to just hop in the galvanized washtub from time to time to wet her skin, but when the tub got too small and the frog could only perch atop it like a cork that came out of the neck of a bottle of wine but won't go back in again, they had to find an old bathtub and move that into the yard for her. Nan would have preferred a green one, or even a blue one, but you don't pick and choose at the municipal dump—you take what you find, and it was a pity that what they found was a pink bathtub that clashed terribly with the frog's natural colour scheme. Nan was busy collecting worms and bugs, Sam was busy, George was busy, Sister Superior came over every night with a donation from the student body at the Academy, friends, neighbours, even strangers dropped by with crickets, June bugs, flies, mosquitoes, grasshoppers, mealy-bugs, weevils, maggots and you-name-it, and fed the frog. Who ate. And ate. And ate. And grew. And grew. And grew. And the bigger she grew, the more food she needed just to keep all that bulk breathing in and breathing out, moving here and moving there.

One day they spread a big square of canvas on the lawn, got the frog to hop onto the centre, managed to tie the ends and attach the bundle to the weight hook of the fish scale. Nan's dad and two of her uncles heaved and got the frog off the ground. The scale read sixty-four pounds, which didn't seem reasonable. They tried again and the scale read sixty-eight pounds. That made more sense. They weighed the frog five times, took the average, then estimated the weight of the square of canvas, subtracted that and finally agreed that the frog weighed in at some sixty-six-and-three-quarters pounds.

For a little while people referred to ''our'' frog or ''the Bright's Crossing Frog,'' but the frog didn't believe any of that and neither did most of the people, especially those most centrally involved in the saga. By the time the furor began to diminish, it was generally agreed that the frog was Nan's frog.

When the nights began to lengthen and the days began to cool, Nan remembered that the frog had hibernated in the mud. She wasn't at all sure her parents wanted a heap of mud in the back yard. In fact, she was quite reasonably sure they wouldn't. The frog solved the problem before the problem actually became a Problem; she hopped down the side steps into the basement, through the door left open while Sam cleared out some trash, and installed herself in a cool, dark corner. The boys helped Nan empty the pink bathtub and then, with the help of all the uncles and three-quarters-grown cousins, moved it into the basement and filled it with clear water. Within a few days the basement was wonderfully free of spiders and other forms of cellar life.

Nan's father built a long box and helped her set up a worm farm, not that he particularly relished the thought of a box of worms in the basement, or a frog in the basement for that matter, but he was sick and tired of people digging for worms in his garden all the time. No matter how careful you try to be, if you're only nine or ten or eleven years old, you're apt, sooner or later, to dig the wrong thing. With the worm farm, things were much simplified for everyone and no need for anyone to look or sound like an old grouch because of the peas and swiss chard and, after all, a garden without worms is no sort of garden at all.

The man who owned the pet store in town told Nan he had some little pellets for sale, and he didn't know if the frog would like them but the trout at the trout farm thought they were the best thing since sliced bread. Ha, ha, said Nan dutifully, knowing the man was only trying to make a joke. She spent part of her allowance on the little pellets, took them home and found that the frog liked them quite well. Nan knew she would not forever want to spend her allowance on little grey and brown pellets and so she began scouring the ditches, looking for discarded pop bottles, beer bottles and anything else she might be able to scrounge.

She went to school, did her chores, practised her piano, prowled the ditches and alleys, fed her frog and sometimes felt her life had become a bit busier than she really wanted it to be; but it was a fact, an absolutely undeniable if somewhat painful fact, that had Nan not told anybody else about her frog, none of the rest would have happened; the bozos wouldn't have wrecked the creek with dynamite and the frog wouldn't be pretending to be quite happy, thank you very much, down in the basement, eating pellets made from God alone knows what. So Nan came face to face with personal responsibility, and found it uncomfortable.

Finally spring came. The creek was still one hell of a mess, what with rocks thrown hither and yon and few fish in it and all, but some things just can't be ignored or put aside or altered, and it was, after all, spring, and spring is when the frogs mate, and to do that, they croak a lot, and there is probably nothing on earth any frog can do about any of it, hormones are hormones and biological changes are biological changes, and that is just about that. And Nan's frog began to croak.

"Well there, just shows-ta-go-ya," said Nan's father. "That frog's a *he*, not a *she*."

"No," Nan insisted, "she's a *she*."

"Can't be. Female frogs don't croak. Only males cut loose like that."

"She's not just any old frog," Nan vowed. "She's special. How many others are as big as she is, how many others are as smart as she is, how many others are as friendly and as beautiful? Maybe ordinary old everyday frogs do things like that, maybe for them only the boys croak, but for her, special like she is, things are different."

They decided to humour her. They nodded as if Nan had convinced them, but they knew what they knew and if they didn't know, there was always the *Encyclopaedia Brittanica*. Which clearly said only male frogs are capable of croaking.

Certainly the swarm of ditch-dwellers who invaded the yard were male; they were all croaking. The ones on the driveway were croaking, the ones on the steps were croaking, the ones on the porch were croaking and the ones who had found their way down into the basement were croaking. The ones that got under Nan's father's feet when he headed off in that gloom most workies call morning were croaking. Right up until the time the workboot came down; then the croaking stopped. The workboot skidded and took Nan's dad with it, ass over appetite, down the stairs, lunchkit launching from his hand, flying through the air, coming to rest in the middle of the rosebush. The frogs on which he landed quit croaking, but all the others continued the serenade.

Poems have been written and long, sentimental reminiscences shared about the soul-soothing sound of the spring croakers pulsing their destiny, but that has nothing to do with what happens when a nearly seventy-pound frog begins to swell her throat and cut loose down there in the basement. The glittering galvanized heat ducts trembled and shook, the floor reverberated, the cups clattered on the saucers, the ornaments on top of Nan's lovely new piano jittered and everybody's eyes got rounder and rounder, wider and wider, as the chorus swelled. Suddenly everyone began racing around, finding the wagon, finding the square of canvas, putting on jackets, dragging on rubber boots, quick, my god, before the windows break or the chimney bricks come down on the greenhouse.

The frog was loaded on the wagon and dragged off through the still winter-mushy meadow to the creek. She let out a croak of pleasure that finished the axle on the wagon and, ker-thunk- splat, she was in the water and letting rip with her mating call. Few people slept well that night. By the end of the week they had grown used to it. Only occasionally did anyone have to lunge to grab Aunt Martha's vase before it hit the floor or save Uncle Jeremy's souvenir moustache cup from destruction.

Fisheries got into the act then. Fisheries is always getting into the act, and seldom on the side of the angels or even the fish. "What's this we hear," they asked, "about an oversized frog of yours back in Haslam Creek?"

"Yes," said Nan, and explained.

"But that's terrible," Fisheries cried, "that creek was nearly ruined just one year ago. We've had fish enhancement projects going overtime, students, unemployed and indigents, grant-getters and subsidy-receivers working there at enormous cost to the taxpayers, and we're beginning to get some return on it. One of our trained observers suspects he saw something shadowy in the water, and it might be a minnow, but if that frog is even one-tenth what we hear it is, we'll be back to square one with a half-dead creek on our hands."

"Why?" asked Nan. "It's her creek, she was there first, she didn't set off the dynamite."

"Maybe so," they said, "but do you have any idea how many fry and minnows a twenty-pound frog can eat in one day?" Nan didn't have the heart to tell them her frog weighed about four times twenty pounds. And when they told her how many small fish one twenty-pound frog could devour, Nan didn't really want to have to add that to her already almost insupportable load of responsibility.

Back to the creek she went, with the new wagon and a growing weight in her chest, her little face set and determined. The frog quite willingly gave up life *au naturel* and rode back to the house and the bags of little brown and grey pellets.

"I think," explained Sam, "they put something in them to make the trout addicted."

"Like in the soft cat food," George agreed.

"I don't know," Nan sighed, "but I have to admit, it's all getting quite out of hand. I hardly have time any more to practise my piano, what with going out on my bike to look for junk and trading it in and buying pellets and bringing them home, and then there's the problem of the dirty water."

"Yeah," the boys agreed, "but even Dad has to admit it's as good as chicken manure for the garden."

"Ugh," said Nan, "I might not eat vegetables again for a very long time."

Aunt Dianne solved part of the problem. "Honey," she said, "within every problem is the seed to its own solution. Now take me. My problem was there was nothing else in the world I wanted to do but play the piano. But you have to eat, you have to pay rent, you have to, from time to time, buy new jeans, visit the dentist, stuff like that. Stuff like that takes money. You have to work to get money. I didn't want to work. I did not want to be a concert pianist or a composer or a conductor, all I wanted to do was play the piano. And that was a problem. But it had its own seed of solution hidden in it; I found a way to play the piano and make enough money to have other things in life as well. And what you have is a problem that revolves around that frog.

"I don't know," Aunt Dianne admitted, "if what you have is an allegorical problem or a problematical allegory, but you sure do have whichever. More and more of your time is spent in providing for that frog, and the more you provide, the more she grows, and the more she grows, the more you need to provide, and it could all become quite intolerable. You don't have time to go to the creek and listen to the music, you hardly have time for your practice, and less and less of that wonderful smile gets shown to the world. The world is fascinated by that frog, the sheer untrammelled size of her, the absolutely undeniable grossness of her. But that frog has the seed of the solution."

So everyone chipped in and helped to build the little park in the back yard, with a pool and a warm rock, and people who wanted to see the frog could see her for a minimum cost of twenty-five cents to defray her food expenses. Any newspaper reporter who wanted an interview had to pay ten dollars, plus five dollars for every picture he took. Television camera crews paid even more. Faced with a need to pay for what they sold, the newspapers and TV backed off and looked for free things to sell to people, like accidents, grief, horror, tragedy, pillage, plunder and all those other things.

What Aunt Dianne forgot to tell Nan was that, while it is true that every problem carries the seed of its own solution, it is equally true that every solution carries within itself the seed of yet another problem. Someone had to collect the quarters, supervise the visitors and generally keep the place clean and tidy, which wasn't easy; each visitor contributed something to an almost unbelievable quantity of trash—gum wrappers, popcorn, chocolate bar wrappers, disposable baby diapers and other things too numerous and distasteful to itemize.

Nan Carson began to despair. Despair is no state of existence for a little girl with a slow smile, a love of music and a piano her favourite auntie is teaching her to play. But Nan knew as well as anyone else that nobody except her was going to sign on for a full-time custodian job, and while brothers, sisters, cousins, parents, family, even friends, would help out from time to time, the full-time job was hers. And if you want a thing done properly, you always wind up doing it yourself anyway. People at all hours of the day arriving to gawk. Paying a quarter to stare, then expecting the quarter to entitle them to use the bathroom or the phone or both. Wanting to know if there were hamburgers and hot dogs for sale. Anything else to see besides the giant frog? No zoo? We brought the kids thinking there might be a zoo. Oh, come on, surely you aren't going to charge a quarter for a two- year-old kid. He won't even *remember*. Well I never, how cheap can some people be, I can see two bits for the entire family maybe, but not two bits each!

The small male croakers came from every direction, hopping along the train tracks, leaping along the road allowance, clambering out of ditches and scrabbling over the woodpile. They died in uncounted numbers under the wheels of vehicles, scooped up by kids and confined to large jam jars, crushed underfoot or rudely shoveled aside. The survivors made it to the pool, where they immediately did their absolute damndest to embrace at least some part of Nan's frog. Thimble-sized green ones clung to her toes, golf-ball sized brown ones gripped her legs, tennis-ball sized tan ones clustered like warts all over her back, and one grimly determined white-bellied swain dangled like a forgotten freckle from the corner of her lip.

Then masses and masses of jelly, a bathtub full of masses of jelly with zuh-billions of little black dots in the mass. It was ghastly. Nan was frantic. She loaded them as carefully as she could into the wheelbarrow and went out along the ditches and streams, shovelling egg masses into the water, praying she wasn't doing something injurious to the future frogs, waking at night with horrifying visions of birth-defected, thalidomide-type tadpoles. Load after load, but when she got home, the bathtub was full again and she had it all to do over again and over again and over again, until she was, quite frankly, so goddamn sick and tired of everything that had anything at all to do with frogs that she almost wished . . . no, she couldn't wish that, what was done was done, and it was, after all, up to her to accept her personal responsibility.

"What's the matter, honey?" her mother asked.

"Oh, nothin'," said Nan, as little girls always say when what matters is that everything is just too big and too complicated to explain, especially when half of the problem is you don't even have a vocabulary with which to explain it.

"Come on," her mother said, "why don't you and I have a cup of tea and talk a bit."

"I am too young for tea." Nan said, "Everyone says so."

"Just goes to show," her mother winked, "that everyone doesn't know everything. Come on, you look like a woman with a load on her mind, and there's nothing for shifting that load like a cup of tea." They sat at the table, stirred honey in their tea, and Nan recited her litany of woe.

"My whole life," she said, tears sliding down her face, "seems to be nothing but frog. And yet . . . I really *like* her momma, she's my most and bestest friend, and it isn't *her* fault. She's always nice to me, she does all kinds of things for me she won't do for anyone else and she's always real glad to see me whether I've got bugs or pellets or nothing at all. She is," Nan insisted sturdily, "the most wonderfullest frog in the whole world ever, but she is ruining my life!" Nan began to cry. Not the little snivels and whimpers of childhood or the brief stormy sobs of adolescence, but the full- bodied, grief-wracked weeping of every woman faced with more on her plate than she can possibly handle. "And I don't know what to do, momma. I don't know anybody who ever had a ninety-pound frog to contend with in all history, and there's nobody to ask."

Nan's mother had no idea what to suggest. She poured Nan another cup of tea, honeyed it and stirred it, then handed Nan some toilet paper to wipe her eyes and blow her nose. "We'll figure something out," she said. "I promise you, Nan, we'll figure something out that's best for you and best for your frog, too."

Nan's mother asked for advice. One or two people suggested "Kill the frog." A few said "Ship it to France," which, considering what the French do to frog's legs, was virtually the same thing. But nobody had any good suggestions.

The eggs in the ditch began to hatch. Tadpoles the size of bananas swarmed and splashed, and by the time their tails had been absorbed and their hind legs formed, they wouldn't have fit in a teacup or even a coffee mug. "Oh my *gawd*," Nan wailed, "I just wish I could die, that's all, I just wish I could die. We're going to be up to our hips in frogs by the time autumn comes! And next spring all those enormous baby frogs will start to croak, then they'll lay eggs and . . . oh, momma, I wish I was dead!"

"This," said Nan's mother, "is *not* your fault! It's one thing to assume your personal responsibility, but you have got to learn right here and now that there are limits. You are not responsible for the state of the entire world."

"Give yourself a break," said George, "call the exterminator and spray them."

'Squish 'em with tractors, bulldozers, skidders 'n such," said Sam.

"Do both," said Nan's father.

"You mean nobody is bothered by the thought of what happens to the baby frogs?" Nan's mother marvelled.

"I don't know them," Nan sobbed. "I don't care if they all dry up and blow away, I just wish something would happen that would make all this fuss disappear so that I can be me again."

They put Nan to bed and left the radio next to her head so she could hear the music instead of the croaking of frogs, then they sat around the kitchen table for hours, discussing any number of possible solutions and quite a few impossible ones too.

In the morning when Nan awoke, her frog was gone.

Nan started to shriek. Her nerves were shot and she had no idea what catastrophe might befall next. "Relax," said her mother, "stop that awful noise and listen." Nan, obedient child, shut up. "Your frog is down in the Nanaimo River," Nan's mother said, "and even for a frog that size, there is a lot of room in that river. It might only be a temporary solution, but at least it's some kind of a one, and we're working on the rest, so just eat your scrambled eggs and go to school and don't spend a single minute of today fretting about any of this.''

''Yes, momma,'' said Nan, feeling as if a huge weight was lifting off her chest.

''*And*,'' said her mother, face serious, tone of voice firm and foreboding, ''for the rest of your life, regardless of who, when or why, no matter moon, June, spoon or croon, if anyone ever says the word *baby* to you, Nan, *please,* think *frog*.''

''Yes, momma,'' Nan promised.

When Nan came home from school, her mother told her, ''Everything is fine, just fine, nothing to worry about at all, it's all working out quite wonderfully.'' Every time Nan asked, she was reassured, yes, everything was fine, Fisheries wasn't concerned with the river, just the creek, it was all just fine. On the weekend Nan rode her bike down to the river and called and called and called and scattered some pellets on the water, and after a while she saw her frog. Bigger than ever, with a smile on her face and a fish in her gullet. Nan knew the frog only ate the pellets to be polite and she wouldn't need to buy any more of them, which was fine by her but undoubtedly was very bad news for the man who ran the pet store.

The hundreds, if not thousands, of enormous baby frogs fared as did frogs of every other size. Birds ate them. Boys caught them. They died in more ways than we can even begin to imagine or itemize, and those few who survived made their way down the ditches to the streams, down the streams to the creek, down the creek to the river, and in the river they encountered their own mother who—zip'plop—solved much of the problem in her own quite inhuman, non-human and undoubtedly level-headed way. The few who survived did so because they were very smart, very fast, very crafty and very, very lucky.

Nan went back to life as it ought to be for any little girl who loves music. Her hands grew. Not as fast as her frog had grown, and certainly never as big as her frog grew, but big enough to span an entire octave and still have some stretch left if needed. High days, holidays and Grandma's birthday, Nan sat at the piano and ripped into honky-tonk and ragtime with Aunt Dianne, and at Christmas and Easter concerts she played as if inspired. Not all the time, but regularly, she would take herself down to the river and sit on the bank to listen to the music in the water as it moved to the sea, and smile her incredible smile. Once in a while she would even see her giant frog.

The spring that Nan was thirteen she went down to the river, and after a very, very long wait, a very tired, very old, very slow frog crawled out of the water and made her way on stiff arthritic legs to Nan's side. The frog was still gi-normous, but nowhere near as big as she had been in her prime. Her green was faded, her white had become grey and her skin sagged in folds and creases. The film over her eyes was no longer clear but opaque, and when she blinked it was as if the light in her eyes had gone out, as if her very life was flickering on and off and on and off and on, and Nan knew that very soon the light would go out altogether.

"Oh frog," Nan sighed, stroking the cool back, "I wish a whole buncha stuff coulda been different. I still don't know what we could have done that would have made it all better somehow, but it really isn't fair that you got such a shitkickin' just for being bigger and smarter and luckier than most frogs. There shouldn't be such an uncomfortable place in the world for the special and different, they shouldn't wind up being looked on as freaks and weirdos."

Bo-o-o-o-rk said the frog, which might have meant almost anything at all. She laid her big head on Nan's knee and blinked, and her sides heaved in and out, and Nan kept stroking and talking.

"They say now we should have started a frog-leg farm with your babies, and made a fortune," Nan said, "and I guess maybe they're right. After all, the price of frog's legs being what it is, there's no way we'd have lost money. And in view of the fact almost all of them got wiped out anyway, what with one thing and another and the birds and boys and all . . . ."

Bo-o-o-o-r-k said the frog, and blinked again.

But Nan knew she was just talking for the sake of talking. She didn't want to run a frog-leg farm. She just wanted to play her music, study her music, listen to music, stroke her frog, live her life as fully as possible and be left alone at least some of the time. And then she realized her frog wasn't blinking. Her frog's eyes were closed and her sides weren't heaving in and out.

Nan took her dead frog home with her. Nan had grown so much and the frog had shrunk so much that it wasn't hard at all. She loaded her dead old frog into the newspaper carrier on her bike and pedalled home, feeling a little tiny bit sad, but not very much, because her frog had certainly had a very long, extremely interesting and adventurous life. She dug the grave all by herself, placed her frog on a bed of leaves, threw in a handful of bugs, just for sentiment, then covered her frog with dirt. At spring planting time, her father put the cucumbers in that corner of the garden. They did so well the entire basement was full of jars of pickles, and nobody had any hesitation about eating them either.

When Nan was sixteen her big brother George got married, and two years later, without anything particularly propitious about the circumstances of her birth, no stars burning in the heavens, no comets streaking across the skies, a baby girl arrived. Nan was thrilled to hear the news. She was studying at the Paris Conservatory that year, and had already had standing ovations for her ragtime and honky-tonk, had played with almost every major symphony in the world, surprising the dinner-jacketed audiences with her jazz solos and inspiring critics to write rave reviews about the teen-aged virtuoso. She sent Welcome Baby cards and hand-knit jackets and books for children in several languages, and part of her could hardly wait to get home.

Nan's mother was Grandma now, and Nan's grandma had passed from this world to whatever waits beyond. Aunt Dianne had almost white hair and her fingers were starting to stiffen, but she could still show Nan a thing or two about honky-tonk.

The birthday party for Nan's father had been an overwhelming success, with lots of potato salad, cold turkey, birthday cake and two kinds of ice cream. Nan was sitting on the back porch, drinking huckleberry wine and watching her new niece toddle unsteadily on the lawn. A shirt-tail cousin, with dark blonde hair and big grey-blue eyes in a decidedly round face, came over, leaned her elbow on Nan's knee, supported her head on her grubby hand and stared at Nan for long moments.

"Aunt Nan," she said quietly, "is it true that you had a frog so big it couldn't sit on both your hands at the same time, but hung over the edges?"

"Yes," said Nan, "I had a very big frog for a friend when I was a little girl."

"Aunt Nan, is it true your frog was so gi-mense you couldn't put both arms all the way around it to hug it?"

"Yes," said Nan. "I know it sounds quite extraordinary, but the truth is, it was a most extraordinary frog."

"Is it true," the child persisted, "that everything was just fine and dandy until other people found out about it?"

"Yes," Nan agreed, "everything was hunky dory until the world insisted on involving itself, and after that it went to hell in a handbasket with startling speed."

''Well then,'' the little girl said firmly, ''I'm not gonna tell nobody at all about my salamander!''

''No,'' Nan agreed, ''I'd turn myself inside out if I was you to keep it all to myself. Here,'' she said, handing over a five- dollar bill, ''just in case you need to buy some of those awful grey and brown pellets.''

''Thank you, Aunt Nan,'' the child smiled, and she walked off, stuffing the money into her pants pockets, her lips pressed firmly together, her secret safe for all time.

NOT PLAYING WITH A
FULL DECK

I

Louella Dixon had no more idea of who or what her father was than your average SPCA mutt puppy. She didn't even know if he had dropped out of her life before or after she was born. If she'd ever set eyes on him, she was so young at the time the memory didn't stay with her, and for all the concern or interest he had ever shown, it hadn't stayed with him, either. No birthday cards, no Christmas cards, no sudden surprise as the postie delivered a big chocolate Easter bunny. Zip-all. She knew her mother, and that was more than enough for anybody. Louella's first clear memory of her mother was of a large angry person pulling her by the hair, hauling her head forward, slapping her on both cheeks, yelling and shouting.

Actually, Louella's mother wasn't a large person at all. In fact, she was very short, quite thin, extremely nervous, and smoked two packs of Buckingham cigarettes a day. If Maddy had a hangover or needed a drink or was in a bad mood or not feeling up to snuff, she'd mutter, "Get me my smokes, kid, willya?" and Louella would start looking. If Maddy was half lit or in a rare good mood, or if there was another in the seemingly endless parade of "uncles" staying at the place, she'd smile brightly and chirrup, "See if you can find those wild pigs, will you sweetheart?" and Louella would buzz off looking for the bucking (wild) ham (pig) package.

· Louella wondered sometimes if her father had been one of the here-they-are there-they-go uncles. She kind of hoped so. From what Louella knew of Maddy, any man who had been interested in anything more than a reasonably warm and tidy place to spend Snow Shutdown, any man actually interested in Maddy herself, would have to have been such a dim-witted, low-life, sag-brained scumsucker as to make a person heartily ashamed of any kind of tie at all, especially a blood tie.

Maddy was what they call a logger's slut. Sometimes they call it Bunkhouse Diana. Mostly they just say whore, which they pronounce hoo-er. Usually she worked on a night-to-night basis, but every now and again some homeless choker setter or rigging slinger would ask, laughing, "So how much a week would you charge me if I was to stay awhile," and Maddy would answer, laughing, "As much as I could get away with." He'd laugh again and ask for a ballpark figure, and Maddy, who already knew what kind of a job he had, how much it paid an hour, and what his pogey would be for the time he was out of camp, would gouge for as much as she could get. "Count yourself pretty costly, dontcha?" they'd laugh. "Was I the one askin' you?" she'd answer. "You're the one brought up the subject, it's your idea. I'm just bein' truthful. You know me, I won't coax and I won't flatter, if you don't wanna, doesn't matter." They usually stayed. Shutdown can last from a month to ten weeks, and the cheapest room in the scungiest hotel is three hundred and fifty dollars, bathroom down the hall, no television, no telephone, no radio, and the sound of drunks puking in the hall and fighting in the alley. Or fighting in the hall and puking in the alley. Maddy's place wasn't much, but nobody was keeping you awake all night horking biscuits past the window.

For what Maddy charged, they got to share Maddy's bed, enjoy her favours, and use the house and its facilities. "Leave the kid alone," Maddy said up front. "I catch you bothering her and you'll wish your mother hadda had a girl insteada you." Meals were irregular, usually good, and sometimes excellent. Louella particularly enjoyed Maddy's meatloaf. She'd stand on a chair, helping her mother, hoping the ash from Maddy's cigarette didn't fall into the big bowl along with the two pounds of ground round, three grated onions, four crushed garlic cloves, salt, pepper, four eggs, a can of tomatoes, and a dozen Christies salted crackers flattened into near powder with the big wooden rolling pin. "Get your hands in it," Maddy would growl. "Mix it up good." And if, as often happened, Maddy decided it was "too dam gooey," there would be the fun of crumbling up and mixing in a few slices of bread. "The secret to meatloaf," Maddy would expound didactically, "is make sure you've got at least three times as much 'loaf' as 'meat.' Just like life," she'd add gloomily. That part of it didn't make any sense to Louella until it was far too late to be of any use to her at all.

The meatloaf was delicious hot, with creamed potatoes and canned corn, and just as delicious cold, between two slices of bread, with mustard and horse radish. It was wonderful when you sliced it cold, then fried it with eggs for breakfast, and best of all when you just held it in your hand and nibbled on it, like an apple, with a hint of salt. Sometimes, if money was tight, Maddy added water and a cup of rice, but that wasn't meatloaf, that was Make Do, and easy to get tired of in a hurry.

Most of the uncles stayed until the snow had melted enough for them to go back into camp again, or until the long summer drought ended in a downpour of rain and they headed off first thing in the morning to get the bus out of town. Some of them came back the next time camp was shut down, but most of them liked a bit of variety and moved in with a different hoo-er in a different miserable wart of a town.

Most of them behaved themselves, big men with soft voices who grinned shyly when sober, widely when drunk. Few of them made much noise; they padded around the house in their big gray wool socks, leaving their boots or shoes at the door, invariably ducking their heads as if afraid the doorjambs would be too low. Working with screaming chainsaws, roaring skidders, howling, stuttering, scree-ching, rending, ripping, and crunching machinery seemed to awe them for life, teach them at an early age that, whatever noise they might dream up, it would be mewly alongside the commonest uproar on the logging slope. However gung-ho and rah-rah-rah they might have been when they headed into the bush, wet behind the ears, with their red strap jeans cut off above their boot tops and their new wide galluses brave in the mist, they came out of the bush at the end of their first season, tamed and civilized by the awesome destruction they helped cause.

The few who caused trouble weren't loggers, they were just bunkhouse bozos, easy to spot once you knew what to look for. Noise. Any time there's noise, you've got a bunkhouse bozo. Any time someone in faded jeans and a gray wool Stanfield's underwear shirt starts off a sentence by saying, ''Yeah, well, let me tell you something. . . .'' you know you've got a bigmouth, all blab and bluster, no more use than an egg-sucking dog.

The loggers took Maddy at her word and left the kid alone; the bozos tried to get cute. ''Hey, kid, how'd you like a quarter for a chocolate bar?'' ''Hey, Lou, do me a favour and I'll give you two bucks.'' ''Don't be so hard to get along with, come on, sit on my knee and gimme a kiss, ain't I your uncle?''

Most of the time Louella could get clear of them. A couple of times Maddy arrived with sparks in her eyes and acid on her tongue. Five minutes later, the bozo in question was on the front steps with his gear flung every whichway all over the yard, his suitcase whizzing past his head, Maddy loudly inviting him to shove his head up his ass and roll right out of her life forever. Inevitably, the time came when Maddy wasn't handy. Lou preferred not to think about that. She told Maddy about it, showed her the bruises on her arms, even sat on the sagging sofa with her head on her mother's shoulder, weeping, grateful that for once Maddy kept her mouth shut and, instead of going off like fireworks, just patted gently and said, "It ain't your fault, kid, don't ever think it is. Jesus, eh. Jesus."

Lou knew at an early age that she didn't like her mother. By the time she was thirteen she knew she not only didn't like her mother, she didn't love her, either. And was very clear in her mind about the difference between liking and loving. "You gotta give me credit for a few things," Maddy would maunder when working toward being shitfaced, "I could'a give you away and I didn't. You gotta give me that much. You could'a got stuck in a foster home, see how you'd'a liked that! But even a bitch dog looks after her puppies, I say. Give it up for adoption, they said, there's always people can't have kids of their own, they'd be glad of the chance. What am I, a brood mare or something? Damn near a year outta my life, and what would I have to show for it? Not a bean, cheap bastards! You want a dog from the pound, you wind up paying, but you want a kid, you get it free. Some priorities, I say! Fat-assed do-gooders, willing to pay five hundred dollars for a six-week-old poodle puppy, but screech like billy-be-damned at the thought of giving someone a little something for the morning sickness and labour pains. No, I said, it's my mistake, it's my problem, my kid, and thank you all the same for nothin'. You gotta give me that much. Believe me," she said darkly, "I know about them dam' foster homes. Buncha freaks and perverts made respectable if you ask me."

That's about as much as Lou ever gave Maddy. Especially when she realized she might have been adopted by a doctor or a dentist, and had a real home, with a proper yard and maybe even a bicycle. On the other hand, she might have been adopted by any of those people who didn't allow their kids to play on the mudflats at low tide, or walk on the hot rails of the train track between trains. People who shoved their daughters into pleated skirts and middy tops, put silly little fake sailor hats on their heads, made them wear white gloves and carry stupid little patent leather purses to match their stupid patent leather shoes. People who seemed to start every sentence with Don't get dirty, and who called their kids darling and dear one and my sweetling. If even one of them had been willing to give Maddy so much as a penny an hour for the time spent pregnant and in labour, if even a one had been as willing to invest money in a baby as they were in a flat-faced, asthmatic, constantly shedding Persian cat, life might have been one whole hell of a lot different. But, she consoled herself, different doesn't mean better.

She went to school because it was a good place to go to get away from Maddy and her louts. She learned to read before Christmas, could keep up with the others in arithmetic, and if she cared that she had few friends, nobody knew, especially not Maddy. There were always a few others like herself, kids whose clothes were a bit too worn, a bit too faded, a bit too small, or a bit too tight, kids with tough, wise eyes and smart-cracking mouths, kids who pretended as hard as Lou did that none of it mattered. Kids who decided early on that if the Goody Two Shoes and Susie Creamcheeses wouldn't play, to hell with them, who needed them, and anyway, was it any skin off anybody's nose one way or the other? Who wanted to stand around on the playground keeping clean when you could run, shove, push, yell, screech, holler, and play Ante-Eye-Over and Run Sheep Run.

She didn't have any of what the teachers called extra-curricular interests; there was no money to rent an instrument for band, and even if there were, neither Maddy nor the uncles were going to want to listen to the caterwaul of practise. She would have liked to have learned the piano, but that was about as likely as learning to tightrope-walk over Niagara Falls. Anyway, who cared, not Lou. No more than she cared that she never got invited to pyjama parties or to join the cheerleaders in their ziss-boom-bah bullshit.

Louella started messing around the summer she was thirteen. There was nothing particular about the boy. He was tall, he was muscular and well-built, he had sandy blond hair, blue eyes, and a happy grin, he was sixteen, and he could not believe his luck. Left on his own they might have spent the summer doing nothing more than packing their lunches and walking together to the swimming hole, maybe once in a while holding hands. Left on his own, the biggest moment of June, July, or August might have been a couple of dry kisses under a hawthorne tree. But Louella had a few ideas, too. And some questions. And while any one of the purported uncles might have been more than glad to answer the questions and even demonstrate, Bob was controllable, he was safe, he was less experienced than she was, and Louella had some control.

Which was more than Bob had the first few times they stripped to the skin and lay together on the picnic blanket. "Oh, God," he groaned, eyes welling with tears. "I'm sorry!"

"I'm not," she grinned, feeling safer than ever. And she kissed him, cuddled him, stroked him, and felt like a million bucks because there was nothing the least bit scary about him or about what they were doing.

They went together for almost a year, and then Bob got a job for the summer on his uncle's wheat farm, some place on the prairies Louella had never even heard of before, and she went to the depot with him, and waved goodbye as the bus pulled off, and even answered his letters when he wrote. But she didn't spend the summer waiting for the postie; she was no fool. Rocky was eighteen and had a car and honked at Louella every time he saw her. He'd stop and ask, "Give you a lift, sweetheart," and as long as Bob was in the picture, Louella said, "No, thanks, I've got a steady." Predictably, Rocky would laugh and say, "Hell, you ain't married to him!" or "Hey, just because you're on a diet don't mean you can't at least look at the menu," but she'd just keep smiling and walking and shaking her head, and Rocky would drive off, promising he'd keep trying. And with Bob off doing whatever it was you did with wheat, the day came when Rocky stopped the car, honking, and yelled, "Hey, sweetheart, give you a lift?" and Louella walked to the passenger's door, opened it, got in, grinned, and said, "Hi, can I see the menu now, please."

She wasn't in control with Rocky the way she had been with Bob, and at first that left her feeling scared—not so scared she couldn't have fun, but scared enough to add excitement and an approximation of adventure to their times together. The world expanded because of the four wheels, the gas tank, the twin beams of the headlights, and Louella no longer had to wonder what all the older kids did at the big old dance hall ten miles from town. She was there every Friday and Saturday night, and if Rocky couldn't dance and didn't want to learn, he didn't mind if other boys danced with her. In fact, Rocky would saunter over to someone he knew could dance, grin cockily, and say, "So, you gonna do me a favour? Get out there and dance with my woman, make sure she has a good time, okay?"

She danced and laughed, she felt as if the whole world was moving to music, the cigarette smoke swirling around the bare light bulbs looked like magic mist, the old bare board floor with its thin film of powdered wax was the ballroom, and if Rocky wasn't exactly Prince Charming, she was still whoever she decided she wanted to be, right up until one a.m. when the band began to pack away the guitars, accordions, fiddles, and the saxophone that only got played once in a while. Then she was Louella again, pulling on her coat, hurrying toward the car, Rocky's arm around her waist, his hand hot and possessive on her hip.

The Lakes Road wasn't much more than a dirt track following the river from small body of water to larger; each pond, lake, and wide spot on the river was rimmed with small cabins, just temporary shelters, some of which had been there for fifty years. Nobody could buy the land, but you could buy a twenty-year, fifty-year, or ninety-year lease, so much a year, and at least you could say you owned the cabin you built there. Fishermen, hunters, bird watchers, nature lovers vacationed there, some spent every weekend they could in their cabins. Nobody locked their doors, it was a point of honour. What if someone got hurt and needed a place to shelter overnight; what if someone was lost and had to get warm, grab a bite of food? It was expected whoever had to use the cabin would replace any food eaten, leave the place clean and tidy, and, maybe, if he had any kind of class at all, leave a note with his name and phone number, and a ''thank you.''

Rocky's parents had a cabin, and after the dance he drove up the road, his car radio blaring, one hand on the steering wheel, the other rubbing Louella's thigh. A small, metal, acorn fireplace, some crumpled paper, dry kindling, a piece of seasoned alder or fir, and the place began to warm up in minutes. The sleeping bag spread open on the floor in front of the fireplace, a beer open for Rocky, a soft drink open for Louella, and if she smiled and closed her eyes she could imagine there was something romantic about it, something sweet and special, although even she knew it was all make-believe, like little kids in a sand pile. Only tackier. There's nothing particularly low class about kids in a sand box.

She learned that if she wasn't in open control of the situation, she could manipulate Rocky, make him think it had all been his idea from the start, get him to decide they were going to do things he himself would never have even thought of doing. Drive ninety-two miles to see the Ice Capades. Stay in a cheap motel, spend the next day looking at acres of flower beds, huge pens with strutting peacocks or brilliantly plumaged pheasants from every corner of the world. Back to the motel for an hour or two, then fish and chips at a small cafe smelling of boiling fat, then to a converted church to listen to two american blues musicians. Back to the motel with a half pack of beer, and drive back the next day, each of them content for very different reasons.

Maddy knew Louella was messing around, and Louella knew Maddy knew. What is more, Maddy knew Louella knew that Maddy knew. And both knew nothing was going to be said. As close as they ever got to talking about it was when Maddy left several pamphlets on birth control on Louella's pillow, with a small appointment card on which was written Louella's name, the day and hour of the appointment, and the name of the doctor she was supposed to see.

At first, unreasonably, Louella was angry and insulted. She sat on her bed, overwhelmed with mental muttering, but that didn't last long, and when it was over, she thought about being lucky, unbelievably lucky. She thought about life for her if she were to find herself up-the-stump, thought about everyone saying ''Apples don't fall far from the tree,'' thought about giving her baby up for adoption, thought about trying to keep it, came dangerously close to understanding more about Maddy, and certainly didn't want to do anything like that. She went to the doctor, listened to her explanations, then got herself fitted for a diaphragm. It was annoying, it was messy, it put a decidedly planned and deliberate aspect to the whole groping and heaving session, but once she was past feeling awkward and self-conscious, even when alone in the bathroom with the pale blue plastic case in which the diaphragm was kept, she made herself believe that knowing her rubber armour was in place added a certain degree of spice to the entire evening. She didn't really believe it, but it helped until she got to the point in her life where she wasn't at all concerned with any of it.

When things wound down with Rocky, as Maddy had always known they would, Louella was seventeen, bored with school, fed up with the situation at home, and less enthralled with Maddy than at any other time in her life. Maddy was thirty-eight and getting desperate, she wore more make-up than ever and had decided to frizz her hair into a haystack imitation of an Afro. Louella knew her mother had always had a problem with alcohol, but it was obvious the problem was winning and Maddy was often so sozzled she could do nothing but sit in the sagging stuffed chair and stare at the blank wall with eyes that looked bottomless. She maundered verbally, talking non-stop through meals Louella cooked alone, talking about things, people, and situations Louella did not even try to understand, and more than once Louella found herself strongly resisting the urge to just get up from her chair, lift her plate of supper, and slap it into, onto, and all over her mother's face. Instead, she packed her few things in two small Carnation milk boxes, bought a bus ticket, and left with her few dollars of savings.

Small town kid or not, she knew about the YWCA and how you could get a room there cheaper than anywhere else, providing you were willing to live by their tightassed rules. Louella was willing to pretend to be whatever she had to pretend to be until she had a job and some money saved.

Her first job was about what anybody would have predicted: waitress in a small greasy spoon. It paid the absolute minimum possible, the hours were terrible, the boss a misery, but it was a job, and she could get a big free meal and ten minutes to eat it when the boss was out of the place, taking his deposit to the bank. The cook wasn't going to tell, would even make sure there were a couple of meat patties simmering in the canned gravy so that, as soon as the boss hauled on his coat and picked up the imitation-leather, zipper-closing bag, Louella could begin to make her way toward the kitchen. As the boss went out the front door, the cook started putting food on a plate. Louella had caught him rolling a big flank steak in a piece of tin foil and stuffing it in the inside pocket of his jacket. She had said nothing at all, not to him, not to the other waitresses, certainly not to the boss, and the cook knew how to ensure her silence.

The older waitress got the afternoon shift, the shift that had the best tips, and that left Louella on straight days, with workies dropping in for a coffee, and rooming house pensioners coming in for the Special. Not much in the way of tips. She started at six-thirty and finished at three-thirty, and could hurry back to the Y, grab a quick shower, and head out looking for a proper job.

The stores and offices were closed by the time she got downtown, but that didn't matter to Louella; she had no experience of any kind for those jobs. The restaurants were open and busy, and the bars starting to fill up with thirsty people. Louella figured she had lots of experience with thirsty people, having grown up surrounded by the chronically parched. It took more than two months of searching, but she got herself a job in a nightclub. Not a nice one, not one full of society people in diamonds and tuxedos; the Birdhouse leaned more to bar girls, lower-middle-class husbands out with the boys, and out-oftowners in for conventions of one kind or another.

She worked both jobs for three months, then gave up both of them and started as a hostess in a not-too-tacky club, where the bar girls didn't look like bar girls, and the conventioneers were less apt to guffaw loudly and tip over an entire table of drinks. The bouncers were less obviously bouncers, the police dropped by less often, and if there were drug deals going down at the tables, they at least weren't obvious.

She moved out of the Y, got herself a very small, very cheap place to live, bought herself some decent clothes, got her hair done the way she had seen other women wearing theirs, and went to a manicurist to get her nails properly shaped. She invested in several expensive magazines and practised their tips on proper make-up, discovered for herself that none of the tips worked unless you bought expensive make-up, and quite willingly paid more money than she thought possible to get the very best. Once she had it on, it was invisible, and that, too, told her something she vowed to remember.

All she had to do was smile a lot, speak softly, and show people to their tables. It didn't pay much, but Louella wasn't there for the money. She was watching, getting the education school had never provided. She gladly threw aside Maddy's example and watched how the well-dressed walked, how they held their heads, how they laughed, how they lifted the glass, how they sipped, and she made damned good and sure everyone else who worked in the place liked her. She listened far more than she talked, she took no sides, initiated no debates, expressed no personal opinions, and gave no information about herself at all. Nobody here knew she was the daughter of a logger's hoo-er, and nobody here was going to know.

When she was ready to move on, she had references and letters of recommendations, and better still, she had contacts.

The piano player at her new club had been there since Cartier left St. Malo, but the singers came and the singers went, sometimes for a month, sometimes two, sometimes male, sometimes female. They might arrive with a little leatherette case full of their own arrangements, but after two nights they sang the same songs and sang them the way the piano player knew how to play them. Rumour was the piano player was a silent partner in the club. The other rumour was the piano player was a silent partner in several clubs.

Whether he was or not, the piano player sat on his bench and sipped steadily, never seemed drunk, and played no better and no worse at the end of the night than at the beginning. Some of the singers were something else again, and the worst of them were the perpetually boyish crooners in their out-of-date tuxes who tried to seem as casual and easy-going as Tony Bennett, and managed, instead, to look merely disinterested and sloppy. Louella also noticed that most of the nightclub entertainers had thirsts that rivalled those of the bunkhouse bozos Maddy had been quick to off-load. And she knew that overpowering thirst made most of them about as dependable as a boar coon in springtime.

Louella couldn't play the piano or guitar or any other instrument except two spoons held in one hand and slapped against her knee. Her voice wasn't really any better than anyone else's, except maybe Maddy's, and Maddy's throat was burned to gravel by cheap gin and cheap rye. Louella's sense of rhythm was no better than anybody else's, but her survival skills were honed to razor sharpness, and she had brass. Whatever else, Louella had brass. She had spent so many hours alone, with nothing and nobody for company but the radio, that she knew the words to almost any mouldie-oldie you would care to name or hear. With a smile on her face and steel in her spine, Louella waited, memorising the words of all the standards the piano player preferred, memorising the phrasing, singing along inside her head, practising and auditioning every night while showing strangers to tables, and craftily waiting her chance.

It came, and it came exactly as Louella had known it would. She showed up for work ten minutes early, as always, and the manager was frothing at the mouth. The singer was in his dressing room, half dressed and totally shitfaced, grinning stupidly, legs as floppy as the ears on a much-loved bunny.

''Jesus Christ!'' the boss screamed. ''What do I have to do around here? Gimme a fuckin' break, willya God? Where do I get a replacement at this hour of the goddam night, middle of the week? I'd kill the bum but I'd do time the same as if I'd killed a human bein'.''

''I'll go on,'' Louella said quietly, shoving the leatherbound drink menu at the boss, her tone so reassuring he forgot to ask if she could sing. He didn't even think to ask if she had a proper dress to wear.

She went out in her plain black dress with her little string of fake pearls, moved to the piano, smiled at the squinty-eyed old man seated on the bench, veined and mottled hands moving across the keys. The pie-eyed crooner's list of tunes was on the music stand, the old man grunted and reached out to turn on the mike, and Louella nodded. A brief musical intro and she was singing, not in her head any more, but softly, calmly, and surely.

She wasn't a huge hit, she wasn't an overnight success, there was no angel in the audience with a recording contract in his pocket, it wasn't the start of a big-time career, and nobody held a parade in her honour. The audience didn't even know it was the first time Louella had stood up in public and put voice to the music in her head. The boss and the piano player heaved huge sighs of relief and stood her to a drink. "Helluva fine job," the piano player grunted.

"Thank you," Louella said sincerely.

"I mean it," he added.

It was a hell of a lot better than standing for ten hours a night, six nights a week. She worked an hour on, twenty minutes off, and didn't have to drink any of the free rounds the customers told the waiters to deliver to her. Louella drank soft drinks, but the bartender doctored them to look like long cool gin of some kind, and split the profit with her, seventy-five cents to her, twenty-five to him. She didn't mind—it was better than nothing, and added up at night to almost as much as her wages. After the boss decided he wanted her long-term, she bought a little goldfish bowl and placed it on top of the piano, empty, and it took no time at all for the customers to realize that, if they wove their way over to ask blearily for a request, they might not get to hear it. But if they wrote the request on a scrap of paper and sent it with some money, the waiter would drop both into the goldfish bowl, Louella would smile, lift out the scrap of paper, show it to the piano player, and the request would be sung almost immediately. At the end of the night, she split the money in the goldfish bowl with the old man, fifty-fifty.

For five dollars on sale she got a two-inch-thick, eight-by-eleven book of songs, complete with diagrams of guitar chords, piano arrangement, and all the words to all the verses. And in the window of a pawn shop she saw a little piano-type keyboard, not the full eighty-eight keys, of course, not even forty-four, but twenty-two is still better than none at all. She bought it and she had something she could at least start trying to figure out for herself. It didn't sound like a piano, and she could only use it where there was electricity to plug it in, but it was a start, and all Louella had ever asked of life was the occasional chance at a start of some kind.

Six months after she started singing, the piano player told her she was being taken for a ride. "You could get better money," he said, "and do a lot better for yourself," and he handed her a slip of paper.

"Phone this guy in the morning, tell him I told you to call."

"Will you come with me?" she asked, suddenly very frightened.

"No," he shook his head, laughing, "I sure as hell won't."

"I've never had any other piano player," she twisted the paper nervously between her fingers, wanting desperately to have a better job, but afraid of leaving the old man.

"Do us both a favour," he growled. "Fuck off before you start calling me dad and I start wanting to believe it."

"Yessir," she agreed.

She phoned, had brunch with the voice on the other end of the line, and wound up with an agent and business manager. A month later she was on a plane, booked into a club in Edmonton for six weeks. From there she went to Vancouver. From Vancouver she went to Winnipeg. A month here, two weeks there, six weeks somewhere else, never a headliner, never a big club, never buckets of money, but she saw a lot of country, met a lot of people, and lived far better than she would have if she'd stayed at home, finished high school, and gone to work for the telephone company. She traded in her twenty-two key electric piano keyboard for a forty-four key, and practised with the help of several how-to books.

William Devereaux was a piano player who had once thought of being a singer. He might have managed, except for his unfortunate habit of shouting and yelling when he lost his temper, which happened with predictable unpredictability as soon as he had more than three drinks. There was never a night went by that Sweet William didn't have at least six or seven drinks, and the yelling and roaring, as well as a couple of punches to the adam's apple from people who did not appreciate Sweet William's sweetness, had written finis to a career that had never taken off anyway. But he could play the piano like a son-of-a-bun, provided, of course, someone could keep him halfassed sober until the bar sent the last satisfied customers on their way.

Louella had it out with him the first time he got loose. Their third break he reached for his glass and she knocked it out of his hand, then had him by the front of the shirt, backed against the wall, the bouncer standing there obviously more than willing to back her up. "Not on my time you god damned two-bit lush," she gritted.

"Hey, back off, bitch," he managed.

"Keep the act together until the place closes," she snarled, "or so help me god, you are going to have to cope with a very angry person."

"Easy." He smiled what was usually considered his most charming smile. ''Easy on, old girl, no need for rash moves and harsh words.''

''Coffee,'' she ordered.

The next afternoon he wandered into the lounge and caught Louella at the piano, practising and frowning with dissatisfaction. He sat at the bar, watching, then hauled his chair to the piano, sat beside her, and demonstrated, slowly.

''Try this,'' he said softly. ''Here, your wrist is wrong. You're getting in your own way. See?''

''Thank you,'' she managed a smile.

''Do it slow as you need to,'' he sat back, waiting. She hesitated, then did as he had demonstrated. ''Great,'' he nodded. ''Twenty times slow, then we'll speed'er up a bit.''

A week later they moved into the same room, and for the next year and a half, Louella travelled with him, sharing the cost of meals, minus the price of whatever kind of alcohol he wanted with his lunches and suppers. Sex was not a big issue between them. Louella didn't really care one way or the other, and Bill's thirst was more apt than not to immobilize him. Eventually, he began to find ways to get booze in spite of her babysitting him, and the immobilization moved from where it didn't bother her to where it did. His fingers began to fumble.

She phoned her agent and got herself booked into a place in Toronto. Solo. Sweet William was still asleep when she checked out of the room and took a cab to the airport, and he probably neither knew nor cared that she had photocopied every score and arrangement he had gathered over the years.

She learned enough about playing piano in a year and a half that she could get by accompanying herself. That meant she got a better pay scale. Afternoons, when the bar was closed, Louella would practise for three hours, learning new songs, learning new arrangements to old songs, knowing she would never try anything very unique on stage. What they heard on the hit record was basically what Louella tried to give them. She had no illusions about her job. She wasn't there to break new ground; she was there to be entertaining and invisible, to provide backdrop only, to smile, to sing, to play requests, and to put as much of her money in the bank as she could manage. Any cutting loose she did, she did on her own time.

Year followed year, musical fads came and musical fads went, other people's careers took off like meteors, flared, and faded, and Louella played the clubs. No first-class airline tickets; she travelled by bus and train until she had enough money for her own car, in which she kept all her worldly goods. Men came into her life and were left behind, their faces becoming one face, their bodies becoming one body, and if there was a joke she hadn't heard, she didn't want to know about it.

She took up for a while with a very pretty young man who played guitar, and her interest in him led to an interest in the instrument he played so well. She paid three hundred and fifty dollars for a guitar and took lessons, in secret. When she realized the young man was dividing his time and energy between her and another young man, she phoned her agent, altered her schedule, and drove off out of his life with her guitar packed in her car and took the scenic route, leaving the freeway and following the line which, on the map, looked like a secondary road. She wound up stuck in a mudhole, unable to go either forward or back. She got out of the car, looked at the mess, knew she wasn't going to get out by herself, and swore colourfully. Whether she went back the way she had come, or walked around the mess and headed on foot in the direction she had thought she was going to go, she was in for a long walk. On the other hand, sooner or later, somebody had to come along the road. So she waited.

Three hours later, a mud-smeared crew cab pickup with a huge gas tank in the bed roared along the road and stopped two feet from her rear bumper. A stubble-faced man in dirty work clothes leaned his head out the driver's window and grinned. A filthy baseball cap was squashed on his head, he had a thick, woolen, gray, Stanfield's longjohn shirt pulled on over top of a faded red-and-black checked doeskin flannel shirt. Wide orange galluses thick with mud, a lower lip obviously stuffed with Copenhagen snuff, and eyes so blue they seemed to jump out of his face, he sat in his mess of a truck and grinned at her. Just before she got mad and told him where to go, he spoke. ''Got bogged down, did you?'' he roared over the coughing howl of his pickup engine. ''Real sorry about that!''

He came out of the truck all of a piece, went to the front, played with some kind of cylinder there, then calmly walked forward into the mud, as unconcerned as if it wasn't even there. He hunkered, muttered, fumbled, then went back to his pickup, did something else to the cylinder, got into the pickup, put it in reverse, and backed down the road, hauling Louella's little car out of the mudhole.

''There you go,'' he shouted, grinning. He turned off his pickup, stopped shouting, got out and unhitched the cable, played with the cylinder, and the cable rewound on the front of the truck. He wiped his muddy hands on his muddy pants, turned aside politely, spit out his snoose, hauled a red kerchief from his pocket, wiped his mouth, then turned to smile again.

''I'm real sorry,'' he ducked his head. ''There's a spring under there, I guess. It all happened just this morning. We were hauling out a load of logs and the bottom fell outta the road. One minute she's hard-packed earth, the next there's this funny lurch and -splash-! Truck made it through, but. . . looks like she's been getting worse all day.''

''Oh well,'' she sighed, ''back to the freeway, I suppose.''

''Hang on a minute and we'll have you past the hole and well on your way. We'll just run us a tow cable from the back of the pickup. Then I'll put 'er in fourwheel and we'll bounce around 'er on the mess they laughingly call a road allowance. No problem.''

It was easier said than done, but it was easily enough done. Two hours later, only slightly mud-smeared, she was checking in at the Roadway, being shown to her room, welcomed by the manager, introduced to the staff. Three weeks at top scale, with her own room, two three-quarter sized beds, a TV and bathroom, two free meals a day, and a key to the laundry room, the pool, sauna, and gym.

She unpacked, used her travel-iron to get the creases and wrinkles out of her clothes, then had a good long soak in the tub and a three-hour nap. When she wakened, she phoned for a pot of coffee and started getting ready for work.

Halfway through her second set, Dave walked into the lounge. No redstrap jeans and work boots, no flannel shirt and Stanfield's, no baseball cap, no red hanky, no Copenhagen snoose. Brown slacks, white shirt, tweed sport jacket, and shy grin, he was shown to a table near the piano and sat himself down, smiling. When his drink arrived, he made to pay for it, nodded when the waitress explained it would be put on his tab and he could pay when leaving, then he put his wallet back and sipped his drink almost daintily, watching Louella at the piano. He tapped his thick forefinger against the side of the glass, listening to every word, watching her.

Between sets she went to sit at the table with him, and when he asked if he could buy her a drink, she told him she only drank soft drinks. He would have paid for champagne and thought himself lucky, and the waitress gave Louella a look that said clearer than words that she thought Louella had lost control of a major portion of her brain cells. When the lounge closed, Dave thanked her for a real wonderful time, shook her hand, and headed out to the parking lot with a grin wrapped from ear to ear. Louella watched him as far as the door leading out, then shook herself and moved toward the kitchen to see if the chef had thought to keep something aside for her. The chef had, and she took the loaded plate back to her room, sat on her bed eating supper and watching the late show, almost ready to agree with the opinion expressed in the waitress's look.

II

She slept well and wakened just before noon. Instead of showering and going for something to eat, she ran a brush over her hair, pulled on her swim suit, took her keys and a towel, and headed off in her least comfortable, most presentable robe.

She was alone in the pool room for almost an hour, and swam back and forth lazily, up and down the short tank, carefully keeping her face, eyes, and hair out of the chlorine-stinking water. She soaked in the swirl, then swam again, went back into the swirl and almost fell asleep, but a mom'n'dad entered with three children, one of them not yet old enough for school, the other two committed to being cute. Hey, mom, look, hey dad, see, watch me, you aren't doing it right, what do you know about it smartie, oh yeah, yeah.

Their voices echoed in the cavernous room, their laughter shrilled piercingly, obviously both mom'n'dad had grown immune to the noise. They raced past the ''no running'' sign, skidded on the wet tiles, one of them fell and bruised a knee, began to howl and screech, sitting on the tile hugging his leg, face red, mouth open, eyes squinched shut. Mom'n'dad ignored it all. Louella wished she could. She got out of the swirl, pulled on her robe, grabbed her towel, shoved her feet into her thong sandals, and headed for the door. Mom'n'dad looked at her and both smiled, as if all the adults shared a secret the kids would one day learn. Louella looked at the yowling brat, then looked at dad and shook her head disapprovingly. ''They have rubbers to avoid mistakes like that,'' she snarled. His eyes lidded, he suddenly looked like nothing more nor less than a soft-bodied pale lizard, and he turned his face away, a move which was supposed to insult her more thoroughly than any words. ''Shut up!'' she told the kid as she walked past him. He shut up, glared at her, waited until she went through the exit door, then he started yowling again, but, blessedly, the door closed and silenced his racket.

She had to shower off the chlorine or risk dry and uncomfortable skin rash, then she dressed and went down for something to eat. A mom was sitting at a table with two kids, no sign of dad, but the kids were at least half trained; neither of them was throwing food or pitching tantrums. They just sat eating quietly.

After lunch she got pamphlets from the front desk, and headed off in her car to see the local sights. It gave her some idea of where she was and what the local people were like, what they considered important, what they thought worth preserving or setting aside safe from industrial development.

She was back at her room with plenty of time to check over her clothes, use her little steam iron again, and then she got herself ready for work. It took longer, now, than it once had; her hair could no longer be trusted to do what she wanted it to do, she had to engineer it, mousse it, and blow-dry it into place. The face did not look forty if judged alongside the moms, who all looked, somehow, tired and more used to being cranky than being happy. The lines at either side of Louella's mouth were smile lines, not the grooves of deliberate control; the wrinkles at her outer eye lids were from laughing, not from squinting in an attempt to attain or retain patience. But alongside the television forties, Louella looked forty, and it was no consolation to know that if she had one of the five most skilled make-up artists in the world working on her team, she would look thirty-two.

He arrived even earlier than he had the previous night, and asked if he could buy her dinner. She explained she had a free meal coming to her as part of her contract.

''Could I order my own and eat with you?'' he pressed politely.

''It would be a pleasure,'' she smiled. And again the waitress looked as if she thought Louella was a few bricks short a full load.

She knew she was showing off for him, playing not only the mouldies but also some of her favourites, pulling out the stops and playing the way she did when she was alone and practising in the dim, deserted lounge. She ignored the talking and laughing, the getting up and going to the john or jane, ignored the waitresses moving from table to table, ignored the table of partying townies out to celebrate somebody's retirement. She played for the big quiet man sitting with a drink, listening, watching, and smiling happily.

''You're very good,'' he said softly.

"Competent," she corrected, "but not inspired, not top-drawer, not big time."

"You could be."

"No," she shook her head, smiled honestly. "No, I don't have what it takes to do what has to be done to make it in that league. I didn't start young enough, and when I did start, I wasn't aiming for anything more than what I've got now: a job I enjoy doing."

"Can't ask for much more than that," he agreed. "I got a brother-in-law aimed for the bucks, eh, and he got them. Made sure about his pension plan, his benefits, his medical and dental, his superannuation, the whole nine yards, and got the best he could get. To get them, he took a job that's left him looking like life is a bitch."

"You know what they say," she teased, "life's a bitch and then you're dead."

"Yeah. A long time dead. That's why I figure I'm real lucky. I get to play with the big toys and I don't have to stay in the sandbox to do it—they let me go out and around the corner. Hell," he laughed, "I even get to cross the street on my own!"

"The boss is giving me the look that means he thinks it's time I got back to work," she smiled, and began to rise. "Anything special you'd like to hear?"

"Well," he laughed quietly and she knew he was testing her, daring her, "you wouldn't happen to know the logger's song, would you?"

"Hey," she chortled, "do I look like a townie, or what?"

"You know it?" He was surprised, and it showed.

"Do I know it? Is the Pope Catholic?" and she went to her piano, laughing at more things than she could have found words to explain.

She switched on the mike, did her fanciest intro, then leaned forward, her laughter riding on her words, tinting them with silver and making all the eaters, drinkers, talkers, and laughers pay attention. "I'd like to do a song I haven't done in so long I'd be ashamed to admit it," she said clearly. "If any of you know the words, sing along. And remember what the lady said: if you can't sing good . . . sing loud."

They were shy, but only for as long as it took her to sing the first verse and then, by ones and twos, they joined in, until even the busboy was singing, the celebrants going so far as to stand up, link arms around shoulders, and ruin the very concept of barbershop quartet.

> I see that you're a logger and not just a common bum
> 'Cause nobody but a logger stirs his coffee with his thumb
> My sweetheart was a logger, there's none like him today
> If you poured whiskey on it he would eat a bale of hay.

Her goldfish bowl started filling up, and not just with ones and twos. They didn't want the middle-of-the-road mouldies and goldies, they wanted the low-rent, somebody done somebody wrong songs, they wanted the innocently racist Squaws Along the Yukon, they wanted Iceworms Nest Again, and they wanted to cheer, to yell, to cut loose and have a good time. She was in the mood to help them have a good time, and if she fumbled some of the notes, and faked some of the notes, or even took her hands off the piano because she couldn't find the notes, and instead of playing, stood up and pretended to be the conductor, they clapped and cheered. For her last piece she had one side of the lounge trying to outsing the other side, the piano pounding, the drinks flowing, the owner grinning from ear to ear as the beer slid down thirsty throats and the rye loosened vocal cords. Every one of them would tell at least three friends, and by the weekend he'd be hauling it in hand over fist.

She almost couldn't believe it when Dave again shook hands with her and went to the parking lot, looking like a kid at Christmas. Louella went back to her room alone, had a bath, watched the last of a movie on TV, then went to bed.

She spent a lot of the next day sitting, thinking, wondering all the things anyone ever wonders when life is obviously about to take some kind of a turn.

Friday night he showed up again, they had supper together during her main break, she went back to her piano, and the boss grinned until his face felt as if it was going to split.

> He kissed me when we parted, so hard it broke my jaw
> I couldn't speak to tell him he forgot his mackinaw
> The snow came from the east and the wind came from the west
> At ninety degrees below zero, he buttoned up his vest.

When the lounge closed, Louella invited Dave to her room for a drink. Both of them knew he was going to spend the night.

By then she knew everything about him she wanted to know. His name, his age, his occupation. Dave Riley, fifty-two, owner of a small logging company.

''Gyppo,'' he said, and waited.

''Gypsy life, huh?'' she smiled, and he grinned and knew she was coast, knew gyppo had nothing at all to do with being cheap.

In her room that night she learned that, huge as he was, he was gentle, and if the palms of his hands were calloused from hard work, his touch was light; his face, close-shaved and free of stubble, was weathered almost red, but his lips were gentle. Louella had never compared lovers but if she had, Dave Riley would have wound up in the top two or three. On a scale from one to ten, she gladly gave him a nine point six.

''I gotta go pick up my kids,'' he yawned in the morning. ''You wanna come along?''

''You married?'' she asked carefully.

''Was.'' He looked her straight in the eye. ''My wife died four years ago. Cancer. Helluva thing. Awful way to go.'' He shook his head, still baffled by the awfulness of it all. ''You'd'a liked her,'' he said. ''There was none of this goddam phony will-of-god stuff when she found out. We went to the beach and she raised a stink. Got it all out then and there. And from then on, it was just one son-of-a-bitchin' rotten break after another. Good woman.''

''Who looks after the kids?''

''My mother. Mostly I live in camp, except for snow and fire season. Send 'em money, of course. See 'em as much as I can. You wanna come?''

''No thanks.'' She lay back down on the bed, shaking her head. ''I don't much like kids. Hardly seen any of them since I was one.''

''Okay,'' he nodded and smiled, accepting her honesty. ''Can I see you later?''

''Sure. There's a spare key over there on the dresser. Just in case they keep you playing cowboys and indians until midnight.''

He came into the lounge at eleven-thirty at night, took his regular seat, ordered his regular drink, and sat grinning. When she was finished, he went to her room with her, and it was better than the night before, better than anything she had known. He left at eleven-thirty in the morning to drive two hours to see his kids, and Louella rolled over on her other ear and slept until suppertime.

She changed her routine on Sunday night, took her guitar into the lounge with her and played it, soothing their expectations, doing what little she could to make things easy for herself—after all, it was the Sabbath and, anyway, most of the rowdies and noisies were either broke after two nights of roaring at the moon, or tired and at home, going to bed early to be ready for the early morning ring of the alarm clock.

Dave came in at ten-fifteen, looking tired and preoccupied. Instead of rye, he had a beer, and he had to leave at the ungodly hour of five in the morning, but she was so glad to see him, to snuggle against him, to feel the warm bulk of him, that it didn't annoy her to be wakened in what, for her, was the middle of the night. He pulled on his clothes quickly, kissed her cheek, told her to go back to sleep, and headed off to wherever it was he was staying, to get into his work clothes.

Monday night he showed up to tell her he wasn't going to be able to stay. "I'm kind'a whacked," he confessed sheepishly.

"Small wonder," she drawled, and he blushed.

"You could," she suggested, with an idleness she did not feel, "just go to the room and fall on your ear. After all, you're up early and we're both past the age of being able to burn the candle at both ends."

"Yeah," he winked, "I'm not even sure I've got any wick left in my candle."

"Ask someone who knows," she laughed. "The wick is fine and the wax more than adequate. G'wan, y'old goat, catch up on your rest."

For the rest of her three-week stint he went from work to his Atco hut, changed, had supper with the rest of the crew in the cookhouse, then drove the three-quarters of an hour to the lounge. Sometimes he had a couple of drinks before going to her room and crawling into bed, sometimes he stopped only long enough to say a word or two, and then hit the pit until she came in after work. They had their own private time then, when the lounge was closed and most of the world asleep; they had time to talk softly, to laugh together, to thrill each other physically and sleep soundly, limbs entwined. He learned the position of the furniture and the location of the bathroom so well he could even wake up in the morning, pad in the darkness to the bathroom, turn on the light, get dressed, brush his teeth, turn out the light, walk quietly to the door, and leave without fully waking her.

And then her stint was finished and she was in her car, going somewhere else, feeling as if all the colours were fading from the world. She lectured herself, she gave herself stiff mental kicks in and up the butt, and none of it did any good. She jumped out of her skin when the phone rang, would willingly have talked to him for hours, and if it wasn't him phoning, but the photo shop to say her prints had come, or the local arts council to ask if she would like to attend their monthly meeting and give a talk on music as a form of self-discovery, her disappointment was a physical pang.

She told herself it was the crush she should have had when she was a teenager, it was what she ought to have experienced at the time she was learning to manipulate Rocky. She told herself it was time to smarten up, calm down, and generally sweep her shit together.

And two months after that, to her agent's surprise and dismay, she was living with Dave in a two-bedroom house in a coast town as scungy as the one she'd been born in, working from eight to midnight five nights a week in what passed as the best place in town. Twenty tables, salad bar, good food, and if it was a lot pricier than the Pizza Parlour, the people who went there expected it to be.

They actually didn't see an awful lot of each other. Dave had to be up and off by five in the morning, and obviously couldn't spend every night in the lounge. He was in bed asleep when she drove home; she was sound asleep when he crawled out of bed, but they had supper together every night, and time to talk together before she left for work. And it was so nice, so damned nice, to come home, shower off the stink of other people's cigarettes, then crawl into bed and snuggle up against his burly, fuzzy body, warm and smelling of clean soap and faint salt tang. However tired he was he would grunt, then grin and roll on his side, his powerful arm reaching for her, pulling her tight against him. "Ssssh," she would smile, "go back to sleep," and he would mumble something, then slide back down into that warm, wonderful place. Or blink, nuzzle her ear, and whisper, "Ssssh, yourself, I've got better things to do with my life than sleep."

Three weekends a month were bliss. She would wake up before he did and slip out of bed to make coffee and something special for breakfast, then take it all in to him on a cookie sheet covered with a striped tea towel. They would eat breakfast, grinning openly, flirting with each other, then, for hours, they would stroke and kiss, smile and talk, and only when there was no more need, no more longing, no more energy, only then would he get up, shower, dress, and phone long distance to talk to his kids.

The fourth weekend he headed off right after work on Friday night, to drive down to see the kids. Louella didn't mind admitting she was glad she was working and couldn't possibly take the time off to go with him. ''I guess the only experience I have with teddy bears is the song about their picnic,'' she said, and blew it all off; it was none of her business.

Then the trees were cut and shipped to the mill, and the whole show was moving somewhere else, to some other contract, almost always in some wart of a place so removed from anything remotely resembling a bright light that the kids would have cut the noses off their faces before agreeing to visit, let alone move there. Anyway, it's no life for a kid, following a gypsy logger; they're better off with their grandma and some stability. After all, a kid can't transfer from school to school to school and still keep up a decent grade average.

Never a big contract, never a job that would allow them to think seriously of settling down, buying their own place, none of it actually very different from being on the road going from lounge to lounge, but they were together, and life was smooth, there was time to buy *The Joy of Cooking* and set about practising Maddy's meatloaf, learning that Maddy's recipes weren't even the start of what you could do with two pounds of ground round and some onions, even getting house plants and a little brass ring-a-ding to spray them. Time to get to know a few people, to visit outside the lounge and see more than the few tourist sites featured in the chamber of commerce maps.

She made less money but expanded her repertoire; she began to care about more than merely entertaining the crowd and getting them to buy drinks. She read more newspapers and magazines, and spent less time sleeping away the hours between sets.

''Would it scare you if I told you I loved you?'' he asked.

''Terrify me,'' she admitted. ''I don't want to hear any of that. I don't know what it means. I like you better than I've ever liked anybody in my entire life, and you're the first person I really wanted to live with. The best thing that ever happened to me was getting stuck in a mudhole, but that other stuff is nothing I know anything at all about.''

''Okay,'' he kissed her and stroked her hair, needing no more than whatever she could willingly and openly give.

It might have gone on for years except Dave's mother was found on the bathroom floor, a look of utter surprise on her face, and the world turned itself inside out, then flipped upside down. Louella couldn't understand how a person could know something and still not understand what it really meant. She felt like one of those numb-brained toots who know there is no way to survive a nuclear war and still insist we have to stay ahead of the enemies we aren't even sure we have. Okay, so she'd known Dave hadn't been a young man when he got married, and she had known he'd thought for a while he and his wife might not have kids, and all right, so she knew how old he was and you could figure to add twenty years to that and not be far off how old his mom had been, but none of it came together until that seventy-three-year-old woman dropped dead and the chickens came home to roost.

She went to the funeral with him, you can't find some casual way to slide out from under a thing like that. Not without looking and feeling like the world's prize Poop. But she left home with her brain on Disengage; she never once thought of what it was really going to mean. Besides, even when the other person never once uses the words obligation, responsibility, or duty, you hear them echoing in your own head if you've done something you've never done before in your life and fallen head over heels for the first time.

Dave had sisters, and the sisters looked at Louella with carefully appraising eyes. Louella tried not to look back at them in the same calculating way. She vowed she would be so polite and so amiable and so helpful and so invisible, that they would either approve of her totally or forget about her altogether.

The sister married to the successful brother-in-law who looked as if he thought life was a bitch, waited until after the service before she broached any of the harsh realities. They were back at the old woman's house, serving buffet to the neighbours and friends, and Louella was in the kitchen, refilling platters of sandwiches, when Karen moved to stand beside her, poised like a bird on a branch, ready to take flight.

''I can keep the girls until school lets out,'' she said conspiratorially, ''but after that, well, other arrangements will have to be made. It's bad enough for them that they lost their mother and now their grandmother. I can't really stand to think of them losing cheerleading and band, as well.''

''You'd better talk to Dave about it,'' Louella said.

''Dave?'' The sister looked as if she had never heard his name before in her life.

''Dave,'' Louella said firmly. ''He's their father.''

''But you're their step-mother now!''

''No,'' she turned, shaking her head gently, and not smiling at all, ''I am not now, nor have I ever been, nor do I intend to become in the future, any kind of mother at all. Not mother, not step, not foster, not in-law, nothing.''

''But you and Dave are as good as married!''

''No,'' Louella smiled. ''No, as a matter of fact we're nothing like married at all. That's something else I do not ever intend to be.''

The other sister tried later on, when Louella was busy at the sink washing up the plates, cups, saucers, bowls, and cutlery.

''Karen's got some idea in her head that you can't stand Dave's kids,'' she said forthrightly. ''They do something to tick you off?''

''I don't know them,'' Louella sighed. ''I haven't talked to them as much as I've talked to you, and we've hardly said more than six words.''

''Karen's not very good with kids,'' Alice confided. ''Especially not with her own. For my money, those kids of hers are too much like their dad for anybody to be able to put up with them for long, but as you might have guessed, Al and I don't exactly see eye to eye. I wish,'' she said more cheerily, ''it was him we'd buried today instead of mother. The guy's been more dead than alive most of his life, anyway.''

Louella made one of those sounds that might mean anything from agreement to a new formula for a cure for the common cold, and carefully washed and rinsed a crystal bowl.

''You and Dave getting along okay?''

''Yes.''

''You've been together a while now, haven't you?''

''Yes,'' Louella answered, wondering when it had happened that families had assumed they had the right to ask any kind of question at all, simply because a person happened to be shacked up with one of the relatives.

''So what has he got in mind for the kids?''

''You'll have to talk to Dave about that,'' Louella smiled again, and decided the old lady had looked surprised because she had been allowed to die without first being interrogated.

Even the discontented brother-in-law tried to get in on the inquisition, but Louella sidetracked him by handing him the dish towel and suggesting he dry the cutlery. And when, by sheer reflex, he took the dish towel and gaped at it, she left the kitchen, hoping briefly that he wouldn't cut himself on a sharp knife.

People she didn't know assumed they knew her and gave her their most heartfelt condolences on the death of an old woman she hadn't even met; other people mistook her for one of the sisters and told her she was holding up beautifully. When the mourners and visitors left, finally, and the family began to discuss the old woman's will, Louella excused herself and went for her jacket.

"You okay?" Dave asked, putting his arm around her shoulders.

"I'm fine," she smiled, "but you look like hell."

"I feel like hell," he admitted.

"I'm going to the motel," she said, not looking at him. "Do you think you could take a cab, or maybe get one of the others to drop you off later?"

"Sure," he was puzzled and she knew it, but she didn't really care. "You sure you're all right?"

"Yeah. You just make sure that you're all right, okay?" And she kissed his cheek, then left the tidy little house, got into her car, and drove gratefully to the solitude and comparative quiet of the Blue Skies Motel.

Dave came in before two in the morning. She was sitting up in bed with a box of pretzels and a half pack of beer, watching television and expecting all hell to bust loose. Instead he flopped next to her, hauled off the tab on a beer, and sucked on it gratefully.

"Gillian and Patsy are staying over at Karen's," he said. "It feels weird to think of the house being empty. But not as weird as it would have felt if we'd stayed there tonight. I'm glad you insisted on this place."

"I didn't insist," she countered. "I just said I was staying here. If you'd wanted to stay at the house, you could have. You still could."

"No. Christ, who were all those people?"

"Nobody I know," she grinned.

"That damned Al," Dave yawned, "I never did much care for him, but I never knew why until today. Do you know he's got a goddam scale and everything he eats has to be weighed? That stupid goddam sister of mine actually cooks two different meals, one for him that's measured as if it was gold, and another one for the rest of them. When I found that out," he laughed harshly, "I wanted to ask the tightassed prick if he had another scale in the bathroom to weigh his shit and make sure it's all in the proper proportions."

"Now, now," she teased, "let's not get uppity here, the man is a big success."

"The man is a big lugan," he corrected, finishing his beer and dropping the can on the floor beside the bed. "Oh well, I never much liked that sister, anyway."

Louella somehow managed to assume a solution to everything would just up and present itself with no need for any sweat on her part at all. And she went back to the cluster of houses and trailers at the foot of a denuded, muddy slope, unpacked her suitcases, did a laundry, made supper, dressed herself, and went back to the piano bar to do a few more nights of Carolina Moon.

And then the kids arrived on the bus with some of their gear, and right away the house shrank so small it felt as if everybody was living in everybody else's pockets.

"What the hell . . . ?" she managed, when the cab deposited them and she had to dig in her purse to pay the cabby.

"I *hate* Uncle Al!" one of them shrilled. "And I'm not going back!"

"Me neither," said the other.

"Listen, don't lay it on me," Louella evaded. "Your dad will be home for supper in two and a half hours. You can tell him all about it."

"Where's the bedroom?" the older one glared at her.

"Just down the hallway and to your right, you can't miss it," Louella glared right back. "The bedroom is the one that doesn't have the toilet and bathtub in it."

Thirty seconds later she was hearing how small the room was. "I thought at least there'd be twin beds. Are we supposed to sleep together?"

"Either that or you can take turns sleeping in the bathtub. Probably lots of room up on the roof. I've known people to sleep in old cars, there's a few of them out at the dump. Personally, I prefer a bed, but it takes all kinds to make a world, as the old woman said."

"What are you talking about?"

"Well, that's open to interpretation, too, isn't it?"

Dave looked as pole-axed as she felt when he came home and found them sprawled in the living room watching television. "School's not out yet, is it?" he asked.

"I *hate* Uncle Al!" Gillian wailed. "I just hate him! And Aunt Karen is almost as bad! She believes everything he says and never believes anything anybody tries to say, and I'm not going back, not ever, and if you try to make me, I'll run away, even if the police catch me."

"Easy on there, Sapphire," he drawled. "One crisis at a time, okay? So what happened?"

"Never mind," she snapped, glaring at Louella.

"I don't need the roof to fall on my head to give me a hint," Louella shrugged, and went into the kitchen. She tried hard not to listen, but the sound of wailing and snoffling, arguing, and entire sentences constructed in italics was not easy to ignore.

As it turned out, neither of them liked meatloaf, only one of them would eat creamed potatoes, and she'd committed the sin of using garlic in the salad dressing.

"Don't you have any food to eat?" Patsy asked, peering into the fridge.

"If I'd known you were comin', I'd'a baked a cake," Louella chanted, "but nobody said a word to me about any of it so I was caught, as they say, short. Have a sandwich."

"Sandwich? For supper?"

"Sit down," Dave said firmly, "and eat what's on the table."

"But I don't *like* meatloaf!"

"Tough shit." Patsy watched him carefully for a long moment, then went back to the seat she had vacated, sat down, and for someone who didn't like meatloaf, she did a very good job of packing it away.

They never really talked about it. There wasn't very much to say, anyway. They were, when all was said and done, his kids. Which left Louella with only two choices: get used to it or hit the road. She wasn't sure she could get used to it, but she knew she didn't want to hit the road. Unless she could hit it with Dave, and the chances of that were growing less every day and at best had been about the chance of a fart in a windstorm.

Dave left for work at five in the morning, and the kids were up by eight. Seconds later the godawful noise started issuing from the shiny metal ghetto blasters. Louella grimly stuffed cotton batting into her ears, pulled the pillow over her head, and tried to stay asleep, but even if she managed that, when she got up the kitchen looked as if a horde of ravenous roof rats had invaded the place. Jam on the side of the toaster, margarine smeared on the cutting board, egg shells in the sink, toast crumbs on the countertop and floor, dirty dishes on the table, and the milk carton never put back in the fridge but left in the sunlight coming through the kitchen window. Louella would have breakfast, clean up the kitchen, and the kids would be home for lunch.

"Hey, you might think about tidying up after yourselves, okay?" she suggested. They looked at her with eyes as blank as pale blue marbles, jaws moving, chewing their way through loaves of bread, mountains of lunch meat, kilograms of cheese, truckloads of hothouse tomatoes, entire groves of apple and orange crops. And when they headed off for school again, Louella would, again, clean up the mess in the kitchen.

They left their clothes on the bathroom floor, they left the top off the toothpaste, they never rinsed out the tub or basin, and they seemed to expect clean clothes to appear by magic in their closets and dresser drawers. No matter what Louella said to them, or how pleasantly she said it, they stared at her with those glassy eyes, as tuned out as if they were sitting in front of the TV watching a cartoon they had already seen five hundred times.

"There's something I think we should all talk about," she said at supper. "It has to do with all of us trying to live together in this house."

"Yeah? Something bugging you?" Dave asked.

"Not bugging exactly, but . . . yeah. Yeah, something is bugging me." And she looked around her kitchen, tidy in spite of the business of cooking supper. "This is how the kitchen looks when it hasn't been cleaned up," she said. "Before I leave for work it will look the way I want it to look, the way I'm used to having it look, the way I think it ought to look."

"Okay," he agreed pleasantly. "What are you saying?"

"I'm saying the only time it looks like that is when I do it." She put down her knife and fork, picked up her cup of tea. "This is the third or fourth time I've asked the kids to clean up after themselves, and they don't do it." She told him about the toast crumbs, the jam cooked to the toaster, the sour milk, the soggy mess in the bottom of the sink.

"You heard her," he said firmly. "Clean up your mess."

"We're out of peanut butter," Gillian accused.

"Doesn't anybody around here ever buy any Coke?" Patsy asked.

"Doesn't anybody around here ever pick up their laundry?" Louella countered. "I did laundry two days ago, washed it, put it through the dryer, folded it, and left it on the shelf in the utility room. I put mine away. I put his away. Yours is still there."

Nobody answered. Dave asked could someone please pass him the mashed potatoes and Louella passed them. He said thank you, spooned a mound onto his plate, and asked if someone would please pass him the corn on the cob. Louella passed him the corn on the cob, took the bowl of mashed potatoes, and found a place for the bowl on the table between the pickles and the apple sauce. Dave asked if there were any more pork chops and Louella said yes, there were, in the oven keeping warm, and she moved to get them. ''I've got them,'' he smiled, and went to the oven, got the platter, brought it to the table, and put two pork chops on his plate. ''I don't know what you do to them,'' he told her, ''but they sure are good.'' Gillian took three pork chops, Patsy took two, they reached for the corn on the cob, ignored the mashed potatoes, squabbled over the apple sauce in the bowl, finally put the empty bowl back where it had been, and started chewing their way through their second helping.

''Bathroom's a mess, too,'' Dave said. Louella got just about set to yell at him. She'd scoured everything the day before, dammit. ''I've never seen any kind of mess in our bathroom before,'' he said conversationally, rising from his chair, going to the stove for the tea pot, refilling Louella's cup, then his own, and replacing the tea pot on the stove. ''I don't want to see no more mess,'' he added. ''I try to get my whiskerbits out of the basin, and if I can take the time to make sure there's no ring around the tub, other people can, too.'' Then he looked at Louella and scratched his head. ''You figure they need hearing aids?''

''God, I don't know,'' she sighed. ''It's those blank stares that are starting to drive me around the edge. It's like living with Orphan Annie and her dog Sandy! But maybe you're right, maybe they have eyes like that because they're deaf.''

''Kind of a change, huh?'' He tried to grin, and she thought she just might break down and cry. He wasn't any more at ease with any of this than she was.

''I used to read those articles in the magazines about child abuse.'' She felt her appetite returning, the knot in her stomach easing, with the realization that even their own flesh-and-blood father considered them an alien form of life. ''I'd wonder how anybody could be such a bastard as to chop a kid up with an axe. I mean, they're the hope of the future, right?''

''Right,'' he agreed, his shoulders loosening, his grin taking hold.

''Little bundles of joy, right?''

''Straight from heaven,'' he agreed. ''Fulfillment of your destiny, for chrissakes.''

''You wouldn't happen to have an axe at work, would you?''

''Bring it home with me tomorrow, for sure,'' he promised. ''Single or double-bitted?''

''Double,'' she winked at him, ''there's two of 'em!''

The grisly humour got them over that one; it bridged their feelings of isolation and padded the jaws of the leghold trap closing around them, but it didn't make any difference to either of the girls. They were still putzing around with the dishes when Louella left for work, and when she came home, the kitchen didn't look any better than it had looked in the middle of supper. The plates were stacked in with the platters, the big bowl was perched on top of the smaller one, the pot lids were heaved in willy-nilly with the pots, and the silverware looked as if it needed to be done all over again. She glared at the kitchen as if it was its own fault it looked so goddam much like Maddy's kitchen, but instead of leaping into the breach and doing it all over again, she turned out the light and went to bed, feeling not so much tired as bone weary.

When they finally gave in and stripped their bed, the sheets were so filthy she had to use bleach strong enough to make her eyes sting. The clean sheets stayed folded on the end of the bed, and they seemed content to curl up in a nest of twisted blankets on top of the mattress.

"Gran made our beds," they said sullenly.

"Well, you're going to make it now," she said, and showed them how it was done. They didn't bother trying to learn how to do it, they just stared at her. They left their clean laundry on the shelf until Louella gave up and took it into the bedroom. Then they left it heaped on the dresser tops. "Gran put it away," they protested. "I don't know which is whose," she said sharply, "and you do. Besides which, it won't kill you to put your stuff away." And when they didn't make even the hint of a move toward their room, she yelled, "Do it, damn you!" and they scuffed and muffed and sauntered into their rooms, backs stiff, to open their drawers and scoop clothes inside and ram the drawers shut again, sock cuffs showing, sleeves draped loose and hanging free.

"Were your kids toilet trained before they were ten?" she asked wearily. It was Saturday morning. They ought to have been snuggled in bed, they ought to have been caught up in hot sex, they ought to have been smiling and laughing and enjoying each other, and instead they were sitting up in bed with lukewarm coffee, their door shut, the sounds of argument and loud music destroying any hope of passion.

"Yeah. Why?"

"Listen, this is embarrassing as hell and I wish I didn't have to say anything but . . . dammit, there's limits! They aren't babies. They could do their own damned laundry if they weren't so determined to win this war of passive aggression!"

''Tell me,'' he said, his voice controlled, and she couldn't look at him as she told him.

''They wear the same underwear until, honest to god, instead of even trying to wash it, I throw it out. They're almost full-grown women. There's no excuse for it. I. . .I just can't handle this, Dave. I've never experienced anything like it. I'll do a lot for you, but those two kids sure know where my lines are drawn and how to step over them.''

''Oh fuck,'' he groaned. He got out of bed, pulled on his clothes, walked out of the bedroom, and the next thing she heard was the sound of his pickup driving away from the rented house. Nothing else to do, she got out of bed, took the coffee cups into the kitchen, took one look at the godawful mess, and started to run water into the sink. He came home half an hour later with a brand new laundry basket.

''This is for our clothes,'' he said loudly, ''Lou's and mine. The other is for your clothes. Lou and me will take care of our stuff, you two take care of your own.''

''What?'' Patsy squealed.

''You're kidding!'' Gillian snapped.

''Dead serious,'' Dave said coldly. ''You want to act like pigs and sluts and put filthy underwear out for someone else to have to touch, you go right ahead, only nobody else will touch it. Even a god damned pig will try its best to stay clean,'' he roared, and they both blushed and looked away. ''You two's actin' like goddam assholes.''

''That's right,'' Gillian yelled, ''take her side of it.''

''I never yet hit you,'' Dave said, ''but you are pushing it, lady. Now turn off that goddam racket comin' outta them goddam radios and get into the kitchen and make it look like it did before you two went in there to make breakfast. And if it don't look like it did when we went to bed last night, I'm takin' them radios to the bridge and droppin' them in the river.'' He looked at Lou, a long look that felt like a nice, round, bright orange life saver thrown to her from the deck of a rescue ship.

''Why don't you and me get the hell outta here?'' he said. ''Even Smitty's pancake house oughta seem quiet after this bullshit.''

''And we get to stay home!'' Patsy accused. ''We get to do the work and you two get to go out for breakfast!''

''God damned right!'' he roared, and Patsy backed down, went into the kitchen and began to slop water around on the countertop, ostensibly washing it clean.

Within a week, everything the two girls owned was dirty, they had no clean clothes for school, and they were fighting over who was supposed to do what. "Thank you, God," Louella said loudly, "for making me a barren woman!"

When she left for work the washer was going, the excess suds were spilling up out of the little trap where the detergent was supposed to be poured, and both young ladies were howling and crying, accusing their father of not loving them, dramatically demanding to know why their mother had to die, why their grandma had to die, and what were they supposed to do for the rest of their lives anyway. When Louella came home, the kitchen was clean and tidy and she knew Dave had been the one to do it. She felt sorry for him, but only briefly. They were his goddamned kids, not hers! So what if he worked hard all day. She worked too. And even if she didn't, it wasn't her mess to clean up! If he wanted to do it for them, that was up to him.

She got up in the morning, feeling as if she hadn't had any kind of sleep at all. She showered, dressed, made up the bed, and tidied up the bedroom before finally going to the kitchen for the first cup of coffee. It was a mess. Worse than it had ever been. Her stomach clenched, she felt as if every drop of blood in her body was about to burst through her ears, she had a wild inner vision of herself swinging the broom, smashing every bowl, cup, saucer, plate, window, teen-aged face in the house. Instead she got her jacket, got her car keys, and left. She went to town, had breakfast by herself at the workie's cafe, then walked up one side of the street and down the other, window shopping. She went into the shopping mall and toured every store, shop, and supposed boutique. She had lunch by herself and enjoyed every moment of silence, every bite of her toasted tuna fish sandwich. She walked the beach all afternoon, resolutely ignoring the logged slopes, the eroded hillsides, the exposed rocks, the accusing acres of stumps and sunbrowned slash. Just about the time Dave was due home from work, she went to the liquor store and bought a bottle of dry white wine and a twelve-case of beer, then drove to the Pizza Parlour for a House Special with double cheese and extra pepperoni.

With the wine bottle under her arm, the beer case in one hand and the pizza box in the other, she walked from the front door, through the living room with its overlayer of comic books, abandoned music tapes, and apple cores, to the bedroom. Dave was standing in the hallway, looking back and forth between the living room and the kitchen, his face tired, his eyes like chips of coal. She walked in front of him, winked even though she felt like screaming, and said, ''Hey big fella, the party's in my room,'' and he followed her into the bedroom.

It wasn't an expensive bottle of wine, she didn't have to worry about a corkscrew, she just twisted off the metal cap and handed him the bottle. He swigged from it as if it was a cold beer, even managed a grim smile. She opened the pizza box, he nodded, left the bedroom long enough to go to the kitchen for paper towels, then returned and they sat on the floor, leaning against the bed, eating pizza with their fingers, saying very little to each other.

''Not a bite of it,'' he growled. ''I don't care if they fuckin' starve.''

''I can't live like this much longer,'' she said. ''I'm sorry. I love you like I never loved nobody in my life, and I'd sooner lose both tits than lose you, but I'm god damned if I'll live like this. I know it's not your fault, and I know you don't like it any better than I do, and I know I ought to be rolling up my sleeves like a good little housewife and wading into this mess with a smile of love and determination, but honest to jesus, honey, I'm about to bust one of them little bitches right in the face!''

''I'll help,'' he promised, chewing as if his pizza had bones in it. ''I don't know what'n hell's goin' on. Their mom would'a raised blisters on'em for half what they been pullin' around here. And I bloody well *know* my mom wasn't their upstairs and downstairs maid. Jesus Christ, she was past seventy—she couldn't have catered if she'd'a wanted to!''

''I've read the magazine articles. Even bought a book about it.''

''Anything in there that might be any help?''

''Shit, I didn't understand the half of what they were saying. Words as long as my leg! Repressed anger, feeling of impotency . . . one asshole said it was because they grew up in the shadow of The Bomb.''

''Who didn't? My whole fuckin' life the bomb's been the boogyman. What did they say to do?''

''Wait. They'll outgrow it.''

''Fuck that,'' he sighed. ''I won't live long enough.''

''Hey!'' the voice came from the other side of the door. ''Hey, what's for supper, anyway?''

''Make it,'' he roared. ''Then clean up your god damned mess in the kitchen and in the living room.''

Dead silence. They stayed in the bedroom burping pizza and holding hands, trying to smile at each other, until it was time for Louella to get ready for work. With her luck, she thought, she'd wind up with a room full of singalong wonders who wanted Danny Boy and My Home by the Fraser.

She was dressed for work and almost at the front door when Gillian said something. Louella had no idea at all what it was Gillian said. The words didn't register. What registered was the look on the face, the tone of the voice, the set of the shoulders. Louella swung. She didn't know she was going to swing, she just swung. The open flat of her palm hit Gillian's face and knocked her sideways, stumbling, until she hit against the big nougahyde recliner and fell into it. "And you're another," Louella heard herself say. Then she left, slamming the front door behind her.

When she came home from work, the house was halfway tidy and Dave was sitting in front of the TV with what was left of the twelve-case of beer. He looked at her, then looked back at the TV.

"Guess I'm the villain, eh?" she managed.

"You think it'll do any good bruising her face?" he asked, voice cold as ice.

"Made me feel a whole hell of a lot better," she flared.

"Makes me feel like shit."

"A while ago you were talking of a double-bitted axe."

"That was a joke, dammit!"

"Ha ha, pardon me."

"Christ, it can't be easy for them either, you know."

"Yeah, and when push comes to shove they're *your* kids, right? Anybody's gonna hit 'em, it'll be you, right? Only you won't hit them because you feel too bad. Lost their mom, lost their gran, now they're scared they're gonna lose you, too, right?" He looked at her, mouth gaping. "Well, darling," she gritted, "fuck that. And fuck them. And fuck you, too, I guess. The whole thing gives me a huge pain in my royal canadian ass."

If they had lived any closer to civilization, she would have packed her car and headed off, bugger the lot of them. But no matter how angry you are, you don't load your stuff into a tired car and head off over a hundred and fifty miles of potholes and hairpin turns at one in the morning.

Instead, she ran a bath and sat in it until she knew Dave had gone to bed. Then she got the sleeping bag from the hall closet, spread it on the rug in the living room, crawled in with the sofa cushion for a pillow, and grimly willed herself to go to sleep.

In the morning, of course, he was gone, and both girls were pretending to tip toe around the house. There were great shows of co-operation, much clattering as the morning dishes were done and put away properly. Gillian even took an SOS pad to the table top, then washed off the soap, rinsed the table, rubbed it almost dry with a clean tea towel, and when it had dried in the morning air, she carefully, too carefully, rubbed it with vegetable oil to even out the colour and protect the wood. Louella could cheerfully have strangled them both.

She rolled up the sleeping bag, put it away, changed the sheets on the bed she usually shared with Dave, did their laundry, folded it and put it away, then vacuumed the living room and headed toward the bathroom.

''I'll do it!'' Patsy squealed, pushing past Louella at the door, hastily diving for the beneath-the-basin cupboard, hauling out cleaning cloths, scouring powder—the local charwoman looking for first prize in the international competition.

She had so much help preparing supper she wondered if she'd ever get anything done. There was no grumbling about who ought to set the table and who had done it the night before, no bitching about who had done more dishes than who else, and she could have swum in the amount of tea each and both offered to make for her. Supper was quiet, but pleasant. After supper they nearly fell over each other in their eager attempts to get the dishes started. It all sickened her so much she went into the bedroom to lie down for a while before getting ready for work.

He came into the bedroom in clean jeans and fresh-smelling white tee shirt, sat on the bed next to her, put his huge paw on her backside, and rubbed gently. ''It won't last,'' he warned. ''I give'em about three days and then it'll be back to that bitchin' awfulness.''

''I'll hit'em again,'' she threatened.

''I'll probably yell at you when you do.''

''I'll yell right back,'' she agreed.

''I guess next time it's my turn to sleep in the living room. Seems only fair.''

''Why don't we find a three bedroom?''

''Because they'll start bitching they want one room each and we'll still be stuck with the sleeping bag in front of the TV.''

''Tell'em to eat shit,'' she screamed. ''Dammit four out of five people on the face of the goddam earth don't even have half a bedroom let alone a full one!''

''Easy, easy,'' he sighed. ''Chrissakes, I'm too old for this.''

''I was too old for this before I was twenty,'' she mourned. ''God, if I'd'a wanted kids hanging off me snotting and snivelling I could'a done it before the veins in my legs started to ache. I mean, christ, honey, look at us. We ought to be grandparents, for crying out loud, and instead . . . the romper room playhouse is turning the kitchen into a disaster zone!''

''Gimme a smooch before you go to work, okay?'' he grinned.

''Talk me into it you silvertongued bastard.'' She moved against him, tears burning her eyes. ''Oh, shit, here I go,'' she mumbled. ''It's downright grisly.''

''How come you never did have kids?'' he asked.

''I hate them,'' she answered honestly. ''I have absolutely no use for them. I think they should be hung on meathooks at birth and left there until they turn twenty.''

''Twenty-five,'' he amended.

''It don't matter what you do, you know,'' she consoled him. ''No matter how you raise'em up, permissive parenting or spare not the rod, by the book or by the boot, they hit an age where they stop being people and start acting like assholes. And they're still acting like assholes when they leave home. And they keep on acting like assholes until they're past twenty-five. And then, if you're lucky, maybe one out of ten of them turn into okay people.''

''How'd you learn so much about kids?''

''I was one,'' she sighed, ''and honest to god, until this very minute I didn't really understand a friggin' thing my mother said to me. If she was alive and I knew where she was, I think I'd send her flowers and a card saying, Okay, Maddy, god damn it, I give you that much!'' Then she was crying openly, and he was holding her and saying all those dumb things like there there now, it'll be all right. And from the kitchen there was a crash of breaking glass, two voices raised in mutual accusation, and the loud hideous ungodly awful cacophony from the ghetto blaster.

HERE KITTY, HERE KITTY . . .

Sometimes Louella Dixon wondered where her brain went when it clicked off and she had to function on automatic. There she'd be, normal she thought, doing what had to be done, going to the supermarket for food, bringing it home, putting it away, taking it out again to cook it for supper, heading off to play the piano and sing the mouldy oldies for a few hours, then back home to sleep until it was time to get up and try for square one again, and all of a sudden some little thing would clue her in to the fact part of her head had been on ''hold'' for quite some time. The little thing was lying on the footstool, between the recliner and the TV, staring at her with deep orange eyes.

''What in hell,'' she asked clearly, ''is that, and how'd it get here?''

''It's a kitten,'' Gillian admitted ''It's been here . . . oh, quite a while.''

''What do you mean quite a while?'' Louella demanded. ''How could it have been here quite a while, it hasn't been alive quite a while! What is it, a month old?''

''Two,'' Gillian corrected carefully.

''Two months old,'' Louella stared at the kitten. ''How long's it been here?''

''Oh, a week or so.''

''How come I haven't seen it before now?''

''Usually it's in our bedroom.''

''The bedroom.''

''There's a litter box in there!'' Patsy added hurriedly.

''When was the last time anyone cleaned it?'' and silence dropped on them like a cement overcoat. ''Go clean the litter box,'' Louella sighed, ''and start training that little sucker to go outside. Every time.''

''Okay,'' they nodded eagerly.

''And get it some shots. Phone the vet. Find out what it needs. Get it fixed.''

''Fixed?'' the two of them wailed. ''*Fixed!*''

''Yeah,'' she said stubbornly, ''fixed. You know. If it's a female, get it spayed, if it's a male, get it neutered, but I want to see the certificate that says that damned thing will not suddenly become seven others as ugly as it is.''

''Ah, she's *cute*.''

''Fixed,'' and then the front doorbell was ringing, and since it seemed God had passed a law insisting only Louella could answer the doorbell or clean the toilet bowl, she hurried to get it before the sound sent her brains running out her ears. It was some earnest young man with big gray eyes and a smile he hoped would warm her heart, handing out an information sheet about whales and wolves, trees and watersheds, peregrine falcons and some other damn thing. She took it, nodded, asked him to wait, dropped the information sheet on the coffee table as she hurried to her bedroom to get five bucks from her purse to give to the door-to-door tearjerker. When she got back with the five, Patsy was talking to the young man. Louella supposed it was someone she knew from school, basketball player maybe, from the height of him. ''Thanks a lot,'' she smiled, leaving the door half open because Patsy was standing in the space, waiting for Louella to get lost.

The kitten was meowing and screeching in the kitchen, so she got it a saucer of half'n'half and, when it had lapped it all up, she put it outside in the back yard and introduced it to grass and dirt. Maybe the idea of digging holes and burying crap would occur to it naturally, you never know, instinct is a wonderful thing.

In no time at all, of course, it was howling to get back into the house, climbing up the screen door, hanging by its claws, eyes wide with rage or terror, yowling and squalling and generally making so much noise Louella closed the kitchen door in spite of the heat and left the little christer hanging on the meshing. It got up, it could learn how to get down again. If God intended cats to live in houses she wouldn't have equipped them with fur coats and the selfish instincts of solitary predators.

Patsy came back in the house carrying the kitten, glaring accusingly at Louella. "Don't try to guilt trip me," Louella snapped. "I've got better things to do with my life than babysit a wormy cat."

"Hey, she isn't wormy!"

"You phone the vet yet?" That initiated a fifteen-minute, two-part dramatic recitation on the unnaturalness of surgical sterilization, the thwarting of maternal instinct, the possibility of consequent neuroses, and anyway, wouldn't it be nice to see the miracle of birth.

"You want to see the miracle of birth," Louella replied, "buy a pregnant guppy, keep it in a jam jar full of water, and when the miracle has happened, flush the whole damn family down the toilet." She dialled the vet, made the appointment for the shots, and hung up, disappointed. "Have to wait until it's a bit older," she confessed, and they grinned. "But I want you to know, it will happen. And if kittens happen first, the cat, the kittens, and the box they're living in will all wind up in a sack half full of rocks off the end of the pier."

"You wouldn't," Gillian whispered.

"You just try me," she dared. "All nine lives in one swell foop, so help me God."

Halfway through pot roast and vegetables with mashed potatoes and a lettuce-tomato-green onion-mayonnaise salad, somewhere between a tidy bite of meat and a neat forkload of gravied potato, it happened again. If asked, she would have said she'd been listening to a quiet family conversation. If asked, she could have given no explanation at all. Suddenly Dave was glaring, Patsy was on her feet shrieking, and Gillian was looking at Louella as if whatever it was, it was all Lou's fault.

"It's people like you," Patsy accused, "who are ruining any hope for people like me."

"Horseshit I am," Dave replied. "All I'm doin' is m'job. Don't you start criticising until you've learned how to do a job, got one, and are doin' it."

"There you go again, nothing constructive to say, just criticism and argument and blaming me for everything! Is it my fault *you* decided I should stay in school?"

"Is it *my* fault you can't even go to school, sit on your ass all day, and bring home a half decent report card? Anybody as has been sitting mooning over books for ten or eleven years and can't even for chrissakes pass a test in the language she grew up talkin' isn't much of a candidate for a goddam job! I could see it if you failed french, but for chrissakes you been talking goddam english for how many years and you still can't pass a test!''

"There! See! You don't even know how *old* I am! You don't even know what grade I'm in! And what's more, I know you don't!''

"Gillian, would you pass me the pickled beets, please,'' Louella said quietly, but not so quietly she couldn't be heard.

"Well, and what do *you* think?'' Gillian asked, passing the pickled beets with no more grace or charm than she had to.

"Think about what?'' Louella countered, smiling the most phony smile since before she left home to seek her own way in the world.

"Well, you're the one kicked it all off!''

"Me? Kicked what off?''

"You're the one gave Kevin the money! You're the one put the handout where everyone would be sure to read it!''

"Who's Kevin?'' she gaped, wondering if that was what they'd decided to call the kitten. "What handout?''

"Jesus H. Christ on a blue suede cross,'' Dave groaned. "Now it's m'own wife bringing this environmentalist bullshit into the house.''

"First off, I'm not your wife,'' she corrected, "nor am I ever likely to be; I've seen marriage and believe me it's not working. And if someone doesn't tell me what this entire hoo-rah is all about, I am apt to just jump into it feet first and attack wholesale.''

"*This!*'' Patsy screamed, waving the mimeographed sheet about whales and wolves.

"Oh, that.''

"Is that all? 'Oh that'?'' he frowned, looking as confused as a bulldog pup expected to think. "Why'd you want to buy a thing like that?''

"I didn't actually buy it. This kid came to the door, is all. Collecting for something or other.''

"Something or other? You give money to people and you don't even know what in hell it is they've got their hat in their hand for?''

"Hey, calm down, Davie-boy,'' she smiled coldly, her eyes narrowing dangerously. "Let us not start poking our nose into personal things like where I do or do not spend my own god damned money!''

"You had to, didn't you?'' Gillian glared at Patsy. "Now we're due for a rerun of the sleeping bag on the living room floor routine.''

"That was *your* fault, not mine,'' Patsy defended, "you're the one got her cheeky face slapped.''

"He was a polite young man with a pleasant smile," Louella said to nobody at all in particular, "and politeness is something in damned short supply around this place too much of the time."

"Pleasant smiles," Dave sighed, "also seem to be a thing of the past."

"Perhaps you might set an example." They glared at each other.

"Oh buggersquat," he forced a death's-head grin. "Let's try to go back a bit in this here go round. Maybe we can avoid mass murder."

"Maybe someone could tell me what the fight is all about," Louella said coldly.

"You paid some kid for some kind of paper," Dave said carefully, "and the girls read it and now they think I'm raping the land and squandering the resources and destroying wildlife habitat and besides that I'm a shit."

"And?" she went back to her cooled pot roast.

"And god damn it, all I'm doing is going out there and doing the only goddam job I know how to do the best way I know how to do it so I can bring home enough money to keep this goddam circus fed and in forty dollar a pair designer jeans!"

"Stop yelling at me," she suggested, "because if you don't I'm gonna throw something at you."

"Oh my sainted aunt!" He took a deep breath, heaved himself out of his chair, went to the stove, refilled his tea cup, held the pot out to her with an inquiring look. She nodded, he moved to the table, refilled her tea cup, and started back to the stove.

"See," Patsy said to Gillian, "I told you. Didn't I tell you? Invisible. Both of us. Utterly absolutely and positively invisible," and she got up from the table, grabbed the tea pot from the stove, moved to the table, and poured tea for herself and Gillian. "You never," she complained, "refill our cups. You refill your own, you refill hers, you never refill ours."

"I might think of it," he replied, "if ever I saw *you* doin' anything you wasn't either asked to do or told to do. I bet I haven't once heard anybody say Hey I'm gettin' a glass of juice, anybody else want one . . . never heard anyone say I'm makin' a sandwich, anyone else interested . . . *She* does things for me without making a big deal of it, so I do things for *her*."

"She," Louella murmured, "has a name, and so does her."

They all sat over their plates, eyeing everyone else carefully, a room full of high stakes poker players without a card in sight.

"Logging," Patsy said, "destroys more timber than it ever ships to market."

"Cow cack," he answered inelegantly. "Timber isn't timber unless it's fit for market. What gets left behind is garbage. Glorified firewood."

"Then why don't you cut it up and sell it as firewood?"

"Because I got better things to do with a million dollars worth of equipment and gear than cut goddam firewood for sixty dollars a cord is why! Let those snotnosed young punks with their father's borrowed chainsaw go out and ruin the family pickup truck hauling firewood. I got payments to make and crew to pay, and I hauled my goddam share of cordwood. You're worried about it? You get the financing together, get yourself a saw and a gas tank and a good three ton and a steady market."

"There!" Patsy sounded as satisfied as a dog full of cream cheese. "I knew you'd do that. We start to talk about something that's been proved time and time again, and you turn it into a personal criticism."

"What I'm saying is, if more of these long-haired, wet-eyed, whimpering Marys had ever had to get out there in salal and oregon grape, with rain dripping down the back of their necks, trying to make a dollar or two, what they have to say might make more sense. What I'm saying to you is, don't take their word for it, find out for yourself. If you really think there's enough waste wood left lying around to have a stove wood business . . . do it for chrissakes! I personally do not think it's worth the wear and tear on my aching ass, but if *you* do. . . ."

It was so quiet and peaceful at work that night, Louella almost wished she could do a double shift. Some dishwater blond took several solid thwacks at the side of the cigarette machine, making it spew out a half dozen or more packages of assorted brands, which he happily dropped on his friends' tables as he paraded back to his own. The table waiter objected to the foul treatment given the cigarette machine, and the warrior loudly declared he'd lost enough quarters to enough machines over the years that the goddam company owed him a new car. One word led to another, as always happens; the table waiter decided one more word like goddam or asshole and he'd cut the dishwater blond's beer supply off, leave him dry at his own table. The dishwater blond invited the table waiter outside to settle it all in the parking lot. The bartender pulling draft hollered if anyone was going outside it was going to be him, all six foot four and a half. The dishwater blond said he, by christ, wasn't afraid of any christly freak of a giant. His buddies at the table suggested he shut the hell up before they were all cut off, and the entire argument subsided into whispered hisses and growled insults.

Two tighties tried to use their big sisters' identification to get into the bar, and the table waiter sighed and said, ''sure, dearie, sure,'' whereupon they both got insulted and stalked out, vowing not to return there to spend their money again. The same owl-eyed schoolteacher fell asleep in the same corner, so pickled you could almost see the booze dribbling from the pores of his skin, and the same dentist asked for Tiny Bubbles, then, again, tried to sing along with Louella. He was an absolute pain in the root canal, but was in the lounge from five until at least midnight six nights a week. He paid his tab every night, and the weekly profit from his middle-class addiction went a long way toward paying off the mortgage. Louella vowed she wouldn't take any of her teeth to him.

It all calmed down, but she wasn't fooled. It was the trough between waves, it would all bust out again, sure as there's shit in a goose, and she waited, emotional shoulders hunched, for the next spray to issue from the fan.

The screen door at the back of the house started to look like a torn spiderweb. The kitten had found a way to squirm through the holes she had made and get herself caught between the frame of the screen door and the main door, and would yowl piteously for someone to please open the door and let her in. Patsy turned hurt and reproachful eyes on Louella each time she let the skittering ball of fur into the kitchen, but wisely said none of the things she was expressing with her eyes and mouth.

Gillian's tactics leaned less to the hurt eyes and pouting mouth, and more toward the lofty disregard of anything in the world of which she did not approve, which seemed to be damned close to everything. She became so expert at loftily raised eyebrows that Louella became convinced the little minx was practising in front of the mirror.

But the mess in the kitchen seemed under control, at least part of the time. The laundry problem seemed to be, if not solved, at least on hold, and if the mess behind the bedroom door was festering, Louella didn't care as long as the door remained closed so nobody else had to see it, and as long as there was no slithering green current of foul air wafting down the hallway to poison the house plants.

''Got something to drop on you,'' Dave said quietly, spooning his peach upsidedown cake with whipped cream toward his mouth.

"Drop?" Louella sighed. "Is this news bad?"

"Well, maybe not bad," he hedged, "but different."

"Everything about our life," Gillian said dramatically, "is sure to be different."

"Yeah. Well. What it is," he finished his dessert, lifted his cup and stared into it as if his speech was written on the bottom. "We're two weeks away from finished here. So we got the news today that we've got the subcontract to haul stuff out for the BushGobbler. Three years steady work except for fire and snow of course. Problem is," he raised his eyes, looked at Louella as if he had just heard the last trump, "it ain't exactly close to home. Nor anywhere's else, either."

"Oh God," she sighed heavily, "what are you saying?"

"I'm saying . . . New Stockholm."

"Sweden?" Louella heard her voice hit a new high note, crack, and waver.

"Damn near," he agreed. "Except I think Sweden is a bit more what you might call civilized."

"This sounds better all the time. How do we get there? Safari?"

"Just about. If we go, we'll load our stuff on a barge and send it on ahead. Then we'll go in by float plane."

"Are you talking about living on some kind of glorified raft?" She felt her eyes widen, knew she was jammed, nose flat against the window, against one of the more major decisions in a life which had energetically avoided as many decisions as possible.

"There's a town," he assured her. "Kinda nice, actually, from what I remember of it. Of course I haven't seen it in ten or fifteen years. Some houses, a big trailer park."

"Trailer!" Patsy yipped.

"Trailer!" Gillian echoed.

"Trailer," Dave said firmly. "But they got doublewides now, just like them nice modular homes, pre-fab, whatever they're calling it these days. And there's a cedar mill and a hemlock mill. And, of course, the pulp mill. But the company's run the electricity from the mill power plant to the town site, and there's running water and all like that. Recreation centre. Movie house. It is, however," he looked slowly at each one of them individually, "pretty much what you might call isolated."

"Let me guess," Louella said slowly, "there's no place I could get work, right?"

''Well, there's two or three bars,'' he said, ''but I don't know as what there's a piano or anything much like a lounge. Besides,'' he gulped, his face reddening, ''what I wanted to talk about was this: if I take a crew in there and have to put'em up in the hotel and pay their meals, there's no damn profit in it for me. And I can't ask guys to go to the asshole of nowhere and pay their own keep or they'd be out there working like dogs just for a chance to buy their food and pay their room. And so what I was thinking of was taking in a cook, maybe, and renting half a dozen of those Atco huts. Put'em up on the outskirts of the trailer park, use'em for bunkhouses. Then,'' he jumped from the table, went to the stove, picked up the tea pot, swirled it around, put it down, lifted the lid, peered inside, shook his head, got the kettle instead, went to the sink and filled the kettle, took it back to the stove, put it on a burner, turned the ring, and watched the propane flame as if it was the most interesting thing in the world.

''Ahem,'' she said clearly. He turned, looked at her, eyes dull.

''Then rent one of those singlewides, put a half dozen picnic table things in it, and use the kitchen as a camp set-up and feed the men there.''

''Take in a cook,'' she repeated.

''Yeah. A cook makes good wages.'' He cleared his throat. ''And all she has to do is turn out three meals a day. And, uh, do the, uh, sheets and pillowcases once a week. And, uh, if she, uh, wants to, uh, make a deal with, uh, some of the guys, well, uh, she can put their stuff through the washer, too, and, uh, charge'em so much for doin' it.''

''Take in a cook,'' she said very slowly.

''Yeah. Except,'' he swallowed desperately, ''so far I haven't found anyone who wants to, uh . . . cook.''

''Oh christ,'' she said. ''Oh my sweet suffering lord jesus christ, son of mary and joseph, brother to all humankind, who died to redeem our souls, who suffered to absolve us of sin.'' The girls gaped at her, she felt hot tears scalding from her eyes, slipping down her face. ''Why in the name of all that's holy did I have to decide to take the scenic route? Mother of heaven, couldn't I have stayed on the freeway just that once, avoided the mudholes, not needed to be pulled out by some silvertongueing son of a bun with shoulders as wide as the average pool table is long? New fuckin' Stockholm, if you please. Or if you don't, actually! Atco huts, doublewide trailers, and the only job to keep me from going apeshit seems to be a job boiling potatoes for a bunch of weak-minded buckers and fallers.'' She looked at him, then at the girls, staring round-eyed and absolutely disbelieving across the table at her. ''We're sending our stuff in by barge,'' she sobbed, ''and going in by float plane. Either that, or he goes and I stay and watch the only pink cloud in my life just fucking walk itself away, caulk boots and all. *Fuck it!*'' she shouted, leaving the table and running for the bedroom.

She slammed the bedroom door, flung herself down on the bed, sobbing into her pillow, crying for everything in her life she had never allowed herself to cry for, crying because she had never even known, let alone liked or loved Maddy, crying for too many hours in too many smoky bars singing too many third-rate songs for too many fourth-rate people, crying for the kids she never even wanted to have, for chances discarded rather than lost. When the bed sagged she thought it was Dave come in to try to comfort her, and she refused to lift her face to look at him. A hand touched her shoulder lightly, stroking, patting, but it was Patsy's voice, not Dave's, that said, ''Hey there, it'll work out, it'll be okay, you'll see. You just cry it all out, I'll phone work and tell them you've got the Asian Flu or something, he needs his thick head examined is what he needs, and Gilly's giving it to him right now! The audacity,'' she mourned, ''the numbskulled aw-dass-ity of the man.''

She didn't want to go to New Stockholm. But she knew she was going to go. Every time she thought of *not* going, her stomach knotted into cramps, her throat closed, her hands trembled, and she started to cry. If she had to see him leave without her, she knew they'd have to find room for her in the closest psych ward. She'd spend months sitting in a corner crying into a teddy bear or a stuffed giraffe, swallowing little blue or pink capsules, maybe trying to explain to some pointy-bearded, all-wise, know-nothing jerk why it was every word of every low-rent, down-home, somebody done somebody wrong, fifth-rate, honky-tonk, moaning, gutbucket whiner seemed more true than the words of the Magna Carta.

They packed all the dishes in layers of newspaper, then put a layer of towels in the bottom of a cardboard box, packed a layer of dishes, more towels, more paper-wrapped dishes, more towels, until the box was full, then they folded the flaps, taped them with duct tape, and marked ''Dishes'' on the side of the box. Then pots and pans, kettles, cookie sheets, roasting pans, and there was the kitchen, denuded, empty. The beds were taken apart, stacked near the front door, the bedding packed in boxes, labelled, and piled in the hallway. The living room rug was rolled up, tied with strong cord, the ornaments packed, the pictures carefully wrapped in sweaters and packed in boxes. Within days the house looked like a cluttered campsite, only the TV, the sofa, the recliner, and footstool still in their usual places.

The truck arrived and four brawny men started lugging things from the house, packing them in the truck, moving in pairs back and forth, taking her life, bit by bit, and hiding it under thick brown quilts. The kitten screeched and yowled, spat and clawed inside the travel cage, regularly jumping into the litter box and scattering the crumbled clay, disdaining it, discarding it, throwing it at everyone who dared to disturb her life. Louella wished she could draw herself in, become small enough to get in the cage with the kitten and heave handfuls of kitty litter at Dave, at the movers, at the world at large.

A week and a half in a motel, each of them trying hard to stay out of everyone else's way, and then a taxi to the airport with their suitcases and the again enraged kitten.

They flew roughly northward, following the jagged outline of the coast, leaving behind the usual hints of civilization: paved roads, electric towers, brown-frothed stains at sewage outfalls. Within minutes, the crisscross of brown slash below them thinned and vanished, they flew over miles and miles of deep green, dark green, bright green, light green peppered with tall, thin spires of bleached silver snags. The sea to the left was marked with the white capped wakes of fish boats, sail boats, recreational yachts, tug boats, and large freighters. Twice they saw small islets heaving with the brown bodies of sea lions. The pilot dipped low over a pod of killer whales, the girls craning their necks anxiously, oooh'ing and aaah'ing and starting to smile for the first time in days. Dave reached over, took her hand, squeezed it, and grinned; the loggers sitting in the seats behind them pretended not to see the boss acting sappy. Louella tried to smile, and it must have been at least a good approximation of the real thing, because Dave winked at her, nodded his head approvingly. Louella stared out the window and wondered how long it would take a person to die if the jouncing little glorified kite shook itself apart and the passengers hurtled down through clear nothingness to bash against the miles-deep water heaving beneath them.

Three-quarters of an hour later they were landing in Stockholm Bay, taxiing toward a cement pad sloping from the hardpacked, graveltopped runway, down to and into the water. The floats under the plane had rubber-tired wheels set into them, the plane landed on the waves, spray flooding against the windows, obscuring the view, and then, amazingly quickly, they were bumping onto the cement slope, riding up it and along the crunching, salt-and-pepper crushed rock on the runway.

They climbed out of the plane and looked around, like castaways on a desert island: a small, white-painted shack with several air company decals flaking on the side of it; to the right, a number of houses, everything from small, unpainted, two-room, shake-roofed wonders to three-bedroom, split-level, stucco-sided family dwellings which would have been more at home in a Lazy Acres subdivision near a small town; to the left, the trailer court, with deceptively manicured lawns, brave shows of geraniums and hanging baskets of fuschia and begonia, singlewides, doublewides, and some aluminum-sided pre-fabs. The two sections of town were joined by a two-lane gravel road which passed over an ancient bridge spanning a wide expanse of gravel and rock, over which ran a few inches of water.

Directly behind the town, within feet of the bank of the three-quarters dry creek, the mountain started, climbing upward at an impossible angle, tapering at the top, snuggled against even bigger mountains to the left and to the right, and those mountains were cuddled close to other mountains as far as the human eye dared try to see, from north to south, cutting, in some places, right into the ocean.

"It looks," Patsy laughed, "exactly like what you'd get if you tried to do one of those cut-out silhouette dolls of Queen Victoria!"

"And there's good old QE2," Gillian agreed, pointing at a mountain that was short and stubby compared to the massive grande dames on either side.

"What a god damned mess," Louella decided. The mountain behind New Stockholm was rock and moss, rock dull and gray, moss burned red and brown by the dry season. Black, sooty, jagged windrows sulked miserably where the skidder had pushed slash into a long wall and the crew had tried to burn it. Stark stumps, jackstrawed trunks and limbs, and deep eroded gouges where the rain had turned the scanty layer of topsoil to mud and the mud had slipped wearily down, down, down until it lay piled in a useless heap, not a stone's throw from the creek bank. To the right and to the left, the slopes were a hundred shades and tones of green.

A pot-bellied, half-bald, grinning barrel of a man heaved himself from a dark blue van, waved cheerily, and stomped his way toward the plane. "Hi," he hollered, "guess you're the new people. This here's as close as we got to a taxi," he waved at the blue van, directing the pimply faced teen-aged boy who was lackadaisically lifting their suitcases and boxes from the belly of the plane. From inside, the moans of the kitten issued, and Louella guessed from the sound that the kitten had been screaming and yowling so determinedly for so long that her throat was sore, probably raw and bleeding.

She left everything for the pimply faced youth to contend with and steered her short self to the van, climbed in, and sat, hands folded on her lap, lips pressed tight against a sound she knew would imitate the sound the kitten was making. So this is what you get for thinking you've fallen in love, she lectured herself bitterly. This is what you get for thinking pink clouds and pastel sky are anything but a manifestation of advanced early senility.

The driver was the only one who did any talking in the four-minute trip from landing strip to three-bedroom doublewide trailer. Dave sat loose and easy in the bucket seat in front, Louella sat by herself on one bench seat in the back, Gillian and Patsy sat facing her on the other. The inside of the van smelled of cigarette smoke, chewing gum, garlic, curry, wet sweaters, and old gumrubber boots; the floor was so thick with dried mud there was no hint of where the benches bolted to the flooring. Louella decided she wouldn't even look at anything.

The doublewide was, thank god, unfurnished. One look at the orange-flecked nylon rug in the living room, the striped orange-and-white fibreglass drapes hanging in the picture windows that looked out on nothing, and the blood-red carpet with black fleck through the rest of the house (exactly like the carpet you'd expect to find on the floor of any beer parlour, bar, hard bar, lounge, or pub in the province), and Louella knew if the furniture originally provided with the trailer were still there, she would never enter the glorified sardine can, but would fling herself to the ground, sobbing and begging to be taken to the psych ward.

And not a sign of any furniture. Not a sign of any crates of dishes or mattresses or bedding or anything at all that might have been of any use to them, except for a three-quarter length, gray tweed sofabed waiting tiredly against the wall in one of the bedrooms.

''I'll, uh, go, uh, check on our stuff,' Dave blurted, racing for the door, waving, flagging down the dark blue van before it vanished.

''This isn't real, is it?'' Gillian asked softly.

''How did all that sawdust get in the yard?'' Louella asked stupidly.

''There isn't really any yard,'' Patsy warned, ''I already looked. Those few bits of grass and weed are growing out of that sawdust stuff.

No dirt.''

''You're joking, aren't you?''

''Would I make a joke like that?'' Patsy asked, and she tried to grin. ''Come on, Lou, you could at least give me credit for a better sense of humour than that.''

''I apologize,'' Lou tried to answer Patsy's rapidly failing grin. ''So we're perched on a heap of hog fuel, is that it?''

''Per-effin-zactly,'' Patsy nodded. ''And I have five dollars that says what this used to be was a swamp. Anyone want to make a bet?''

''Not me,'' Louella sighed, heading for the sagging tweed sofabed, and flopping onto it with a prayer that she die within two minutes. ''I think we'll be lucky if the swamp doesn't swallow the hog fuel, the trailer, and us. Don't!'' she blurted. ''Don't let the cat out yet, or the last you'll see of her will be a streak heading away from this place.''

She sat for three-quarters of an hour, legs crossed, hands gripped on her lap, staring at her fingernails. Patsy and Gillian wandered around the tin box, looking at the sprung door frames, the protruding screws, the dangling or sagging cupboard doors, the unusual ripple under the garish carpet, and the pillar, covered with cheap wallboard, which, on curious inspection, turned out to be hollow and empty except for one bare shelf and a dozen imitation brass coat hooks like the disembodied snouts of elephants. There was no squabbling about who ought to have which bedroom, no complaining that only the master bedroom, obviously intended for Dave and Louella, had an en suite, not even any quibbling over who ought to get which elephant trunk coat hook in the hollow pillar that sat in one corner of the living room.

The only one who made any noise at all was the kitten; she lay in her dirt box in her travel cage, hissing and moaning, tail switching, ears laid back, eyes distended. Louella agreed with the kitten. Completely.

She hauled herself from the tweed sofa, went to the pile of stuff placed just inside the door, heaved her suitcase out of the pile, and walked with it down the Death Row corridor to the master bedroom. It was enormous, the entire width of the trailer, not very long, perhaps, but with width like that, who needs length. There were two windows, one at each end, the bed in front of one, and a long arborite counter in front of the other. There was a long, narrow, supposedly walk-in closet with an insubstantial-looking overhead shelf, and there were also several drawers, ill-fitting and almost impossible to open and close, under the arborite-covered counter. The ''en suite bathroom'' contained a tub with a shower nozzle hanging over it, and a toilet so crammed into the room you had to sit sideways on it or you couldn't close the door.

As soon as the girls had a role model, they leaped into some sort of activity, bringing their suitcases and cardboard boxes from the pile, taking them down the hall, turning, without any discussion at all, into different bedrooms, each just about big enough for a bed and a wastepaper basket. Louella went back to the much diminished pile and hauled Dave's soft-sided gym bag and canvas duffel bag down to the bedroom and dropped them next to her own much-travelled suitcase.

Still no sign of furniture. No sign of dishes, pots, pans, kettle, coffee mugs, can opener. Louella went to where a chipped phone sat on the gold-streaked arborite of the bar in a cubicle off the living room, lifted the receiver, and could hardly believe there was a dial tone. She dialled for the operator and waited. Waited. Waited. Finally a tiny, disembodied voice that sounded as if it was coming from the bottom of a dry well identified itself as the operator.

"Is this the Stockholm Bay exchange?" she asked.

"What number are you calling?" the voice evaded.

"The taxi company."

"One moment plee-uz," the voice intoned. There were clicks and burps, blips and sizzles, and then what might well have been the very same voice cleared an invisible throat and gravely intoned, "Stockholm Bay taxi may I help you please?"

Louella didn't know her address, but the driver did. Within minutes he drove up in the same dark blue van, wearing the same forcedly cheerful smile. "Come on," she sighed wearily, "the least we can do is see if there is anywhere in town we can get some groceries. And a can opener."

Four and a half minutes later they were in the store. The Store. Shelves of canned goods, shelves of dehydrated goods, shelves of toothpaste and cleaning fluid. One wall was commercial freezers, waist high, almost empty except for packages of bacon, wieners, sausage, and very tired-looking pork chops. There were two frozen chickens, looking so puckered and withered Louella decided they had been frozen by the Ice Age and kept in the store until a space could be found for them in the National Museum of Civilization. From sheer bloody-mindedness, and for no reason other than to thwart the anthropologists, archaeologists, and sociologists, she bought both relics.

She bought a cardboard box full of potatoes, little white tendrils issuing from the eyes. She bought beets so wrinkle-skinned they looked like shrunken heads from some Amazon village. A can opener. A couple of bread tins. Two packages of frozen bread dough, pre-formed into loaves. She bought a black, cast-iron frying pan, she bought a case of tomato juice. She bought all six two-pound packs of ground round, the entire dozen assorted plastic packaged anonymous lunch meats, almost a yard and a half of garlic sausage, and both badly bruised tomatoes. She refused to consider what the sum total meant in terms of any vague concept of budget.

Another four-minute ride, another three dollar taxi bill, and they were back at the carpeted coffin. No sign of beds or mattresses, no sign of dressers or plates, no sign of forks or toothbrushes, but she had oven cleaner and scouring pads, she had TuffWipe synthetic wash cloths, and with three of them grumbling, muttering, snarling, and bitching, they got the stove and oven cleaned, even got the layer of gray grunge off the stainless steel sinks in the kitchen—if you dared to think of it as a kitchen, a brave hollow square of too small, too short, too dinky chipboard cabinets with the hinges already coming loose, several screws protruding graphically. And installed in this planned obsolescence, a gleaming new huge dishwasher.

"If someone will just scrub those potatoes, I'll start trying to figure out something to do with these pork chops."

"What are those white wormy things?"

"Sprouts. If they'd been planted they'd have grown into better potatoes than these are."

"You mean they're kind of like a vegetable abortion?"

"You've got it, kiddo. But don't tell anyone or we'll be cleaning barf off the floor."

"God this place is awful."

"Gross."

"Disgusting."

"Unbelievable."

"Listen, you two," she tried to laugh, "don't knock it. It ain't much, but, as the man said, it's all there is."

"What man."

"That was a joke, sweetheart. Or used to be."

"Oh, God, how can people *live* like this?"

"Most people don't have any choice," she said idly, busy with the faded pork chops, the bacon, and some tired garlic.

"Lou?" Patsy asked tentatively.

"Yeah."

"How come you know so much about . . . this place? This kind of place . . ."

"It isn't much below where I grew up," she answered, her voice matter-of-fact, her smile pleasant. "We had a few more buildings, a lot more people, but believe me, that was no improvement." She slid the pork chops and bacon into the oven and turned on the electric element, swearing wearily as she picked up a slight but absolutely unpleasant shock from the oven dial on the stove.

"Was your dad a logger?" Patsy probed.

"God knows what he was. Or who, for that matter. Those potatoes should go in the oven as soon as they're ready, okay?"

"How many?"

"Oh, shit, do 'em all. Someone'll eat them, I hope!"

"What do I do with this bread guck?"

"Slap some grease of some kind on those tin pans, put a loaf of guck in each pan, set the pans over here, shove the rest into the freezer. And thanks, Gilly. Who knows, we might even get the damn stuff cooked tonight!" She looked around, suddenly more tired than if she'd been working for hours. "Holy fuck," she breathed. "If there was a shrink in this town I'd be parked on his doorstep with all my Freudian slips exposed."

"Just the hem of them," Patsy murmured. "Maybe one shoulder strap. But not the whole thing, surely to god you got more class than that, eh?" Louella stared at her and started to chortle. Patsy flashed a shy, pleased grin.

"Way to go, kid," Louella approved. "Way to be."

Dave walked in alone long after dark, looking as bewildered as a bull who just blundered into a wasps' nest. Big as he was, burly as he was, powerful as he was, he looked helpless.

"Lou . . . kids . . . listen, I'm sorry, but . . ."

"Never mind," she snapped. "Don't bother. Just call 'em in and tell 'em it isn't much but it's hot."

"And, as the man said," Gillian parroted, "it's all there is."

They sat on the orange carpet in the living room, trying to make the best of the whole dipshit situation, eating overcooked food with their fingers, grinning suddenly, briefly, nervously, as if even their faces couldn't believe what was happening.

"So where's the chrislemighty barge?" one of the loggers blurted.

"I can only hope to god," Dave prayed, "that the bugger's sitting on the sand under six hundred feet of water. Because no other excuse is gonna do'er.''

''Diddlysquat, huh?'' a narrow-faced, bitter-eyed kid gritted, shaking his head, gnawing his bottom lip. ''Honest to god! If it wasn't for bad luck there wouldn't be no luck at all nowhere for no one.''

''Terry,'' Dave said gently, ''if I had a bottle of rye, I'd give it to you. If I had a sleeping bag, it'd be yours. All I got is egg on my face. You want it, you can have it.''

''I got my own egg on my own face,'' Terry answered. ''Oh well, what the hell, I can't dance and I'm too fat to fly, right?''

''You said'er.''

And with no more fare-thee-well than that, Terry drained the last of his styrofoam cup of tomato juice and started to sing. ''If I had the wings of an angel, or even the wings of a crow,'' and the disgusting trailer echoed to the combined voices of everyone, including the girls, ''I'd fly to the top of a spar tree, and shit on the people below!''

They took off their boots and shoes, and lay on the ugly orange carpet with jackets and sweaters for covers, their own tired arms for pillows. They no more than managed to get to sleep and someone was pounding furiously on the door, yelling at them to get themselves down to the dock, the bloodybejesus barge had arrived and what in hell was supposed to be done with all the goddam gear on it.

They drove the company equipment off the barge and left it above the high tide mark, parked wherever they could find a space to park it. Then they quickly hauled the boxes and crates of household gear out from under the bright orange tarps, loaded them into pickups, and drove as quickly as they could to the doublewide.

Louella stood in the trailer, looking at the incredible mountain of boxes and crates, at the wet mattresses leaning against the walls, the dressers, water-stained and humidity-blistered, the TV with its screen and tubes imploded.

''Sweet Christ,'' she mourned.

''My *bed*,'' Patsy wailed, and Louella knew if the bed hadn't been in pieces, soaking wet, Patsy would have flung herself on it and howled.

''Come on,'' Louella said firmly, ''put a lid on it until there's time. And then, I promise you, we're going to sit down somewhere and bawl like calves. But until then. . .let's get at'er. Those guys'll want breakfast in about three hours.''

''The condemned,'' Gillian growled, ''insisted on a hearty meal.''

''Oh *damn*,'' Louella shouted, ''who in *hell* let the cat out of her cage?''

The cat still hadn't showed up when breakfast was ready, and the men were standing with loaded plates, shovelling scrambled egg into their hungry maws. The sun was coming up over the lofty heads of the mountains, exposing again the unbelievable shoddiness of the entire town. Louella moved to the sliding glass doors, looked out past the hog fuel, the other aluminum boxes, past the dry creek bed, the ridiculously oversized bridge, past the various styles and sizes of houses, past even the massive stain pluming from the smoke stacks of the mill, following the wind stream out over the bay, up toward heaven itself. Somewhere out there a half-grown kitten was trying to convince itself it really was related to the mighty cougar. Somewhere out there people were trying to civilize a wilderness. Trying to pretend something good was happening. Trying to think in terms of progress.

"Anybody seen the cat?" she asked, unheard.

THE TURKEY CATCHER

I

The folding wooden chair was getting harder by the minute. One of the cross-slats got her in the small of the back, the sharp edge digging into her, pressing either on the hard nub of vertebra, or, worse, into the softer flesh between the bones of her spine. What had been merely uncomfortable three hours ago was past painful and well on the way to agonizing. The edge of the seat pressed against the backs of her legs, slowing the flow of blood, numbing her toes and feet. Her ankles swollen and numb, she wiggled her toes frantically, but all that got her was a sharp pinch above the elbow. There would be a blue bruise there within minutes. No wonder so many of the Family had varicose veins, phlebitis, fluid retention and dropsy! No wonder so many suffered paralyzing strokes! If God had intended them to sit all day Sunday on spartan chairs, their legs would disconnect on Saturday night.

Doug O'Leary was well into his lesson. He'd been talking for almost an hour, carefully tracing some obscure trail that had started with the quotation, "A thousand years are but a day in the sight of God." Doug seemed to think at this point that he'd effectively disproved carbon-dating techniques and the theory of evolution and was zeroing in on something else. Probably yet another prediction of the day the world would end.

It was supposed to have ended March 21, 1843, according to William Miller. And when March 22 rolled around, the founder of both the Jehovah's Witnesses and the Seventh Day Adventists decided he'd been out half a year in his calculations and rescheduled the event for October 21. So, as the dawn broke, the Millerites went to the rooftops, ever nearer my God to Thee, with celebratory picnic lunches, just in case the great event was closer to twilight. They ate their lunches. Those who had leftovers ate them for supper, and on the 22nd they came down from the roofs, their faith still intact, and waited for the next prediction.

Doug had at least made it to the First World War. The world was supposed to have ended in 1914 too, but obviously hadn't. Doug seemed convinced that what had *really* been predicted was that those born in, or at least near, 1914 would live to see the end of the world. Unless, one could only suppose, a runaway bus intervened. Or disease. Or, oh-oh, wait a minute here, back up, each and every person born in or before 1914 is going to have to *die* before the last days arrive. Including those old Russians who live on yogurt and grain and show up in the pages of *National Geographic* looking translucent and calm, claiming to be one-hundred-and-six or two-hundred-and-four or whatever. Actually, she suspected, they were only sixty-three, but living in that place on that diet, it all seemed so much longer, so endless and unremitting.

And now he's reminding us about four score and ten. Ninety years. So 1914 plus ninety is . . . what? 2004. Well, that'll give us a bit of time. We can all carefully choose our picnic baskets, start planning the menu, practising our recipes, so that when we go up the aluminum ladder to the roof, we go up with something more in keeping with the occasion than mere peanut-butter sandwiches in a brown paper bag.

Look at Beth McRae staring up at him as if the sun rose and set only because he told it to. So much for upright whatever. He's married, got four kids, and his wife is as alive as anyone else. Bloody hypocrites. The most upright thing about Doug O'Leary seldom sees the sunlight. Two-faced ungodly righteous! Nobody looks at anybody else that way unless there's been encouragement. These are the same ones quote the Sermon on the Mount and say if you sin in your heart, you're guilty, even if you don't *do* anything about it.

She wiggled her toes again, got pinched again, but the Hand of God intervened and Doug O'Leary finished his lesson. People did not clap, but they did nod firmly, approvingly, before rising and moving to the hallway. Ten minutes to get the blood moving, pee and get back to your seat before the next session.

She waited politely. Pregnant sisters first, then elderly sisters, then those sisters trailing children. And finally it was her turn, and none too soon; she felt as if she were going to flood. And, by God, there it was again! Something . . . different . . . about that knot in the wall. Just as she'd thought last Sunday. Well, at least this week she was ready. Last week she hadn't been sure. Well, not true exactly, she had been sure, but what do you do? Yell, and have everybody look at you as if *you* were the pervert?

She bent forward, opened her purse, took out what looked for all the world like a tampon, then, just as she'd rehearsed a dozen times in her head, she pulled down her underpants and stepped out of one leg hole, letting the cotton wisp dangle. She put one foot on the toilet seat, leaned forward as if to insert a tampon and, instead, jammed the counterfeit tube through the knothole and squeezed. Then she hit the end with her other palm as hard as she could.

The squeeze bulged the hidden balloon, the slam sent a ballpoint pen through the end of the distended, fluid-filled party favour and a mixture of India ink and household bleach squirted out through the hole.

Calmly, then, she took the real tampon from her purse, pulled out the sodden one, inserted the fresh, dropped the used one in the toilet, then stepped back into her cotton underpants. She pulled her sniper's revenge from the knothole, dropped it in the toilet and flushed. Then left the Sisters. Not the Women's or the Ladies', heaven forbid, everyone here was a Sister or a Brother. Except for the Servants and Elders, of course. They stood *in loco parentis. Loco* for sure, *parentis* probably not.

She walked quickly back to the hard wooden chair and sat down, hiding her intense satisfaction. She had no idea what would happen next. Her stomach tingled and knotted pleasantly, her face and hands felt warm in spite of the chronic chill in the room. "You'll enjoy this next part," her mother promised with a satisfied smile, whose meaning was made amply clear once the congregation was resettled. Anton Vaymer moved to the podium, his sheaf of notes at least an inch thick. Beside her, bladder still miraculously undrained, her mother sighed contentedly.

Daleth sighed, then wished she hadn't. Her mother was sure to misinterpret the sigh. Her mother misinterpreted everything, her capacity for revision practically astounding. He'll talk about how a widow had to marry her husband's brother to protect the purity of the tribe and ensure no quarrel over inheritance. Then he'll talk about what a great idea it is and how men should marry a sister-in-faith. And throw in some St. Paul, "better to marry than to burn," and probably the part about a good woman being more dear than pearls. And he'll look at me. In between every paragraph, he'll look at me. And she'll look approving and proud and suitably aware of her improved position.

And soon they'll all be looking at me. She wished the floor would open, the roof fall or the Last Day arrive.

Anton Vaymer was a Servant, forty-five years old at least. His first wife took the kids and left him. Anton found her, reclaimed his sons and his daughter and reported her to the Elders. Her name was read out and she was Shunned. Anton divorced her and kept the children, and when she tried to fight him for custody the Elders of the congregation appeared as character witnesses for Anton. Anton re-married, to a seventeen-year-old sister-in-faith who immediately became mother to a ten-year-old, an eight-year-old and a four-year-old. A year later she had an infant to care for too. Three months ago she had died of post-partum haemorrhage, giving birth to her second child. Twenty-one years old, worked to death and fucked to death and not even cold in her grave, but Anton is on the prowl again. And even the poor dead woman's family approves of the prowl because she has been guaranteed her place among the Saved. When the world ends she will be raised to life again, one of the Chosen, and there is no marriage for the Chosen, they will spend Eternity in the service and worship of God, completely unconcerned with the things of this earth and the flesh. Besides, her two little ones needed a mother.

Daleth didn't want to marry Anton Vaymer. She didn't want to be mother number three to five kids aged from infant to fourteen. She didn't want to graduate from high school to a life of cooking, laundry, housework, child care, pregnancy and more of the same.

High point of the day: the Head of the House comes home from work, has a bath, changes his clothes, is given a cup of tea and gets a report on everyone's behaviour so far. While he's having his tea and punishing the errant, the wife cleans the bathroom, hangs up his clothes, sets the table and serves supper to those not banished to their room . After supper, home study. Then bath and bedtime for the children. Then dishes and clean up the kitchen. Then bath and bed and a bit of the old bounce on the bones. Tuesday night, the same, except dishes have to be done right after supper so everyone can run around like fools and get ready to go to Group Study. Two hours of that and home for the bedtime rush and, of course, more bone bouncing if the Head of the House wants. Wednesday night, the same as Monday night; Thursday night, the same as Tuesday night; Friday night, Hall Study for three hours. Saturday, all day it's ''go ye unto the highways and byways and tell the good news in my name.'' Sunday, back to the hall for hours of folding chairs and listening ears.

Anton Vaymer finished, the faithful nodded, some of them sliding their eyes to where Daleth was sitting, hands folded on her lap, eyes downcast, face pale. The faithful were reaching for their books and their coats, getting ready to leave, and then Einair Swensen was up front, face nearly purple.

"Brothers and Sisters," he said loudly, "Servants and Elders. A moment please." His accent thickened. "We are much accused of being clannish, of ignoring other people, and of being unfriendly. Small wonder." He jabbed the forefinger of one hand into the palm of the other. "God said we should avoid the unrighteous, and so we do. And this often means we are martyrs in His name." He shook his head, his jowls quivering. "Young Brother Bill McMillan went outside at mid-break, to get some fresh air and contemplate what he'd just heard. And was set upon in the parking lot of this, our very own building. Set upon by thugs! By Philistines who willingly do not know our Father. And right now, as I speak to you, young Brother Bill McMillan is in the hospital, seriously injured."

She almost laughed. But she had more sense than that, and besides, old Einair Swensen was glaring right at her! "This was the foul act of a devil worshiper!" he thundered. Still glaring at her.

My God, she realized, he knows Bill McMillan wasn't set upon by Philistines. *He knows what happened.* And he knows he's telling a lie!

II

Everyone tsk-tsk'ed and oh-dear'ed and oh-my'ed and told each other martyrdom in His name for His sake automatically brought apotheosis and was required if one hoped to be among the blessed in Heaven.

"Oh, sweet Christ," she thought, "Bill the peeping tom is a martyr. And I suppose he sitteth on the left hand of God Himself." She couldn't stand it. She hurried down the hallway, ignoring Anton, who moved toward her, smiling widely. Past old Einair, still glowering, and outside, to sit in the car and wish there was an extra door in the near-new vehicle, a door marked EXIT, a door that would open and let her step through to a new life.

What kind of new life? Nobody can leave home and just walk in the front door of the university and be accepted as a student. You need money. And no member of the Faithful is going to encourage a young person go to university, where the devil worshipers abound. Too many young brothers had gone and been lured into temptation, and nobody had ever allowed a girl to go and waste all that money.

Go to Jubilee? And get nothing but more of the same, ten or twelve hours a day. And even if you top your class, you don't become a Servant; the best you can hope to be is the wife of a Servant. Oh damn, if that was what she wanted, she could marry Anton. At least he had a good job, a new car, a brand new house. Servants hardly got paid, they lived with Brothers and Sisters and Elders while giving their lives to the Truth.

What then? Lion tamer in the circus? If Holy Rollers could handle poison snakes on faith alone, maybe one of the not-so-faithful could . . .

"Brother Anton is catching a ride home with us," her mother beamed. Anton grinned. Teeth like that belong on television, she thought bitterly, or in the Mormon Temple with the rest of the Osmond family.

Anton got in the back seat, the scent of his after-shave rich in the closed space of the car. "Sister Stacey is taking the children," Daleth's mother purred, "and Brother Anton is having supper with us."

Sister Stacey has those kids all the time, Daleth thought. She's had that baby almost twenty-four hours a day, seven days a week, since it was born. Sister Stacey would give her teeth to be the third Sister Anton, but Sister Stacey isn't eighteen, she's thirty-two, and she doesn't have curly brown hair with red tints in it. Sister Stacey's hair is light brown, not quite blond, mousy actually, and starting to fade. She has pretty eyes, but you don't see them in the dark. You wouldn't see curly brown hair either, but it's probably more fun bouncing on eighteen-year-old bones.

"You're very quiet today." He leaned forward, his breath warm on the back of her neck. He had been sucking peppermints again; the smell mixed with his after-shave, not pleasantly. "What do you think about when you're so quiet?" he persisted. She shook her head, saw her mother throw an arrow glance at her; the wave of disapproval almost burned her skin.

"I don't think," Daleth said quietly, "that people's thoughts should be exposed to other people. I think if God had intended us to share our thoughts we'd only be able to think out loud, so other people could hear us."

"Ah," Brother Anton said easily, "but if God hadn't wanted others to ask about our innermost thoughts, He wouldn't have made us respond to the mystery of the silence.''

''Some of us don't,'' she said stubbornly. ''Some of us never ask other people what they're thinking.''

''But if you ask me,'' he persevered, his voice still pleasant, the skin around his eyes tightening and betraying his disapproval.

''I'm not asking,'' she said loudly. And again her mother glared at her, and this time Daleth had sense enough to shut her mouth before the balloon went up.

Brother Anton sat in the comfortable chair, pretending to talk hockey scores with Daleth's father. The old man was sober for a welcome change, and lucid, too. He wasn't one of the Faithful, never had been, never would be. Her mother had found the Truth after the marriage, but her father, so far, had avoided the honour. Nobody even bothered shunning him. He wouldn't have noticed, or cared if it was pointed out to him. Shunning only works if the one being shunned is affected. Most are. It's hard to lose your entire world and everyone in it. Not quite as bad as Total Expulsion, but Total Expulsion was reserved for those who had accepted Salvation, then fallen away, discarding Truth in favour of false doctrine. Or worse, free thought, which was no doctrine at all.

She ate supper quickly, silently, declined dessert, and started the supper dishes. When they were done, she quickly showered, changed to fresh clothes, and was ready to go back to the hall for evening service.

She saw her mother slip the car keys to Brother Anton as they moved down the front steps. She knew they expected her to move to her usual place in the front seat, then be unable to gracefully get herself into the back once Anton slid behind the wheel. They would arrive at the hall appearing to be what they were not, appearing to have reached an understanding Daleth had no intention of reaching.

She sidestepped awkwardly, moved behind her mother, and had the door to the back open before they knew what she was going to do. She closed the door, leaving her mother with no choice but to sit where Daleth usually sat, next to Brother Anton, who looked not at all pleased. As soon as the car was parked, Daleth was out of the back seat, her books in her hand, moving purposefully toward the hall, leaving Anton to walk with her mother. She knew from the looks people slid at her that her message was starting to get across to them. Her deliberate physical separation from Anton was telling them more clearly than any words would that Daleth Fisher was not moved to share the marriage bed of the righteous.

Sister Stacey brought the children into the hall fed, bathed, and in spotless clothes, their hair neatly brushed, eyes downcast and modest. Brother Anton, mercifully, joined them and sat proudly as his oldest son, Barry, moved to the podium and gave the opening prayer. The boy's face was chalk white, but his voice was firm; his first public move on the path to Jubilee had been rehearsed so many times he could probably have given the prayer in a coma. And considering the amount of time Barry had endured under Steadfasting, there was always the very good chance the kid really was in a sort of a coma. Not that Barry was a bad boy. Considering the furor kicked off by his mother's fall from Grace, the boy was doing well. But he had tried to run away three times and he had tried to make his way to where she was living, and he had stolen money from his father's pockets to buy his bus ticket, and it had taken the combined love of the entire congregation to drive the devil from Barry's soul. Daleth tried not to remember what her Social Studies teacher had told them about North Korean 're-education' sessions.

They were looking at her again, watching to see how she responded to Barry Vaymer's first solo presentation. Was she smiling with maternal pride? They knew Brother Anton had eaten supper with Daleth's family, eaten even with her unbelieving father. It almost overshadowed Brother Billy's damaged eye. An engagement ring couldn't have said it more clearly. Brother Anton had laid claim as surely as a dog pissing on a post. The fact nobody had yet asked her so much as the time of day didn't count. Nobody ever asks the post how it feels.

She had to stop doing nothing, and find a way to do something. "Silence means consent," her mother had told her. "What you condone, you accept, and that's as much as agreeing."

Five kids. One of them almost as old as herself. A house half the size of the Taj Mahal. Square yards of carpets to vacuum, square metres of painted gyproc walls to scrub. And windows to wash. And laundry. And the hard, wooden, folding chairs. Fun-filled family vacations at week-long assemblies with hard, wooden, folding chairs, hard benches, ten-hour days of truth, truth, truth. With Daleth looking after children not her own and Brother Anton busy saving souls not his own.

If the Sermon on the Mount was true, Daleth was already damned. What do you do when you don't Believe? What do you do when, no matter how you pray, the spirit does not move into your heart?

Everything Daleth could do, Daleth did; she prayed, she read the daily scripture, she studied the articles and magazines, she observed the rules. Daleth tried not to listen to the music coming from the radio her father insisted on having in the house, and Daleth never watched the television. Not because she was afraid her mother would find out and strap her, but because the Faithful were not supposed to listen to radios or watch televisions or go to movies or in any way allow themselves to be influenced by the purveyors of temptation. The only songs Daleth sang were songs of praise, the only books she read were school textbooks or the books the Faithful published at Jubilee. Daleth did not read the novels recommended by the English teacher. She wrote her book reports, not on *Lord of the Flies* but on the Book of Ruth. And still Daleth did not Believe.

Daleth knew all the quotations, she knew the stories, she knew chapter and verse. She was like a parrot in a cage, because she did not Believe. And God, how she ached to Believe! What can you do if you don't Believe? Without faith, all the rest is dross. Without faith, there is no salvation. Without faith, all the praying and studying and obeying and submitting was a lie, and a lie was a sin, and the longer she prayed and lied and sinned, the more damned she was. It made no sense! The more obedient and faithful she tried to be, the more damage she did to her eternal soul, simply because she did not Believe.

When she tried to talk to them about it, they told her to pray and have faith. How can you have faith if you don't believe? Ask the Father, they said, and she asked, and for all the good it did, she might as well have asked her shoes!

Just before she went to bed, her mother put it right out in the open where it could at least fester honestly. ''Brother Anton is interested in Daleth,'' she said. ''He's what?'' Daleth's father lifted his head slowly, his bloodshot eyes puzzled.

''Interested in Daleth.''

''Son'a'bitch is older'n I am!''

''He is not!'' her mother recoiled.

''I tell you he is. When I went into grade one, that sucker was in grade three. 'Sides which, he's got more kids now'n he can look after.''

''He does not!''

''She's eighteen. I'm thirty-nine. You're forty-one. He's not only older'n me, he's older'n you, and he's got at least five kids.''

''None the less, he's interested. And he's a good catch for her,'' her mother said primly, abandoning the arguments about age and the number of children.

"Make'im sound like a fuckin' rock cod. A good catch!"

"He's got a very good job, a fine house . . ."

"And five kids."

"He's a warrior for God!"

"He's an asshole. Any man who wants to get close to a kid is a goddamn asshole."

"You understand nothing. There's more to marriage than . . . that. There is . . ."

"Bullshit. He don't want no adult woman who might have some idea of what it's all supposed to be about, he just wants some kid who don't know what a ball-less bastard he is!"

"Brother Anton is one of God's chosen . . ."

"He's a goddamn queer freak with the hots for a kid young enough to be his own daughter. And that's all he is."

"You understand nothing."

"I understand, right enough. He ran one off, killed the other . . . what's he going to do to Dally? Launch her into outer space?"

"He wants to marry her."

"Fuck'im."

"You're sick!"

"Not so sick as some."

"Brother Anton . . ."

"Brother fuckin' Anton is gonna wind up drinkin' soup with his fuckin' jaws wired together if he starts sniffin' around my kid. If you'd'a tole me Daleth was innerested in *him*, that'd be one thing, but you ain't said a word about that, and what's more, neither has Dally. And until *Dally* wants him, he can go suck rocks. And you tell'im. He ain't dealin' with no mealy-mouthed psalm-singer here, eh? He's dealin' with me. You tell'im, y'hear?"

Well. Her father had done more than anybody to stop the entire stupid thing. But what had she done? Not even back him up, agree with him, confront her mother and her mother's ambitions. Just floated off to bed feeling wan gratitude that someone had protested.

Spring moved inexorably toward summer. Toward graduation and the black void of after-grad. Other people, girls her own age, knew what they were going to do. The telephone company, nursing school, computers. But after the end of the world, none of that would matter!

No phones, no computers, no hospitals, "for there will be no sorrowing nor crying, no sickness nor dying." Everyone will have their own vineyard. Fig trees. The lion will lie down with the lamb. Everyone will have their own gardens, and the gardens will bloom all year. And no need for gardeners or horticulturists because the earth itself will bloom and celebrate the glory of His Love.

All they're going to do is worship! And Believe. Which Daleth could not do. And if she couldn't Believe and Believe Fully, she wouldn't make it through the great upheaval, she would die with the sinners and the ungodly, and have no need of any kind of career, trade, or job.

Brother Anton's oldest son, fourteen-year-old Barry, brought his lunch to her table in the cafeteria, and sat across from her, smiling shyly. "Hi," he said quietly.

"Hi," she answered, opening her cardboard carton of milk.

"You really going to marry my dad?" he asked.

"No," she said, and his face fell.

"Damn," he hissed. "I was hoping you would. If you don't he'll probably get Phyllis Fraser to marry him, and she hates me like poison."

"Phyllis Fraser is only sixteen."

"Well, you know what my dad says." Barry shook his head in a terribly adult gesture.

"What does he say?"

"Get'em young and teach'em only that which you want'em to know."

"Yuck," she blurted.

"Yeah." He bit into his tuna fish sandwich. "I really like what you did to dear old Brother Bill." He chewed the sandwich as if it were cardboard and paste. "Someone should'a given him a poke a long time ago."

"What do you mean?" She put down her sandwich, her stomach twisting.

"Oh, a lot of people know," he laughed, "they just can't say anything because if they do, they're admitting that the pride and joy is a snoop, and if they admit that... there goes the great hope for congregational representation at Jubilee."

"What?" she gaped.

"Sure. I told my dad months ago what BillyBoy was up to, but you know the moral obligation; you have to speak to the person himself before you go to anyone else with the problem, and my dad asked if I'd spoken to BillyBoy and I said no and my dad gave me the two-hour lecture on the dangers of false-witness and rah-rah-rah three bags full. I,'' he shook his head again, ''am not going to walk up to BillyBoy and say hey, guy, don't you think it's a bit tacky watching through the knothole. He'd just pound on me some more.''

''Pound? You mean . . . fight? But that's a sin.''

''Yeah?'' Barry raised his eyebrows. ''Boy, must be nice to be a girl.'' He opened his milk carton, drained half of it. ''Actually, I'd rather he married Sister Stacey, she's more like a mom, you know? But . . . failing that, I was hoping it would be you. You're sure you won't change your mind?'' he smiled, ''I promise I'd help with the dishes and the little kids. Do the lawn, rake the leaves and . . . no, eh? Well, there you have it, the best offer I can make and you're shaking your head. Rejected. Must run in the family,'' and he laughed easily. ''Have to figure something out myself. Castrate him, maybe. If you do it to a tom cat they stay home more and don't smell so bad.'' And then they were both laughing softly, suddenly closer to being friends than they had ever been.

It wasn't enough to say nothing do nothing be nothing. Even Barry knew what was happening. Knew that they were all quite capable of making all the arrangements, holding the ceremony, and smiling contentedly at the end product of their determination. The end product being, of course, that Daleth, the way she was going, would just puddle along, doing what she did not want to do, becoming what she did not want to become, letting her mother make her choices, buy her dress, stuff her into it, and stand mute while the words got spoken and she let them turn her into what she did not want to be, had never intended to be.

''Momma,'' she managed, ''Momma, I do not want to marry Brother Anton.''

''Don't be ridiculous,'' her mother snapped. ''Just finish the dishes and get ready for Group Study.''

''No,'' she whispered, feeling her knee bones jump up and down, her entire body go cold.

''What?'' Her mother stared at her.

''I'm not marrying Brother Anton,'' she said shrilly.

''Don't be silly,'' her mother snapped. ''Of course you are.''

''No,'' she choked on the lump in her throat, swallowed, and blurted, ''I'm not.''

"And why not?"

"He's old," she whispered. Then cleared her throat nervously and said it again, louder. "He's old, and he's got a pack of kids. And I don't love him. I don't want to marry anybody."

"He's not old," her mother contradicted, "his children are well-behaved, and, as for love, you'll learn to love him after you're married."

"No," she said flatly, cursing herself for having been so stupid as to make her stand when she was alone with her mother. No sign of her father, no sign of anyone to stand beside her, to back her, to agree with her. No sign of anything except the increasing anger in her mother's face.

"It's the best chance you'll get in your whole life," her mother flared, "and you are *not* going to make me look like a fool, young lady! This stupidity of yours just goes to prove how much you need a strong hand on the reins, someone with a cool and mature head, someone who can provide the things you, yourself, are not capable of providing."

"I'm not a horse!" Daleth wailed. "I don't need reins or a firm hand on them! And there's nothing cool and mature about the head of a man who chases after girls before his poor wife is even decently buried! Let Sister Stacey marry him." She was sobbing now, shaking pathetically, her voice shrill and out of control, proving everything her mother said about her lack of maturity and need for someone to control her. "I won't," she repeated hysterically, "I won't, I won't, I won't!"

Her mother's hand connected with the side of Daleth's face, and for a moment Daleth hoped she was going to just fall on the floor, knocked cold. But all she did was stumble against the counter, knocking several glasses off of the drain rack. The sound of their breaking was like another slap, and she ran for her room, sobbing, nose running like a five-year-old. She supposed her mother cleaned up the glass before she went to Group Study, because it was all gone when Daleth finally left her bedroom and went to the sink for a glass of water to wash down the three aspirin she hoped would stop her headache.

The Sisters arrived home after Group Study, and the Steadfasting began. All night they sat with her, and in the morning, other Sisters arrived to take their turn. The only time she was alone was when she went to the bathroom, and even then, her mother stood outside the door, and when she figured enough time had elapsed for any bodily function, she pounded on the door until Daleth gave up and went back to the on-going educational session. They didn't even allow her to go to school. Every time she tried to go to sleep, they pushed another cup of strong, sugared coffee into her hand, lifted her hand to her mouth, almost pouring the coffee down her throat. By mid-afternoon she felt as if she had sand under her eyes, and by supper time her throat was so tight with fatigue and fear it hurt too much to swallow. Several times she heard her father's voice slurrily demanding to know what'n hell was going on, then her mother's voice answering softly and calmly, followed by the shuffle and lurch as the old man made his way back to his television room with the bottle the women kept replacing with a new one any time the bottom began to show in the one he was drinking.

By the end of the third day it wasn't just her hands were shaking, it was her whole body. Colours were too bright, sounds too loud, and everything seemed to be coming to her down a long tunnel. She stumbled when she walked, and inside her head she heard someone shrieking for help, screaming for them all to go away and leave her alone, but she couldn't speak, she couldn't even believe that the voice in her head was her own. Her face was chalk white, her eyes as dark-ringed as a raccoon's, and nothing at all made any sense any more. They helped her dress, led her to the car, drove her to the hall, and sat in a protective circle around her all afternoon. Everyone stared at her. Everyone knew she was being Steadfasted. And everyone knew Steadfasting never failed. Even Daleth knew Steadfasting would work on her. It had worked on Sharon Givvons. She had wanted to accept the scholarship she had won, had wanted to go to University and become a vet, but two weeks of Steadfasting changed all that. Sharon had married, the way a girl was ordained by God to do, and less than a year after that happy event, she had a child, then another, and was now pregnant again, and as happy as any other obedient soul. Of course she was happy, she smiled all the time. Steadfasting never failed because they wouldn't stop it until she agreed with them, did what they did, said what they said, thought what they thought, believed what they believed, and, most important of all, did what they told her to do. They would Steadfast her until she agreed to marry Brother Anton, and then she would be married before she had any chance at all to change her mind. Within minutes of agreeing, she would be married, Sister Stacey would take the children to her home for a week, and Daleth would be alone in Brother Anton's house with him, her husband, the man who would have the right to do anything to her he wanted, anything with her he wanted, anything on her or in her he wanted. Wives, be thou in subjection to thy husbands, for the husband is head of the house as Christ is the head of the church. Except Christ never made anybody marry him, never held them down and took off their clothes and bounced on their bodies, and put it to them, like it or lump it.

"You leave my daughter alone!" the voice bellowed from the doorway. Daleth tried to turn around, to see her father, but her mother's hand was suddenly on her neck, forcing her head down, and all she could see was her own lap, her own trembling hands. "A man's home is his castle," her father shouted, striding to the front of the hall, his heavy work boots thumping the bare floor. "And my home is my castle. I'm the goddamn king there. And Daleth is my daughter, she's the princess in my castle, and you psalm-singing, scum-sucking freaks aren't going to brainwash her into marrying some pervert who gets his kicks by fucking children!"

Old Einair was on his feet, saying something, but her father wasn't listening, and Brother Bill, one eye covered by a black plastic eye patch, was rising, with several other of the young warriors, moving forward menacingly. Then Brother Anton held up his hand, the young warriors obeyed him and stopped their advance, and Brother Anton took it upon himself to reason with the father of his intended. "I hold no hard feelings toward you for this interruption," he said charitably. Daleth's father let go with a short one; it travelled no more than six inches, but the full power of his body was behind it, fuelled by years of simmering resentment. Brother Anton went ass over appetite and landed on his back on the floor. Brother Bill and the warrior brothers moved forward, then stopped. Daleth's father faced them with a tight grin on his face, his hard-knuckled fists ready. "Daleth," he said loudly, "get the hell outta here right now! And you nice ladies better let'er go because I ain't no gennulman, I'll kick female ass as quick as any."

They rode home together in her father's car, then he told her to go to bed, and he locked every door and window in the house. "You got ten hours sleep coming to you," he belched, "then you'd better do something to save your own ass."

Daleth couldn't say anything, she just stumbled down the hallway and fell on her bed, fell into a dark cloud. She wakened to the angry shrill of her mother's voice. Daleth sat up, terrified and adrenalizing. Her mother's face appeared at the window of Daleth's bedroom, one hand banging insistently on the thermal pane. Daleth obediently got out of bed and moved to the window, unlocked it, and slid it partway open. Her mother was standing on an aluminum ladder, held against the side of the house by Sister Warren and Brother Anton Vaymer. "Daleth," her mother demanded, "you stop acting like a moron! Open the door, let us in, and just stop this."

"No," Daleth said. She put her hand on the aluminum ladder and pushed, and, without waiting to see what happened, slid the window shut, locked it, and ran to the living room. Her father was sitting in his chair, an empty bottle of whiskey on the carpet beside him. Out colder than a clam.

Sister Stacey arrived, weeping and howling, running from her car to the back yard waving a piece of paper. Daleth watched as Brother Anton, Sister Warren, and Brother Einair moved, with several of the warrior brothers, to meet Sister Stacey. Brother Anton took the piece of paper, read it, then raced up the back steps of Daleth's house, and yelled at her, enraged.

"Now you've done it!" he screeched. "You've set an example of disobedience that the congregation will be years overcoming. My own children have been taken by the devil. My own first-born son has given his allegiance to Beezlebub. Oh, you'll pay for this, Daleth, you'll pay for this! You owe me three children!"

"You hear that, Daleth?" Brother Bill shouted. "You hear that? They've run away! The Lord Most High will make you pay for this."

"Wicked, wicked girl," Anton roared. "You've caused Barry, Patsy, and Phillip to run off to join their harlot mother!"

Daleth ran to her bedroom, looked around wildly, then ran back out again, and raced down the steps to the basement. She rummaged in the downstairs closet and finally came up with her father's old army rucksack, the one he used when he went on his annual two-week fishing trip. It smelled woodsmoky and musty, it was stained and almost shapeless, but it was as close to a suitcase as she could think of, except for the moulded plastic matched set her mother used when they went to Assemblage. Daleth wanted nothing to do with her mother, Assemblage, or any reminder of either.

It took five minutes to pack, and the whole time Anton raved on the porch, her mother wailed and howled at the front door, and the Faithful trampled the flower beds as they circled the house, looking for some way in, some way to get at her without actually breaking windows and running the risk of having someone, her father probably, call the police.

"Wait a minute or two," her father slurred. "Make yourself a fried egg sammich. Give'em a while to work off their steam and impress each other with their bravery."

"A fried egg sandwich?" she gaped.

"Yeah." He lurched to his feet. "Go out there now and they'll eat ya."

"But. . ."

"Dally," he looked at her apologetically, as if he felt he was personally at fault for the circus unfolding all over their yard. "Just do'er, willya?"

So, because he told her to, she made a fried egg sandwich and ate it. Then another. Somewhere between the first sandwich and the last bite of the second one, the Righteous piled into cars and took off, yelling to each other that if they hurried they might be able to head off Barry, Patsy, and Phillip before they got too far.

"Oh," she dithered. "When they catch them, they'll whip Barry because he's a boy and the oldest and ought to have stopped the others."

"They ain't gonna catch nobody," her father grinned. "One nice thing about havin' a life-long reputation for bein' useless is that when you finally decide to make yourself useful, you can get a lot of arrangin' done before anybody clicks in to what's happenin'."

"Huh?"

"Well, there's booze in the basement to last me for weeks. That was their mistake. None of them cheapskates ever bought a drink for nobody, and I ain't so dumb as a fool might think me to be. Figured if they were busy keepin' me drunk, then best I sober up and listen in on the proceedings. Phoned Sue Vaymer—she's Sue Fleming again, took back her own name and everything. While that bunch was hasslin' you, she drove up and waited outside the school until Barry came out of the place at lunch time. Guess it didn't take'er more'n six minutes flat and all three of them kids was in the car with'er. They been gone long enough now to be halfway to any goddamn place at all they wanna go. And them kids is old enough, now, to be able to stand up in court and have their say about custody."

"Oh."

"You better learn to stand up and have your say, too," he lectured.

"Yes," she agreed. "I should have spoken the first time you . . ."

"So ya didn't. What's done is done. Ya ready?"

"I don't know what to do," she blurted.

"Why, leave town o'course," he laughed. "Listen, Dally, my old man was the same kind of mean bastard this bunch is, only he didn't pretend to be religious. And one night he slapped my mom and I blew up. Beat the supreme shit out of him. Then left, because I knew I'd never be that mad again, and I'd been so scared of him for so long that without the mad I'd still be scared. It was a habit I was in, bein' scared. And when you're scared, that kind wins. Any time you beat those bastards, it's time to leave, because when it comes to wearin' ya down, they got a patent on the process."

"But. . . ."

"You want to marry that psalm-singing fart?"

"No!"

"Then let's get a wiggle-on, kid. Standin' in one place is a lot like doin' nothin'."

She nodded, he patted her shoulder, then reached for the rucksack. Daleth followed him, and would have left without her jacket if he hadn't reminded her. As numb as her bum had ever been after an all-day study session, she left the house and moved toward the pickup truck.

Her father stopped at a gas station, filled the tank with high test, then drove silently, hunched over the wheel. When the gas tank had dropped to half full he sighed, a deep shuddering sound, and took the highway turnoff to the next town. "Gotta go to work in a few hours," he muttered. "Gonna have ta leave ya to your own devices, babe." He looked at her apologetically and shrugged. "If I'm gone too long, they'll know I helped. If I'm back and at work on time, they'll forget I even existed. Gotta do ever'thin' as close to normal as I can."

He found the bus station, they went inside, and he handed her the old rucksack. "Here," he mumbled.

"Thank you," she wept. "I love you, daddy."

"Yeah. Well," he pulled a large roll of bills from his pocket. "Here. Little somethin' I had put aside for a rainy day," he managed. "Guess she's pourin' cats'n'dogs today. Hell," he tried to joke, "some of it's drippin' offa your face."

"Daddy. . . ." she felt panic rising in her, making even Brother Anton seem preferable to this awful emptiness.

"Easy, kiddo," he warned. He pressed the money into her hand, patted her face. "Lemme know where you are and I'll send you more. Phone when you get settled, okay? Phone when your mother's at meeting, keep'er in the dark long as we can. And don't you take any wooden nickels, y'hear?''

She watched him leave, her ribs still feeling the force of the tight squeezing hug he had given her. She wanted to howl like a homeless pup, fall to the cigarette-butt-strewn floor and wallow in the dirt and grime, grovel on the chewing gum flattened onto and become part of the vile linoleum. She wanted to bay like a hound and roar like a bull, but instead, she went into the women's washroom and carefully shut the door of a cubicle, then leaned against it, shaking, not seeing the stained toilet directly in front of her, not reading the witless graffiti on the walls.

She took most of the money her father had given her and stuffed it under the waistband of her underpants, as safe as she knew how to make it. She adjusted the pantyhose she wore over her underpants, grimaced at the uncomfortable crinkling of bills against her skin, then went as casually as she could to the ticket counter, and stood there in her over-long skirt, her out-of-date and out-of-style jacket, and her sensible, low-heeled oxfords.

''Do you have a schedule?'' she asked. The sleepy clerk nodded, handed over a timetable, and Daleth wandered with fake unconcern to one of the benches in the depot. She sat and pored over the timetable. What good did it do to know what time all the busses were going if she didn't know which bus she wanted to take or where she was heading?

She looked at the big clock with its hour, minute, and sweep-second hands, then at the timetable again. There was a bus leaving in twenty minutes. Well, what did it matter where the bus was headed as long as it didn't go back where she'd just left? She had time for a hamburger in the coffee shop, maybe even a bowl of soup as well. And then, oh, ta-ra-rah-boom-de-yay, a new life.

III

Her mother was pulling at her sleeve, yammering at her that she'd turned the wolf loose in the flock and the lambs were being slaughtered. She jerked awake, recoiling, and the bus driver grinned down at her. ''Hey, lady,'' he said, ''you might want to take advantage of the half-hour stop here. There's soup and sandwiches and stuff for sale inside. You wouldn't get much sleep anyway, they're going to vacuum the inside of the bus.''

''Thank you.'' She stumbled to her feet, followed the driver off the bus, and made her way inside, to the women's room. She fished the money out of her underwear, used the toilet and replaced the money. She washed her hands and face at the basin, looked at her rat's-nest of hair, and cursed herself for not having thought to bring her brush and comb, toothbrush and paste.

She ordered soup and something called Quick Grill, which turned out to be mashed potato, watery overcooked carrots, canned peas at least lukewarm, and three very thinly sliced strips of liver with a strip of crispy bacon laid on top, the whole thing smothered and drowned in canned gravy. She ate it all, amazed at her own hunger.

They sold dry-goods and novelties, too. She got a brush, a toothbrush, a small toothpaste, a roll of adhesive tape, and a package of envelopes. Back in the women's room she fished out her money, put it in the envelope, and then taped the envelope to her stomach. She brushed her teeth, rinsed her mouth, brushed her hair, and decided she looked like something brought back from the grave by a mad scientist.

She couldn't get back to sleep, but couldn't quite wake up, either. It was like one of those dreams where you know you're dreaming, but can still see the headlights of passing cars arc across the bedroom ceiling, slash across the walls. They were following the natural valley created by a wide and muddy river. On the right, the road ended and a two-hundred-foot drop began; on the left, the meadows stretched upward, ending in sheer granite cliffs which merged into the skirts of massive mountains, still capped with snow. New spring grass and occasional dwarf crocus, and everywhere the tractors were out, plowing the soil, preparing the fields for the first seeding of hay.

The road widened, then widened more, and they were speeding along a multi-lane freeway, through a national park, where rhododendrons bloomed wild, and everything looked clean, almost groomed. A stocky woman, with thinning grey hair pulled into a severe bun, got on at a gas station, moved to squeeze herself in next to Daleth, nodding pleasant but private greeting. Daleth nodded in reply, even managed a wan smile, then turned her gaze to the scenery beyond the window. The bus started up, the heavy woman heaved herself comfortable, put a big brown bag on her lap, opened it, then pulled a book from her pocket, found her place, and began to read. One stubby-fingered hand reached into the bag, brought out a pickled egg, lifted it to the stern mouth, and the woman bit decisively, chewing determinedly.

An hour later, the woman began to fart. Amazingly, she seemed unaware of the purple explosions, and just kept turning the pages, her lips sounding each word, her hand still bringing pickled eggs from the bag. Daleth reckoned the woman had eaten three dozen pickled eggs without so much as a drink of water.

People sitting in front and behind began to squirm. Oh God, Daleth thought, they think she's reading and I'm farting! The ghastly farts fought a pitched battle with the stench of pickled eggs, and Daleth's stomach began to squirm and lurch. Oh God, if I puke they'll be sure it's me. She swallowed, slid the window open a crack, and prayed for fresh air. Just before Daleth's stomach emptied itself, the woman reached over and up, grabbed the cord, yanked on it, closed her book, folded the top of her brown paper bag, heaved herself to her feet, and moved down the aisle. Daleth sagged against the seat, almost weeping with relief.

The bus stopped, the pickled egg woman got off, and the bus started up again. The beer-swilling, skinny young man with reddish hair, sitting across the aisle from Daleth, stirred in his sodden half-sleep, then stood up, grabbed the back of the seat, leaned forward, and pee'd his pants.

Daleth didn't know whether to laugh or cry, to ignore it or go tell the driver. The young drunk, convinced, obviously, that he'd managed to find the washroom on the bus, sighed with relief, then sat back down on his seat, the stain spreading all over the front of his brown gabardine pants. Someone in the back of the bus began to sing, ''the squaws along the Yukon are good enough for me.'' Several others joined him, and when they had roared their discordant way through at least ten partial verses, they switched tunes. ''In the land of the pale blue snow where it's forty nine below and the polar bears are roaming o'er the plains . . .'' And Daleth decided it was another nightmare, the imps of Satan come to punish her for tipping the aluminum ladder and dumping her mother in the compost bin.

There were more stops now, people on'ing and off'ing, and the wet-lapped young drunk was snoring loudly, sprawled on the seat so effectively nobody even tried to sit next to him. A sullen-faced man sat next to Daleth and took up more than his share of the seat, forcing her closer to the window. At first she thought it an accident, then she realized it was purposeful, and not because he needed more room. He was just snuggling up to her. She wanted to move, but all the seats were full, and she had no intention of winding up standing in the aisle because of someone else's disgustingness.

"You're crowding me," she said quietly but clearly. He grinned at her, his eyes daring her to do anything about it. He knows, she thought, he knows I'm a coward. He knows I'm not going to jump up and make a fuss. In his own way, he's exactly like Brother Bill, he just doesn't bother making sure there's a wall around the knothole. He doesn't need to hide; he's already hiding behind my gutlessness.

"Shift over," she said loudly, "you're annoying me."

"Hey buddy," a young logger said quietly. "You want a knuckle sammich?"

"Get lost," the man growled.

"Move *over*," Daleth shrilled. The man moved as far to his side of the seat as he could and glared at the floor. The young logger grinned, shook his head, fished a round can from his pocket, carefully stuffed snoose under his lip, then closed his eyes and leaned his forehead against the arm hanging from the hand clinging to the support bar.

The sullen-faced man got off the bus, and the young logger sat down next to her, nodded politely, then slumped in his seat, his peaked cap pulled down over his eyes. Daleth wondered what he had done with his snoose. Swallowed it? He hadn't spit it on the floor. She hadn't seen him spit into a hanky. Christ, to swallow snoose!

She realized with cold horror she had almost taken the name of Christ in vain. And, earlier, had spoken the name of God without due respect. What was happening? Was it true the companionship of the Faithful was like a loving golden cord, and once you started moving away from it, you weakened it, and your life and mind began to unravel? The further she got from them, the looser her mind and tongue became! Arguing with strange men. Using the name of the Lamb as an exclamation. She was a worm. A disobedient, evil worm.

She huddled in her seat, miserable, as the city began to form on either side of the freeway. Exurbs first, then suburbs, then, finally, the incredible sprawl and stench. She saw more cars in the first half hour than she'd seen in the sum total of her life to that point.

"Where you off to?" the young logger asked, yawning.

"No place special," she answered. "I mean, I have to find a job and a place to stay and then . . . well, you know . . . settle in, I guess."

"Any particular kind of job?"

"Anything," she shrugged. "I don't really have any kind of training."

"Tell you what," he said, leaning forward slightly, looking

sideways at her, face pleasant. "Just a bit of advice. You can take'er or leave'er. Don't stay in the city. Everybody comes to the city lookin' for work, but the only people who do good in the city are people with training. It's the last place people without training should go."

"Oh," she said, almost relieved.

"And get rid of those clothes," he grinned, "they're a dead give-away."

"Give-away?" she echoed stupidly.

"Give-away. Let me guess. You've never been out on a date, you've never smoked a cigarette, let alone a joint, you've never tasted beer, gone dancing, or . . ." he stopped suddenly, blinked rapidly. "Or like that," he finished lamely.

"How did you know?"

"Your clothes. Your face. I'm psychic," he laughed.

"Oh," she felt chilled again. Psychic. Thou shalt not suffer a witch to live. Souls pledged to Satan. Strange rituals and rampant evil.

"What's wrong?"

"Nothing," she lied.

The bus pulled in to the depot and they all got off. She stood in the main room, watching the people. Mothers with cranky, whining children, teenagers in dirty, patched clothes. Several Indians in jeans, denim jackets, long hair, and bright red headbands. Well-fed laughing young men and women in bright-coloured jumpsuits, lugging skis as long as the bus itself.

"Come on," the young logger said, chortling to himself.

"Huh?" she blinked.

"Come on," he waved two tickets. "Can't leave you just standing here waiting to be mugged or arrested. Or both."

They took another bus, drove through the city, parked briefly, then drove onto a ferry. She wanted to protest, and she didn't want to protest; she wanted to ask where they were going, and didn't want to know. Someone else was taking control. Just as well, she obviously couldn't control anything. What did she know?

They got back on the bus, drove off the ferry and into a town, then transferred to another bus and headed south. She had been twenty-three hours on busses and boats, and her mind had been left behind six hours ago.

"Come on," he said, pulling the cord and standing in the aisle. He got his pack and his big heavy boots, handed her the old khaki pack, and they left the bus. She stood on the side of the road, watching the bus pull away and trying to get used to the idea she had no idea at all where she was. And was afraid to ask. Across the highway from the bus stop, a yellow-and-red neon sign flashed and flickered. "Islander Inn," it bragged.

He led the way to the small hotel, went to the desk, signed the book, got the key, then led the way up the stairs to the first floor. And Daleth just followed, too numb and too confused to be able to ask questions or think. There were two beds in the room, and an adjoining bathroom. She looked longingly at it.

"You first," he agreed. He tossed his pack on the bed, stuffed the key in his pocket, and headed for the door. "Me for a beer," he said.

She filled the tub with warm water, got in, soaked until she nearly fell asleep, then scrubbed herself thoroughly. She let the water drain out, dried herself, cleaned the tub, and put on clean clothes. She wasn't surprised when the door unlocked and opened, and the young logger came in with a paper-wrapped package that smelled so good she would have fought for the chance to break into it.

"Began to feel pretty hungry," he laughed, "so I figured you probably were, too," and he handed her the parcel. She put it on the small table, unwrapped it, and gazed happily at the pile of deep-fried fish and chips. "Got you some pop, too." He handed her two cold cans. "Didn't figure you for a beer drinker." But he had been drinking beer, she could smell it from six feet away. Well, so what, Jesus turned water into wine, what was wrong with one or two beer? "Listen," he munched happily, "I asked around. There isn't much in the way of work anywhere right now, but there's a part-time dishwashing job in the hotel here. Four bucks an hour. You'd work from seven at night until one in the morning. It's only six hours, but . . . it's a start. You'd get a meal and a coffee break, and you can start tomorrow night if you want the job."

"Thank you," she managed a smile.

"It's a bitch for work," he warned. "Lots of lifting and stuff. And they kind of save up the dishes all day, so you'll be doing mountains of them."

"I'd be willing to give it a try." She could feel the knot unwinding in her stomach, and wasn't sure if it was the food or the chance of work.

"The only other thing is the poultry farm." He pulled a face. "It's a stupid job, a stupid useless job. Nobody does it but tards, retards, and goofs."

"Poultry farm?"

"Yeah. You bop around in a big barn up to your arse in feathers and shit, chasing down chickens and stuff. Stupid job."

The fish and chips went down easily and sat comfortably, the pop was cold and cut the grease from her mouth and tongue. Life was starting to look like something worth living. And then the young logger's grin took on a different shade of happy, and Daleth knew that every warning she had ever been given was about to come home to roost. "Well," he stood up, stretching, "what say we turn on the radio and, uh, dance a bit?"

"Radio?" she gaped, at once relieved and horrified. "Dance?"

"Yeah, you know, one-step, two-step, cha-cha-cha, three-step, four-step, rah-rah-rah . . ."

"Oh, I can't." She had no idea what she looked like from his perspective, sitting on the edge of the bed, ankles politely crossed, hands folded in her lap, clutching the wad of toilet tissue which had served for a napkin.

"You can't dance?" he laughed softly. "I'll teach you."

"No!" and then it was all blurting out, uncontrolled. "The Believers don't have radios or TVs, or listen to popular music. It's all devil inspired!"

"Devil?" The smile left the young logger's face, he looked around the room nervously, obviously wondering what kind of loon was between him and the door.

"Well, my father had a TV, but he was a Satan worshiper. He still is, in fact. And we never watched his TV, or listened to the noise coming from it, prayed extra hard to overcome its influence on our lives. Not that prayer seems to have done much good for me," she mourned.

"Uh, listen, I didn't mean to, uh, upset you at all," he said soothingly, moving slowly and carefully across the room.

"And we never dance. Never. Nor sing, either. Except to make a joyful noise unto the Lord Most High God. Dancing," she told him sincerely, "is a sure path to perdition."

"Oh, yeah?" Again he licked his lips nervously.

"Oh, yes," she assured him. "We are enjoined to be apart from and not part of the empire of Lucifer."

"Lucifer." He backed to the other bed, reached out, grabbed his pack and his warm jacket. "You mean like, the devil, huh?" And he wondered in his heart why it was always *him* had to find the weirdoes and loons, the oddballs and goofs.

"The very one," she nodded. "People think he's ugly, but how could he be, it says right in the Bible he's Jesus' big brother, the most beautiful of all creations, God's favourite, the Star of the Morning . . . how could he be ugly?"

The young logger grabbed the doorknob, twisted it, pulled the door open, and stepped into the hall, nodding frantically, certain now he had somehow managed to escape having his throat slit. Or worse. He closed the door firmly, and headed down the hallway toward the steps to the lobby. Inside the room, Daleth listened to him beating a hasty retreat, and she knew he wouldn't be back. She wished she had thought to give him some money for the room and the food, but knew the worst thing she could do was go after him. It would only frighten him more, and frightened people sometimes got violent. Well, it was a good work, and you shall be known in heaven for good works done here on earth.

"Thank you most Merciful Father." She carefully packed up the remnants of the uneaten fish and chips, put the still unopened second can of pop on the floor, locked the door securely, then climbed onto the bed and slept the sleep of the blessed.

IV

She was considered staff, even if her part-time status entitled her to virtually nothing in the way of benefits. No pension deductions, no medical or dental insurance or coverage, just minimum wage six hours a shift, and a free meal. And reduced rent on one of the overnight units in the small annex that jutted from the Inn and tried to become part of the bush. Given her choice of the several empty little places, she chose the back corner room, where the window pressed against the elderberry bushes and the door opened to a small path that twisted idly down to the creek where the water burbled, surprisingly clean in spite of the discarded black rubber tires, several rusted and junked bicycles, and a fluttering, dangling array of plastic liners from disposable diapers.

There wasn't much in the unit, and Daleth certainly didn't have anything of her own to move into it. Most people would have found the amount of empty space neither appealing nor comfortable, but Daleth didn't know her place was barren; she had never had pictures on the wall, books, or magazines, what with books conveying devil-inspired ideas, magazines furthering satanic thought, and pictures violating the injunction against graven (or any other kind of) images.

She thought her first few shifts were going to either kill or, at the very least, cripple her. Huge plastic bins filled with coffee mugs, soup bowls, small and large plates, dessert dishes, water glasses, an attached plastic-webbing container imprisoning the knives, forks, and spoons. She lifted the bins, carried them to the enormous sink, and lowered them into steaming hot water. Without the red rubber gloves she wore, the water and caustic soap would have dissolved the flesh from her fingerbones.

Everything was washed by hand, then separated into heavy, plasticized metal racks, plates here, mugs there, glasses somewhere else, then the plasticized racks were put on the belt and fed through the machine that sprayed boiling water on everything.

The first night she wore her usual clothes, and within two hours knew she had to seriously consider the advice of Bella, the cook, who took one look at her and grunted, ''Best you wear jeans for this job, girlie.''

She breathed steam and the stale odour of food until she could barely taste her free meal. She washed dishes until long after the dining room and coffee shop were closed, then she scrubbed tables and mopped floors. By the time she got back to her unit, her skin and hair stank of grease, food, detergent, and disinfectant.

She slept until it was almost time to go back to work, but on the second night she wore the only jeans the Faithful had allowed, old maid jeans, cheap fabric, saggy-assed, allowed only for the most messy of jobs. God had ordained that women, and of course girls who were good women in training, wear dresses, long stockings, and sensible, low-heeled, lace-front shoes. Jeans and pants were only allowed for jobs which required the climbing of ladders and trees, jobs like cleaning eavestrough gutters, picking fruit and berries, or painting the ceilings. Daleth had been the one who had done the upkeep and chores at home. Your legs are younger than mine, her mother had said, and certainly nobody in her right mind would have sent a sozzled drunk up a ladder. Daleth had several pair of old maid jeans, and had never before in her life even thought briefly of wearing them where anyone outside the family might have seen them. But it was much easier to haul loads without the restriction of the straight-cut skirt.

Her hands sweated inside the rubber gloves, and when she finally got a chance to sit down for her meal, and removed her gloves, her hands were bleached and soft, her fingers swollen and clumsy from the gripping and lifting. Her shoulders ached and the small of her back felt as if two oval pads of burning coals had been set on either side of her spine. The muscles in her legs hurt, and her feet wanted to crawl out of the heavy leather shoes and curl up in the corner behind the big string mop. She stared down at the bowl of soup, then made herself eat it, but when the cook asked if she wanted anything else to eat, Daleth shook her head dully. The soup had tasted too much like the disinfectant she poured into the boiling hot wash water for her to dare try anything more substantial.

She stumbled the last few yards to her little cabin, fumbled the front door open, and lurched to a chair. She knew she should have a bath, get the stink of grease from her skin and hair, but she also knew she absolutely could not do it. She sat on the side of her bed and even managed to get her shoes off, but the rest of the undressing ritual seemed beyond her. She lay back on her pillow, planning a little rest before she got ready for bed, and when she wakened it was past ten in the morning, and a carload of tourists was hoo-rah'ing out on the parking lot. She got out of bed long enough to have a bath, wash her hair, and make herself a cup of tea, then she went back to bed and slept until three-thirty in the afternoon.

On pay day she got a teapot so she wouldn't have to put the tea bag in the cup, and an electric kettle because the one in the unit took forever to heat water. She got a toaster, a big packet of tea bags, some bread, some cheese, jam, and several kinds of crackers. She also got nicely scented shampoo and soap. Anything that would get rid of the smell of old kitchen grease was worth whatever she had to pay for it. When she got back with her purchases, she realized she could have used some of the money her father had given her and made herself more comfortable two weeks earlier. Had she been asked, she wouldn't have been able to explain why it was she had waited until she had her own money from her own job. Daleth wasn't used to asking herself questions like that, or answering other people's questions. That's just how it worked out, and she was reasonably content.

The elderberry thicket grew along an almost forgotten path that led down the gently sloping bank to Haslam Creek. Small fingerling trout darted in the clear water, zigging and zagging between the water-tumbled rocks and round stones of the creekbed. Kingfishers screamed and scolded, a family of mink lived in a burrow in the bank, and cats gone wild prowled in search of squirrels and mice. Huckleberry and salmonberry, twin berry, salal, and oregon grape grew thick, and tiny, jewel-like wild strawberry climbed over the rock and clay. As the days grew longer and warmer, Daleth spent more and more of her time watching the water, and the small scurrying animals began to relax in her presence, probably because Daleth was quite unaware of them. If asked, she could not have said what it was she thought about as she watched the moving water.

"How ya doin', Dal?" he slurred, and she knew he'd been drinking heavily.

"Fine, daddy. Fine. I've got a job," she told him, "and a place to stay."

"Got a boyfriend?"

"You know you're my only boyfriend." She could almost hear him grin proudly. "How is everything?"

"Fine as silk. Never better." There was a chuggling sound as he drained a quarter of a can of beer. "The whole freakin' congregation is shittin' razorblades," he laughed. "Alice Stacey stood right up in the meeting, from what I can understand. Said either Farthead married her or she was writing to whoever or wherever it is they get their orders from."

"Jubilee," she supplied.

"Wherever." Again the sound of a gurgling can. "Said something about the wise and the foolish virgins, and something else about steadfast handmaidens, and hit'em with something about if any of ye are the reason one of my lambs go astray then it is better for you that you never were born. Or whatever."

"Oh, my," Daleth breathed, awed by Sister Stacey's courage.

"But I think you should stay gone a while yet," he laughed. "The whole bunch of'em is in a tizzy and Farthead ain't married Alice Stacey yet. Does he see you, we're all back to square one."

The radio played constantly in the kitchen, the music softly tempting her ears. She knew about temptation. Beautiful and inviting, wearing the face of innocence. She had to concentrate not to listen to it, and even so was horrified to find herself working to a rhythm she didn't know she was hearing.

"Hey, Dally," the boss chided, "you gonna hold me up over a few minutes?"

"Three hours, almost," she said softly, watching her toes wiggle in her cheap canvas sneakers.

"Oh, hey now, I mean, is that fair? Don't you get a meal worth six bucks at least?"

"But it isn't really worth that," she wished her voice wasn't so shaky. "I mean, you charge that, but . . . that's not what it costs you," and she knew it wasn't going to do any good to talk to him. She was part-time, he paid minimum wage, she got a meal, and if she worked fifteen minutes overtime each night without getting paid for it, well, it was ten or fifteen minutes, that's all.

"Tell you what," he offered, "I'll let you have free lunches Saturdays and Sundays, how's that?"

"Supper on Sunday," she bargained.

"You're gonna kill me," he laughed. "But okay, I'm gonna show you I'm a good guy. Free supper on your day off."

"Not free," she said clearly, and the cooks grinned at each other. "Not *free* at all. Two hours overtime at four dollars an hour means that meal is costing me eight dollars. More if you figure that overtime is supposed to pay extra." The boss eyed her warily, then grinned. An uneasy, I'll-keep-my-eye-on-you sort of grim grin.

"Beneath that reserved exterior," he mocked, "beats a cold and calculating interior."

"That man," Bella said softly, "would steal the gold from a corpse's teeth. Amazes me he doesn't scrape the plates into the soup pot. You broke, Dally?"

"No," she blushed, "not broke. But I don't like being cheated and I work two nights just to pay my rent. Rent on a very small room!"

"They hardly ever have any call for those units in the annex," Bella snorted. "But you'd think they were giving a body space in Buckingham goddamn palace the way he goes on about it. Colder'n a well digger's knee in wintertime, too. No insulation."

"But it's close to work," Daleth whispered, "and I was glad to get it."

That night, when it was her meal time, Daleth was too tired to want more than a bowl of soup. "Never get fat that way," Bella said loudly, looking at the boss. He bit his lip and went back into the dining room, face flushed. But not before he heard Daleth say she was too tired to be hungry.

As she left for her room at nearly two in the morning, Bella handed her a take-out bag, still warm. "Say nothing," she hissed, winking.

Daleth didn't open the bag until morning, and by then the grilled steak was cold, but it was delicious, and so was the garlic bread, spotted now with drippings from the meat. Much more satisfying than toast and peanut butter. She ate sitting on a warm rock by the stream, and when she had eaten as much as her stomach would hold, she flipped the bone and gristle into the bushes where she knew the cats made their lair.

"How's it goin', babe?" he slurred.

"Fine, daddy, how are you?"

"Just fine," he coughed, a thick, phlegmy bark. "Great."

"That sounds like a bad cold."

"You know what these summer colds are. Sound like hell, but if you think I'm bad, you should hear my buddy at work. Sure you're okay?"

"Fine. Really. How's work?" She wished she could talk about something real, something that said any of the things she felt and couldn't put into words.

"Same old thing. Yourself?"

"Same thing, I guess. I suppose that's why they call it 'work'."

"Yeah." He laughed, then coughed again. "Yeah, that's a good one. That's why they call it work."

"I love you," she blurted.

"I love you, too, Princess," he coughed again. "Goddamn," he wheezed, "guess I'll have to try some of that vitamin C. Anyway, I love you lots. You're the only freakin' thing in the world I loved that didn't turn around and kick me in the teeth."

"More vitamin C, less cigarettes," she lectured, not daring to look too closely at the rest of his words unless they vanished from her mind and his heart.

"Yeah, well, you know how it is." He sounded sleepy, and she told him not to work too hard, and to be sure to get lots of rest.

The wild cats were getting used to her; they no longer raced away when she went down the path to the creek. The young orange tom let her get six feet away from him before he started to back into the brush, gliding smoothly, ears flattened, tail fur fluffed in warning.

"What do you do with the scraps?" she asked Bella.

"Give 'em to my hens. Why?"

"The cats . . ." she gestured beyond the window and the black pressing against it.

"Why'n't you take the meat?" Bella suggested. "Damn hens are overfed, anyway."

The orange tom waited, nose twitching, until she moved away from the pile of food, then he raced forward, growling, gobbling, and chewing frantically, almost choking. "Easy, easy," she soothed, and he hissed at her, swiped warning, his claws extended. Bits of beef sausage, half-eaten hamburger, steak scraps and bones, an untouched tuna sandwich: enough calories to keep an adult fed for a day, and the orange tom gluttoned until he could hold no more. Then he backed off, still snarling, and the other cats raced in to grab something and race off again, savage, untrusting, more vicious than guard dogs, more dangerous than their size would suggest.

"You want to make a few extra dollars?" Bella asked.

"Sure," she answered.

"You didn't ask how," Bella teased.

"Is it legal?"

"After work," Bella laughed. "I'll wait for you. Wear old jeans, old shirt, old gumboots if you've got'em, sneaks if you don't."

She finished quickly, raced back to her unit, changed her clothes, and raced for the parking lot where Bella's old car was waiting, exhaust misting white in the moonlight. It was warm in the car, and it smelled faintly of the lavender sachet hanging from the rearview mirror, and of Bella's hand-rolled cigarettes.

"There's fresh coffee in the thermos," Bella offered, tooling the car easily, the steering wheel become an extension of her strong hands, sturdy wrists. "I figure the boss would rip us off for everything we own if he could get away with it, so . . . turn about's fair play, I say."

The sheds were unexpected. One minute they were moving along an unpaved road, flanked on both sides by tall evergreens, the next they were on a large, hard-packed parking lot, dominated by a huge flat-deck truck stacked high with metal cages, their doors held open by stiff latches. And behind the flat-deck, the long sheds, each looking to be a half-mile long, a quarter-mile wide, with the area just under the eaves open and heavily screened. At regular intervals in the heavy screening, huge metal squares, ventilation fans, hummed softly.

A door opened, a thick-bodied young man came out, lit a cigarette, nodded, wordless, at Bella, and ignored Daleth.

''The lights'll be on inside, but they'll be turned real low,'' Bella warned, ''so when you first go in there, take a few minutes to get your eyes used to it. Can't turn'em up,'' she grinned, ''or we'll be beaten to death in the panic. If there's anything stupider than birds, damn if I know what it is.''

The place stank, but you don't keep several thousand chickens in a huge barn without having a few pounds of shit festering, no matter how well you wield a shovel. The birds sat on roosts along the walls—tiers and tiers and tiers of roosts—and in the centre of the shed were food bins and water troughs, the stink from the feed almost as eye-watering as the stench of chicken shit.

Daleth peered in the dim half-light, recognizing, without needing to be told, that most of the set-up was as automated as technology, ingenuity, and money could make it. Conveyor belting under the roosts caught most of the droppings and took them through the end walls to the outside of the building. The water troughs were at a constant level, the water replenished from the main pipe as demanded by the float-valves, and the food bins obviously could be refilled from above, the weight of the stinking, pelleted mass constantly dropping food into the big feeders. The warmed air of so many breathing, feathered bodies rose to the screening, pushed upward by the falling colder air, pumped from outside by the steadily humming fans.

The chickens blinked drowsily in the dim light, perched on their roosts, their feathers fluffed, their skinny heads reddish under the thin layer of bedraggled feathers. Dozy looking, stupid, there was something vicious, rat-like in the yellow gleam of their round eyes. Daleth knew they would as eagerly peck to death and eat each other as gorge themselves on the pellets of feed.

They worked five hours that first night, grabbing two hens by the ankles, then two more in the other hand, walking from the barn to the parking lot where the flat-deck waited. Hand the four hens up to the driver standing on a ladder, stuffing stupid white birds into the cages, where they huddled, lost in the dark of night. Then back to the poultry shed, breathing deeply of the clean outside air. Blink as you enter the shed, your nose and throat tightening with that first, harsh bite of stink, move quietly to the roosts, grab two more hens by the ankles, then two more again in your other hand, and head for the door to the outside and the waiting truck.

Back and forth, back and forth, with four birds weighing seven to ten pounds each, heads down, poor, stupid, cannibal eyes blinking in confusion. Trip after trip, from barn to truck, from smell of shit and mash to smell of evergreen trees and night mist, back and forth, feeling the encrusted and scaly legs, the rough-skinned, shit-scarred feet, back and forth, hands cramping, arms aching, legs heavy, fingers increasingly stiff and swollen. Back and forth, feathers sticking, shit smearing, and if one hen starts to squawk and flap, fifty others reply, cackling hysterically, and you have to leave that corner, let them settle down, start in another area, lifting hens from their perches and taking them out to the cages on the truck, cages where they are crammed twelve to fifteen per container, jammed too tightly to flutter or fight, comforted and consoled by the presence of other doomed birds, snuggling together, chirring and soothing each other, even contentedly dozing, locked securely by the metal snib on the door.

They worked without a break, catching chickens, taking them to the truck. The first load Daleth carried felt as if she were carrying twenty pounds in each hand. By the end of two hours, it felt like fifty pounds in each hand, and from then on, the weight increased until it felt as if she had a ton of dead weight hanging off each elbow. The truck driver was built like a beer barrel on boots, standing balanced on an aluminum ladder, reaching down, grasping forty pounds of mildly fluttering birds, lifting the weight to the cages, ramming it in, reaching down for another forty pounds. Daleth couldn't believe what the human body could do, hour after hour after hour. Lift her birds, lift Bella's birds, lift the birds of the two Salish men, lift the birds of the pinched-faced teen-aged boy whose teeth told of a diet of neglect, a lifetime of hard times. And others she didn't notice, men and women, moving back and forth, back and forth, from roost to flat-deck.

When the shed was empty of all except three dead birds lying on and in the mess of shit and feathers, they moved to the next shed. When all the cages on the flat-deck truck were full, they stopped. The driver quickly tightened some wide woven belts holding the stacked tiers of cages in place, waved, grinned, and was in the cab of his truck. The engine roared, the headlights flared, and the truck was driving away with six thousand roasting grade chickens, on their way to the processing plant.

''Turn you off?'' Bella asked, yawning.

''It's two dollars an hour more than I get for doing dishes.''

''But pretty gross, huh?''

''You ever take a look at a cigarette butt stuck black end down in a heap of mashed potatoes?'' Daleth asked dully. ''Or have to fish a napkin out of a cup where it's mashed on the bottom and sodden with cold coffee? Anything that has to do with food is pretty gross.''

''You up for tomorrow night, again?''

''Yes,'' she said firmly.

The tub in the cubicle the boss referred to as a bathroom wasn't long enough for Daleth to stretch her legs. She sat partially jack-knifed in the warm water, scrubbing her hands with a blue-bristled nail brush. Even with all signs of chicken muck washed off, her hands and fingers felt slippery, slimy, her skin abraded by the scaly yellow legs of the roasters. She scoured her skin, she washed her hair and rinsed it, then washed it and rinsed it again, and finally realized the smell was not on her, but caught in her nose and throat. She tossed her socks, jeans, and shirt into the tub and swished them with the red rubber plunger she had to use every third day on the balky toilet, then let the water out of the tub and rinsed her clothes a second time. She twisted the worst of the water out of the clothes, carried them to the hand basin to drip while she pulled on clean jeans and a warm shirt, then slipper-footed her way out into the first light of dawn and put the sodden clothes over the rope strung between two small trees, a clothesline the boss insisted was for guests to use to dry their bathing suits and towels. He'd complain about it if he saw it, but chances were he wouldn't even go to the back of the place before Daleth had the clothes back in her little unit.

Then, of course, she had to go back into the steamy little booth and clean out the bathtub. Bits of feather, bits of what she knew in her heart was probably re-constituted chicken muck, strands of her own hair, bits of twig. . .she scooped it up and dropped it into the toilet, then used some antiseptic smelling cleanser she'd bought, not so much for its cleaning power, but for the smell of it. It came in an aerosol spray can and, with a silent apology to the ozone layer her geography teacher had been so worried about, she sprayed the foam liberally on the tub, cleaned the stained and cracked porcelain, then sprayed the guck again to combat the musty smell that pervaded the place, even in the warm, dry, summer weather.

Only then could she begin to think about going to bed. Her back ached, her legs ached, her shoulders ached, her arms ached, and her hands were in torment, but she slept until four, then took her cup of tea and the scraps from the previous night down to the creek. The young orange tom sat watching expectantly, his tail puffed warningly until she put the scraps on the grass. She moved five feet away and sat on a rock, sipping her tea, watching him stalk the scraps.

"You don't have to pay for them by being nice," she said. The cat glared, hissed, showed his fangs. "You can have them even if you never make friends."

The dishes seemed to weigh five times as much, and it took half the shift before the stiffness worked out of her back, but she had the satisfaction of knowing she got her full value from the meal the boss kept calling her free one. Bella wisely cooked three hamburger patties, smothered them in fried onions and gravy, and heaped two scoops of mashed potato on to the plate, and Daleth packed it all away easily. "Pie?" Bella urged, but Daleth couldn't manage it, didn't want to be stuffed for the last half of the shift. She wanted to be able to move quickly, get it all done as fast as possible, then run home and change.

The second night was a rerun of the first, the same flat-deck, the same cages, the same driver, the same co-workers doing the same job. They might well have been the same chickens, lifted from their perches, loaded into cages, driven by the ferryman of hell, returned by magic for one more last, doomed day, one more condemned night.

And again she scrubbed herself and her clothes in the too-small bathtub, put the clothes on the rope line to drip, then fell into bed so tired she didn't even care that the muscles in the calves of her legs were twitching with fatigue and stress.

She went into town on her day off, both paycheques in her pocket, her father's money in her sweaty grasp. It was easier starting a bank account than she had thought it would be. She deposited the cheque from the boss and the cheque from the poultry farm, then handed over most of the money from her father and deposited that, too. Most, but not all.

She bought a pair of rib-soled rubber gumboots for chicken catching, and warm heavy red socks to wear inside them because Bella had warned her about cold feet. Then she took a deep breath, and another, and walked into Workwear World. Daleth had never had a good pair of jeans, a real pair of jeans, and Daleth determined she was going to join at least part of the rest of the world. She was tired of looking like a shapeless lump, tired of looking as if she agreed with those who thought the female body shameful.

She wasn't quite ready for designer jeans that hugged her butt and made her feel more naked than if she was standing there without her clothes, but she got three pair of heavy, denim, straight-legged, fly-front jeans, with brass-riveted pockets. In the same store, she got half a dozen cotton work shirts, pale blue, with dark blue buttons and long sleeves. She still had lots of money left, so she went to a different store and got half a dozen pair of cotton underpants, four cotton tee shirts, and three packages of athletic socks, fifty percent cotton, fifty percent nylon, three pair of socks per package. That left her enough money to buy a bag of groceries for her little cell, and catch the bus back to the Inn. And left enough time for her to take her week's laundry to the coin-operated machines in the Inn basement, and wash her clothes. Especially the jeans she had worn when she had been catching chickens. The rinsing in the tub had not rid them of stains, nor of smell, and she had the good sense to put them in a load by themselves.

Another week of work, another week of lifting heavy loads, another week of cleaning the kitchen, and three nights of that week she went with Bella to the poultry farm and carried idiotically blinking birds from their stinking perches to the slaughterhouse truck.

''Want to see something?'' Bella invited, and led the way to the first long shed they had worked. Daleth peered inside and knew it was the expression on her face made Bella chortle softly. Huddled on the floor, too young and too small to make their way to the roosting perches, four thousand baby chicks slept in the dim light. Another fifty or sixty lay crumpled, dead, on the crap-speckled floor.

She had her little room set up more like a proper home, now. She could make coffee or tea, she could make toast, she could keep her milk cold by putting the carton in the water tank of the toilet, she could heat canned soup or canned pork and beans or canned spaghetti on the little one-ring electric hot-plate. She had cheese in a mason jar, she had jam, she had peanut butter, and she had some *National Geographic* magazines to look at.

The cats no longer raced away when they saw her, and she prowled the banks of the stream every afternoon. She picked a breadbag full of blackberries and took them to work with her, intending to share them with the others, expecting they would just sit on their break and eat berries. Instead, Bella took the entire bag load and made two blackberry pies, and the boss, as eager as anyone to have a slice of fresh berry pie, donated from the depths of his charitable heart a scoop of vanilla ice cream each. He sat with them, grinning and saying over and over again how much he enjoyed the pie, how much he appreciated Daleth's thoughtfulness, and so, of course, they all had to say how much they appreciated the free scoop of ice cream, but what did that cost them, and it made the boss jovial for the rest of the night.

Upstream from the Inn there were rocks ringing a deep pool, and Daleth went there to swim, or to sit on the rocks, watching the children and young adults diving and splashing, calling rudely to each other, their summer holidays more precious as each day brought them closer to the start of school. Daleth spoke to nobody, and nobody spoke to her, but it made her feel less lonely to be at least on the fringes of a laughing group, if not actually part of it.

And on pay day she put her dishwashing money in the bank, took her chicken-catching money in cash. She bought a denim jacket like the ones the Salish men wore, with pockets to stuff her hands into, and other pockets with snap-front closures where the Salish kept their tobacco and rolling papers, their penny matches, and their registration cards with their status number and identity picture. Then she bought herself her first pair of real sneakers, white leather Nikes she vowed would never know the slipperiness of the crap-smeared floor of the chicken shed.

Once the denim jacket was washed and tumbled in the dryer, and the first shiny glow on the sneakers was white-polished off, Daleth could put on her jeans, her blue cotton shirt, her jean jacket, and her sneakers, and look like any other teenager. Except, of course, for her clean-scrubbed, cosmetic-free face, and her hair which had never known gel, mousse, curling iron, or hair spray. But Daleth didn't know she looked different, she was happier than she could remember being.

Back in her cell again, she waited until six-thirty, when the long distance rates were low and she knew her mother would be at Service. She phoned home for her weekly visit with her father, and listened numbly as her mother hissed over and over again, ''It was worrying about you brought on the heart attack. You did this to him. You.''

V

He was lying in bed with a little clear-plastic tube up his nostril, an intravenous dripping fluid into his arm, flanked by an array of machines. She thought he was either dead or asleep, so slipped quietly into the wooden chair.

''Hey, Sugar,'' he breathed, opening his eyes and trying to reach for her hand.

"Hey yourself," she answered, taking his hand, kissing the bruised back of it, blinking rapidly because she knew it would upset him to see her cry.

"How ya doin'?" he managed.

"Fine." She cleared her throat and tried again. "Fine as silk. Never better."

"How'd ya find out?"

"I phoned and . . . momma answered . . ."

"Son of a bun," he sighed, then coughed, that thick phlegmy rattle she had heard through the phone. "I was hopin' to be able to make'er down the hall to the pay phone," he whispered. "Thought maybe I'd phone your boss, leave a message or somethin', but . . . helluva way to find out. She raised the roof, I guess . . ."

"Oh, you know . . ."

"It ain't your fault, Dally," he gasped, then fumbled with the plastic tube in his nostril, turned a small knob on it, increasing the flow of oxygen. "Fucker," he coughed again, and she realized his chest was just bones with skin draped over them, she could see the knob of his wishbone through the thin cotton of his pyjama shirt. "I know she likely yammered at ya about that. But it ain't your fault at all. Or hers, either, prob'ly," he admitted. "It's just how it is, ya know?"

"Don't talk too much," she urged, "save your strength."

"Tell me about your job," he asked, his eyes pleading, wanting something she could only pray she would be able to give him.

"Well," she settled herself in the chair, hitched it closer to the bed, leaned forward, his hand held against her cheek, "well, if this is the first rung up the ladder of success, it must be an awful high ladder." She smiled, and he nodded, a smile flickered brief as a candle flame. "All I do is sling dirty dishes into blistering hot water, then use a long-handled brush on them, put them in even hotter rinse water, and, when the rinse sink is full, I pull the plug and load the dumb dishes onto this moving thing that takes them through the sterilizer spray. And when they come out the other side of it, they've been dried by this light and this blast of hot air, and guess who gets to stack'em up and put'em away again."

"Pearl diver," he teased. "Grade twelve education and she's a pearl diver."

"What's more, she's a sanitation engineer," Daleth laughed. "I'm all checked out on a twenty-pound string mop, too."

"Impressive," he agreed, his eyelids fluttering.

"And about half the time, after work's done, I go catching chickens."

"You're shittin' me," he tried to laugh, and the cough burbled, stopping all conversation for long, nerve-wracking minutes.

"No," she forced herself to continue, watching him struggle, exhausted by his fight with the fluid in his lungs. "No shit, except for the heaps of it on the floor, of course. The idea is," she hoped if she talked enough he'd go to sleep, "that once or twice a day, the guy tosses this switch that starts the conveyor belt moving. It's supposed to catch most of the crap and take it through this hole in the wall, to a bin built along the end of the wall. And the belt, of course, goes back underneath and into the shed and round-about, round-about, catch a little mouse, endlessly taking chicken crud out to the bin. Except someone forgot to train the chickens, and they don't seem interested in running over to the belt and dropping their load on it. So the floor is more than a bit what you might call . . . ripe."

"Skater's Waltz," he whispered, and again his smile flickered, his lips grey, his face ivory-coloured, fallen in on itself, cheeks sunken.

"There's me and there's Bella the cook, and we work together real well," she let her voice drop, almost crooning the story to him, telling him about the Salish men, the ferret-faced boy with the bad teeth, the truck driver built like a weight lifter. And even when she knew he was sleeping, she talked to him.

The nurse came in regularly, checking on the machines, on the amount of oxygen being fed by the clear plastic tube. She told Daleth about the dining room in the basement annex, and eventually, when she knew her father was sleeping soundly, Daleth made her way down and got a tray, took her place in the line-up, and got supper.

She was back in his room, sitting on the chair, holding his hand and telling him about the creek and the orange tom cat, when her mother came into the room with two of the Sisters flanking her like bodyguards. They ignored Daleth completely.

"Is there anything you need or want?" her mother asked her father.

"I'm fine, thanks," he said clearly. "Got everything I want now that Dally's here."

"Well, then . . . I . . ." and for a moment the crusty exterior almost cracked, but the unbending spine kept everything in place and her mother recovered. "I hope you're responding to treatment," she said politely.

"Well, not much chance of that, I guess," he answered, shaking his head slowly.

"They have television sets available," she blurted, "and if you would like one, I would make arrangements."

"Thanks, Lynnie," he smiled, "but I'm not sure I could concentrate on anything. But it was real nice of you to think of it," he smiled, and Daleth watched, amazed, as her mother smiled back, even patted his leg comfortingly. Had there been a time they had been friends? Had there been a time when they had held hands, smiled often, and could hardly wait to see each other? What had happened to change that? What story did they each keep locked in their memories, hidden from the entire world? "You take care of yourself, you hear?" he whispered. "Don't take no wooden nickels or nothin'."

"You take care as well," she replied, then she and her Sisters left the room, and nobody said a word to Daleth. She hadn't expected it would hurt so much.

"I could read to you," she offered.

"Where you stayin' tonight?" he yawned.

"Right here," she grinned. "I'm going to haul another chair in here, put my legs up on it, and save the cost of a hotel bill."

"You go down to the solarium," he suggested, "they got these big plastic jobbies you can . . . recline in." He tried to laugh and coughed instead. "Shouldn't be too hard to shift one of'em in here."

The nurse helped her move the big blue plastic chair, and then brought her a waffle-weave white cotton blanket to wrap herself warm. "If you need anything, dear, you just ring his bell," she said gently. Daleth thought the nurse very kind and understanding, and had no idea at all that it was her father's terminal condition got her such consideration.

"You comfy?" he asked repeatedly.

"Just fine," she assured him.

"Sure do love you, Dal."

"Sure do love you, daddy."

"Glad you're here. Wish it could be different, though."

"It'll be different," she assured him. "When you get out of here we'll take the bus together. We'll get a double unit at the Inn. You can sit on the bank of the creek and catch fish, and when I come home from work, we'll dig into the take-out Bella makes for me."

"Sure, Princess. You just bet your bottom dollar on that. I can see it all now. Gonna get me one of them floppy hats and put my flies in the band of it, just like those rich muckymucks in the magazines do. Wish to Christ I could smoke me a cigarette.'' He yawned again and closed his eyes. Daleth watched him sleeping like a child, and when she was sure he wasn't going to waken and need something, she closed her eyes and let the exhaustion of the past two days wash over her.

It was the insistent noise of the cardiac monitor wakened her, and she knew he was dead by the look on the nurse's face.

''Oh no,'' she breathed.

''I'm sorry dear,'' the nurse said. Daleth got out of the blue plastic chair and moved to stand at his bedside, looking down on him, wasted and waxen, and so very very still.

''He needs a shave,'' she managed. And then the nurse was holding her, patting her back, making all the right sounds, saying all the right things, but Daleth couldn't cry. ''You made him so happy,'' the nurse told her. ''He was so much more comfortable once you got here.'' But that didn't help thaw the huge lump of ice that had taken up residence where Daleth's belly used to be.

She got a hotel room, after all, and sat in it numbly. She had never thought of her father as an organized man, a businesslike man, but he had all the bases well and truly covered. A lawyer, a will, a list of his possessions, including serial numbers and registration papers. And a clear, legally binding, unshakeable, and unbreakable disposition of his lifetime's accumulation. And when it all got to be too big to handle, too horrible to bear, Daleth phoned Bella.

''You hang on, kiddo,'' Bella said easily. ''I'll be there before the funeral. What hotel and what room number?''

They gave him a Believer's service, knowing full well that, in life, he had hated them. Which just went to prove, she decided, that funerals and everything involved in funerals are for the living, not for the dead. All the pomp and ritual, all the public grief and pious-faced prayers, all the beauty and bullshit of it. Somehow they had managed to convince themselves that by smoking himself into emphysema and heart disease, and drinking himself into a bleeding ulcer, a perforated liver, and an early grave, he had been called to Glory, and would be among those who would rise again, whole and healthy, the day after Rapture.

They had to give him his Believer's service without his earthly remains. He had anticipated their hypocrisy and left a signed and witnessed legal document with his lawyer, and that piece of paper kept him out of the clutches of the Sisters and Brothers, and put him, instead, into a small sealed urn in the bottom of Daleth's pack.

''You want to go to the service?'' Bella asked casually.

''No,'' Daleth said firmly.

What the Believers couldn't explain away with out-of-context quotes and manipulative interpretation was the last will and testament which gave Daleth's mother the use of the house for her lifetime, but not the right to sell it, gave her his work pension and insurance, but left the big insurance policy, and all his savings, to his daughter. All his personal effects, including his guns, fishing rods, tools, pickup truck, and camper unit went to Daleth, as well as his little green-painted punt and the oars he had made himself.

He also specified that if Daleth's mother remarried or died, the house went to Daleth as well. Daleth was not the only one who understood that her father had done the best he could to ensure that none of the old, widowed Brothers would marry her mother just to get the house, garden, furniture, and the comfort of the work insurance policy. If anyone married her, he married her, not her house and money.

''I don't know what to do about all the . . . stuff,'' Daleth confessed.

''Leave it for now,'' Bella advised. ''Nobody can take it or sell it or anything rotten like that. Your old man nailed everything in place. We'll come back in a month or so, after all the probate business is done, when you've got a better idea of what it is you're up against.''

Her job was waiting for her when she got back, and the hard work helped ease the hot ache of loss in her chest. She washed and rinsed dishes, stacked the clean dry ones in their proper places, and tried to erase the memory of the resentful eyes of the people she had once considered to be her real family here on earth, her Brothers and Sisters in love, those same ones who now shunned her for not doing what they had decided she ought to do.

Shun her, would they! Not even a chance to explain. So much for the injunction about false witness. So much for the mealy-mouthing that before you accused anybody publicly, you had to go to that person and discuss with them your doubts, feelings, thoughts, evidence. What good would it do to go to them and make them listen? They knew why Brother Bill wore a black patch over his blind eye, and they were still going to send him to Jubilee. If the right eye offend thee, pluck it out, and it was out and the offence forgotten. They knew why she had been Steadfasted. They knew full well what Brother Anton had in mind. It had nothing at all to do with any of her reasons; what they had their shirts in a knot about was the success of her actions. Every girl in the congregation knew, now, that all you needed was twenty dollars worth of bus ticket and you were spared a cold marriage bed and pregnancy diabetes and varicose veins and a lifetime of being treated like a mindless child. And the custody case had been underway before Brother Anton had time to recover from his blind rage and put on his conciliatory and reasonable face; the judge decided the children were old enough to make their own choices, and they chose, all three, to live with their mother. Brother Anton was ordered to pay child support. That probably griped him as much as anything else. The two support pillars of his empire had been gnawed by the rats of doubt and defiance, he had lost both control and money, and without them, you do not have power.

They had taught her you do not get good fruit from a bad tree. If the Brothers and Sisters, the Servants and Elders, were allowing, condoning, and doing things which weren't right, might they not be saying things that weren't true? If part of the congregation were two-faced, might they not all be at least . . . what? Some of them believed. Many of them Believed. To the pure, all things are pure, and there were Sisters whose purity of thought was undeniable. Sweet-faced, kindly, and forgiving, they looked for the best in others and always found it. Yet, did they? They weren't looking for the good in Daleth, let alone the best in her. Their blind faith short-circuited their intention, and they believed those they had allowed to have authority over them. They would mourn for her, they would have compassion and supportive love for her mother, they would pray that she be returned to the fold, but they would never consider, even for a moment, that the ones they had allowed to be appointed as their leaders would lie to them. And would never question what was told them about doctrine and belief, either. Might not some of the doctrine be false? What if those young brothers who had gone to university and then fallen away had not been led into perdition by Satan? What if they had seen for themselves what she had realized?

And yet Satan wears a beautiful face and can argue so skillfully that even the angels have difficulty resisting him. Isn't that why we aren't supposed to argue, debate, or enter into discussions with the sinful? Doesn't Satan come to help them, to confuse the mind and soul?

She stood at the sink, in hot water to her elbows, scrubbing dishes with a brush, her thoughts coming back, always, to the shunning, nibbling at the edges of the knot she could not untie. And when the nibbling got painful, her mind jumped away, surfacing long enough to notice some bit of what was going on in the world around her. "Is the boss mad about something?" she asked Bella.

"Him? Don't worry about him. He's not from around here, anyway, he's from one of those places in California named after lady saints. Those kind come, and those kind go. Soon as it isn't all jam, they run back home to their rich families."

"Lady saints?"

"Yeah, you know, Barbara, Monica, Anna . . . like that. Must be an awful thing growing up in a place that constantly reminds you of the need for sanctity and the punishment waiting if you don't have what it takes."

"Tell me about it."

"Guess my feeling on it is that, if it's true doing some particular thing or thinking some particular way gives you a key to eternity and forever, then I want to be sure the people I'll be living forever with are people I can get along with. I mean, Christ, who wants to spend Forever stuck with a bunch of people who make your arse ache?"

"You sure you don't know Brother Bill the One-Eyed Wonder?" Daleth asked, and they both laughed softly, companionably.

Two and three nights a week, from just before Thanksgiving through Christmas and New Year, they worked five or six hours carrying chickens or turkeys from poultry shed to truck. Anywhere from twenty-four dollars on a short night with chickens, to fifty-four dollars on a long night with turkeys, and if the short days of winter were spent mostly in near-sodden sleep, what else do you do when the sky sits on your head, leaks over the world, and twelve to fourteen hours of every twenty-four are spent working.

"So, what are you gonna do with all your money, Daleth?" the boss said pleasantly.

"I don't know," she answered honestly.

"You could buy this place. I'd give you a good price."

"Me?" she laughed, "I don't know the first thing about this business."

"Neither did I. But I've made a good profit, and so could you."

"If you've already made a profit," she teased, "why not just give it to me. Then, when I've made a profit, I'll give it to someone else. Bella, maybe. And when Bella's made a profit, she can give it to Carol, and . . ."

"Whoa, whoa," he laughed, "the socialist serpent raises its ugly head."

"Ugly," Bella said firmly, "is in the eye of the beholder."

"Philosophy at the stove," he shook his head, pretending wonder. "It's more than a man can stand. Tell you what," he grinned, winked, "why don't you marry me, then what's mine is half yours anyway."

"And what's hers is half yours, too, right?" Bella teased. She laughed, gave her boss a jolly nudge, held out a spoon for him to sample the sauce. He tasted, nodded, smiled approval, any sign of bad mood gone completely. "Boy," Bella said admiringly, "have you ever got a sense of humour." He laughed and left the kitchen still smiling. As soon as the door swung shut, Bella's smile disappeared. "Be careful," she said, "he's too nice too fast. He's after something."

"I know," Daleth said easily, "but there's nothing in it for me."

"That will stuff been settled yet?" Bella asked.

"Just about," Daleth grunted, lifting another heavy rack of dishes. "Sure takes time. Makes you wonder, sometimes."

Eventually the paperwork was done, the lawyer paid himself what he thought he was worth, and there was less money than Daleth's father had thought there would be, less than her mother thought there should be, and more than Daleth had expected. "I don't know how he managed to save all that," she marvelled, "it's kind of scary."

"So marry me," her boss invited, "and I'll invest it for you."

"Sure," Daleth agreed, "and in five years you're back in La-La land and I'm still washing dishes. Besides," she said, with what looked like a wide, happy smile, "it would ruin a fine friendship if we got married."

"Why should it ruin anything?" he parried. "I'm a nice guy. I'm house-broken and toilet-trained and very very affectionate. Never had anything but compliments," he bragged.

"But right there we'd have a big problem."

"How so? Satisfaction guaranteed or double your lust returned."

"I'm not interested in lust," she said flatly, "or in passion or any of that glup."

"You're kidding," he gasped.

"No." She put the plug in the sink, squirted in the detergent, turned the tap to full open, and let the hot water gush into the big sink. "I'm not kidding at all."

"What a waste," he mourned.

"There are worse wastes," she smiled outside, but inside she was thinking of a twenty-one-year-old obedient Sister, dead at twenty-one, her replacement chosen immediately.

VI

The boss was amazingly cheerful about it all, called in the relief cook and a relief dishwasher, and even offered to go with them if they thought he'd be needed. They thanked him for his consideration, promised to phone if he was needed, then flagged down the bus and rode into town. They transferred at the bus depot to the bigger bus that drove them right onto the ferry, then, on the other side, drove them off the ferry and down to the city terminus, where they had a wait of an hour and a half before the bus left for up-country. To fill the time, they grabbed a cab and rode down the hill to Chinatown, where Bella introduced Daleth to a whole new taste sensation. Some of it Daleth wasn't too sure about; most of it she enjoyed, especially the crunchy vegetables.

"I thought they always used cat meat," she whispered worriedly.

"If I could make cat taste this good," Bella hissed, laughing, "there wouldn't be a feline left to yowl on my back fence at night."

They took a cab back up to the bus terminus, bought some chocolate bars, chewing gum, and magazines, then got in line and bought their tickets. That left just enough time to get on the bus, find their seats, and settle themselves comfortably for the long trip.

The bus tooled slowly through city traffic, swung left onto the freeway, and headed east and north. Four seats behind them, a broad-shouldered, blond-haired man in his mid-twenties loudly and enthusiastically discussed with the woman sitting next to him the intricacies of running a Burger Mart.

"The trouble nowadays is that the unions have ruined it for everyone," he said positively. "You get these kids come in looking for a job and the first thing they want is union wages. They haven't got the first idea of how to do the job, I've got to train them and everything, but they sure want their money."

"Damned unreasonable of them," Bella whispered.

"Mostly I try to hire fourteen and fifteen-year-olds," he confided loudly, "that way you can keep their hours down, wind up actually hiring three of them for the price of two old enough to qualify for minimum wage legislation coverage. Then, before they turn sixteen, I let them go," he laughed smugly. "I always give them a good letter of recommendation, and once they've got job experience, it's easier for them to find something else, their attitude is different just because they know what a job is and what it all means.''

''Remind me never to eat at a Burger Mart,'' Bella said softly, shaking her head. ''Son of a bitch sounds as if he's doing them a favour by firing them!''

''What you have to do is keep the volume up, stay a jump ahead of the competition, and always look for marketing advantage; you'd be amazed how much money you can save, for example, just by doing a big push on open-faced bunwiches. Instead of using both halves of the bun, you just add another tomato slice, an extra layer of sliced lettuce, and push an olive onto a toothpick and stick that in like a little flag; that leaves you the other half of the bun. Doesn't sound like much, maybe, but believe me, half a bun costs a lot more than a slice of tomato, some fine-sliced iceberg lettuce, and one little olive. Another way I upped the profit, I did a thing on chunk-its. The usual order of fries costs a specific amount. So what you do is, you use big chunks; and you don't save a lot, but you get three potatoes worth of orders out of two potatoes if you chunk them. One potato saved isn't much, but you save fifty potatoes a day and you've saved, oh, maybe four dollars. And that isn't much, but you figure four dollars a day for ten days, and it makes a difference.''

The woman sitting next to the chatty, loud-voiced Mart manager nodded politely, and murmured something he didn't even pay any attention to; instead he began to tell her how a few extra ice cubes in a paper cup could save ten dollars worth of drink mix in a month. Half an hour later, Bella decided she had heard as much marketing advice as her health could tolerate, and she got up, moved down the aisle, leaned over, said something very very softly, and then returned to her seat in silence so thick you could almost see it spreading throughout the bus.

''What did you say to him?'' Daleth asked hesitantly.

''I told him I'd had enough of his loudmouthed yap,'' Bella said with a wide smile. ''And then I told him to keep his voice and his exploitive ideas to himself. And then I told him he might think he sounded real smart, but to me he sounded like two pounds of shit crammed into a one-pound bag.''

''You didn't!'' Daleth marvelled.

''Did so,'' Bella laughed shortly. ''Suckers like that make me want to get violent. Yap, yap, yap, the story of the big I-Yam. Probably makes minimum wage himself, but he loves having all that control over other people's lives. One of these days, so help me God, one of them jerks will start in like that and I'm gonna be sittin' behind'em. Then I'm gonna accidentally-on-purpose barf down the back of their neck.''

The bus stopped for ten minutes at a small, lighted depot squatted on the side of the highway. The bus driver got down, fished a key from his pocket, unlocked the heavy glass door, went inside, checked a sheaf of papers, went to the shelves, and brought four parcels back to the bus. He relocked the glass door, got on the bus, checked the parcels sitting on the front seat, then closed the bus door, checked his mirrors and turn signals, and pulled back onto the highway. An hour later, he pulled in at another small, brightly-lit depot, and announced there would be a ten-minute stop. Nobody got on the bus, and only the smokers got off, to light up and puff desperately in the cone of light from the depot. The driver unlocked the door, and several people rushed inside to use the toilets, but there were no parcels to put on the bus.

When the bus started up again, the driver reached out, flicked a hidden switch, and music softly filled the interior of the mobile metal tube. Old-timey country and western-y music, and the passengers smiled, spoke softly to each other, pushed the buttons in their arm rests to lower the backs of their seats, and relaxed visibly. Then, softly, happily, bonding themselves in some kind of companionship Daleth could only watch and not share, they began to sing, softly, ''Happy Trails to you, until we meet again, happy trails to you, keep smiling until then . . .'' Bella smiled, singing and tapping her foot, and Daleth noticed the driver watching in his rearview, smiling at the reflected smiles of the passengers.

She slept briefly, wakened when the bus stopped to let off a woman and three sleepy children, then couldn't get back to sleep again. She turned on the dim overhead light, dug a crossword puzzle book from her pack, found her pencil, and ate one of the chocolate bars while almost off-handedly filling in the squares in the puzzle.

Her body was tired, her mind darted desperately, thoughts she couldn't have put into words, feelings she didn't recognize, something about damnation and what it meant, salvation and what it meant, and the difference, if any, between the two.

When the bus stopped at the depot-diner, she was glad to get off, to go inside to the Women's, drain her bladder, wash her hands and face, pull her toothbrush in its plastic container from her jeans pocket, and scrub her teeth. Bella grinned, nodded approvingly. "Atta girl," she teased, "never be without the toothbrush. Or the contact lens case if you wear contact lenses. You never know when you're gonna be presented with an offer you don't want to even think of refusing." And at Daleth's blank look, Bella laughed again. "My God," she sighed, "I never thought the day would come."

Daleth opted, this time, for liver and onions, expecting one or two razor-shaved slices of paper-thin meat. She was pleasantly surprised, instead, to be served three thick and tender slices with real, not canned, gravy. The potatoes were real, too, boiled, buttered, and garnished with finely chopped parsley, and when she had eaten, she felt almost human again, almost able to choose between waking and sleeping.

The driver had an extensive selection of tapes, none of them screaming the praises of vampirism, drug abuse, or drunkenness, and as the sky tinged with dawn light, Daleth drifted in and out of a half-sleeping state, where the words of the songs echoed in her head more clearly and loudly than when she was awake, and where she was aware of the hum of the wheels, the rustle of newspapers, the soft conversations, and strange hiss every time they went through a puddle on the road.

They retrieved their packs from the luggage bay under the body of the bus, took a cab to the hotel, checked into a small room with two single beds, and flipped a coin to see who got the bathtub first. Bella won, and while she was happily scrubbing the smell of travel from her hair and body, Daleth stood at the window, looking out from her second-storey height at the town she had thought to be her home.

There was the store that had once specialized in musical instruments, sheet music, records, and tapes, become, now, a furniture store advertising microwave ovens and dishwashers. Next to it, a medical-dental complex in what had once been the movie theatre and, before that, the opera house. A pharmacy, shelves stocked with cigarettes, hair colouring, perfumed soap, and travel-sized blow dryers and curling irons.

It took less than half an hour at the lawyer's office. A few forms to sign, some words of unnecessary explanation, and then they took the city bus across town, got off at the corner, and walked the half block to the four-bedroom, split-level, stucco exterior house that had once been home.

Daleth rang the front doorbell and waited. Rang again, and waited some more. And, finally, turned the knob, opened the door, shrugged, and stepped inside. She wondered how it was she knew the house was not empty. There was, of course, no sound of radio or television, and this early in the day no need for electric light, but she knew her mother was at home and ignoring her.

The other people were busy ignoring her, too. They sat, all six of them, at the kitchen table, their Bibles open, softly reading aloud together.

"The lawyer said he had contacted you," Daleth said politely. Nobody looked at her, nobody spoke to her, the soft voices blended together, reading at measured pace. "He said everything was packed in boxes and ready to go." Daleth stood straighter, her legs slightly apart, her weight balanced easily on both feet. And the people at the table ignored her totally. "Since I don't see any boxes here, I can only suppose they're either in the basement or in the shed." She turned and headed down the stairs, Bella following, eyebrows raised.

The boxes were stacked by the side door from the basement to the carport. And on top of the boxes, the keys to her father's truck and camper. It took an hour to move the boxes and pack them securely in the camper, and when they were finished doing that, Daleth returned to the house, went to the kitchen, put on the kettle, and made a pot of tea, then looked through the cupboards familiarly, as if it was her food, as if she still lived here, as if there was nobody else in the house but herself and Bella. "Doug O'Leary has been flirting with Beth McRae for over a year," she told Bella conversationally. "I don't think either one of them has actually done anything about it, just cow-gazes and simpers, but he's married and certainly knows better, and she isn't married, but she certainly knows better. Right in the meetings, too. Probably, if he wasn't the promising young respectability he likes to pretend he is, he'd be taken aside and cautioned, but . . . and Brother Bill of the Black Eye Patch got that way for peeking through knotholes to watch what was happening in the women's toilet. He beats up on the younger boys, too, but they're afraid to tell anyone about it. When I was younger," she confided, "cornea replacement was new, and people said how wonderful it was, to think that some blind mother would be able to see her children's faces again. But then the word came down from Jubilee, you see, and people had to stop thinking for themselves, depending on their own ability to judge things. And now it's considered a sin to give organs for transplant, or take transplants. You see," she smiled, "if God had wanted you to have a functioning liver, he'd have made sure you were born with one. However, it doesn't also hold true that if God had wanted you to roll down the highway, he'd have had you born with rubber wheels on the soles of your feet. Things equal to the same thing are not always equal one unto the other. Unless Jubilee dictates it.''

''Good tea,'' Bella smiled.

''Yes, but if God had intended us to drink it, it would grow in our own back yards and not need to be picked by underfed oppressed pagans who are damned for all eternity, then shipped here by ungodly fornicators, and sold to us by those who would be money-lenders in the temple. For by purchasing and using it, we support those who do not honour the one true path, which means we condone their devil worshiping ways, and, as we all know, who condones sin is himself a sinner.''

When they finally left, the silence in Daleth's mother's house was too thick to be cut by anything so ordinary as a sharp-honed knife. It would have required a Stihl chainsaw to even begin to make a dent in that deafening lack of sound. The women sat at the table, Bibles open in front of them, not reading aloud, probably not even reading silently, refusing to look at Daleth, at Bella, or at each other.

Bella drove, of course, because Daleth still hadn't applied for her learner's licence or begun to practise driving. Less than two blocks from the house, Bella reached out, flipped on the radio in the dashboard of the truck, and the Mouldy Oldies drifted into the cab. ''Hello, darkness, my old friend, I've come to talk with you again.'' Daleth felt something akin to, but not quite, grief closing in her throat, she could smell, faintly, the tobacco her father had smoked, she could clearly remember the times she had driven in the truck with him, the times he had not turned on the radio because he knew how dead set against music the Brethren were.

''You okay?'' Bella asked quietly.

''Yeah,'' Daleth said. ''Yeah, I think I am.''

They drove until long past dark, then stopped, got a hotel room for the night, locked the truck in the hotel parking lot, went to their room and cleaned up, changed clothes, and went down for the hotel Seafood Smorgasbord. ''I do love a Smyorgybyorgy,'' Bella teased, and Daleth laughed, softly at first, then louder, until even she knew it was nothing Bella had said had kicked off her laughter.

Late the next afternoon they off-loaded the still-packed boxes, watched as they were taken into the storage warehouse. Daleth signed the papers, paid the first three months' storage in advance, and went back to the truck. Bella drove them to the Inn, picked up her own car, and drove off alone, waving.

"How long do you plan on leaving your stuff in storage?" the boss asked.

"I don't know," Daleth shrugged. "First I have to learn to drive the truck. Then, when I know I can get myself back and forth to work with no trouble, I can start looking for my own place. When I've got a place to put the stuff, I can take it out of storage, but until then . . ."

"I meant what I said," he urged, "I'd give you a good price on this place."

"No, thanks," she said strongly, "I'm not interested in the hospitality business."

And then it was back to the same thing and more of the same, lifting heavy basket loads of dirty dishes, swinging the mop across the floor, eyes stinging with disinfectant.

"If you get it," she heard the boss say, "we could maybe work a deal . . . people are always looking to spend money for a 'country experience.' We could put in a campsite or maybe a couple of rustic cabins . . . let'em pick fresh vegetables from the garden or feed the chickens and collect the eggs. City people like their kids to have those kinds of experiences."

"You gonna go down, gather up the bedding, bring it here, do it, and take it back?" Bella teased, "because I sure won't have any time for that."

"Oh, come now," the boss snapped, "you're not as run off your feet as you make yourself out to be!" He shook his head, insulted and more than a bit disgusted. "You people, honestly," he mourned, "you're sitting here surrounded by the most saleable scenery I've ever seen, and you act and sound as if tourists were the third worst thing in the world, just half a step behind Bubonic plague and AIDS."

"I'd rather have AIDS," Bella snapped. "At least with AIDS you have some fun getting it. Tourists are no fun at all."

"No wonder you people never get anywhere," he shook his head and left the kitchen, went to the bar to polish his glasses and bottles, and glare mournfully at the nearly empty dining room.

"You buying something?" Daleth asked, more for something to say than from any deep curiosity about Bella's life.

"Trying," Bella laughed, "but you know the banks . . . by the time you're acceptable to borrow money from them, you don't have to borrow money from anyone."

"My dad says . . . said . . . banks were like tapeworms."

"Yeah," Bella agreed. "But I can't see any other way to buy this place than to get a loan from the bank."

"Is it a nice place?"

"Hey, I'm smiling at the bankers, aren't I? Would I do that for a not-nice place?"

The house was small, square, with an old-fashioned, four-slant roof and a wrap-around, all-weather, roofed verandah. Two floors, bedrooms upstairs, kitchen, living room, bathroom downstairs. Neglected rose bushes with main stems as big around as Daleth's arm, lilac bushes twelve feet tall, ten acres gone back to grass, and three sturdy but long-abandoned big sheds.

"Oh, Bella," Daleth grinned, "it's beautiful!"

"Yeah," Bella agreed happily, holding up both hands, fingers crossed.

"Oh, look, a creek . . . and a little pond."

"Well, it used to be a pond. But it needs to be cleaned out and deepened again."

"You could get in a backhoe," Daleth enthused. "You're gonna need one, anyway, to dig fence post holes. You can't possibly replace all that fencing if you have to dig post holes by hand." She stuffed her hands in her pockets, turning slowly, falling in love with the little farm. "You could have ducks," she dreamed, "they'd eat the slugs, keep the weeds down, keep the pond from going scummy in summertime."

"Could do a lot of things," Bella agreed, sitting on the front steps, squinting in the warm sunlight. "Take a year of damned hard work before you could move in much in the way of critters, though. Gotta get the fences fixed, get the place dowsed so that one wonderful day, when I'm so rich I could buy bottled water if I wanted it, I can get a well drilled. There's a couple of dug wells on the place, but . . . every now and then we get a couple of summers where it's so hot and dry the wells empty. But . . . " she shrugged. "Oh well, if we didn't have unrealizable dreams, some of us would never have any dreams at all, I guess."

"Why is the bank being difficult?"

"Oh, you know . . . single woman, middle-aged, no other assets . . . bad mortgage risk."

"How much do you need?"

"I've got a little more than half what I need, but that doesn't give me any money to do any fixing up . . . "

"How much?" Daleth insisted.

"What do you have in mind?" Bella asked quietly, her fingers nervously twisting the tail of her shirt.

"I've got money in that bank," Daleth hardly dared speak. "We could go half'n'half on this place."

"I'm not the boss," Bella growled. "I didn't invite you here to put the arm on you for money."

"I know." Daleth sat next to Bella. "But why should I pay storage on that stuff, or rent a place and put my money in someone else's pocket if. . ." she looked at the old rose bushes, the buds straining to open.

"What terms?" Bella asked, her face tight, her eyes hungry.

"Like I said, half'n'half. You've got more than half the price. . .I'll put in the other half. You've got no family and neither have I, so we make a will or whatever they call them; if I get hit by lightning and killed, it's all yours, if you get hit by a runaway hearse and killed, it's all mine."

"And if you get married?" Bella asked.

"It's yours," Daleth laughed, "because I'll get married over my own dead body."

They drove into town, went to the real estate office, and in less time than Daleth believed possible, the papers were signed, the money transferred, and the farm was theirs, joint ownership, immediate occupancy.

"Did you have the roof checked?" the boss nagged.

"Yes," said Bella.

"Electricity?"

"A friend of mine is a small-time contractor, he checked the place out," Bella said patiently. "There's some stuff needs to be fixed, but not right away, and what's there is sturdy. No dry rot, no bugs, no major leaks, and it's clean."

"You should have had me check it out," he grumbled. "Those real estate guys are notorious. And until you've been stung a couple of times, you don't really know what to look for. Why was it just sitting there?" he probed.

"The old-timer who owned it couldn't look after himself any more," Bella said, "let alone look after the place. So he moved into one of those senior citizen lodges, and. . ." she shrugged. "Poor old guy, it must be a real sorrow to have to leave your place just because you're old."

"You could have got it cheaper," the boss insisted. "Those old guys don't know the real value of anything."

"I think we got a real fair price," Daleth insisted sturdily.

'You're a sweet kid," the boss dismissed her with an indulgent smile. "Now when you marry me, we can go to the farm for our honeymoon."

"It's going to take me a while to get over my broken heart," Daleth laughed. "You know how it is, when a woman's been disappointed in love, it takes her a long time to dare risk it a second time. When you've seen the love of your life, the man of your dreams, off and marry someone else . . . ."

"Yeah?" The boss looked startled. "You? Who was he?"

"Prince Andrew." She shrugged. "But he likes them with reddish hair, so . . . tough luck for me."

The storage company delivered the still-sealed boxes, and Daleth unpacked them in her bedroom. Plaid work shirts, dark blue work shirts, dark green work shirts, brown work shirts. Jeans, work pants, winter longjohns, grey work socks, red work socks, green work socks, cotton undershirts, long-sleeved cotton winter tops, jockey shorts, two dark winter jackets, one obviously for work.

"Boy," Bella said quietly, "your mom sure didn't want anything left around to remind her."

"Most of it," Daleth said, her eyes flooding, "is still real good. I can use almost all of it. Not the jockey shorts, but . . . nice socks," she sniffed. "But Bella, he's got . . . he had . . . almost nothing that wasn't for work. A couple of light blue cotton shirts . . . a couple of white cotton shirts . . . three ties . . . and . . . two pair of dressy pants is all. Oh, and a pair of dressy shoes. Not even a suit," she mourned. "All he did was work and . . . sit in front of the TV drinking beer and . . . ."

"He must have done more than that," Bella argued. "Those fishing rods are about as fine as a person can find. And those guns didn't just roll down the street, either. There's a camera in there that's worth at least five hundred dollars, and enough lenses, filters, and whatever-in-hells to set up a portrait studio. You look at your old man's life and you start to cry, feeling sorry for him. I look at it and I see a guy who had some stuff in his life gave him real satisfaction. So he drank too much," she shrugged, "that's how they get extra taxes out of you."

Of course the television set was in with his stuff, and the sound system he had bought for himself for Christmas two years previously.

A yellow plastic milk case full of music tapes, two other yellow plastic milk cases full of LPs, and a big box of pictures and negatives. Daleth put them aside for some time when she could bring herself to sit down and look at them. She stacked his clothes neatly on the shelves in her closet, took his work boots, gumrubber boots, and hiking boots down to the mud room, just inside the back door.

"They fit," she laughed. "Isn't that..." she shrugged, unable to find the word she wanted.

They used the pickup to move Bella's things into the house, then stood looking at all the empty space. "We sure don't have much," Daleth laughed. "You really think we can do it?"

"Sure," Bella yawned. "A couple of pieces of foam, a couple of sheets, a sleeping bag, and we're fine...until we can get to a Sally Ann and buy some stuff."

"I notice," Daleth said sourly, "that her royal self wasn't in any hurry to get rid of his big leather chair or his bedroom stuff! She'll probably fill the house up with old bachelor Brothers, charge them room and board, let them use his stuff..."

"I'm sure," Bella laughed, "that their mere presence will sanctify it all. Maybe she'll marry one of them."

"Not if it means losing all that good stuff, she won't," Daleth laughed. "Anyway, I don't think she thought much of the state of matrimony."

"A woman after my own heart," Bella grinned. "I didn't think much of it, either."

VII

The young orange tom yowled and screamed the entire ten-minute trip, the old striped tabby growled, the grey-and-white pregnant female purred happily in her cage. Daleth left them inside their cages, in the small wood-shed, and gave each of them a bowl of cream, an opened can of sardines, and a plastic bowl of cat chow. The evening of the second day, she let the females out of the travel cages, and they headed immediately for the boxes of sand she had moved inside the shed. The next morning, when she found the females waiting for her, ready to rub against her ankles and purr as she refilled their food dishes, she let the young orange tom out of his cage. If she had thought he, too, would be tame, she had another think coming. He streaked from his cage, snarling defiance, backed into the farthest corner, and showed his fangs. "So be like that," she said, suddenly bored by his constant nastiness. "See if I care." She left them all in the shed another day, then risked leaving the door open so they could come from the darkness and begin exploring the acres of new territory. The tom, predictably enough, refused to step outside; he sat just inside the door, growling and guarding his food dish.

The walkway to the front steps was lined with crocus and daffodil, with narcissus and hyacinth, and the rose buds had begun to open in the long, soft spring. Daleth and Bella were up by ten every morning, busy clearing out the weeds and the blackberry vines that were trying to invade the grassy fields. They spaded the garden space, covered it with the mess in the huge compost bin, bought two fifty-pound sacks of sterilized steer manure and spread that, and sat poring over seed catalogues, dreaming of begonias, but ordering cabbage and broccoli.

Every day for an hour there was a driving lesson, then back to the farm to get ready for work. Hours of steam, disinfectant, heavy loads, and more steam, then into Bella's car after work. Some nights they drove home and went to bed, other nights they drove to the poultry farm and worked until dawn, lugging chickens or turkeys out to the truck, socking away as much money as they could.

They were busy at the Inn, now the first summer people were arriving in the big American cars, some of them dragging their own boat trailers, others looking to rent or charter, all of them wanting seafood platter or captain's choice or fisherman's luck dinners.

"How much a pound do you charge for your prawns?" Bella asked one of the Salish men at work. He looked at her, his face impassive, then smiled. "For you, three dollars a pound, no heads."

"For the Inn," she corrected, handing her hens up to the driver.

"For the Inn," he laughed, "four dollars a pound *with* the heads."

"I'll let you know," she promised.

"You sell any to the Inn," he laughed, "and I'll give you commission. Every ten pounds prawns you sell that cheap shit, I give you a pound, no heads, jumbo size."

"Cheap shit, huh?"

"Always lookin' for a way to gouge a fellow," the man agreed. "Pisses me off, that guy."

"How much a pound you paying for prawns?" Bella asked the boss.

"Five dollars a pound," he grumbled.

''With or without the heads?'' she probed.

''With,'' he admitted.

''Who you getting them from?''

''The wholesaler,'' he answered, ''why?''

''Want to save a dollar a pound?'' she asked.

''Without the heads?'' he bargained.

''No, Mac,'' she said flatly, ''don't try to gouge people all the time. You only wind up getting the worst of it. Four dollars a pound with the heads is still a dollar a pound cheaper than you're paying now.''

''Where you gonna get'em?'' he asked suspiciously.

''Where I'm going to get them doesn't matter. Saving a dollar a pound is what you should be looking at.''

''You making a buck on it?'' he asked coldly.

''No, I am not making a buck on it,'' she snapped, ''I'm making friends on it. You could be one of them if you weren't so goddamn proddy.''

''Okay, okay, I was just askin','' he protested. ''You must be workin' too hard or somethin', you're getting real snarly lately.''

The Salish man grinned, nodded, and grabbed the turkey by the ankles, pulling it from its perch and swinging it upside down before it could react. Once its head hung down, the turkey went limp, blinking sleepily, lost in a world turned downside up and strange. ''When you're sick of prawns,'' he laughed, ''you let me know. I'll pay you in salmon or something.''

In the beginning of August, suddenly and unexpectedly, the boss sold the Inn. The new owner had a teen-aged son and a teen-aged daughter, and between them, they took over Daleth's dishwashing job. Bella's hours were cut because the new owner and his wife were both cooks, and the assistant cook was let go entirely. He shrugged, went into town to register for Unemployment Insurance, and immediately began going to other places, leaving his name in case a job came up somewhere else.

''You gonna make enough on pogey?'' Bella asked Daleth.

''Oh, it'll buy groceries,'' Daleth shrugged. ''I'll find something.''

''Not many jobs around,'' Bella warned.

And there weren't. Not many jobs at all, certainly not for someone whose entire experience was as limited as Daleth's was. She left her name at all the restaurants and cafes, but knew she was going to wind up depending mostly on the chicken catching job. But she had time, now, to get her driver's licence, to get her fishing licence, and to take the little green punt up to the lakes and start learning how to catch fish with her father's gear. The first three times she went out, she came home skunked. The fourth time, she caught five fish, the fifth time she went out, she got her limit, and from then on, it was as good as guaranteed she would do well.

''Beginner's luck,'' she insisted.

''You ever go fishing on the chuck?'' Al asked quietly.

''No.'' Daleth grabbed her second turkey, moved for the door with them.

''I could take you,'' he offered. ''See how you do out there.''

''Yeah? When?'' she grinned.

''Soon as we're finished here,'' he grunted. ''I only got a small boat, that's why I work here, too. If I had a big one,'' he dreamed, ''I could go where the fishin' is really good, do it full-time. But like the man says, no money, no candy.''

''Not me,'' Bella yawned. ''I start at two in the afternoon, tomorrow. And I'm gettin' too old to do without my beauty sleep.''

''You don't need beauty sleep,'' Silas laughed, ''you just need some of what makes life worth living.''

''Yeah?'' Bella yawned again. ''I tried it once, cost more'n it was worth.''

''Ain't that the truth,'' Silas agreed. ''Wish I'd been born when the best things in life was free, like the song says.''

Daleth drove home with Bella, stripped off her chicken-catching clothes, had a quick shower, changed into clean jeans, a short-sleeved tee shirt under a long-sleeved flannel work shirt her father had once worn, and her comfortable old sneakers, then she drove down to the dock, parked her truck, and ran for the small troller. Al was waiting on the deck, grinning and drinking thermos coffee from the red plastic thermos cup. He grinned, held out an enamel mug and the big, stainless steel thermos. ''Have one,'' he offered, ''helps keep you awake until we get out where the big ones are. After that, I pray to God you'll be too busy haulin' them in to have time to feel sleepy.''

Half an hour later, he was showing her how to trail the trolling lines out behind the *Osprey*, explaining trolling speed, even checking her out at the wheel, telling her how to line herself up and how the compass worked. And when the little bell began to ding, he grinned, slapped her on the shoulder, and headed on deck happily. ''Some people smell 'em out,'' he explained, ''but that's not what you're doin', because I'm just trollin' around where I always troll. People who smell'em out, they say go here, go there, try someplace else. So you got to be one of those people the fish . . . respect. Some people, they sing to the fish, a few don't even have to do that.'' He smiled up at her. ''You got a special gift, Daleth.''

''I don't know anything about it . . .'' she blurted.

''And best you don't even try to find out,'' he said firmly. ''Forget ever'thin' I told you about setting lines! You just sit here and let'em know where we are. I'll do the rest of it.''

''But I don't know how to . . .''

''Don't think about it,'' he warned. ''You'll think it to death and it'll go away. Just have fun. That's what they like, someone who enjoys bein' on the water, someone who has . . . respect for them.''

''But if they know that, how come they don't know . . .'' She looked at the salmon flopping on the deck as Al pulled them from the hooks.

''Bein' dead isn't scary for them,'' he said shortly. ''They know they were born for only one thing, and that's to die. They know lots more than we think they know. And they like you, Daleth. Just feel good about that. We're making ice cream money, now!''

Daleth hunkered on deck, watching the sunlight sparkling on the water, the small, tree-covered rocks some people called islands, the other boats out on the water. The gulls were screaming and circling their boat, hoping for guts and scraps, and other boats, seeing the fuss the birds were making, were starting to move toward them. ''Won't do'em no good,'' Al laughed. ''Them fish came here to find you, and they know!''

She tried to forget everything Al had told her about setting lines, about steering the troller, about the compass and how it worked, but, of course, it was like being told not to think about the purple cow sitting in the corner of your living room. She sat, she thought about the fish, about schools and swarms of them, all telling each other that Daleth herself was sitting on the deck of the *Osprey*. Fish, making their way through the waves, swimming through forests of bull kelp, past mountainous rock formations hundreds of yards beneath the surface, moving along unseen, uncharted rivers, seeking that dot on the surface that was the bottom of the fishboat. And she watched Al, moving with all the grace of a ballet dancer, his bright red, hand-knit woolen toque holding his jet black hair back from his face. And soon, within mere hours of leaving the wharf, she began to anticipate what Al would do next, what adjustments and corrections to course, what study of compass and depth finder.

"If you start to feel sick," he suggested, "the thing to do is watch the horizon; it doesn't ever move. Some people, they get sick in the bathtub, other people, they don't seem to be bothered. But if ever you are, just find the horizon and fix yourself on that."

He pulled a plastic milk case from under a pile of sacking, turned it downside up, pulled a small plastic tool box to a convenient place by his feet, opened it, and pulled out a long, thin-bladed knife with a spoon set into the handle. He lifted a circular whetstone from the tool box, spit on it, and began to hone the knife, humming softly to himself. And then, when it was sharp enough to suit him, he put the whetstone back in the tool box, wiped the knife blade on the leg of his jeans, reached down, lifted a silvery salmon from the decking, and deftly slit the belly open, spilling the guts to the planking.

"You leave the head on?" she asked quietly.

"It weighs, too," he laughed, "and some people like to use it for soup."

"Got another knife?"

"You don't have to, Daleth. It's more than enough that you just sit there and bring them to the lines."

"Gets boring just sitting," she laughed.

They cleaned the fish, took them below and laid them in fish boxes, a layer of fish, a layer of crushed ice, another layer of fish, another layer of crushed ice. They hauled in the lines, took hooks from mouths, dropped the fish on deck, re-set the lines and unrolled them behind the troller, then sat gutting fish until it was time to haul in the lines again.

"Better roll down your sleeves," he advised, "it's getting on to the real hot of the day. Even if you don't burn, it isn't good for you," and he went to a bucket of clean sea water, scrubbed his hands with a small brush, dried them on a reasonably clean piece of towelling, and rolled down his own sleeves, buttoning them around his thick-muscled wrists. He pulled the collar of his shirt up over the back of his neck, hauled a clean hanky from his pocket and knotted it, cowboy-style, around his neck, then removed his bright red woolen toque and dippered water onto his head. It cascaded through his hair, down the sides of his face to his shirt, soaking him from shoulders to waist.

"Gotta keep yourself cooled down," he said conversationally, "or the next thing you know, you'll see islands floating above the sea. And if it's really hot, you'll see people on the islands, and cows and horses, even. And if you're in real trouble, you'll steer for those islands, and they might find your boat and your catch, but they'll never find a sign of you. But the next time someone goes boil-brained, there you'll be, waving with the other people, standing on the beach of an island that nobody ever put on any map.''

''Yeah?'' She rose hurriedly, moved to the bucket to dipper water on her head.

''Over there,'' he pointed at a small barren island, ''that's where my grandparents' mother and dad were buried. Well, not buried, exactly, they didn't put'em in holes, but that's where they were taken when their bodies were cold.''

''What did they do with . . . the bodies?''

''They had platforms in the trees, put'em on the platforms with their best stuff, and left'em there. Some people went back a year later and gathered up the bones, wrapped the bones in bundles and put the bundles in, oh, like those sandstone caves, over there . . . see, them holes where the waves eat at the rocks?''

''But there aren't any trees on that rock,'' she said slowly. Al grinned, shrugged, then managed a short, harsh laugh. ''You're right,'' he said softly, ''but there used to be. Great big suckers. And from the time they were little ones, the people trained the branches. Sort of like that bonsai the Japanese do, only lots bigger. Trained the branches so's they could lay the platform planks and tie'em down securely. And then the loggers cut'em all down. Someone told me they paid a bunch of people big money to plant new trees, but by the time they got around to it, all the dirt had washed off into the chuck, and so nothing grew.''

''What happened to the bones and . . . ?''

''Don't know,'' he shrugged again. ''We weren't allowed onto the rock, by then. Go to jail if you go there.''

Daleth dippered more sea water onto her head, shivering and blaming it on the sudden change in temperature as the water soaked her shirt. She sat back down on the plastic milk case, reached for the whetstone, spit on it, and sharpened her knife, then put the whetstone back in the tool box, wiped the knife blade on her jeans, and reached for another fish to clean.

The sky was beginning to streak with pink before Al pulled in the lines for the last time. ''You wanna take'er back?'' he asked softly. ''I'll finish up those fish.''

''You think I can be trusted not to take it up on the rocks?'' she asked, hesitating.

"Oh," he grinned, "I think so. Not too many rocks out this way anyway."

He took over as they approached the channel into the harbour, and slowed the troller to less than five miles an hour, ignoring the speedboats, pleasure boats, and haughty tourist yachts.

He tied up in his usual place, then lifted the hatch cover off completely. He disappeared in the hole, then clambered back out again, holding a number of strong ropes. He reached up, grabbed a small clip hook, passed the knotted loop ends of the ropes through the clip hook, tested it by tugging, then went quickly to the wheelhouse. The engine was still purring noisily, the prop not turning, and then the engine raced slightly, the slip hook began to lift, the ropes tightened, and the overhead winch lifted the fish box from the bowels of the fish hatch. It hung suspended over the decking, then Al was there, pushing, swinging the fish box from the *Osprey* to the wharf planking.

Three boxes of fish and ice, and then they were hauling buckets of sea water, rinsing out the fish hatch, scrubbing it down with long-handled, heavy, bristled brushes, and when the fish hatch was cleaned and rinsed, the deck was still to be cleaned.

Daleth drove home, stripped off her clothes and hung them on the back yard clothesline, walked into the house in her underwear, and headed immediately for the bathroom. She soaked in a tub of hot water, scrubbed her hands several times, then, finally, cut open a lemon and rubbed the lemon on her skin to try to get rid of the all-pervading smell of fish. She drank four glasses of cold water, thought of making herself a sandwich, yawned, and decided what she really wanted to do was sleep like a baby.

Her bed had never felt so good to her. A four-inch-thick slab of light green foam rubber, cotton sheets, and one cotton blanket: it felt to Daleth at least as comfortable as a bed of dandelion fluff. She lay belly down, her head turned to one side, aware she was falling asleep, drifting down into a place cool and dark and friendly, a place where she would be safe from unseen rocks, safe from uncharted islands where ghost people waved welcomingly.

The lights of Bella's car arced across the bedroom walls, slanted down, and touched Daleth's face. She opened her eyes, heard the sound of the car door closing, of footsteps crunching on the gravel, then touching the back steps, crossing the verandah. When she heard the back door open, Daleth sat up, yawning.

"Well, you look like a cross between a sunburned tourist and an exhausted workie,'' Bella said tiredly.

''I feel like a dehydrated piece of old leather.''

''Get much sleep?''

''Yeah, I think I did,'' Daleth nodded. ''You think we have time for a coffee?''

''Sure,'' Bella pulled off her light jacket, moved toward the staircase to the upstairs. ''I have to change. Christ, that place is going nuts!''

''Busy?''

''Dis-freakin-organized. Maw'n'Paw get along like two badgers trapped in the same sack, and neither Junior nor Sissy think it's fair that they have to work when their friends get to go . . . lah de dah dah.''

''God, nice to have the choice, eh?''

''Never mind the choice, make the coffee and let's go grab turkey ankles. Some people,'' Bella shouted from the second floor, ''some people get to reach out and grasp the glitzy golden ring . . . others get to reach out and grab turkeys by the ankle. Just shows to go ya, that's what I always say, just shows to go ya!''

Six days of fishing and three days closed, four days of fishing and four days closed, two days of fishing and three days closed, no rhyme or reason to it that Daleth could see. The fisheries department would let them fish one day in a certain place, then close that area for whatever length of time they had decided to close it, then open it again. The sports fishermen seemed to move over the face of the sea at will, the commercial boats were as carefully herded as pedigreed sheep. And Daleth was out there with Al, helping, learning, working, and, to her surprise, making very good money.

''I think,'' Bella said firmly, ''we should buy a freezer.''

''Yeah?''

''Yeah. Or do you want to spend the month of September with vats of boiling water, two hundred dollars worth of jars and lids, and . . . because I don't! I feel as if I have too much to do, already.''

The salmon they caught were cleaned, packed in ice, loaded onto the wharf, then rolled to where the buyer waited in his refrigerated truck. The fish were carefully lifted from the ice, placed gently on the weigher, and the empty fish boxes taken back down the pier decking, fastened to the winch, and lowered back into the hatch. Those salmon too small for the buyer were supposed to be tossed back into the water, but by the time they had been caught, hauled in, and the hook removed, they were invariably dead, or almost dead, with no chance to survive. Thrown into the water, they were immediately attacked and devoured by dogfish, by seals, or by the gulls who followed the fishboat constantly. Sometimes an eagle would plummet from the sky to grab a dying small salmon, and it enraged Al to throw back what ought to be food. "If you kill it," he raged, "you're supposed to *eat* it." They packed the small fish in a picnic cooler, with crushed ice, and prayed to all the good luck either or both them had, that the fisheries inspector not stop them and demand to see what they had in their cooler.

Cod, tommy cod, ling cod, dogfish, even small octopus, got caught on the hooks, too, and while much of this "trash fish" got put in a bucket and taken to Al's freezer to be cut up for bait, much of it wound up in Daleth's picnic cooler and taken home to the freezer.

"We could bring the fish guts home," she offered, "and bury them in the garden for fertilizer."

"Spare me," Bella groaned. "It'd be in the dirt only so long as it took those goddamn cats to dig it up again." She glowered fiercely, shaking her head. "The cat had her kittens, and now the kittens are getting ready to have kittens. I never saw so many fat, overfed, underworked, useless cats in my life. Half the world hasn't even *tasted* fresh fish, and these pampered arseltarts are getting choosy; they don't want perch, oh my no, they want ling cod."

"Right," Daleth agreed.

The vet wouldn't spay the females until they had all had their shots. There was no discount for bulk customers, and Daleth was shocked and angered at the sum total of what it cost her to have them fixed. By the time they had been given their inoculations, their anaesthetic, and their spaying operation, it was close to one hundred dollars per cat—several nights' worth of hauling chickens or turkeys off their perches and carrying them out to the truck load of cages.

"Pray God," she groaned, "that's the end of that!"

"Keep hoping," Bella laughed, "the word is out, the toms head off every night to fight and gossip, and when they meet a sweet young unspayed thing, why they just bring her home to this magic land where fish dinners are put out twice a day. Keep workin', Daleth, from where I sit it looks like you're running like hell and still fallin' behind."

She bought proper rubberized deck boots, she bought rain gear, she bought a rain hat and rubber gloves. Her stainless steel thermos cost over forty dollars, but the cheaper ones didn't last two weeks.

Summer days were long, but barely long enough. The garden had to be watered at least every second night, the produce picked at least every second day. They trimmed, blanched, and froze plastic bags full of green beans, yellow beans, peas, and raspberries. They cut the kernels from the cobs of corn, tossed the cobs onto the compost pile, picked and froze broccoli heads, filled breadbags full of ripe tomatoes and put them in the freezer for spaghetti sauce or soups. One thing after another, and still they made time to go swimming in the creek or river, take sandwich lunches with them on their days off and walk the beaches, or lie, smeared with coconut oil, on the hot rocks, sweating contentedly.

The first storms brought days of rain and wind, and Daleth learned the other side of fishing. The rain hat she had paid fifteen dollars for collected the water that fell on her head, and funneled it back and down her rain-slickered back. Which worked fine until she had to bend; then the water sluiced down the back of her neck, soaking her clothes, or dumped off the front of the hat onto whatever work she was bending to do. Her dryback, rain-repellent pants hindered her walking, made her sweat like a pig in spite of the bitter cold that lashed her cheeks, and somehow the small of her back was never warm.

"What you need," Al suggested, "is to get one of the old women to knit you a long sleeveless vest out of natural sheep's wool. Still got the sheep oil in the wool, so the water runs off. Of course," he warned, grinning widely, "it's gonna stink!"

But the stink didn't matter, the vest came down to her hips, she could bend and not feel her clothes pull up, the cold, waterproof slicker touching her unprotected back and kidney area. The leg warmers fit over her heavy wool pants, under her gumrubber boots, her waterproof pants hanging over the entire rig, swishing and rubbing when she walked, bending unwillingly in the endless cold.

"Christ," she growled, "if I fall overboard, I'll go down like a stone!"

"Better that way," Al agreed, "because no matter how well you swim, that water's so cold it'll kill you in twenty minutes. Even those survival suits aren't going to help."

And then salmon season was closed, the *Osprey* was hauled out of the water, and Daleth had her days to herself again. The first week, all she did was eat and sleep, and soak for hours in a tub of hot, soapy water.

Two weeks into the slack season, the lawyer contacted her to say her mother was getting married and, under the strict terms of her father's will, the house would be Daleth's, to rent or sell or move back into again, if she wanted.

"Oh," she said, feeling suddenly off balance and more than a bit hollow. "Oh, well, I'll have to think about it."

"The wedding is set for next month," the lawyer said, voice friendly, "and if you want me to handle things, I would be glad to do that. There is," he reminded her, "the matter of the furniture."

"Isn't that hers?" she asked stupidly.

"No."

"Oh. Well, she might want a few things like her china cabinet and . . ."

"I'll mention it to her."

"Thank you. If she wanted to stay on in the house that would be okay."

"Your father's will specified . . ."

"I know. And we both know why he did that. But if the house is going to be rented, what difference does it make if it's her that rents it?"

Daleth realized how far from home she had come when she found herself washing dishes and humming the music line to one of the commercials on the television Bella was watching in the other room. She stood still, her hands in hot soapy water past her wrists, waiting for the great finger to come from the clouds, through the roof, and squash her flat as a bug. The last sound she would hear would be the voice of Doom saying, "Now you've done it!" and then—splat—no more sinful Daleth. No more backsliding, devil-worshiping abomination humming a ditty about the number of scoops of dried grapes in a box of breakfast cereal.

She had never listened to the television or the radio when her father sat with his cans of beer or his bottles of liquor, she had developed an ability to deliberately ignore even the most cleverly hidden and trickily constructed subliminal temptations. But the ability had withered without the constant shoring up of the faithful and devout, and she realized with shock she knew the tunes of probably dozens of ditties, selling everything from dental decay to possible renal failure. And the great finger had not come from the clouds to wipe her out for eternity.

She finished the dishes, scrubbed and rinsed the sink, dried and put away the pots and pans, tidied the kitchen, and listened deliberately to the sound from the living room. Yes, she did know the music to the commercials. She even knew the dialogue of the commercials. Even more astounding, although she had never looked at the TV, she recognized the voices of the actors and knew the basic premise of the program. Knew who those imaginary people were, what their living conditions were, their problems, their personalities, their individual ways of coping.

She made a pot of tea, took it with two cups into the living room, put the tea and the cups on the coffee table, and, almost defiantly, sat on the sofa, poured herself a cup of tea, and waited. The finger didn't come through the roof of the living room any more than it had come through the roof of the kitchen.

"Ah," Bella sighed, "this is good." She lifted her feet onto a small, faded, Salvation Army thrift shop footstool, rested her head against the back of the old chair. "I've been laid off," she said, her voice deceptively casual.

"You've been what?"

"Laid off. Not enough work, they said."

"Oh, for Pete's sake!"

"Yeah. If they were going to lay me off, I wish they'd done it right at the start, when they first bought the place. I'd have got better pogey, because I was working full time. Now . . . ." she shrugged, "pain in the ass."

"I thought they were doing okay . . . ."

"Oh, they're doing okay." Bella laughed a short, harsh laugh. "They're just cheap is all. He's going to do all the cooking, she's going to do everything else. And while she's doing everything else, she can ram a broomstick up her arse and sweep the floor! Junior and Sissy don't want to go to school. They don't," Bella looked over at Daleth and grinned, "find it . . . meaningful."

"Washing dishes is meaningful?"

"So everybody has been let go because of lack of work, but really, what it is, is that his brother has showed up, and he, of course, needs a job, so . . . ."

"That's not fair!"

"No, but it isn't the first time in my life it's happened. Maharishi say true peace in life come with financial self-sufficiency."

"Confucius say who work for self have fool for boss and idiot for employee," Daleth countered.

"Maharishi say who hire brother-in-law pay wages for family fight."

"Daleth say it all suck slime."

"Bella agree."

Every day Bella headed off to town to make the rounds, applying for jobs and checking the board at the Employment office, and every day she came back without a job and out the money it had cost her in gas.

"So where are you going?" she asked, as Daleth headed for her truck, gumboots, dryback, and rain pants over her arm.

"Wanna come?"

"Come where?"

"Digging clams."

"Digging clams? Dally, it'll be dark in an hour!"

"Doesn't matter if it's light or dark, it's the tide that counts." And Daleth laughed softly. "I sound like an expert, huh? Harumph, harumph, a lecture on clams . . . all I know is what Al told me when he phoned. Meet him at the *Osprey* and go digging clams. For money."

"For money?" Bella grinned. "Give me half a minute and I'll be with you!"

Someone built a fire on the beach, but it was psychological warmth only, the wind gusted and snapped, the late autumn cold found every gap in their clothes, and the ankle-deep water numbed their feet in spite of the heavy wool socks and waterproof rubber boots. They dug the sodden sand, lifting clams and putting them in buckets, taking the buckets to their sacks and emptying them in, then back to the flats to bend over and dig more clams, following the retreating tide, digging with numb feet, with increasingly aching backs, their fingers, in the green rubber gloves, swollen and stiff, their hands cramping and sore.

They stopped once for coffee and stood by the fire, trying to get warm, past shivering, and Daleth thought her guts were going to cramp her double with the knotting. The coffee was hot and sweet and welcome, but when they left the fire to go back to the sand flats, the wind felt colder than ever, and she almost regretted having stopped for ten minutes.

"Hell of a way to do a person a favour, eh?" Al grunted, digging stolidly.

"It's money," Bella managed, her face red and swollen, her lips numb.

"Gonna seem damn well warm in that turkey shed tonight," Al tried to smile, then sniffed, his nose plugged, eyes streaming in the biting wind.

They quit when the tide came in, and rode back to the *Osprey* in a rubber zodiac. The deck of the fishboat was covered with sacks of clams, and they huddled together in the wheelhouse, grateful to be out of the frigid wind, drinking hot soup Al had brought in a huge picnic thermos.

"In my next life," Al promised, "I'm going to be born with blond hair and blue eyes, and I'm going to learn to play three musical instruments, sing, and dance, and then I'll go on TV and never have to work a day."

"Haven't you noticed?" Bella grumbled. "All those guys singing on TV have dark, curly hair, big spaniel eyes, and gold chains hanging around their necks. They also have hair on their chest that grows up their throat almost to their chin. And they can't sing a goddamn note!"

"There you have it," he agreed, "I can't do anything right. No chest hair, no curls, stupid bugger like me deserves to have to freeze his ass digging clams!"

They hauled the sacks to the buyer's shed, had them weighed, then drove straight to the poultry shed to start loading turkeys, working until the sky had lightened and the long winter night was definitely gone, replaced by the pale and all-too-brief winter day.

"Jesus," Bella sighed, settling herself on the seat of the pickup. Daleth slid in behind the wheel, turned on the truck, and drove home, wordlessly. There was nothing to say. It wasn't the worst work in the world, and it wasn't impossible, lots of people did it, why should she feel cheated? And yet she did feel cheated. Here she was, and how long had she been on her own, and what did she have to show for it? Everything she had was because her father had left it to her; what bits of furniture she had, the truck, even her share of the house and land. On her own, what had she accomplished?

They stumbled into the house, hung their rain gear in the little mud room to dry, then, while Daleth put the water on for coffee, Bella filled the tub with hot water, got in, and scrubbed herself clean. Halfway through Daleth's second cup of coffee, she and Bella traded places, and Daleth sat in the tub and tried to untangle the knot the bitter cold had tied in her gut.

"You want bacon?" Bella called.

"Yes, please. Lots of it."

"How do you want your eggs?"

"By sixes."

She was out of the tub, dried, and in her clean, warm clothes when the phone rang and the lawyer told her that her mother had agreed to rent the house, providing Daleth did not think that gave her the usual landlord's rights to go there and check on things.

"Tell her," she said carefully, "that I can only trust her Christian morality as far as things like damage and repair are concerned."

"I'm sure she won't object if I make arrangements and go out from time to time to see if there is anything requires attention," the lawyer said, just as carefully.

"Sure. Whatever," Daleth agreed. "Who did she marry?"

"The name on the lease . . ." The lawyer paused. Daleth heard the shuffling of papers. "The name on the lease is Swensen. Einair Swensen."

"My God," Daleth could barely speak, "he's old enough to be her father!"

She was eating her scrambled eggs and cheese when the laughter hit her.

"What's the joke?" Bella asked.

"My mother," Daleth managed, "married this guy who's got to be almost old enough for his pension. He's probably older than my grandfathers, and they're both dead!"

"Maybe he makes her feel safe," Bella shrugged. "Some women prefer it that way. Get'em with one foot in the grave and the other on a banana peel, then . . ." She made a shoving gesture and Daleth laughed harder.

"She spent years of her life moaning because my dad wasn't religious enough," she explained, "and now she's gone and married the most religious of the religious. Which leaves her nothing to complain about. Although I'm sure she'll find something."

"She's your mother," Bella said quietly.

"Huh?"

"She's your mother. Whatever else, she's your mother."

"People who say things like that usually grew up orphans," Daleth snapped. "If you'd had my mother for your mother, you'd know better."

"Maybe so, but she's still your mother."

VIII

Uncomfortable is a word to describe the numb feeling in those private parts of the body when your stiff new jeans prove to be just a little bit too tight, and the unyielding, double-stitched inseams run up both legs and meet in exactly that place no woman would ever have designed them to meet, which may prove that women are not designed by God to wear jeans, or it may prove male designers hate all things womanly, or it may mean nothing whatsoever. Uncomfortable is the first few times you wear your new leather shoes, before they have been trained not to rub or pinch. Uncomfortable has nothing to do with being cold for so many hours you feel as if your flesh will never forget the pain and misery, your mind never thaw enough for you to think rationally or feel emotional again. Uncomfortable has nothing to do with scorching your lips simply because your hands were too numb to warn you how hot the mug of coffee really was. There has to be another word for that dreadful condition that borders on hypothermia.

It is a way to buy food, pay the hydro and phone bills, buy heavy flannel shirts and triple-thick wool socks, and put gas in your truck. Heavy woolen clothes you wouldn't need if you weren't out there in the cold, digging in icy sand and mud for clams to sell by the pound to get the money to buy the gas to drive your truck to and from the dock where you catch the boat to take you to the mud or sand flats. Like a crazed wheel of fortune, where the players don't dare dream of winning, but pray every night that they not be forced by shithouse luck or asinine stupidity to join the ranks of the losers.

Two days off for Christmas, two days off for New Year, and the days spent mostly sleeping, trying to make up for the extra hours in the turkey sheds, lugging the birds out to the cages, walking with them, walking until their feet were shambling, even stumbling, their minds curled up on themselves, trying to ignore the stink of fear-sweating birds, the mustiness of feathers dropped in terror, the acid smell of shit and puzzlement, the eyes with their accusation of betrayal. The growing conviction that it is not true the creatures we murder and devour have no concept of death, no idea what awaits them when the cages are trucked to the poultry processing plant. The questions nobody dares ask, the thoughts nobody dares speak: do they know they are being taken to their death? Why do they not resist, leap at human eyes with sharp, curved beaks and crap-encrusted toenails? Why are there so many terms in the language to insult those creatures we cannibalize? Do we need to convince ourselves they deserve no better fate than to be munched, digested, and shat, flushed through sewer pipes and dumped in the ocean, washed onto beaches where people sit eating picnic sandwiches, chicken salad, turkey salad, ham salad, cold roast beef... Why so many words of praise for the wild animals...noble stag...proud bull moose...and such insults for the domesticated animals...silly cow, filthy pig, mindless sheep...?

The turkey grower gave them each a holiday bird, thank heaven not still walking, breathing, staring, but anonymous, depersonalized, plucked, cleaned, and ready for the oven. Or the freezer, which is where Daleth and Bella put both of their birds. Their Christmas dinner was the pepper-smoked salmon Al had given them, with baked potato and a huge salad; their New Year dinner, the ling cod feast Bella prepared with all the skill of fifteen years' professional cooking. And then they were back at work again, with the bitter wind blowing the sleet in their faces, the tide retreating and advancing with no interest at all in their presence, and the clams they dug and sold by the pound for less money than you'd believe a person would accept after all that misery.

"Who was the guy who asked about, if winter comes can spring be far behind?" Bella shivered, huddled in the wheelhouse, holding her cup of hot tea close to her face, the steam slowly warming her top lip, her chronically red and chapped nose.

"Asshole," Al said of the poet.

"If you can fly off to Hawaii and sit on the beach," Daleth muttered, "the answer is no, spring can't be far away. Out here, by Christ, it feels as if spring will never arrive."

"Daleth, you terrible thing," Bella sipped noisily, "you took the name of Christ in vain."

"I do a lot of things in vain," Daleth answered. "Try to balance my chequebook, try to save money, try to keep an optimistic outlook...all in vain."

"Fuck it," Al agreed.

"What are you complaining about?" Bella asked. "After all, civilization arrived on these shores and you've got television and penicillin and welfare and medical insurance and all kinds of things you never had when you were stone age people with no concept of Christianity."

"You're right," Al agreed, "and every day I get out of bed and thank Baby Jesus and the three wise men for being allowed the benefits of progress."

"One good thing about it," Daleth decided, "when your bum's been numb with cold for as long as mine has, you can forget that what you're doing makes your ass ache.''

And then, just when they were convinced it would never happen, spring arrived, with daffodils and hyacinths, lilac and narcissus, apple blossoms and primroses. They scraped the *Osprey*, painted her, took her on trial runs, and then they were out there again, setting lines and bringing in fish, as cold as they had been on the clam flats, but making slightly better money and, best of all, they were standing upright like people, not bent over with their noses in the mud, their bums pointing at the sky, backs aching, Achilles tendons stretched painfully, guts cramping.

Two weeks into the season, Al's brother-in-law got a trolling hook through the palm of his hand, and because it was his right hand and he was right-handed, he couldn't manage the wire snippers well enough with his clumsy left hand, so couldn't cut off the eye and pull the hook through. He had to make himself take his boat back to the wharf and get someone else to tie it up while he took a cab to the hospital. They managed to remove the hook, and Charlie went home, but was back two days later with such a grossly swollen hand, they admitted him to hospital. The fourth day after the accident, they operated on Charlie's hand, and when he came out of the anaesthetic, he was missing his baby finger and his ring finger.

''So what I had in mind,'' Al said quietly, ''was that maybe Bella could go out with you and I'd take Charlie's boat. Because there's too much for you alone on this boat, and Bella can't take Charlie's boat and . . . what do you think?''

''I feel a bit scared about it,'' Daleth admitted. ''I've never had the full responsibility. I mean . . . I think I could, but . . . ''

''Tell you what,'' Al said, ''anything comes up that I think you don't know about, I'll get on the mickey mouse and warn you. Like if the weather is going to change or whatever . . . we'll fish tandem, each of us there in case the other needs help.''

Bella grinned from ear to ear and headed into town right away to take money out of her sadly depleted bank account to buy the clothes she would need to work the fishboat. Charlie sat in his hospital bed nodding, his face mustard yellow, his lips faintly blue, his system boiling with antibiotics that killed off all the flora and fauna in his intestines and gave him a case of the shits that weakened him more than the staph infection had.

''God,'' Bella gasped, face pink with windburn, eyes wide and nervous, ''I'm never going to remember what all to do! I feel as if I'm running around in circles, undoing what few things I managed to do.''

''Tell you what,'' Daleth said easily, ''you just sit down on deck with a knife and a sharpening stone, and gut fish. I'll handle the rest. You forget everything I told you about what it is needs doing. Forget it all together. All you have to do is gut fish.''

But, of course, Bella couldn't sit on the deck and gut fish any more than Daleth had been able to sit on the deck and attract the fish for Al. There is nothing gets done on a fishboat for no reason at all, everything has its own order, its own logic, its own time to need attention, and the gutting knife gave Bella's mind time to get over being afraid, gave her time to calm down, stop trying to do the best job anybody had ever done, stop trying to anticipate what might be needed, and just catch on to the rhythm and order of the day's work.

During days of closure, they prepared the garden, fertilized the few fruit trees, and gazed, sometimes, at the television, but nothing they saw on it seemed to have anything to do with them. Or with anybody they knew. They slept a lot, sometimes on the beach, sometimes by the river, sometimes at home in their own beds, sweating in the growing heat, and then closure was over, fishing was open, and they were once more out on the sea, setting lines, hauling in fish, gutting them and icing them, over and over again, as monotonous as housework, as adventurous as slinging hash, as romantic as driving cab, over and over again.

They harvested their garden, used their days of closure to freeze vegetables for winter, to put away cod and salmon, squid and prawns, and then it was again time to haul the *Osprey* out of the water, and truck her to Al's front yard, where he could attend to such minor repairs as he felt like doing through the winter.

''Uh, Daleth?'' The voice came through the phone thin and nervous. ''Uh, this is, uh Sister Vaymer. . .I used to be Sister Stacey, and, uh, well, I think you should try to come and see your mother. She's in hospital.''

''In hospital? What's wrong?''

''I don't know exactly.'' The voice trembled, and Daleth felt her stomach drop down to her ankles. ''I know you and she haven't. . .I know. . .the past two and a half years have been strained, but. . .''

''You going to get into trouble for phoning me?'' Daleth blurted.

''No.'' There was the sound of a very weak laugh. ''No, I'm alone right now, it's not going to cause any trouble. But I think you should try to get to the hospital to see her.''

Bella was even more forceful about it than Sister Stacey Vaymer had been. Within hours, Daleth was packed, her truck topped with gas and oil, the big metal thermos filled with strong sweet coffee. ''You take care,'' Bella said, ''and phone me when you get there.''

''Sure,'' Daleth nodded.

''I mean it. Before you even go to see her, you phone me, no matter what time it is. From the pay phone in the lobby of the hospital. Collect, if you please. That way you can't put it off because you're six cents short for the coin phone.''

''Nag, nag, nag,'' Daleth teased.

''Nag nag is nothing to what you'll get if you don't phone!''

''I'll phone,'' Daleth promised. ''I'll phone for sure.''

Daleth had a C.J. Cherryh book for the ferry, and a Stephen King for backup, and she had a shoebox full of music tapes for the player in the pickup. She stopped every two or three hours to stretch her legs, step off into the bushes to pee, or to take pictures with her birthday present camera from Bella, a much less complex thing than the one her father had left her. All you had to do with this one was aim it and shoot. To use her father's camera you first needed a six-week course at the provincial technical institute.

Her mother wasn't in the regional general hospital, but in a private clinic on the far side of town. When Daleth arrived, the ornate, wrought-iron gate was shut and locked, the sign firmly proclaiming there would be no visiting except at visiting hours or by prior arrangement. She was tempted to take a kick at the gate, but, instead, took a picture, then drove back into town to get something to eat. She phoned the clinic to warn them she was coming, then phoned Bella, and they laughed together about the sign on the gate.

''Und ve haff vays, ja?'' Bella teased. ''You phone me again after you've seen her.''

''Worried she might be nasty to me?''

''Damned certain she will be.''

Daleth drove back to the clinic, left her pickup on the parking lot, and walked to the main door. Just inside was the Reception/ Information desk, with a coolly smiling young woman in white, who nodded, told Daleth which room her mother was in, and reminded her, in case she needed reminding, that visiting hours were only from six-thirty to eight.

Daleth walked quietly along the hallway, past closed doors with numbers on them, past a closed door with "Ladies" written on it, past another with "Cleaning" marked in prim black print. And then she was at door number 14 at the very end of the hallway. She opened it without knocking and stepped inside, closing the door behind her.

Her mother lay in bed, seeming to be asleep, and a well-dressed, pleasant-enough-looking man in his late forties was sitting on a straight-backed wooden chair, reading the Bible to himself. He looked up, saw Daleth, and smiled.

"Daleth," he said softly, "I'm so glad you could come."

"What's wrong with my mother?" she asked.

"She's fine," he soothed. "You obviously don't recognize me. I'm Einair Swensen, your mother's husband."

Daleth stared, then shook her head, grinning in spite of herself. "I thought," she blurted, "I thought my mother had married *old* Einair!" and she giggled.

"No," the well-dressed man laughed. "No, she married me. Although Uncle Einair did introduce us." He stood, offered Daleth the chair. "I knew you when you were only, oh, so high," he measured a spot somewhere between his knee and his hip. "Such a serious little girl, you were."

Daleth sat on the chair beside the bed, turning it so she could look directly at her mother. Her mother lay on her side, her back toward Daleth, her hair loose on the pillow. She didn't look as if there was anything at all wrong with her.

"Momma?" Daleth said softly. "Momma, it's me. It's Daleth."

She heard the door open, turned to see who was coming into the room. She had a quick flash of Sister Stacey Vaymer and old Einair, with a woman in a white uniform. And then, suddenly, Einair the younger was behind her, his arms pinning her to the chair, one hand over her mouth, and someone was jabbing a needle into her arm. Daleth heaved her body desperately, was almost off the chair, and Old Einair had her. She could feel something very very cold moving in her upper arm, she kicked frantically, had the satisfaction of hearing Einair the younger gasp, but then her mother sat up in bed and looked at her with wide-open, lucid eyes, and Daleth froze, pinned where she was by the look of total satisfaction on her mother's perfectly healthy face.

There was nothing she could do. Whatever they had rammed into her made her mouth taste sour, her spit bitter. She was aware of everything going on around her, with her, and to her, and she couldn't do a thing.

The women stripped her, pushed her arms into an open-backed hospital gown, pushed her down on the bed, and pulled the blankets up under her chin. Her mother moved to the closet, took some clothes from inside, walked to the small, adjoining bathroom, and went inside. It seemed the same second, she came back out again, fully dressed, and smiling that same satisfied smile.

The men came in, then, and there was someone else with them, someone in grey pants, white shirt, a grey tie with a diagonal burgundy bar on it, and over all that, a long-sleeved, button-front, white starched coat. He had a shiny metal flashlight the size of a fountain pen in his left breast pocket, and used it to peer into Daleth's eyes. He pulled a stethoscope from his right front pocket and listened to her heart, then nodded, and two nurses began fritzing around with Daleth's left arm, inserting and hooking up an IV.

She could see the doctor talking, but nothing he said made any sense to her; he was standing at the end of a spyglass, and the tunnel was getting longer and longer, narrower and narrower, until there was only this endless circular blackness with a tiny pin-prick of light at the other end, the doctor trapped in the pin-prick, his mouth moving as he explained something to some people.

She went to sleep then, and stayed asleep for longer than you would think a human person could survive. While she was asleep, they inserted a catheter and rectal tube. As one bottle of clear fluid dripped into her veins and was emptied, another bottle replaced it. From time to time, they came in with hypodermic needles and injected fluid into the bubble on the IV tube. Sometimes they injected sedatives, sometimes tranquilizers, sometimes other drugs, the names and purposes of which we can only pray none of us ever need to know. They added trace elements, they added vitamins, they added whatever the doctor took it into his head to tell them to add, and Daleth slept. The blinds were pulled on her window, the door shut to her room, there was no radio, no television, and none of the staff who went into the room spoke, not even to each other. Sensory deprivation more complete than if she had volunteered to climb into the legendary tank.

Bella waited until two in the morning, then decided everything was hunky-dory and she could go to bed. She convinced herself Daleth and her mother had established a rapport, had healed the rift, had mutually agreed to forgive and forget, then had sat talking together until it was too late to even consider phoning someone who might well be in bed sound asleep. Bella made herself believe she would get a phone call in the morning that would tell her love had bridged all gaps, healed all wounds, and accomplished all miracles.

Her determined optimism lasted two full days, then the feeling in the pit of her stomach would not be ignored. She wasn't constipated, she didn't have indigestion, her morning coffee wasn't sitting in a sour puddle . . . she was scared. Scared for Daleth, scared of what she did not know, might never suspect.

The police had no reports of an accident involving a camperized pickup driven by a young woman. The general hospital had no record of Daleth's mother being admitted as a patient. The private clinic refused to give any information, and none of the hotels admitted to having Daleth as a registered guest.

By week's end, Bella was as close to frantic as she had ever been in her life.

"Did you phone her mother?"

"She won't talk to me," Bella said sourly.

"Won't talk, huh?" Charlie rubbed the new pink skin. "Usually when people decide to not talk it's because they're hidin' somethin'."

"I'm scared, Charlie."

"Me, too," Al agreed. "I'm always scared when the holy and righteous get their shirts in a knot."

"Phone the lawyer," Charlie suggested. "Phone the lawyer and make sure that there's a stop put to anything cute."

"You're a genius," Bella sighed with relief.

"I ain't no genius," Charlie contradicted. "I've seen what happens when the ones with the Bibles decide to deprive you of everything you've got. For the good of your immortal soul, of course."

The lawyer asked very few questions and said nothing that could in any way be interpreted to mean he thought Bella had her head up her ass. "This won't be cleared up overnight," he warned. "And we have to make sure we do things legally."

Day after day of sensory deprivation, night after night, one week, two weeks, three weeks, and then they began to deprive her even of her dreams. Electrodes were attached to her temples and forehead, to her wrists and the backs of her hands, even to her waxy closed eyelids, and every time the machine registered the rapid eye movement, or the increased heart rate, that told of a dream, a mild electric current would be zapped to her, disrupting the dream, stopping it.

Without her dreams, her mind began to come apart at the seams. She lost weight in spite of the nutrients they poured into her. Her hair started to come out when the nurse brushed it, her skin took on a yellowish tinge that warned of liver complications, and still they kept on with what they were doing. Except now they began to play the tapes, over and over and over again, the same few phrases, the same careful editing of fact. What she knew, they tried to prove a lie; what was a lie, they tried to convince her poor, battered brain was truth, and when she started squirming and twisting in protest, clenching her fists and trying to raise her arms, the good Doctor Campbell had them load her on a stretcher, push her down a hallway to a different, more openly diabolical room. They removed the IV, put her on a rubber-covered table, slid an airway in her flaccid mouth, and put electricity through the lobes of her brain.

There was too much sedative in her to allow her to thrash in convulsions in an honest and natural way. She gagged, she bit down on the rubber airway, her spine arched slightly, she balanced on her shoulders and heels, then her bladder emptied, her bowels spewed air, she collapsed, and her fingers and toes twitched madly.

Every day for a week and a half they took her for Electro-Convulsive Therapy, then returned her to the room and the tapes played. The tapes played. The tapes played. And the good doctor took his notes, kept his records up to date, and sent copies of them off to the people south of the border, the people paying for all this fancy treatment.

The spyglass was there again, but it wasn't working properly. She could hear their voices, but she couldn't see them, not any of them. All she could see was the little pin-prick of light. They were talking about lawyers and about an airtight agreement, and someone, was it Sister Stacey or her own mother, someone was angry, and someone else, the young one, not the old one, was being cautious. Saying the terms of the contract clearly stated that if either of them died or was in any way at all incapacitated, the other got it all, saying this a second time, and warning them that any attempt to have someone—who?—declared incompetent, would only make it easy for someone else—who?—to wind up with everything, possibly including the house they lived in. Who lived in? What house? What did a house have to do with a spyglass?

A house. Daleth thought of a house. It was no house she had ever seen in her life, she knew that much. Houses here were made of wood or of stucco, not of soft, red brick. But this house was made of brick and it was old, very old, rickety-rackety, roof-blown-off-one-corner old. The rooms where the roof was ruined were mildewed and mouldered, the floors rotted, leaking rain down onto the rooms below, but someone had lived here once, someone had been happy and sad, had laughed and cried, and in the other part of the house, where the roof wasn't ruined, things waited.

She was in a small house, or shed, or barn, or . . . something. There were cages, so many cages, wire mesh cages, and in this one a white rabbit with black paws, black ears, black tail, and black nose was lying like a sphinx, with six, seven, eight babies climbing on it, jumping over it, lying beside it, snuggled and warm. And in this cage, a pheasant, the body the colour of butter, the tail silvery white, curved and curved and curved, such a tail, and behind it, a speckledy brown one sat on eggs, crooning softly, crooning deep in her throat chrrrrruik, and chickens, and another rabbit, and someone—who?—was feeding them, talking to them, scratching the rabbit's ears, stroking the pheasant's back, and then her mother was there, her mother in a faded cotton dress with an apron over top, her mother was there and she was starting fires, in the straw, in the hay, in a pile of empty feed bags, starting a fire, and oh God, they were all dying, the bunnies and the chicks and the rabbits and the pheasants, all dying, and she was yelling at her mother, yelling and swearing and trying to get her poor animals out of their cages, pulling them out and tossing them through a window to the ground, tossing them and turning them loose, better they run away, go wild, be lost in the bush, better even they be eaten by owls or hawks than to just sit here in these cages and smother, and her mother was saying it was cruel to deliberately try to take a child away from its mother, but better it go than be burned up, and she turned to her mother and yelled and yelled and yelled, you dirty rotten puke, you dirty rotten puke, you . . .

They thought she was dreaming, of course, and zipped her with a little bit of electricity to break the pattern of the dream. The fire vanished, the mesh cages vanished, the little shed vanished, but not the echo of dirty rotten puke, dirty rotten puke.

And then she was in the old brick house, in the part not ruined, and anyone would know this had been a beautiful place to live, the walls were wood, not too dark, and there was an old clock, not ticking now, of course, but it would again, all she had to do was wind it up herself and it would tick. It might not tell time, but it would tick. An old old desk. She watched herself lift the sloped lid of the desk, and there was no writing paper inside, but she could get some. There were nibs, brass nibs, slightly touched with rust, nibs and an ink well and a bag, a beaded bag, pursed shut with a drawstring, and on the drawstring a bead, an amethyst bead. She watched herself open the beaded bag and pull from inside a triple strand of pearls, and she knew they were real. A strand of crystal beads, and another, and a string of coloured crystal beads, not cheap glass, hand cut, catching the light and breaking it into prisms.

Again they thought she was dreaming and sent the shiver through her head to disrupt the dream. All they did, although they didn't know they did it, was turn the prisms into shimmering colours, a floating rainbow. It drifted around in the room, and the young Einair was wrong when he droned that in his father's house were many mansions, he was a fool, a total fool, it wasn't his father's house, it was her father's house, and the mansion was where she was, and it was a bit of a wreck, but it could be fixed again, because brick didn't rot the way wood did, or minds did, brick just got weathered and more beautiful, and down in the basement, down where they didn't even know anything existed, there were trunks full of clothes to wear and a smaller trunk full of books, hand-written journals, the woman who had lived here before had sat at the upstairs desk and used those nibs in a long black pen, she dipped those nibs in that inkwell, and wrote those stories, and nobody but Daleth knew anything about any of it, certainly not these people, these stupid stupid people. They didn't even know that under the floor of the basement there was the skeleton of a woman, and cuddled in her bone arms, the skeleton of a baby, buried forever, buried and pressed down by the weight of the floor, the floor made of lies, and of injections, and of trips down a hallway to a terrible place where the Inquisition was alive and well and wearing white smocks.

All she had to do was pay more attention to the stories in the little trunk, the box, the Pandora's box, all she had to do was pay more attention to them than to the needles in her arm.

She had a camera. Somewhere. She had a camera and her friend had given it to her for her birthday. Birthdays were just another day, only the devil worshipers bothered with birthdays, the Faithful knew that it was just another way to try to tie your loyalty to this evil world, to try to take your mind off the real day of celebration, the day when destruction rained from the skies and the Faithful were raptured to heaven, safe from the flames of that last cleansing time. But her father had always given her something for her birthday, and even if her mother snatched it away, Daleth knew her father hadn't forgotten. Sometimes he would be crafty and a week before, or a month afterward, would pile her into his truck and drive down to the ice cream store and get her a huge, gooey creation with marshmallow and whipped cream and banana and bright red maraschino cherry and chocolate sauce and two kinds of ice cream in a long, pressed-glass dish, and she'd be eating it, happy and laughing, and he'd say "Happy Birthday old kid," and she was a sinner, a go-to-hell sinner, because she just grinned and nodded and ate and ate and he sat there across the table from her, grinning, his eyes bright and damp, watching her pig out on her sinful ice cream. And her friend had given her a camera and she had taken pictures with it. A picture of an orange cat. A picture of a boat. A picture of a man with straight black hair, brown skin, and slanted black eyes.

Who leaned over her bed, smiling and saying "sssshh." A picture man telling her to "sssshh." A picture man or a man in a picture? Lifting her, carrying her to an open window, passing her through the window to another man whose face she couldn't see.

And they were walking through the night, and someone climbed a fence, then she was handed over it to him, and he carried her to a car. Someone opened the back door and she was passed in, a woman held her like a baby, held her tightly, and all Daleth had to do was rest her head on the woman's shoulder, feel the woman's lap beneath her ribs, her stick-out arch of ribs, and someone tucked a quilt around her skinny legs and corpse feet, there was the sound of a door closing, then two doors opening, and then those doors closed, a car engine roared to life and they were moving.

"Oh, Daleth," the woman sobbed, "oh God almighty damn what have they done to you?"

"I have a camera," Daleth whispered. "I have a camera. For my birthday. My friend gave me a camera and they took it."

"We've got your camera, Daleth. It was in the pickup truck and we stole the truck from them about an hour and a half ago," a man's voice said from the front seat.

"Dirty rotten puke," she said conversationally. "Took my stuff. Took it all."

"Oh, baby," the woman gritted, squeezing her tightly. "Just go to sleep, babe, it'll be okay, we'll have you home in no time."

"My house," Daleth said with conviction. "Not theirs."

"No. Not theirs," Bella promised.

Daleth opened her eyes because someone was sticking something down her throat. She raised her hand, tried to grasp the arm holding the tongue depressor.

"It's okay," the voice said calmly. "Just checking you over."

"Check the oil," she whispered. "Fill it with unleaded, please."

"Atta girl," the voice approved.

"I have a camera, you know," she said confidentially. "I really do."

Bella sat on the bed and held Daleth's hand while the new doctor checked her reflexes, peered into her eyes, sat her up and thumped her chest, her back, her shoulders, then placed her back on the pillows and watched as she drifted off to sleep again.

The next time she wakened, the new doctor was there with Bella, and in the doorway there were two policemen she didn't know, and someone she thought she might know, a man who might or might not be a lawyer.

"Dally," Bella said clearly and slowly, "this is important. Do you want to stay here or do you want to go live with your mother?"

"Home," Daleth said.

"Here or with your mother?" Bella insisted.

"Here. Home. Here," she managed.

"Did you hear her?" Bella asked.

"Ask her if she knows what day it is," a policeman suggested.

"Why, it's my birthday," Daleth said, smiling faintly, "and I have a camera."

"Is it her birthday?" the policeman asked, suspiciously.

"No, it's not," the lawyer admitted.

"Doesn't sound too compos mentis to me," the policeman insisted.

"Hungry," Daleth smiled at Bella. "Very hungry."

They stood around in her bedroom, talking to each other, while Bella hurried to the kitchen to warm up canned chicken noodle soup. Daleth didn't really know what they were talking about, and she didn't really care. Until she heard one of the policemen mention "pickup" and "stolen."

"That's my truck," she said firmly. "My pickup. My camera was in it. My suitcase. Not stolen now." She tried to sit up and couldn't, but the lawyer smiled at her as if she had just managed to skip to the top of Mount Everest.

"Where do you live?" the doctor asked.

"Here," she said, gripping her comforter with skinny fingers.

"Where's here?" the policeman asked.

"Go away," Daleth said clearly. "Bugger off. Dirty rotten puke."

"Easy, babe, easy," Bella soothed. "Your soup is ready. Just sit up on these pillows, that's it, now drink slowly, real slowly, you haven't had anything in your stomach for nearly three months, so don't gulp or be greedy.''

Less than half a cup of broth and Daleth was full, getting sleepy and, suddenly, very very warm. When she wakened several hours later, there was more broth and a welcome sponge bath. She even managed to brush her teeth, then was asleep again, as if she had spent twelve hours on a heaving deck, working as hard as she ever had. The doctor was there in the morning, telling her she could try some Cream of Wheat, and then it was supper time and she'd slept through lunch and knew it. Al was there that time, and he lifted her from the crumpled, sweaty sheets, carried her to the living room, sat her in the big chair with her feet on the coffee table, protected from the sharp edge by a pillow. He sat talking to her, telling her what he was doing with the *Osprey*, and she knew she knew him, knew, in fact, she knew him quite well, but she could not find the time in her life when she had met him, become acquainted with him, began to feel he was her friend. He was just there, full-blown and accepted as a friend, someone who had come through a window to carry her away from that awful dead place.

Bella stripped and remade the bed, then she and Al carried Daleth back to bed, and Al waited in the kitchen, drinking coffee and muttering to himself, while Bella again supervised the sponge bath.

''Should have done this before we changed the bed,'' she grunted.

''You're very kind,'' Daleth responded. Bella looked at her, opened her mouth as if to say something, then closed it again, words unsaid.

Al brought in her supper, a half cup of broth and a poached egg, and nobody scolded when she could eat only part of the egg. When the soup was almost finished, Bella had some oily drops Daleth had to swallow, less than half a teaspoon full, and Daleth couldn't begin to identify the strange taste.

''Vitamins,'' Bella explained without being asked.

''Pills?'' Daleth eyed them warily.

''The doctor says you have to be weaned off whatever it was they were sticking into you.'' Bella controlled her voice as carefully as she could, the rage didn't show, but anger and disillusionment peered around the edges.

''What?''

''I don't know,'' Bella admitted. ''The doctor had blood samples taken, and he could pretty well tell from that.''

''He told us,'' Al contributed, ''but it was all Greek to me.''

Daleth slept again, and in the morning it was Al's wife Sally who was there with warm wash water and soft towels, speaking quietly and soothingly, helping Daleth with her sponge bath, helping Daleth into fresh pyjamas, helping Daleth out of bed and into the big chair that had been moved to the bedroom.

She sat propped by pillows, staring at her skinny stranger hands and gaunt forearms. Big knobby bones where her wrists used to be muscled; pale skin where she had once been tanned. In the mirror above the dresser, she saw a face and knew it was her own, but she did not recognize herself.

Every day she was able to sit up for longer periods of time, every day she was able to eat a bit more, to take notice of things around her, and before too long, she was on her feet, walking around, as stiff as a stick woman.

''How did you know?'' she asked.

''You didn't phone again,'' Bella said, and knew by the look on Daleth's face that what she had said meant nothing to her. ''You were supposed to phone me, and you didn't. By the next afternoon I was getting anxious, by night I was worried, and the third morning, I phoned the hospital. Instead of answering my questions, they asked if I was a member of your family and, like a fool, I said no. That was it. They wouldn't tell me anything. So I phoned the police. A week or so later they told me they weren't going to tell me anything because I wasn't a member of your family, your family was 'taking care of you,' and you were 'improving.' So I went to the lawyer.''

''Lawyer?'' Daleth tried fishing in the jelly of her mind. What had she heard about lawyers when the body and mind began to adjust to the massive doses of reality altering drugs. ''Incompetent,'' she guessed.

''That was later,'' Bella agreed, making the mental quantum leap easily. ''First we tried half a dozen different things. I thought if I could just get in to see you, talk to you, maybe find out why . . . and then they started making noises about you not being able to take care of your own affairs.'' She laughed harshly. ''That's when we whipped out our contract about the house. And,'' she grinned, ''suggested it wouldn't be at all hard to include everything else registered in your name. Truck, other house, the whole nine yards.''

''We have to do that,'' Daleth said suddenly.

''Yes,'' Bella said carefully, ''but first we have to be able to prove you're . . . we have to be able to prove you've got all your marbles.''

''But I don't,'' Daleth realized. Bella's eyes flooded, she looked away, biting her lip. "I don't, do I?"

"No babe, you don't," Bella answered honestly. "Not yet. But you will."

They started taking her for walks, at first just to the porch to look out at the winter-wet yard, then down the steps and along the walk to the shed where the cats lived, a dozen or more of them now.

"I rounded up the whole bunch of them," Bella said, "and drove to the vet and said I wanted them fixed. Said I'd pay him on time. And if even one of them had kittens, I'd stop paying him. So. . . there they are. And so far, no more kittens. Of course," she grinned, "I throw rocks at any new faces that show up for meals."

Some days, when it was clear, they loaded Daleth in the car and drove her to the beach, or took her to the dock to watch the unloading of the sacks of clams.

"You aren't working," she realized.

"I'm okay," Bella lied. "Everyone deserves a rest."

"You'll be broke," Daleth warned.

"Already am," Bella laughed.

"I have money," Daleth realized.

"We have to be careful," Bella explained. "If we do anything too fast, they'll say you're not able to make lucid decisions and I'm taking advantage."

Her appetite returned, and she could eat again without having to fight nausea or revulsion. But her stomach was still shrunken, so instead of three normal meals a day, Daleth had six or seven little ones, and still she didn't gain weight. But she had energy enough to start puttering in the garden, and it was there she decided to start learning something to replace what had been wiped from her memory.

"Did you ever feel as if you believed something you knew wasn't true?" she asked.

"Did I ever. . . I don't know what you mean."

"There are these things I. . .know. . .but. . .I don't believe them." Daleth struggled to explain something she couldn't understand. "And other things I. . .believe. . .but. . .I don't think any of it is true."

"Like what?"

"I have these. . .they're like memories, almost. Or little movies in my head. Me and my mom. And I'm me, I look like I do now. . .or rather, like I did before this thing happened. . .adult face, adult eyes, adult. . .but I'm small. Kid sized. And my mom is big. She's an adult and I'm a kid. Only I'm *not!* And we're having fun. We're swimming and laughing and she's cuddling me and. . .she never did anything like that, I'm sure. My dad did, I think. But. . .but I don't remember him. I know I had one and he was. . .nice. But he isn't in any of these movies. And sometimes I'm with the Faithful, and they are all so. . .loving. Old Einair is like a grandpa or something and young Einair is like an uncle. Even Brother Anton is. . .brotherly! But. . .'' she shook her head, aware she was very upset, her hands shaking.

''You know who I am?'' Bella asked carefully.

''My friend,'' Daleth answered instantly. ''We washed dishes.''

''I cooked,'' Bella corrected, ''you washed dishes. Do you remember how you got to the Inn?''

Daleth tried to remember, but there was nothing, she was just suddenly in the Inn, sitting on a bed, eating fish and chips, and a young man was laughing and then he was hurrying from the room, looking at her as if she was growing snakes instead of hair.

''We could ask the doctor,'' Bella said hesitantly. ''He might know someone who. . .''

''No!'' Daleth flared. ''No more hocus pocus.''

''You're the boss,'' Bella smiled.

They took the little green punt and went to the lake. Daleth sat quietly, waiting for fish and groping with questions.

''How did you get me out of there?''

''Al, Charlie, and I drove up.'' Bella hauled in a speckled trout, carefully removing the hook and putting the flopping fish in the wicker creel. ''Looked in the phone book for Swensens. Christ, must be a thousand of them! We drove around from one address to the other, and then we saw your pickup truck parked in back of one of the houses.''

''My mother's house?''

''No. We didn't even check there. I didn't want her to see me in case she remembered me. Besides which, I didn't think they'd dare have it there. I guess it was at his dad's place.''

''With my camera.''

''Right. So when we knew where that was, we looked for the hospital. Had a hell of a time finding out what room you were in! Finally, Charlie just walked in with a bouquet of flowers and said, 'Is Daleth Fisher in Room 10?' and the nurse looked at him without seeing him and said, 'No, Room 14, but you can't go in there. Leave the flowers here.' So he did. And we left. Went back at night and jimmied open the window. Windows, actually. The first room we tried was empty. Christ, but that was scary! We hadda do'er all over again; go out the window, move along the outside wall, jimmy another window...Thank God *that* was the right one. I don't know if I could'a took much more of the tension.'' She grinned, then winked. ''Wasn't sure you were worth it, kiddo. But there you were, lookin' like Death warmed over...And we swiped you, then drove back to where your truck was. I had,'' she grinned, ''the spare set of keys. Charlie just got in and drove off with it. Nothing very heroic about it at all.''

''Why did they do it?'' Daleth asked pathetically.

''Probably figured it would work. They'd have you back, prim, proper, religious, and, above all, obedient. They'd have control over you and that would give them control over your stuff. Although I really do believe it was you they wanted more than your stuff.''

''Me?'' Daleth shook her head. ''I don't see why they'd bother.''

''Dally, listen to me. And listen good. They think they are *right*. More than just think they're right, they *believe* they're right. Your mother wouldn't have given a fat rat's ass if she hadn't loved you. If she hadn't loved you she'd have just let you walk off down the pike. But she loved you. She probably still loves you. And as far as she's concerned, you're in danger.'' Daleth tried to understand what Bella was explaining, but she could only shake her head and weep. ''Babe,'' Bella tried again, ''Listen...if you had someone you loved and had loved for damn near twenty years, and that person had, say, cancer, wouldn't you do everything you could to save her? Well, she's not just tryin' to save your life, she's tryin' to save your soul, and she really really Believes...she'll do anything it takes, whatever it takes, at whatever cost to anybody. That,'' she sighed, ''is what makes her so goddamn dangerous.''

''No,'' Daleth said stubbornly. ''You don't do stuff like that to people you love. If she had loved me she would never have decided I should marry someone who gave me the flyin' creeps.''

''Why not?'' Bella argued. ''What if she married for love, and then found that the old ghosts wouldn't leave your dad at peace? What if she loved him and couldn't handle the drinking? And then found a bunch of people who didn't drink...and she wanted good things for you...not mistakes and regrets...the guy she picked was sober, he was...successful, and...he didn't have old ghosts?''

''Why in hell do you defend her?'' Daleth screamed. ''Why are you trying so hard to make me see what you want me to see?''

''Because I don't want you to spend as many years walking around under a load of hate as I did,'' Bella said firmly. ''It takes energy to hate, Dally, and as long as you hate them, they're alive in your head, picking at you. Believe me, the hate you hold for them will hurt you more than it hurts them.''

''No it won't,'' Daleth contradicted stubbornly. ''I'll show them!''

The lawyer listened to everything she had to say, then shook his head regretfully. ''Why not?'' she asked.

''Not a hope,'' he said, as if that explained things, instead of raising even more questions.

''You can't just grab people . . . ''

''You don't have any witnesses that you were grabbed,'' he said flatly. ''Their story will be that you became hysterical or violent or uncontrollable or . . . ''

''But I *didn't!* I was sitting on a chair and . . . ''

''No witnesses,'' he repeated.

''They drugged me!''

''No proof of that.''

''What do you mean, no proof of that. Ask the doctor what I was like when . . . ''

''For all anybody knows, any drugs given you were given on your way back home from the hospital. For all anyone knows, you were using drugs before you went to see your mother. For all anyone knows, it was because of drugs they had to keep you in the hospital.''

''You can be sure,'' Bella said softly, ''that they won't admit to anything.''

Daleth wanted to say they were honest people, but she remembered, in spite of the tapes, how they had hidden the truth about One-Eyed Bill. And there was something she ought to know, something she ought to remember, about Anton, too.

''Another thing,'' the lawyer said, and somehow she knew that he, at least, believed her, ''nobody wants to believe that things like this happen to ordinary people in ordinary places. This is tabloid stuff, this isn't home-town newspaper material! This kind of thing only happens in Toronto and Montreal. And,'' she knew it was a gentle warning, ''it only happens to people who have a few screws loose, anyway.''

They rode home in silence, and Daleth felt as if she wanted to either cry like a baby or just relax long enough to let her temper explode. But crying wouldn't change anything, and pitching a fit might only prove she had loose screws and they had been right to do what they had done.

Every day she made sure she did more than the day previous, and every day she regained her strength. A few sit-ups, a few push-ups, some isometrics that left her sweating and wobbly-kneed, and as her muscle tone returned, so did some measure of control over her emotions.

''You think they'll try again?'' she asked.

''Listen,'' Bella said firmly, ''when I was a kid, my grandfather told me something. First time you do me dirt, shame on you; second time you do me dirt, shame on me.''

''I heard a guy on the radio saying the market was up and house prices were higher than they'd been in six years.'' Daleth studied her fingernails, glad her hands no longer trembled with weakness. ''What I'd like to do,'' she took a deep breath, knowing she would drop the idea if Bella didn't agree with her, ''is tell the lawyer to sell that house. I can do it,'' she said quickly, ''because she got married again, and the will said . . .''

''I know what it said,'' Bella soothed.

''Then I'd like to give her thirty brand new silver dollars.'' Daleth felt scalding tears slip down her face, drop from her chin to her blue jeaned lap. ''She'd know what I was telling her.''

''Someone once told me yogurt was the same as pottage,'' Bella laughed. ''Too bad you can't stuff the silver dollars into a quart of plain yogurt, she'd understand that, too.''

''I'm gonna do it,'' Daleth vowed. ''And then . . .''

''Then you're gonna remember what their Belief teaches them: a soft voice turneth away wrath.'' Bella spoke firmly, her eyes drilling through the rage and hate Daleth felt. ''Be kind to your enemies and thereby confound them. You'll do as many of the Right things as you can do in your ordinary life; you won't give them the satisfaction of seeing you go to hell in a handbasket! By your deeds shall ye be known, kiddo; and,'' she winked, ''you will be rewarded in heaven for good deeds done here on earth.'' She took a clean hanky from her pocket, wiped Daleth's eyes, then patted her cheek. ''Phone the real estate agent,'' she suggested softly, ''then phone the lawyer, then get on with your life. That, more than anything will drive those pinch-nosed bible-thumpers right up the wall.''

''Maybe get enough money to buy our own boat,'' Daleth sobbed. She walked to the bathroom, pulled a long strip from the toilet roll, blew her nose repeatedly, then wiped her eyes with the cuff of her shirt. ''I didn't know you knew your Bible,'' she blurted, sniffling tiredly.

''Darlin','' Bella shook her head, ''there's a whole bunch of stuff about me you don't know. Why,'' she winked, ''eye hath not seen nor ear heard, neither has it entered into the hearts of man, the things about me that you don't know.''

''You're gonna go to hell,'' Daleth grinned.

''Yeah,'' Bella agreed. ''With people like your family and mine taking over heaven, I think I prefer hell.''

THE COMMON NAME FOR DIGITALIS IS FOXGLOVE

I

Both of Blackie Williams' parents had been Doctor Barnardo street ayrabs, brought from a life of nothing in Britain to a life of next-to-nothing in Canada. The good doctor got a degree of acclaim, his picture in the paper at least twice a month, an aura of liberal do-good charitability that may or may not have been deserved, and some lucre besides. The streets of London, Manchester, Glasgow, Edinburgh and Cardiff were tidied of ragged, foul-mouthed urchins, and the needs of a relatively new, undoubtedly deserving country for unpaid labour were met. The farmers, shopkeepers and other petty exploiters looked like open-hearted Christians, and only the ayrabs themselves had an alternate opinion. Those who survived told of hunger, cold, overwork, cruelty, sexual abuse and brutality. But who would listen to an ungrateful brat, saved from a life of squalor and lawlessness. Liars, all.

Tom Williams was seventeen, fifteen pounds too thin, barefoot and with only the clothes on his back. Martha Logan was sixteen and in similar straits. But the snow was beginning to melt and the little blue and purple crocuses were already blooming. Soon the gophers would come out of their holes and a well-aimed rock would provide a meal; sage hens would nest and there would be eggs to steal and suck for the nourishment inside; and the jesus awful killing cold would vanish for a few more months.

The sun warmed the earth and stirred the sap in the trees, and the farmer got Martha alone in the barn. Tom walked in some five minutes too late to avert the episode and he asked no questions, not then, not later. He knew Martha hadn't invited this, he knew she wasn't enjoying it and he knew she would be making loud protest if not for the huge, dirty, calloused hand over her mouth. He picked up the axe and used the handle alongside the farmer's ear. Martha rolled out from underneath and didn't bother wasting so much as a minute in hysterics or tears. She knew she could stay and probably wind up wife in name and fact, mother to a brood, and be no worse treated than any other Canadian farm wife. She knew most of the men in the country considered rape tantamount to courtship but she knew, without having the vocabulary to express it, that no ring, no preacher, no Mrs. before her name could ever make rape respectable in her own eyes, or acceptable in her heart.

Martha would have taken nothing but her wages, but Tom had better sense than she did. He knew their wages were pittance and wouldn't last two days in the real world, where you could buy all the food you needed, even all the food you wanted. And he knew, too, that people were going to do nothing but sic the dogs on people dressed the way he and Martha were dressed. So he took reasonably good pants, a couple of decent shirts, a pair of socks, and a pair of boots. He then took the farmer's best shirt and Sunday pants for Martha, and the keys to the farm truck. Watching, Martha's own stupidity began to vanish; she remembered the long, minus freezing winter, her fingers swollen and blue, her body aching with cold, and her stomach knotted with fear. She took her wages, Tom's wages, and then, wisely, the rest of the money she found in the tea canister. It wasn't much, but it was a lot more than either of them had seen in their short, grim lives. And off they drove in the farm truck, even though, at first, neither of them had much idea how to drive. Saskatchewan, however, is flat and wide, and so were the roads, and if they were both unskilled, they were neither of them stupid.

The farmer came to mere minutes after the truck turned from the long driveway to the dirt road that led to the highway. He lurched to his feet, hauled up his pants, and staggered sideways, his head pounding, the homemade schnapps in his belly roiling and trying to spew from his mouth. He waited until his head steadied, then stomped for the house, roaring with rage, expecting to find the two rebels cowering in the kitchen. When they weren't there, he roared some more, settled his stomach with a couple of massive gulps of rotgut, and checked the house. He was so pickled in his own rocket fuel, he didn't even notice anything was missing.

Assured the house was empty, he headed outside, still vowing vengeance, heaping curses on their absent heads, planning exquisite revenge, and assigning the entire country to the care and keeping of the devil. He stomped back to the barn and checked it thoroughly, then, jug in hand, headed back out into the yard. The toe of his heavy boot caught on the splintered lip of the door jamb and, bellowing obscenities, he fell. His large glass jug hit a frost-heaved rock and shattered, his blocky, muscular body dropped onto the shards, and when his exsanguinated body was found two days later, strong men with cast-iron stomachs turned aside, sickened by the sight of sunlight glittering on the jagged glass embedded in his throat.

Tom and Martha knew nothing of any of this. They stalled the truck regularly, but stayed on their side of the road, headed West. By the time they had crossed half of Saskatchewan, they knew how to avoid the stalls, and by the time they entered Alberta, they could drive at least as well as anybody else in the province.

They ate gophers and sage hens, they ate chickens they stole and raw vegetables they bought in towns where they had no choice but to stop for fuel. They did not eat a balanced diet, but it was a lot better than they had been getting from the farmer, and they headed West, hoping only to be left in peace. By the time the exsanguinated corpse was buried, they were on Vancouver Island, which is about as far West as a body can go without winding up in the Orient, and both of them had effectively relegated the ham-fisted, ignorant asshole of a farmer to his proper place in their individual memories. Which is to say, they effectively forgot about him.

Nobody on the Island gave a good goddam about anybody else's background, place of origin, or official schooling. There were forests to cut, stumps to pull, valleys to turn into fields and farms; there was coal to be ripped from the ground and exported; there were houses to be built, towns to be founded, families to be raised, and a future to be carved. Dammit, there was barely enough time for soccer and horse-shoe pitch, for picnics and three-legged races, for singsongs and dances—who had time to snoop and ponder? What needed to be known was obvious. Both Tom and Martha could drive, both knew a cow from a pig, and a dog from either, and both of them were not only willing to work, they prepared to fight for the chance.

Tom got a job driving the Feed CoOp truck up and down the Island Highway, delivering bulk feed. Nobody else wanted the job. The stuff smelled so jeezly awful it was hardly bearable, and there were better wages to be made cutting trees. Martha got a job driving a primitive fork lift around the yard of the local sawmill, until her swelling belly got in the way of the steering wheel.

"We can't live in this truck much longer," Tom suggested quietly, staring through the windshield at the burbling creek beside which they were parked.

"It's okay as long as it isn't raining," Martha answered. "There's lots of room to sleep in the back."

"Heard about a house to rent," he hinted.

Angus and Flora Murdoch had a second house on their property. Flora's parents, Ed and Nora, had built it and lived there, building up a patch-ass farm while Ed worked in the coal mines. When Flora married Angus, Ed and Nora had a brand new house built for them because, as they admitted freely, they couldn't stand the twin thoughts of seeing their only child move off the place and seeing her move into a place built by Angus. Angus, you see, was not what you'd call Handy. He was one hell of a faller, and he made good money, and heaven knew he was kindly and as good a soul as you could hope to find, but he couldn't fix a fence without, in the process, knocking down a shed.

The two families lived happily enough in the two houses on the same piece of land, and Ed and Nora had the satisfaction of seeing their grandchildren grow up and follow every other kid who'd ever been born with gumption, away from home, and, usually, right off the rock. When Ed and Nora died, the house stood empty for three years, but Flora knew she couldn't keep that stump farm from going back to alder all by herself, and Angus, turned loose, would demolish the entire thing, so she put the word out, and Tom heard about it at the Feed CoOp.

"It's very nice," Martha sighed, looking at the house and fields, and yearning, suddenly, for something she had never known. "But could we afford it?"

They moved in on a Sunday, and ever after considered Sunday a particularly lucky day. It didn't take very long to move in; they had practically nothing in the way of possessions, and when the few things they had managed to accumulate were in place, Flora had them over to the big house for supper, and didn't even notice how much they ate.

Tom didn't ask questions, and if Martha had any, she didn't express them. Their first child may or may not have had a brutal Saskatchewan farmer for a father, but their second, third, fourth, and fifth were definitely Tom's. They saved their money, they worked harder than you would think was humanly possible, and they adored their children openly.

Flora helped them adore the kids. After all, she and Angus had openly adored theirs, and that had turned out just fine. Besides, how could a person not fall head over heels for a bunch of spunky little devils who seemed born to grin, laugh, cuddle, and willingly help with chores. And there were chores to be helped with, god knows. Chickens to feed, eggs to gather, coops to shovel, compost piles and manure heaps to turn, duck ponds to drain, duck-pond muck to be shovelled into buckets and packed to the garden, and then the pond to be refilled. There were gardens to dig, seeds to plant, weeds to pull, there was a goat shed to clean, goats to feed, milk to bottle and store in the cooler, which was little more than a strong box on a pulley rope, lowered into the deep well and suspended just above the water line. There was canning to be done and eggs to sort, there were chickens to kill, pluck, and clean, and washing to scrub, rinse, hang on lines to dry, bring in, iron, and put into cupboards and handmade dresser drawers.

Their fourth child, who was named Andrew but called Blackie, was so strange a child he almost broke their hearts. To the consternation of his parents, Blackie insisted on bathing two or even three times a week. When he wasn't playing in the duck pond or sitting in the creek, he was trotting back and forth from the well with pails of water, climbing on a kitchen chair to pour the water into the copper boiler on top of the woodburning stove, then waiting, expectantly, for the water to heat. When the water was nearly ready, Blackie pailed it back out of the boiler, carried it to the tin tub, and dumped it in, smiling happily. When he was old enough to learn how, he whistled like a well-fed canary from the beginning of the process to the end. By the time Blackie was seven, his parents and his erstwhile grandparents, Angus and Flora, expected it would probably be necessary to keep him at home all their lives, as people did with the simple-witted and crippled. What else could you do with a kid who took so many baths, and could spend an entire day pouring water from one cup to another, smiling dreamily.

Then, when Blackie was seven, he redeemed himself. Every so often, the serpent reappears in Eden, and even Vancouver Island has some drawbacks. Red claybank, gray claybank, white claybank, blue claybank. Bedpan two inches below the topsoil, hardpan six inches down or thrusting up in violent outcroppings. Areas where the ''top'' is gravel and, beneath that, bigger gravel, beneath that, rocks, then, beneath that, stones, and under the whole thing, boulders as big as grand pianos, and if a person is daft enough to haul it all away, the only thing that is left is a great christly big hole, that within a year fills up with rocks again. The cataclysm that shook the island loose and scattered the smaller islands around like jelly beans, forced mountains to thrust up like a spine ridging down the centre, and as the mountains rose and fractured, the rock striations did, too, and trapped between the layers of rock, clay, and rocky clay, was the water. There are places on the Island where the soil is rich, black, and three feet deep, and right next to those places are strips of clay bigger than any football field, clay that absolutely defies agriculture. Fractured coal seams hide under cedar forest, and rivers and streams appear from nowhere in particular, to drain into the sea. Spring comes early, winter is just a continuation of endless autumn rain, mist, and fog, and summer is usually pleasant. But sometimes the sun burns down fiercely, rivers dwindle, streams shrink, and creeks and wells go dry. As on any island, water is always a constant awareness and a problem.

The summer Blackie was seven, water was a problem. It was such a problem, it was a pain in the face. Wells dwindled until people were using water more than once, washing clothes in bath water until they stopped wasting water and wore dusty clothes on unbathed bodies. Streams became trickles, swimming holes became mere ponds, and everybody worried about the fish. Even the evergreen trees drooped, and the smell of fir and cedar pitch was ripe on the hot, dry breeze.

Blackie was furious. Blackie was livid. Blackie was thwarted. Blackie wanted his baths. When he understood it wasn't just stubborn, bloody-minded awfulness on the parts of all the adults, he walked off, upset and worried. Not enough water. Not enough water. Blackie tried to imagine a world with never enough water. When he didn't come home for supper, they went looking for him, their hearts in their throats. Everyone knew the cougar and bear were going mad with drought, and Blackie was just one small boy, hardly more than a mouthful for a cougar, less than a snack to a bear.

They found him in a hole to his knees, right in the middle of an outcropping of bluish-gray dried clay, digging with a pick-axe and scooping with his bleeding bare hands. "Water," he insisted, panting and sweating.

If it hadn't been Drought, they'd have hit him on the head with a rock and taken him home unconscious. If it hadn't been Drought, nobody would have listened to anything coming out of the mouth of a seven-year-old. But it was Drought. Two horses were already dead, and a litter of piglets dying, the bush had been closed as tight as a Scotsman's purse for six weeks, and there wasn't a garden left for miles.

"Water," Blackie insisted, and nobody could make him say otherwise. "Water," he sobbed, hacking at the unyielding clay.

So they got Rhys Evans with his bore drill, and they all started helping turn it. Down, down it corkscrewed, the metal tip chewing through clay, bedpan, and even rock, down, down, and they added length to it at the top, sweating and turning and cursing the god damned fanatic kid, the christ cursed weather, and the motherless bitch of a bore. All night they toiled, boring grimly.

"Nothing," Rhys said finally, so they hauled it all out and started glaring bitterly at Blackie.

"Water!" he said, stamping his foot. The earth trembled, then it heaved, and then a gout of mud and rock puked up out of the bore hole. And while the adults gaped and Rhys prayed, the artesian broke through, spewing to the morning sky. Blackie sat down in the spray and grinned as the cold, clean, endless gout of water shot high in the air and fell back, gently bathing dust, dirt, sweat, and tears from his skinny body.

The people stared, their exhaustion and their depression suddenly gone, washed from them by the water, springing from the ground, falling back down from the sky. "A dowser," they breathed, awed. And it was true. Blackie Williams was a dowser.

They didn't just use Blackie to find drinking water, or for stock-watering wells. Nobody would have thought of excavating for a root cellar or basement without first checking with the water dowser. "You'll have seepage," he'd say softly, and they would willingly scrap that site and build their house where Blackie promised the least problem. "Run a ditch here," he'd say, pointing at a piece of land that looked no different from any other, but they'd run the ditch without question, a foot wide, a foot deep, and the sogginess would drain from their field. "Your best chance is here," he'd point, and they'd drill, right in the middle of the rose garden if they had to. They trusted Blackie. Trusted him where water was concerned in a place where water was life, and so, without ever even thinking about it, they trusted Blackie with their lives and the lives of their children.

A witcher uses a witching wand, a diviner finds drinking water, a dowser is the same as either, different from both, and most of what you get told about it all is crap, anyway. A fat woman once held forth at great length about how you'd have to use a willow wand cut from the piece of land you wanted witched, and do the witching before the sun came up, a certain phase of the moon, and she went on and on and on and on about the magic, ritual, and meaningfulness of it all. Some witching wands are willow and some aren't. Some cut a new one each time, some carry a favourite with them. Some use copper pipe. One uses a straightened coat hangar bent into a rough ''U,'' carries it points outward, finds water every time. One carries a glass rod in a case originally meant for a flute. Blackie walked with his hands in his pockets, whistling softly. He'd look at the hills and how they sloped, at the trees, and at the grass. Sometimes he'd lie on his back for a while and watch the clouds, the birds that rode the air currents. If there was a secret, a trick, a magic, or a science to it, Blackie didn't know or care zip-all about that. He just found water. He could have found water in the Sahara if someone had bought him a ticket and taken him there. The soles of his feet twitched when he walked past a ditch, the palms of his hands went pins-and-needles when he rolled up the garden hose, and his entire body glowed and tingled when it rained. Bathtime for Blackie was a near-orgasmic experience, and had been from age two.

''How d'ya do it, Blackie?'' they asked shyly.

''I don't know,'' Blackie admitted.

''You must have some ideas.''

''I like water,'' he confessed. ''I. . .I guess I. . .I guess I respect water. When you think about it, it's just about the most beautiful thing in the world. Especially sweetwater. It's all got its uses; even sulphur water is good for your skin, and salt water is home to more food than we know about, but sweetwater. . .'' He shook his head and blushed deeply. ''I don't know, it's just beautiful, is all,'' and they knew what he meant. Unschooled, ignorant, and not always civilized, they still knew what Blackie was trying to say. They listened intently to his words, watched the expression on his face, and opened their hearts to the words he could not find.

When he was fourteen, he quit school and went to work in the bush, setting chokers for Sidhu, Singh, and Sons, and it was after work, evenings and weekends, that he found water. Even Sidhu, Singh, and Sons respected the special gift given their chokerman, and when they were going to enlarge the camp, they asked Blackie's advice.

''I'd put'er on the other side of where you park the crummy,'' Blackie mused. ''If it was me doin'er, that's what I'd do. Otherwise, you're maybe gonna find one corner of'er settling' and the whole riggin's going off-kilter because there's a pool down there and she won't hold the weight."

"A pool?" They looked at the ground, packed hard by years of heavy machinery.

"Not so big as a lake," he admitted, "but she feels deep."

Sidhu, Singh, and Son didn't hesitate. They changed their plans totally. the new buildings went in on the other side of the clearing, where Blackie had indicated, the crummy park was relocated, and Rhys Evans and his big bore drill were brought in to tap the pond. Blackie was given two days off with pay as a thank-you, and when Sidhu's son came back from India with his new bride, Blackie was invited to the wedding reception. He took off his shoes at the door, just like all the others, ate food that burned his tongue and made his eyes water, and he smiled and blushed until he almost changed some opinions about the eventual possibility of civilized behaviour on the part of some of the strange people on the Island.

"Jesus, Blackie," they'd grin happily, "what do I owe you?"

"Your life, probably," Blackie would laugh.

"No, I mean it. Seriously. Name your price."

"Whatever you think is fair." And Blackie would look down at his shoes, his face again burning with embarrassment. He knew damn well the ones who worked hardest for their money, and had the least of it to spare, would pay more quickly and more generously than those who had the most and got it the easiest. William Baldwin, school trustee, owner of both hardware stores, half-owner of the lumber yard, first person to own a television set, gave Blackie ten bucks for finding him a pure crystal spring. Pete Raboniuk, who worked as hard as any man who ever lived and had no more spare cash than anybody ever has, every year brought a hen with a clutch of chicks in the spring, and a side of pork every fall. "Damn good well you found me," he smiled, as red-faced and shy as Blackie himself. "Good water all the time. Thank you, Blackie, from all of us."

"Oh, any time, Pete," Blackie squirmed, "any time."

Alice McKye brought jars of pickles and jam, Dave Easterhouse stopped by regularly with a string of fat trout, and Bill Colville brought sacks of potatoes and carrots from his garden. Baldwin built six houses and rented them for good money, and all six were serviced by the spring Blackie found for him, but he would pass by without so much as a flicker in his eye, and anything Blackie ever bought from him, he paid for, full price.

II

Blackie was nineteen, and his brother Milt, one up the ladder, took up with Esther Lawrence. Esther was shorter than Milt, who was the stubbiest of the Williams, and she was about the most beautiful thing Blackie had ever seen in his life. She had eyes so blue you couldn't believe it, hair as dark as his own, but curly, curlier even than an Airedale dog. And she laughed. God, how she laughed. Laughed so much and so easily she didn't seem to notice that Milt hadn't so much as cracked a spontaneous smile since his twelfth birthday. Blackie wanted to take Esther aside and tell her Milt wasn't the one for her, but he knew she wouldn't listen, even if he could manage to get the words out of his mouth.

"Of course my hair is curly," Esther teased, her voice singing as she talked, the rhythms of the old country locked in her speech, two generations away from the green valleys and black pits. "It's the Spanish armada, you see," and she laughed softly. "Spain and England had a fight, and England sank the Spanish ships. On them were Moors, kept as slaves, and they swam to shore. We kept them," she laughed again, "because of their singing voices, you see. In return, they gave us curly hair."

Blackie believed her. Believed every word she ever told him. Thought his brother Milt was a lucky mucker to be able to walk by the river holding Esther's hand in his. Blackie wished Milt wasn't such an ungrateful, unfaithful, lying-mouthed asshole, because as sure as there's shit in a sea gull, he'd make Esther cry, he'd break her loyal and generous heart, and no use to try to warn her, she'd never believe a word. All Blackie could do was stand there and hope to God he'd be able to catch the pieces when the whole thing blew apart because of Milt's rotten nature.

"Milt," he tried, "Milt, you've got to change some of your ways."

"Fall on your head," Milt answered.

"Milt, she's a good woman."

"What would you know about it, water-brain?"

"Chrissakes, Milt, she trusts you!"

But Milt had never listened to Blackie or to anybody else. And

Blackie wound up shrugging hopelessly, forcing his face into a smile, and serving as usher at the wedding he had prayed would never happen.

Esther's first child was born in the heat of summer, and didn't look like her mother at all. Milt's features never looked any too good on Milt, and didn't look any better on the round-faced, bald-headed, eight-pound daughter he sired.

"She's got no nose," Blackie observed. "Just a sort of button." He bent closer. "She's got eyes that kind of slant," he frowned, puzzled, "and there's something godalmighty strange about her cheekbones, too. She looks," he realized, "like a bleached Chinee."

"Those damned Moors from the armada," Esther laughed. "Are you afraid of her?"

"No," Blackie lied.

"Pick her up," Esther dared him, "she won't break."

Blackie lifted the odd-looking infant and held her awkwardly. Nothing happened. She didn't snap, crack, or howl. He relaxed, his arm curved more comfortably and naturally, she nestled against the clean front of his best white shirt, worn especially for the occasion. He walked to a chair, sat down, and grinned at his niece. "Sure is pink," he observed. The child lay contentedly, and Blackie felt his stomach warm, his dark tanned arms and hands become suddenly confident. Shirt sleeves rolled just past his elbows, his large tanned paw cradling the child's head, he stared down as the baby stared up, and Blackie wondered at the undeniable truth he, himself, had once been that small. Smaller, for he had weighed seven pounds three and a half ounces, and his niece weighed eight pounds at birth. "You should call her Clementine," he teased, "and then I could call her Clem. Or Ernestine and I'd call her Ernie. Or Josephine so she could be Joe."

"Jesus Christ," Milt glowered, disgusted by such mindless blether.

"No," Esther laughed, "that's a boy's name."

"His sister's name was Jessica," Blackie said, his face serious, his eyes twinkling. "Everyone called her Jessie. Jessie and Jesus Christ, the carpenter's kids," and the baby peed her diaper, soaking the left leg of Blackie's nearly new red-strap jeans.

"Lookit that!" he laughed, "She even baptized herself. And me, too."

"Yeah," Esther agreed, "you always could find water, Blackie. Now you've even got water on the knee."

"You're both goofier than shithouse rats," Milt glared, while

Blackie and Esther howled with laughter. Milt had been attracted to and had married Esther because she was so different from himself, and Esther had been attracted to and had married Milt for the same reason. Milt immediately began trying to remake Esther over in his own image, and it didn't seem to occur to him that, to do that, he'd have to destroy what had most appealed to him.

"Hey, Muffin," Blackie laughed, "nobody pisses on me and gets away with it. You'll be hit with the Dowser's curse for that. You'll have more water'n you can handle in your life. I promise." He chucked her under the chin, then carried her to the table, laid her on her back, and proceeded clumsily but willingly to try to change her diaper. Predictably, he pricked himself with the diaper pin. "Now look," he chided, "you've sealed your blessed curse with blood. Boy, oh boy, are you in for a life of it. Water, water, water, you'll see."

When Jessie was eighteen months old, Blackie realized his brother Milt was regularly laying beatings on Esther. Blackie didn't know what to do about it. He wasn't even sure it was any of his business. A man's home, they said, was, after all, his castle, and all that's within it, he owns. You never interfere, they had taught him, with the way another man builds his fences, trains his dog, or treats his wife. A woman, they joked, is like a violin, you gotta play it every day, and she's like a rug, you gotta beat it once a week, har har.

"Milt," Blackie tried, "them's awful bruises on Esther's arms."

"Why don't you go find a puddle to play in?" Milt snarled.

"Milt, for chrissakes, she's just a little bit of a thing. What kind'a horseshit are you pullin' off, anyway?"

"Did someone ask you to butt your nose into my business?"

"You're my brother," Blackie said honestly, "but you make me ashamed that I even know you. Where'd you learn to act like that? Dad don't beat on mom. Neither of them ever beat on any of us. It make you feel big to pound someone who's smaller'n you are?"

"Pound you if you don't shut up," Milt raged.

"No," Blackie said scornfully, "you won't even try. Because I can hit back, and you're too gutless to take the chance. You'd rather punch on someone who's smaller'n you."

Blackie went to his mother, and asked her what he ought to do about what he knew for a fact was happening. Martha poured tea, stared into it, and blinked her eyes rapidly, holding back her tears.

"There isn't much anyone can do unless Esther either asks for help or leaves him. I wish she'd leave him," she decided, "because there isn't any way I know of for anyone to help her.''

''She's awful pale,'' Blackie mourned.

''She lost a baby,'' Martha sighed, ''and that's harder than having one.''

''Oh, momma,'' Blackie mourned.

''You have to wait for her to tell you what she wants done about it,'' Martha warned, ''otherwise you're apt to just make it worse.''

''I tried to talk to him,'' Blackie confessed, ''but he told me to take a hike.''

Martha tried to talk to Milt, too, and if Milt didn't dare tell his mother what he'd told his brother, he did manage to convey his opinion. ''You live in that house over there,'' he said, pointing, ''and I live in that house behind us. And what goes on in your house is your business, just the same as what goes on in my house is my business.''

When Jessie was two, Esther miscarried for a second time, and she stopped laughing. Milt had punched her out for laughing; he figured she was making mock of him. The first punch bruised the side of her face, the second hit her in the belly and knocked her against the corner of the table, cracking a rib.

Blackie took Jessie for a walk by the river—to give Esther a break, he told Milt—and he picked huckleberries until his peaked cap was full of them, then they sat on a big rock overlooking the deep green river, and Blackie watched Jessie eating berries, one at a time.

''Did mummy cry when daddy punched her?'' he asked, his voice lazy.

''No,'' Jessie answered, more interested in berries than in anything else. ''She just said 'oh','' and parrotlike, Jessie imitated Esther's gasp of pain. ''She said it again when she hit the table and then fell onta the floor.'' Jessie chewed carefully, swallowed, reached for another huckleberry. ''When he kicked her was when she cried,'' she said innocently, licking her lips. ''Not s'posed'a tell,'' she lectured. ''Daddy smack ass if you tell.''

''Not a soul,'' Blackie agreed. ''Look, Jess, up there,'' and he pointed.

''Hawk,'' she remembered from the last time Blackie had shown her.

''Red tail,'' he agreed, his heart cracking.

''Fisher,'' she said, pointing at the flash of blue.

''Kingfisher,'' he corrected, and she nodded, her juice-stained fingers dipping into the cap again.

Milt had been drinking for a week, ugly, mean, and on the prod the whole time, and nobody in the pub was of a mind to cross him. Al, the oldest brother, tried to reason with Milt, but there wasn't a chance of anyone being able to control the miserable bully when he was in an ugly mood, so even gentle, good-natured Al gave it up as a bad job, shrugged, had a beer, and agreed Milt got more and more like a junkyard, rat-killing dog ever day.

''Why'n't ya get lost?''Milt suggested, poking a thick finger into his brother's shoulder, prodding, prodding, trying to kick off a fight.

''Miltie,'' Al tried again, ''why not come with me? We'll pack us up a lunch, get a jug of good stuff, and head up the Lakes, fishing.''

''Get outta my sight,'' Milt demanded. ''Go home and get momma to sing you a song.''

The pub at Bright's Crossing is just across the highway from the railway tracks. If you're in a car or on a bike, you have to follow the road down past Hilton's farm, over the Haslam Creek Bridge, and around the curve, but if you're on foot, you can cut a half hour off your walk home by climbing the bank, going over the trestle, and down the footpath on the other side, avoiding the long slow curve of the road.

''Save yourself a walk,'' Al tried. ''I'll give you a ride home.''

''Get out of here, you gearbox fruit,'' Milt roared, pulling back his arm, ready to heave his beer glass. Al shrugged, finished his beer, and left. ''Go to the beach,'' Milt yelled after his brother, ''and pound sand up your ass!'' When the pub crowd left at midnight, nobody else offered Milt a ride; let the surly bugger walk, maybe the night air would take some of the starch and shit out of him.

Blackie was sitting on the trestle, watching the water below as it shimmered in the pale moonlight. He heard Milt scrambling up the bank, looked up and tried to smile. ''Hi Milt,'' he said.

''Get outta my way, ya fuckin' loon,'' Milt shouted. ''How come every time I look around me, I see your stupid face with that stupid smile.''

''Milt, you gotta do somethin' about that temper,'' Blackie said mildly. Milt suggested Blackie perform an acrobatic and probably anatomically impossible act upon himself, and Blackie ignored his brother's suggestion. ''Milt,''he said firmly, ''them miscarriages of Esther's aren't miscarriages. You hit her. That's abortion, Milt, and it's as illegal as bank robbery, and you know it.''

''Mind your business, puddlebrain.''

''Don't think I will,'' Blackie answered, as mild as a June morning.

"She's my wife," Milt shouted, lurching unsteadily.

"But she isn't a *thing*, like a chair or a fishing rod! She isn't a cuckoo clock you can drop in the garbage when you're tired of it. You murdered two little kids with your bad temper! What's more helpless than a kid still inside its mother?"

"None of it's got anything to do with you."

"It's got everything to do with me. It's got to do with everybody on earth."

Milt swung at Blackie and, of course, he missed. He almost fell back down the embankment, his legs wobbling. Blackie got to his feet, his hands hanging by his sides, trying to talk sense to his brother. Milt pulled his big bone-handled knife, a lock-blade solingen steel special, and took a swipe with it. "Gonna rip your guts out," he promised. "Gonna gut you like a pit-lamped deer and dump you off into the river. Gonna give you all the water there is, and they'll never find what's left of you." He swung his knife again, and Blackie jumped back, saving his own life by less than half an inch. "Then," Milt decided, "I'm gonna go home and cut both their throats."

"Why?" Blackie raged. "Why don't you just bugger off and leave'em if you don't wanna live with'em and enjoy life?"

"Cut their throats!" Milt cheered. "Both of'em!"

"Ah, shit," Blackie sobbed. "Did you have to go and say a thing like that?" He knew Milt meant it, knew the sickness had been festering since before Jessie had been born, knew the beatings had been but the prelude. And knew there was no reason for any of it. Like famine, flood, and war, it just was, and no reason for any of it. "Isn't it enough that we love you?" Blackie evaded another vicious swipe. "Mom, dad, all of us."

"Spill your guts!" Milt laughed, his eyes no crazier drunk than they were when he was sober. Blackie kicked twice, because he believed Milt would do exactly what he said, and there was no way Blackie was going to stand by while Esther and Jessie wound up slashed open like weaner pigs. The first kick landed square on Milt's crotch and buckled his knees, the second, as Milt sagged, caught him under the chin, rammed back his head, and snapped his neck. Milt fell to the trestle and lay there, the knife falling between the ties and down sixty feet to the river. Tears streaming, Blackie walked away and went home to his parents' house to lie in bed, eyes wet, hands behind his head, waiting, staring at the ceiling, until he heard the 3:10 blow and thunder over the trestle on its way south to Victoria.

What they found of Milt wasn't much, but it was recognizable. They wrapped it in a sheet and took it ten miles into town on a rubber tarp in the back of a pickup truck. Tom and Martha wept, Esther's parents wept, Al sobbed, Mavis and Helen cried, but Esther didn't and Blackie had already shed his tears, although only he knew that. He stood bareheaded in the church, holding Jessie on his arm so she could see all the flowers. Jessie only knew some of the words of the songs, but what she knew, she sang, and people vowed, tearfully, it like to broke your heart, hearing that child sending Daddy to heaven with the words of ''Abide With Me,'' and they remembered Esther's jokes about the singing voices of the Moors, then reminded each other about the Welsh, and agreed it was small wonder Jessie had such a voice, why it hardly seemed right that a voice like that could live in the throat of a bittybaby like she was.

Nobody expressed any suspicions of any kind, and the guilt Blackie felt, he kept hidden. There were only three opinions involved anyway: his own, Milt's, and God's. Milt, probably more than anyone else, would have understood completely why his brother had kicked him under the chin and snapped his neck. And God was yet to be heard from about it. In Blackie's opinion, Milt dead was better than Esther, Jessie, and Blackie dead, but he knew he would hear that crack for the rest of his life.

They buried Milt as decently as possible, then went back to the business of getting on with their lives. Esther cashed the insurance policy and put the money in the bank, got herself a job waitressing in a chow mein and chop suey house, and even began to smile again. Martha looked after Jessie while Esther was at work, and if Esther's shift meant she had to sleep while Jessie was awake, there was Flora next door, or Esther's own mother, or one of the neighbours, or, dependably, Blackie when he got home from work. Jessie went with whoever it was, happily from one to the other, no tears, no sulking, no uproar. Inside of a year, Esther was making little jokes again.

Jessie liked to hear her mother laugh, almost as much as she liked to laugh herself. She also liked it when Blackie looked after her. They walked along the river, or went to the lake or to the pond to watch frogs and newts, and Blackie always asked Jessie to sing for him. ''loud as you can, Jess,'' he'd urge, ''just open'er up, kid, and let'er rip.'' Jessie opened'er up and let'er rip, sending her amazing voice out across the water, singing words if she knew them and sounds if she didn't know words.

By the time Jessie was four years old, Blackie, nearly twenty-five, had asked Esther, almost twenty-three, to marry him.

"I'm not sure,' Esther teased, "that the church approves of marrying your brother's widow. That might fall into the forbidden area of consanguinity."

"Better'n marryin' some woman I don't know or like," he grinned hopefully, his heart balanced somewhere between hope and terror.

"What about consanguinity?" Esther asked, still teasing.

"Christly Jesus," Blackie laughed, "I'm not askin' for a blood transfusion, Es. Just your hand in marriage."

"You take the hand," Esther guffawed for the first time in a year and a half, "and you'd better be prepared to deal with the rest."

"I will," Blackie vowed, "try my very best."

"You're sure," she wasn't laughing, "you're not worried about the consanguinity?"

"Woman," Blackie wasn't laughing either, "we know how you feel about consanguinity; how do you feel about love, honour, and carnality?"

"You still gonna try your best?" She was laughing again.

"Count on it."

Blackie's best was more than good enough for Esther. Whatever anyone may have thought of her marrying her dead husband's brother, nobody said anything out loud. And if they had, neither Esther nor Blackie would have given a rat's ass for the unsolicited opinion.

Blackie had some money saved, and Esther had the insurance money, and they pooled what they had to put a down payment on five acres of second growth with an unfinished house and a good-sized garden. Kitchen, pantry, living room, and bedroom downstairs, and one long, half-built room upstairs. A fine well, dowsed by Blackie himself and drilled by Rhys Evans, a dependable pump in the kitchen, a sturdy chicken house, and a respectable woodshed out back. Blackie knew he had the world by the short and curlies, and he promised himself and an obviously understanding God that he'd do his best to deserve it all.

They'd been married a week when, for the first time in her life, Esther experienced the power and wonder of orgasm. She clung to Blackie fiercely and knew nobody and nothing was getting in the way of this, not ever. "I love you, Blackie," she said, for the first time. "I love you, Esther," he cuddled her gently, his eyes streaming tears. "I have loved you since before I met you. You are . . . you're like water to me,'' and Esther knew she would never get a higher compliment if she lived to be a zillion years old, which she did not expect to do anyway.

After a while, most people forgot Milt had ever been in the picture. Tom and Martha, Al, Blackie, Mavis, Helen, and Esther remembered Milt, as did Flora and most of her scattered kids, and Angus, if he thought about anything, but the public at large managed, most of them at least most of the time, to obliterate his memory. Jessie sometimes twisted and turned in her sleep, dreaming of a loud angry voice, the sting of a huge hand against her bare bum, the echo of her mother's deep gasp of pain, but none of it made connection to her life, the memories faded, and eventually she shrugged the dreams off as non-specific and unrelated nightmares.

Nobody could have found any reason to suggest there was anything in the way Blackie treated Jessie that set her apart in any way from his own kids when they began to arrive. Blackie loved kids. He loved most kids, and his own kids more than most; he adored Esther, and Jessie had grown in Esther's body, so how could Blackie not love Jessie. Even better, he liked her.

''Jessie's my buddy,'' he said often. ''My buddy, my friend, and my kid. Eh, Jess?''

''You betcha,'' Jessie invariably replied. ''You just betcha.'' She didn't look like him, she sure as hell didn't look like her momma, and, as everyone's memory of Milt faded, they all became less able to decide who, in fact, Jessie did resemble.

''Herself,'' Esther said coolly, ''exactly like herself. Unique in all the world, that's my Jess.'' Like Blackie, Jessie adored her mother, and, again like Blackie, Jessie believed every word her mother told her, and grew up convinced she was one of a kind. Sometimes it felt wonderful, knowing there wasn't another like you anywhere on the face of the earth, but sometimes it was damned lonely. Occasionally, it was frightening.

''She isn't a dowser like you, Blackie,'' they said.

''Dowsers come and dowsers go,'' Blackie agreed, slipping Copenhagen under his bottom lip, spitting neatly, wiping his mouth politely with his blue-and-white polka-dot hanky. ''Give her time. It might come to her, it might not. Doesn't matter, anyway, because Jessie has her own talents,'' and he smiled. ''Jessie can sing like nobody I ever knew. Jessie can grow flowers where nobody else can, and Jessie knows her herbs and potions. She doesn't need to dowse.''

''You have to watch good,'' the old woman advised sternly.

"Everything that's good has something that looks almost exactly like it that's bad. Honey bee is a friend; wasp and hornet is murder. Some mushrooms is food, some is magic, and some is death."

"Really?" Jessie listened, wide-eyed.

"Now comfrey," the old woman pointed, "that will cure almost any ill you've got. Fine for indigestion, sleeplessness, bad nerves, overwork. And this," she picked up a leaf and handed it to Jessie, "looks so much like it even I might be fooled if I wasn't watching carefully."

"What is it?"

"Your favourite flower," the old woman grinned. "It's foxglove. Doesn't take much of that and your heart just spasms, explodes, and that's it, goodbye, all she wrote, right now."

"Wow," Jessie breathed.

"Sing me a song, Jess," the old woman sat down under a tree, leaned against the trunk, closed her eyes, and waited. "Sing me a good long one." And Jessie sang. She just stood there, hands at her sides, feet planted firmly, and she sang. The old woman nodded, her gnarled fingers tapped time against her old leg, and the birds had the good sense to shut their silly little mouths and listen to real song for a change.

Maybe because of the beauty of her songs, or maybe because God figured she had already seen a sufficiency of ugliness in the first year and a half of her life, everything slipped by quite easily for Jessie. She was six and a half, her brother Peter was almost a year old, and spring was soft and warm on the earth. Blackie, stripped to the waist, was spading the garden, Esther was bringing clothes from the drying line, and in the house, on the big woodburning stove, the water in the copper boiler was bubbling steadily around the last dozen jars of moonlight mowitch Blackie had brought home two nights previous. Pit-lamping was, of course, against the law, and the game wardens, mounties, judges, and other gin-drinking nose-pickers would have you believe it was reprehensible in the extreme, but it was how most people, brown or white, fed their families.

Pete Raboniuk drove into the yard in his battered pickup, stopped politely well back of the house so no dust would blow onto the washing or in anyone's eyes, got out of his truck, reached into the back, and brought out a cardboard box in which sat a clucky hen and her brood of two-day-old peeps.

"Hey, Pete, how's the world treating you?" Blackie grinned.

"Not so worse," Pete answered, "yourself?"

"Can't complain," Blackie laughed, "but I probably will before the day's finished. Could you stand a taste of huckleberry wine?"

"Might save my life." Pete blushed then, and shoved the box at Blackie. "That's a damn good well you found me. Here."

"Thank you, Pete." Blackie took the box, looked inside, cht-chted at the hen and the peeps, and, together, they walked to the enclosed chicken yard. Jessie stared at the peeps, then smiled up at Pete, who patted her head and continued to blush.

"They're beautiful, Mr. Raboniuk," she said, kneeling to watch as the hen fluffed her feathers and the chicks tried to hide underneath.

"Gimme," Peter, the baby, demanded.

"No!" Jessie said firmly, "you'll break them. Look," she repeated her mother's words, "but don't touch."

Esther arrived with tall glasses of huckleberry wine, cold from the storage bin lowered just above the water level in the well. "Thank you, missus," Raboniuk blushed. They sipped, nodded, grinned satisfaction, and watched the young hen parade her peeps around the hen yard.

"I have a favour to ask," Esther said quietly, "a big one. If I take Jessie down to your place, could she see your puppies?"

"I'll drive you down." Blackie's grin widened.

"We could go right now," Raboniuk offered.

"Never rush huckleberry wine," Esther advised, and Pete relaxed visibly. The kids watched the peeps, the adults had another glass of wine, and then both pickups headed down the road to Raboniuks.

Pete's bitch was part Lab, part black-and-tan, and had mated with a white pointer with black spots. The resulting litter was invariably long-eared, big-nosed, and went all colours from black, through spots and patches, to mostly white with some stripes and strips. Jessie, of course, picked the ugliest of the pack, a white-bodied bitch with a dark brown head and tail and a scattering of spots. "Freckles," Jessie insisted.

"Gimme," Peter demanded.

"Okay," Jessie agreed, "but you be careful or you won't get her no more. And if you hurt her, she's gonna bite you. Right on your chin," she elaborated, "and you'll cry and bleed and nobody...not nobody...will tell her she did a bad thing, you hear? So you don't hurt her." Peter must have been careful and gentle, because when Freckles wasn't trailing after Jessie, she was following the baby. Freckles never learned to jump through flaming hoops or ride a motorcycle or dash into burning buildings to rescue injured firemen, or any of the wonderful things you're always hearing about other people's dogs. She came when she was called, she sat where she was told to sit and when, and she raised hell if a raccoon came near the hen house or the garden. She chased after and brought back the sticks Jessie threw for her, she tugged gently on one end of an old rope while Peter pulled on the other, she raced after a thrown lacrosse ball until even Blackie's throwing arm was tired, and she was so goofy looking, with her long soft ears flapping, that no matter how grumpy you felt, you smiled when you saw her.

"Funny looking pup," people said at first, but after a while they stopped looking at her outside and saw how she behaved. "Good dog," they said.

When school started up again in September, and Jessie was seven, Freckles would walk as far as the school bus stop and wait with Jessie for the bus. After Jessie left on the bus, Freckles went back to the house and played with Peter, or lay by the buggy, faithfully waiting for the day Donna would be crawling or pulling ears or walking and throwing sticks.

Blackie was a good chokerman and a good dowser, he was a good husband and a good father, a good neighbour, a good hunter, and a good person. Esther was a good wife, a good mother, a good cook, and a good gardener. She took good care of the chickens and ducks, was a good dancer, a good singer, a good neighbour, and a good person. It never occurred to Jessie she wouldn't do as good at whatever she was set to do, and so school just passed with few problems and even fewer heartaches.

And then Lorcas Dee came to town. For weeks, the entire island buzzed with excitement and preparation. Lorcas Dee was not as famous as Elvis Presley, but a lot handsomer and one hell of a lot more approachable. On top of which, Lorcas Dee travelled with his own amateur talent show, only five dollars to enter, and the top three, chosen by a totally impartial applause meter, got to appear on stage and entertain with Lorcas himself, and were eligible for the annual big prize, a chance to be considered by Lorcas' own recording studio. Some of the step dancers, tap dancers, and contortionists felt discriminated against because, obviously, there wasn't much scope for them on an LP, no matter how good they or their families thought they were, but Lorcas, upon receiving word of their unique concern, solved the problem by making arrangements for the "visual artistes" to have their pictures in the International Inquirer. And only the permanently sour, and those inevitable chronic complainers, made any fuss over the fact the visual artistes wound up in the Oddities column.

Harmonica players huffed and blew and practised sounding like chugging trains; fiddlers sawed and scraped and practised sounding like wailing trains; spoon players clattered and clanged and wished there was some way they could imitate trains. And Jessie Williams stood on the bank by the waterfall on Haslam Creek and practised singing every verse of every song she knew.

"Damnit," Blackie said in a hushed, pain-filled voice. "I don't want Jessie-kins leaving. I don't want her travelling near and far, singing in towns the names of which I ain't even heard, let alone know how to spell."

"Maybe she won't win," Esther soothed.

"Oh for christ's sake, my darling," Blackie tried to smile, "that's a brave lie, but you know damn well Jessie will win. It's because of that damned dumb joke, when I said she'd have all the water in the world for peeing on my leg. She's gonna cross the Atlantic and sing for the Queen'a England, she's gonna cross the Mississippi and the Missouri, the Ohio and the Fraser, the Ottawa and the Mirimachi. There's just no way it can't happen. That bunch will hear that voice and she'll win in Nanaimo, then she'll take the Island, then the Province, then the Nationals, and then that's it, off to Nashville. The shit of it all is," he wiped a tear from his cheek and cleared his aching throat, "we're gonna have to pay at least two hundred dollars for a short wave strong enough to bring in WWVA Wheeling West Virginia."

Jessie practised "Peace in the Valley" for the born-agains and jesus lovers, and "It Wasn't God Who Made Honky-Tonk Angels" for the betrayed wives, bitter mistresses, disillusioned sweeties, and sad-eyed mothers.

The Lorcas Dee show arrived on Thursday morning, and on Thursday evening, the first amateur talent search was underway. The Nanaimo Civic Arena, right at the south end of the George Pearson Bridge, was jammed with contestants, families, and those determined to see the whole shiteree from start to finish and take advantage of the 3 for 2 deal: buy a ticket for Saturday and Friday shows, and get Thursday thrown in free gratis, as they said.

The resulting traffic jam was monumental, even in a town famous for traffic jams; four lanes north and south on Terminal, coming off or going over the bridge; four lanes east and west on Bowen, with two lanes each way trying to get onto the bridge; and then the bottleneck at the arena, with everyone trying to get in at the same time.

Jessie won on Thursday night, and was invited back Friday night to compete against a whole slate of contestants. Lorcas Dee, who would himself end the Thursday night program with a five-minute medley of his all-time greatest hits, smiled at her and patted her nearly white hair. ''Not bad, kid,'' he grunted. Jessie looked up at him in open worship and couldn't think of a thing to say. Lorcas Dee looked down at the memorable little face looking up, and wondered if what he was seeing was an albino asiatic. Actually, what Lorcas wondered was if he was looking at a bleached chink, but albino asiatic is much less offensive a term, even if the thought is the same. Sequins glittering, diamond studs flashing, hair grease glistening, Lorcas Dee picked up his twenty-thousand-dollar, insured-by-Lloyds-of-London guitar, and went on stage to sing of love lost and regained, and Jessie gawked from the wings.

Jessie won on Friday night, too, and with the second, third, and fourth place winners of both nights, was invited back for the Grand Finale on Saturday night. Of course, this meant almost all of every show for the full three nights was amateur talent that anybody could have heard or seen free of charge at any time at all, and that people had paid good money to hear and see Lorcas Dee, who showed up for only a few songs each night, but for one thing, that's Show Biz, and for another, who would deny these young folk, or even the determined and re-attempting repeatedly old folk, a chance to get the hell and gone off the rock. Lorcas Dee, himself, could well understand why so many people were paying five dollars a chance in the hope they would get the hell off the rock. He himself hoped to get the hell off it just as soon as he possibly could. It reminded him too much of his own home town.

Every one of the losers got to sing or play two songs each, and then Jessie went out and sang one song, Peace in the Valley, and on Saturday night, even Lorcas Dee sobered up enough to hear what was coming from Jessie's throat. When the applause died down, Lorcas Dee came on stage and promised the overflow crowd that the second half of the program would be just as good as the first, better in fact, because Jessie would sing more than one song. As the lights dimmed, Jessie was on stage with Lorcas himself, his wonderful guitar held in his left hand, and, in his right hand, her own.

During the half hour intermission, Jessie and Lorcas sat in the dressing room, practising a duet, and throughout the practise, Jessie's eyes were fastened on Lorcas' wonderful guitar. Lorcas' own eyes were fastened on Jessie.

"If you win tonight," he asked carefully, "would your folks let you go to Victoria for the Island championship?"

"Yes," Jessie said confidently. Lorcas grinned and stepped out for a word or two with the engineer who handled the impartial applause meter. His words were quite unnecessary; Jessie won fair and square anyway and when—after being given her fifteen dollar cheque and a certificate suitable for framing—she sang with Lorcas Dee himself, the home-town crowd went crazy. For the first time in more years than he cared to admit, Lorcas was enjoying himself.

"They want more, Jessie," he said clearly into the microphone. "Dare you to sing unrehearsed?"

"With you?" she asked.

"Do you know," he challenged, "Whispering Hope?"

"Yessir."

"Then give it to them, Jessie," and the crowd screeched. "Hear that?" Lorcas Dee said, watching the sweat beading on Jessie's forehead. "That's the audience. It's the only god damned thing on the face of the earth that comes anywhere near being sacred."

"Yessir," Jessie agreed. They sang together, unrehearsed, and the crowd was silent, except for those who wept. And one of the ones weeping was Blackie, because he knew Muffin was almost gone from his life.

The following Thursday, Jessie was in Victoria, staying at the Douglas Hotel, all expenses paid as part of her win in Nanaimo. Half an hour after she arrived, Lorcas Dee knocked at her door.

"Want to practise our duet?" he asked. Jessie nodded eagerly, her eyes fixed on the wonderful guitar. Lorcas watched, and Lorcas grinned.

"Hey, Jess," he said softly, "want to learn C chord?" and he handed her the guitar. Jessie paled. Jessie took the guitar, and, with Lorcas' help, learned C chord. "Hey, kid," Lorcas wasn't grinning now, "how'd you like to have a guitar for your own?"

Jess was a bushbunny; not quite a hillbilly, not quite a cracker, but close to either or both, and she knew what Lorcas Dee had in mind. A lot of boys, and a lot of men, all her life, had entertained the same thought. It wasn't something she'd tried yet, but she knew she would try it on for size sooner or later, and Lorcas Dee was offering more than a two-hour movie and a Coke after, more than a fast wrestle in the back seat of a rust-riddled Chev. There was a bed right there, and there was the guitar. Above and beyond anything else, there was the guitar. And Jessie thought Lorcas was dickering with his own guitar. Neither Jessie nor her family nor any of the people she knew set much store by virginity, and she'd seen enough black-eyed wives and sweeties to know how long love lasted and how much it meant.

"Sure," Jessie agreed.

It wasn't comfortable, it wasn't pleasurable, and she bled, but Lorcas Dee was no fool and had the towel from the bathroom folded under her so the sheets and mattress weren't stained. Lorcas had a lot of practise with what he called Tighties; it was one of what he saw as the main benefits in his line of work. He took his time, he enjoyed himself as much as possible, and by the time he finally blew his wad, Jessie was sore, had a crink in her back, and was quite totally bored. When he got up, dressed, and left with the dream guitar, she was too stunned to speak. Twenty minutes later he was back, and handed her a plain, light-coloured, flat top, better than anything she could have got from the catalogue. "Here, kid," he grinned. "I'll be back after the show to give you some more lessons," and she knew he didn't mean G or D chord. She didn't know guitar manufacturers the world over sent guitars to Lorcas Dee in the hope he would carry one on stage and give them more publicity than they could ever afford to buy. She didn't know, and neither did Lorcas, that the guitar he handed over so easily would, in time, be worth even more than the magic-seeming, insured-by-Lloyds-of-London, twenty-thousand-dollar wonder.

Jessie sat on her bloody towel, looking at what she thought was a third-rate guitar, and thinking. It didn't seem to be a patch on Lorcas' guitar, but she figured it was probably better than anything anybody she knew had, or would ever get. And if she was stiff, sore, and swollen, so what? But still, she did feel as if she had been, to put none too fine a point upon it, had.

Thursday night, Friday night, and Saturday night in Victoria, the audiences screamed, clapped, shouted, hollered, yelled, and roared "encore" for the weird-looking kid with the enormous voice. And before and after each show, Lorcas Dee gave lessons in guitar and humped sweatily, and Jessie moved as he told her, although she wasn't sure why, because she sure as hell didn't owe him anything, and how much goddam boredom did a woman have to put up with anyway? However, she could go over, in her head at least, the finger positions, use Lorcas' bare back as a mock guitar neck, and she really didn't have any other plans, anyway.

She rode home on the bus on Sunday with her guitar, a book of chord and finger positions signed by Lorcas himself, for what that was worth, a cheque for one hundred dollars, and another certificate suitable for framing. She let everyone think the guitar was part of first prize, and she picked up her life where she'd left off, with the minor exception of the two hours a day she spent practising.

Lorcas tried to pick up his life, too, and in most areas he succeeded. He went from town to town to goddam, identical, one-dog town, with his amateur talent scam, and he entertained himself with aspiring singers and musicians. He went on stage, sang in his sequinned suit to entertain the crowds, but there was something missing, and even he knew it. At first it was easy to blame bad publicity and hire a new advance man, or to tell himself some strike or another had made money too tight for people to be able to afford tickets, but eventually, the truth will make itself known.

"The audiences are dropping off," his booking agent said flatly. "They aren't turning out in droves any more; they're barely turning out in trickles."

"Shit," said Lorcas, haunting visions of his home town appearing in front of his bloodshot eyes.

"Been downhill since Victoria," they said coldly. Then showed him the books.

Everything else had been downhill since Victoria, too. So downhill, Lorcas began to think of Victoria as an omen, a glimpse of what could be. He became superstitiously convinced Jessie was his only chance; after all, she was the only thing made Victoria any different from any other wretched dump.

Lorcas grabbed for what he saw as his only chance because he sure as hell was not willingly going back to where he'd started. Not Lorcas. He was as upwardly mobile as a person could be. There would never be too much "up" for Lorcas Dee; he had started too far "down" to ever be satisfied.

Come Christmas, Jessie left to go on tour for a hundred dollars a week, plus expenses. It made a lot more sense to quit grade twelve and head off for that kind of money than to finish grade twelve and go to work for B.C. Tel for sixty a week, minus deductions. Esther and Blackie stood with the other kids, waving good-bye and forcing themselves to look cheerful, but when the bus was out of sight, Esther turned blindly, grabbing desperately, and Blackie was there, holding her, his body shaking with sobs. "It'll be okay," he insisted, "she'll do just fine."

Jessie was not an overnight hit. Lorcas was no fool; he wasn't about to step aside and let some weird-looking kid take the pie out from under his face. But Jessie did half a dozen songs a night, and the crowds began to turn up again. "Hope you appreciate the chance I'm giving you," he said after every concert. Jessie, who knew nothing of the audience size or the gate receipts, nodded, increasingly aware of how the life she had known and thought ordinary, fine, and normal, was considered by most to be less than privileged.

She practised her guitar, took lessons from Lorcas' sideman, and began to realize Lorcas himself was not much of a guitar player. In fact, mostly Lorcas just lugged the thing around for show, and the chord progressions and lilting fingered melodies pouring from the speakers actually came from the sideman.

"Go back to the beginning," Tom told her. "If you make a mistake, go right back to the beginning, not just back to where you got it wrong. All the way back, Jess, time and time and time again. Practise doing it *right*, not just correcting your mistakes."

Jessie practised her guitar, she practised her singing, she even practised her walking and sitting. She chose songs to learn and sing for the people, and others to learn and sing for herself. After a while, she began to learn songs which made the members of the band feel challenged. They responded to the challenge by playing better than they had thought they could. At night she lay waiting for Lorcas to finish flopping because she thought that was the price she had to pay for the big chance he was giving her.

Every week she wrote home, sending money orders to help out with the rising costs of raising a family, her family, her brothers and sisters, her cousins and kissing cousins. Once a month she phoned to talk, but increasingly, the distance between her and home was something more than miles. When Rhys Evans died, Jessie couldn't go home to sing at his funeral, as he had asked. But she had flowers delivered, and sent a tape they played in the church. People said it was a pity Jessie hadn't been able to get home, but hearing Rhys' favourite hymns on that tape was a wonderful thing. Not as good as having Jessie there herself, but at least the next best thing, and wasn't it wonderful the way her little brother Devon had sung along, a chip off the old block and no mistake about it. And nice, too, that Blackie had the money to buy Rhys' business from the Missus. A pity his own boys didn't want to continue the family trade, but there you have it, and at least it wasn't an outsider taking over the way they were taking over everything else lately.

"I don't know," Blackie said doubtfully. "It's an awful risk."

"Nothing ventured, nothing gained," Esther reminded him.

"But it means quitting my job," Blackie fretted. "And that means..."

"If it gets tight," Esther said calmly, "Jessie will pick up the slack. She's doing well."

"Doesn't seem right that Jessie should have to..."

"Why not?" Esther smiled and stoked the frown lines from Blackie's brow. "You saved us." She kissed the tip of his nose. "That lunatic would have made our lives a total horror," she said calmly, "and they'd'a been damn short lives, too."

Blackie stared at her, wondering if he'd been talking in his sleep. But Esther just smiled at him, kissed him again, and started making teasing jokes about the knight in shining armour.

"Esther," Blackie managed, his throat tight with fear and worry.

"Hush," Esther laughed. "You'll get an ulcer if you worry about things. Life was awful, Blackie, and I was so scared I couldn't think, and then the fear was gone and life was just dreary, which is an improvement from horrible, but not much. I thought I'd spend my life carrying chow mein and chop suey to tables full of noisy drunks. And then life started to get better, and it's got so much better I don't see any reason to lose faith now."

Blackie made sure that Jessie understood what the well drilling gamble might turn out to be. "We might wind up putting all our money into nothing but holes in the ground," he said into the telephone. "I know I can dowse, but I don't know about the rest of it. And I never charged no set amount for dowsing," he confessed. "Drilling is different, you charge so much a foot, and that's what scares me. Seems like a body shouldn't charge other people. I didn't have to pay anybody for my gift, why should..."

"Poppa," Jessie laughed, sounding so much Esther that Blackie had to look across the kitchen to make sure his wife was there, and not on the other end of the phone line. "Poppa, my voice is a gift, like your dowsing, but everybody who comes to a concert has to buy a ticket to get in."

"That's different," Blackie objected.

"No," Jessie said gently. "No, Poppa, it isn't any different at all. You break your arm, you pay the doctor. Get a tooth fixed, you pay the dentist. And if you're worried, you do the dowsing for free and just charge for the well drilling.''

''Thanks, Jessie,'' Blackie sighed with relief. ''You're something else, kid.''

Jessie didn't feel like something else, though. If she felt like anything, she felt like one sausage in a whole link of them. One night she watched Lorcas walk down the hotel corridor with his sequinned arm around the waist of a young fiddle player who had taken first prize in the amateur talent show, and she knew she didn't care. She didn't care about or for Lorcas Dee, she didn't care that he was humping and flopping on the fiddle player, and she didn't care about the fiddle player, either. Jessie knew Lorcas would be back. He always had been, he always would be. What she didn't know was why she felt the same way as when she got what she had thought was a third-rate guitar instead of the one she had been expecting. She didn't know why she felt so cheated. After all, for crying out loud, she was getting paid very good money for doing something she'd be doing even if nobody paid her. She was being paid very well indeed for the chance to travel, to learn, and to develop her natural talent. Why should she feel cheated?

Lorcas was not doing well. He looked like hell and sounded like one of his own records after it had been played too long and scratched too often. ''I don't know what's wrong,'' he grumbled, ''I just feel tired all the time. I've hit that note a million times before,'' he mourned, ''but you think I can hit it now?'' He licked his whiskey-wet lips and shook his head. ''Gonna have to rework some of them songs,'' he sighed. ''Gonna have to get rid of them high notes.''

''You're working your throat overtime,'' Jessie said softly. She wanted to tell him off, she wanted to tell him he was burning holes in his throat with cigarettes, booze, and over-loud laughter, but she knew if she didn't handle him properly, he'd tell her to shut her face and maybe even backhand her, so she came in the back door. ''Look how hard you're working,'' she consoled, ''five or six nights a week, out there in the hot lights, turning yourself inside out to give the folks something beautiful to take home with them.''

''Yeah,'' he agreed, feeling like a martyr.

''You've got to start babying your throat,'' she suggested. ''Maybe we should stop expecting so much of you. We all depend too much on you, anyway, no one man can hold up the whole show by himself. Not night after night, week after week, and year after year. You might be super human,'' she grinned, ''but you're still only human, eh?''

"Yeah," he agreed, nodding as if the wisdom of all time had finally been uttered. "Yeah, if it was easy, the whole world'd do it, right Jess?"

"My mom used to make this special tea for us if we had sore throat."

"Yeah?" His face lit up briefly, and for a moment, Jessie saw who Lorcas had once been but would never be again. "Yours, too? Mine always had herbs for tea," and then he cried a bit, talked non-stop about his silver-haired momma, talked until his voice was raw and the whiskey had his words so slurred only he knew what it was he was saying. Jessie figured the chances were that even Lorcas didn't know what he was talking about. Increasingly often, lately, Lorcas said things nobody else could make hide nor hair of, anyway. Jessie didn't let it bother her; she figured if nobody else was going to mention it, she wouldn't be the first to question what looked for all the world like a classic case of brain rot. And if nobody, including Lorcas, knew what in hell was being said, then probably none of it mattered a whit, anyway.

When Lorcas finally passed out, Jessie undressed him, feeling nothing but mild distaste for his pasty skin and the cummerbund she knew was really a fancy form of secret corset to hold in the soft jellybelly. In his fancy clothes, up on stage, with the lights gelled to put him in the most flattering glow possible, Lorcas still looked like a star. Away from the magic of performance, he looked like the Michelin tire man. At the rate he was going, he would soon look like the Goodyear blimp.

Jessie got some pills from the bass player, told Lorcas they were vitamins, kept him in bed for three days and nights, sound asleep, and the audiences didn't even miss him. When he woke up, she gave him a cup of comfrey tea, then had room service bring up a good meal, and Lorcas ate hugely. She nagged him into the hot tub, then poured more comfrey tea into him and tucked him back in bed again. That night, Lorcas Dee hit the notes he missed so often now.

"It was the comfrey tea," she convinced him. "I told you it was good for your throat."

Lorcas lived the clean, pure life for an entire week, then reached for the bottle again. Jessie felt angry, so angry she almost hollered at him, so angry she almost told him the cold, hard truth. But she didn't want a crack alongside the face, she didn't want him to grab her by the shoulders and shake her until she saw spots in front of her eyes. And anyway, you can only babysit an adult so long; then you have to butt out and look after your own life.

Sometimes at night, Jessie would waken from dreams in which she was crying, listening to the sounds of violence, waiting for the violence to come from the kitchen to her bedroom, knowing if her bedroom door opened there would be a huge figure filling the door frame, roaring in a deep voice, calling her a brat and a little bitch, and ungrateful pup and a streetwalking piece of shit just like her mother. Sometimes Jessie almost thought she knew who the huge figure was, but trying to make sense of the dream, trying to solve the riddle of it, was like trying to close your fingers around a handful of water, like trying to hold it tightly, squeeze it, and claim it for your own forever.

"You okay, Jessie?" Tom asked quietly.

"I'll be okay," she answered. "I've been better, mind you." And they nodded, watching Lorcas putting the tap on a sixteen-year-old banjo picker.

"You sound tired." Esther's voice came through the phone so clearly Jessie could almost see her mother's face.

"I am a bit," she confessed. "After a while, every hotel room looks like every other hotel room, but none of them look like home."

"You should come home," Esther said firmly. "Spend the summer here with us. I'll cook all your favourite food, you can go swimming every day, sleep late as you want. And if you get bored, you can go to work with Blackie and the boys."

"How's that going?" Jessie asked.

"Good. Real good," Esther laughed softly. "We'll never be zillionaires, and we'll never show up at the gates of Buckingham Palace telling the royals to just hit the road because we're taking over, but we don't have anything to complain about, that's for sure. You're gonna get your money back, Jessie," she promised.

"I wasn't worried about that, Momma," Jessie laughed. "After all, if worst comes to worst, I'll just move in on you and free-load for the rest of my life."

"Any time you're ready," Esther vowed. "I'll even send the boys down with the pickup and drive you home in style."

Jessie travelled in style all the time, now. She saw New Orleans during Mardi Gras, she saw Calgary during the Stampede, she saw Times Square on New Year's Eve, and she watched as Lorcas ate and drank himself closer and closer to ruined health.

He let her sing on his next record, and even convinced himself it was out of the goodness of his heart, not at the insistence of the producer.

Jessie knew it was more than luck, now. She wasn't as trusting as she had been, she was much smarter than she had been, and the musicians made a point of letting her know what the truth was. The song she sang was so popular, she won an award for Newcomer of the Year, and in her acceptance speech she told the world she owed it all to her mom and dad, and to Lorcas Dee, ''who has been like an uncle to me.'' Then she held up her trophy, grinned from ear to ear, and the crowd went nuts.

''Your uncle, huh?'' Lorcas puffed and wheezed, his body oiled with sweat, his pulse pounding. Jessie smiled up at him, and when he finally finished, she got out of bed, got him a cool facecloth, and wiped his red face. When he was snoring, she went to the adjoining room, took Lorcas' wonderful guitar from its case, then, for the first time, she played it. ''Violins,'' said the guitar, ''have Stradivarius to honour, but who have we? Who knows of our crafters? Who cares?''

''I do,'' Jessie said, and proved it with her playing.

''Aaaaah,'' the guitar sighed, ''you don't know how long I've waited.''

The producer wasn't happy when Tom told Jessie she was being offered a bad deal. ''It's her first record,'' the producer objected.

''Come on,'' Tom grinned. ''We didn't fall with last night's rain, okay? You aren't the only label in the world. And,'' the grin faded, ''you don't have Jessie tied into a contract. Neither,'' the grin reappeared, ''does Lorcas.''

''Christ,'' the producer grumbled. ''What's in this for you?''

''I get to play,'' Tom said happily, ''real good music. And ain't that a welcome change?''

The picture on the album cover was of Jessie laughing happily in the recording studio while Lorcas clowned with the band. What the picture didn't show was that Lorcas was so full of strange substances he was almost completely bent out of shape. The title of the album was ''For My Uncle,'' and Lorcas had straightened up just long enough to sing with Jessie on one of the cuts, just as she had sung with him on his record. It was the last big hit for Lorcas Dee.

''Isn't education a wonderful thing?'' Jessie mused. ''Here's a university just finished a two-year study of couples where both husband and wife work, and neither has any children. They found that these people eat out about twice as often as couples with single income, and about five times as often as couples with single income and more than one child.''

"Wonder how much it cost them to figure that one out?" Tom muttered. "And to think I sent money home for three years so my goddam brother could get him a Bachelor of Arts degree!"

"Another university," Jessie yawned, frowning at the newspaper, "after interviewing five thousand couples who claimed to be happily married, discovered that over seventy percent of them were not as close as they thought they were. They were what the professors called 'pseudo intimate.' They were not," she laughed, "as happy as they thought they were!"

"As long as they never find out they aren't happy, they'll do just fine." Tom joined Jessie's laughter with his. "You phoned home lately?"

"Yeah." She tossed aside the paper, reached for the TV guide. "Everything's goin' real good."

"Your baby brother still got his sights set on the stars?"

"Yes." She dropped the TV guide to the hotel room floor. "Devon wants to be a singer. And I don't know whether to encourage him or tell him to stay in school."

"Don't tell him nothing," Tom advised. "Then, whatever he does, you aren't to blame. Anyway, everybody has to pay his own dues."

"I haven't had to pay many dues," Jessie objected.

"Don't you believe it, kid," Tom shook his head. "Don't you ever believe it. You not only pay dues, you pay taxes on the goddam dues. Let the kid find out for himself."

The night of the country music awards, Lorcas pulled his cummerbund tight, forced his fluid-retaining blob of a body into his sequinned tuxedo, and went to Jessie's hotel room to escort her to the Do of the year. Jessie's room was full of flowers: roses, hibiscus, orchids, and large bouquets of what she insisted on calling foxglove, even if the tony-talkers corrected her and told her it was really called digitalis.

"If you don't win everything worth winning," Lorcas told her, "that's all the proof the world will ever need that the goddam thing is rigged from start to finish. You deserve'em all, Jessie. You're the best."

"Thank you, Lorcas," she managed, unable to believe her ears.

Lorcas Dee ate the rich food at the banquet, and drank the fine wines, the champagne and the Glenfiddich Scotch. He clapped and cheered and patted backsides; he danced and whooped and yelled when Jessie got her awards. He told jokes, laughed at other people's jokes, and drank toast after toast to the future. People who had almost given up trying to be friends with the bad-tempered bozo felt relief; maybe all Lorcas had needed was that one overwhelming, undeniable hit, maybe now he was back up on top again, he'd stop being such an unappetizing freak, such a dreary asshole. After all, how many stars have got the god-damned class to help a hillbilly kid get herself the biggest award of the year.

"Never felt better in my life," he burped, laughing. "Gonna go places, Jessie. You'n me'n the boys in the band. Gonna go far."

"We'll show them how it's done," Jessie agreed. "Come on, Lorcas, let's go back to the hotel and I'll make you a pot of comfrey tea. We'll eat and drink and laugh and make plans and get ready for next year's awards. Gonna take'em ALL next year, Lorcas. Every single solitary one of them."

At the funeral, they all said it was, after all, inevitable. "He was," Jessie said in her eulogy, "the man they had in mind when they said 'Live fast, die young, and leave a beautiful memory.'" After that, there wasn't a dry eye in the place. "He was," she said, "The living embodiment of 'star,'" and they all agreed totally. "His life personifies our business," she reminded them, "and if there is a mystique, Lorcas Dee lived it and died it." They didn't know for sure what a mystique was, but by god Lorcas had lived'er and died'er, and the funny-faced kid he'd given a hand up the ladder had just as much class as he'd had; they'd never heard a better, truer, or more touching eulogy, or one presented with such utter sincerity.

Her next album, a collection of songs most people had associated with Lorcas, was called "Foxglove," and featured a picture of a bouquet sitting in a plain vase on a sun-drenched windowsill. Her sidemen teased her she hadn't left them a whole hell of a lot of work to do, but they knew they had never played better or been more challenged and inspired. Even the ones who thought they knew, when pressed, couldn't say for sure which guitar Jessie used during any particular song.

"It's called cross-collateralization," she told her producer. "The revenue from one helps off-set the cost of the others, which, in turn, off-set the costs of future albums."

"But why, for chrissake?" the producer growled. "How many people want to buy nothing but instrumentals? Especially when some of'em is classical?"

"I've got some of the best musicians in the world working with me,'' she said stubbornly, ''and they deserve to be heard. They also deserve some say in what it is they want to play!''

''Look at this list!'' the producer raged. ''Just look! One asshole wants to do some old-time blues, another wants to try jazz violin, another . . . it makes no sense at all.''

''Then we'll look for a producer who thinks it does make sense,'' she smiled, and the producer knew he was well and truly had.

''Okay, Jessie, but you can go too far with cross-overs. I'm warnin' ya.''

She had a shelf full of awards, money in the bank, a high-priced five-year recording contract, a three-year schedule of personal appearance concerts, and the satisfaction of knowing her parents and siblings didn't have an economic worry in the world. And if the nightmares got too bad, she knew she could get sedatives.

''How's it going, Jessie?'' Blackie asked.

''Busy, busy, busy,'' she laughed lightly.

''You okay? Not workin' too hard?''

''What about yourself?''

''Oh, you know.'' She could hear the amusement underlying his words. ''Same as always. Dowse'em, drill'em, cap'em. Working hard,'' he admitted, ''but everything's goin' good.''

''The kids?''

''Fine. Except,'' he hesitated, ''maybe you could have a talk with Devon?''

''He still wants to be a singer, huh? Well, what's so wrong with that? I guess,'' she admitted, ''I don't understand why you were always encouraging to me, but . . . it's as if you're doin' everything you can think of to stop Devon.''

''Devon don't wanna be a singer,'' Blackie said sadly. ''Devon wants to be a star. And it ain't the same thing, Jess. Not by a goddam long shot it ain't the same thing.''

''It'll be okay, Poppa,'' she soothed. ''He's still young. He'll learn better.''

''You think so?'' Blackie's voice lightened.

''Yeah,'' She nodded, even though she knew he wouldn't be able to see the nod. ''Yeah, he'll find out there's more to it than party-till-you-puke.''

''And you're fine. You're sure?''

''Poppa, I'm sure.''

''Okay.'' Blackie's relief smoothed his voice, she could almost hear him nod his head, and then he was asking about her personal appearance tours. She told him about Britain, about Europe, about the trip to Japan, and Blackie laughed freely. "I told ya," he crowed, "told ya when ya were little and peed on m'leg. Told ya ya'd have all the water ya could handle. Crossing seas and oceans, crossing rivers and lakes, just like I predicted, your life is full of water, all the water you can handle, fresh water and sea water, sweetwater and salt water."

"Sure do love you, Poppa," she told him, before she hung up the phone.

She felt lonelier after the call than she had before the ring had sounded. She sat in her hotel room, looking out the window at the afternoon traffic, wondering about the people in the cars, who they were, what they did, how they lived, what they wanted out of life. She had her evening meal sent up and ate it sitting on her bed, watching the news on television. Then it was time to shower and start getting ready for the concert.

They loved her, of course. She sang the only way she knew how to sing, freely and for them. She gave them their money's worth, and then gave them an extra half hour, and for the time the lights were on and the people were sending her their approval and acceptance, Jessie Williams was fully alive and happy. When the lights were finally out and the people gone home again, she packed up her guitars and went back to her hotel room to try to unwind enough to be able to sleep properly.

"What is it about you and foxgloves, Jess?" the drummer asked, looking at the framed photographs of the meadow out behind the house in Bright's Crossing.

"I've loved them since I was a little kid," Jessie smiled. "You could say, I guess, that they do my heart good."

"They aren't much more than weeds," he decided, starting to yawn.

"Ah," Jessie teased, "but aren't we all weeds in the flower garden of paradise? I mean, look at yourself; you're a bit seedy and weedy," and then they were both laughing, but of course, everybody knows drummers are more than a little bit crazy, and Jessie's mother had laughed right up until the time she was stretched out unconscious on the kitchen floor.

"What in hell are you two laughing about?" the bass player asked.

"Does it matter?" the drummer gasped.

"It's a helluva lot better'n crying," Jessie managed.

EMMA JONSTONE,
THE PIE-FACED CHURCH

There wasn't much laughter in Emma Jonstone's life, but since it's true you don't miss what you never knew, Emma didn't waste much time fretting about it. Some of the Jonstones were good-looking, some of them fair-to-middling, but Emma was downright plain. Her mother, Kay, didn't care what Emma looked like; she loved her. And Emma always knew that. No matter what, all the days of her life, Emma knew her mother had loved her. "How come," Emma asked, "people look at me and grin?" and it was true. Men or women, young or old, they looked at the plain, serious little pie-face and laughed, softly or harshly, depending on what kind of people they were.

"Just looking at you," her mother lied lovingly, "makes them happy." Emma might have been satisfied with that, might even have been happy with it, if the rest of her world had been as loving, but, it appeared, that was too much to ask. "Hey pie-face," they said. "Hey flat-face," they mocked. "Boy, never gonna win any prizes with that puss!" they laughed. "When God said 'head,' Emma thought he said 'bed,' so she took a big flat one," they joked. Emma got so used to being teased about her face she stopped wondering why people did it. In time, she understood why her mother had lied and said what she had about making others happy, but that was one of the very few things about anybody else Emma ever really understood.

Emma listened long before she could talk, so when she started talking her vocabulary was bigger than she was. She didn't always, at first, get the words right. "You shouldn't tease that puppy," she warned the yahoos in the kitchen, "you're going to make her delicious," and the yahoos laughed like hell, made jokes about hot dogs and dog's breakfasts and teased Emma for being three and sounding thirty. They taught Emma more about the word "vicious" than any dictionary could have done, and instilled in her a deep determination to learn words, the power and use of them, and to learn how to manipulate them expertly.

"A is for apple so rosy and red," her mother chanted, holding Emma on her knee so Emma could plainly see in the book both the apple and all the different kinds of "A." "B is for baby asleep in her bed." Emma pointed to the "B" and the picture of the pretty baby.

"Emma," her mother squeezed her gently, "you're a wonder." By the time Emma was five, she was reading the funnies all by herself. "What means 'in-vas-ion'?" she asked. Her mother told her, and Emma went back to trying to understand the front page. "What means 'covet'?" Emma asked. Her mother told her, and she returned to the puzzle that was the Bible. "What means 'begat'?" and that was explained to her too.

"Eat a dictionary or something, pickle-puss?" they asked.

"Hey, you've had your nose in a book so long it's worn to a nub," they laughed.

"Hey Emma," they jeered, "if you're such a good speller, how do you spell 'dishface'?"

"Hey yourself," Emma asked, her face bland and friendly, "do you eat with that garbage can of a mouth?"

"G'wan, you little shit," they yelled.

"You put things in your mouth I wouldn't hold in my hand," she scorned, walking off, her back stiff, pretending they couldn't hurt her, pretending she couldn't hear what they were saying about how she had a face like a festered fig, or a can of worms thrown against a mud wall, or a handful of cat shit dropped on a hot brick.

Coming home from grade two, her big cousin Darryl, who was in grade seven, opened his pants and made her touch his thing, then told her he'd fix her clock good if she told anyone.

"You're gonna be sorry," she said, but Darryl only laughed and grabbed her in a choke hold, and felt under her skirt, and then rubbed his ugly thing against her leg and spit in the dust, but only ordinary spit. Even Emma knew he was too young to make the kind that got anybody in trouble. "You're disgusting," she told him. "It looks like an old, dried-up dog turd." Darryl got mad then and spit at her, and told her she was too homely to bother with. He walked off and pretty much left her alone after that. But that winter Darryl's younger brother Bobby, who was eleven, showed her some fumble games, and she didn't mind that. Then Phyllis Dakins, who babysat her on Saturday nights when everyone was down at the beer parlour getting shitfaced, taught her some others. Emma found out for herself that if she went to the lake and hid herself in the salal and Oregon grape she could watch what was going on in the back seat of a parked car, or on a spread-out blanket if it wasn't raining or the the ground too soggy. She knew what they were doing, and with what, and it was all very interesting in its own way, but she didn't understand why they would bother.

Emma's mother continued to love Emma openly and steadily, and that made Emma's family life very unusual. Emma and her mother never fought, argued or said bitter things to each other. They didn't vent their frustrations on each other and they didn't grow to dislike each other. They helped each other and tried to find nice things to do together, and enjoyed each other's company. But in all other ways, Emma's family life was like everyone else's. She argued with her brothers and fetched cups of tea and bottles of beer for her father, she picked up the stuff they littered behind themselves, and did the dishes, and there was more than just cousin Darryl the dog turd who wanted to touch and feel and fondle, but she didn't actually get fucked until she was fifteen.

Before that year, though, Emma's mother died. Everyone had known for years that Kay had what they called a tender stomach. The doctor said it was a duodenal ulcer, worse, he said, than a peptic, but controllable with proper diet. Kay drank the half milk-half cream, ate the cream of wheat and the poached eggs, and stayed away from spices and onions and tomatoes and cucumbers, but the ulcer didn't heal. Emma blamed this on her dad, whom she privately thought of as That Old Buzzard or The Old Man. He drank every weekend away until he must have almost believed creation had intended a person to go from Friday night to Monday morning without bothering with Saturday or Sunday at all. Most of the time he was a rambling jerk, but sometimes when he was drunk he was almost okay. He might take it into his mind to get down the big aluminum pot and tell Emma to run up to Chinatown for an order of chow mein.

Fong Lee would look up and grin and say, "So, your old man's on another bender, is he?" and Emma would say, "You guessed it, Fong." She'd sit at a round table drinking green tea from thick cups with no handles, and Fong would give her an almond cookie or, if she was really lucky, a doughball with a chip of pork in the middle, and she could watch all the chopping and slicing, the glow of the charcoal in the huge, strange stove with the holes on top where the wok bottoms fit through. Then, after all that work and all that getting ready, it got dropped in this, then that, then the next, and then this, and no more than six stirs and dump it all into the big pot and add the shredded cooked yellow egg and the sesame seed. Then home, hurrying down the hill with the heavy pot held carefully and the change in the front pocket of her jeans, and they would all have a real feast, unless Kay's stomach was on the fritz, then she'd just have some raw egg whipped in her half-and-half.

Other times he'd take it into his head to make pancakes and everyone would have a good feed, but it always took a long time to get the kitchen cleaned up afterward, so that wasn't as good as when he wanted chow mein. Kay would sigh at the sight of all that grocery money going up the hill to Fong, but it was cheap at twice the price if it kept him in a good mood, because if he wasn't in a good mood, look out, donnybrook here we come, chairs overturned, tables tipped, noise and yelling and kids scattering like quail, and Kay always the one to catch it the worst because, as he loudly let the entire goddam world know, it was all her fault anyway, all women were the same, walked around with a bear trap between their legs and god help the poor fool who got his balls caught in it.

"A total paragon of a man," Emma muttered often.

Then came the day when Kay started to sit down suddenly, her face chalk white and sweaty, and then she was in bed, puking into the old dishpan, puking up increasing amounts of blood. First old black blood, then bright red blood and finally it was off to the hospital. The doctor cut her open and cut out half her stomach, and he said that after that she'd have to eat six or eight tiny meals a day, but she'd be all right. That's what he said. He almost promised. But she was dead the next day, so that showed what he knew, the asshole.

The old man blubbered and howled and roared that he might as well curl up and die too. He vowed his life was over, and he spent the entire funeral doing everything he could to attract as much attention and sympathy as he could. Emma thought it was all just a lot of melodrama, but she was too numb to tell him to sit down and shut up and let the dead rest in peace.

For someone who wasn't going to be able to live another day without her, he managed to live quite well. There was a series of women in and out of the house, the whole thing getting tackier by the week, one low-class episode after another. Pretty soon her brothers got involved. The biggest ruckus was when he found his oldest son making out on the couch with his latest live-in wotzit. That fistfight covered a block and a half, with the neighbours all watching and saying as how it was better than the Look Sharp, Feel Sharp, Be Sharp Gillette Blue Blades Saturday Night Boxing on the radio.

But the family decided enough was just about enough and whatever in hell was going on it was no place for a growing girl, so Emma got taken ten miles out of town to Bright's Crossing to live with her Aunt Flo. Emma, if asked, would much have preferred to live with Kay's sister Elaine, but nobody thought it the least bit fitting, what with Elaine not being married and living the way she did, which, god knows, was nothing her mother, god rest her soul, would have expected.

Flo was okay, but Flo was the old man's sister, and blood runs thicker than water. You can change the record but the melody, as they say, lingers on. It wasn't a whole lot different in Bright's Crossing except there weren't a bunch of neighbours to call the cops and you weren't as apt to get your name in the papers for baying at the moon. Flo drank, but she didn't drink in town and she didn't drink anything from the Liquor Control Board store, so nobody ever saw her drink, which seemed to mean she didn't drink at all. Emma learned a lot when she figured that one out.

But Flo did her best. There was always food, most of it good, and there were clean sheets and blankets. Her husband Jack had a pack of cougar hounds and more stray cats around the place than you'd believe any one person could tolerate. They all seemed to live in a shed at the far side of the property, a long way from both the house and the dog pens. "Don't get yourself attached to any of them cats," Flo advised mysteriously. Jack also had chickens. Weird chickens, too scrawny-looking to be meat birds, that laid eggs no bigger than bantam eggs. The second Sunday Emma was living with them, Jack invited her to go with him to a neighbouring farm and help with the chickens. Emma figured he was going to sell them or trade them for Rhode Island Reds or something useful, but no, every other chicken in the place looked the same as his own. Ugly.

"Hold him for me, will you?" He handed her a bird. He reached into his pocket and brought out two shiny things. Then he brought out a whetting stone and spit on it and stropped the shiny things a while. He slipped the shiny things over the big thumb-spur thing on the chicken's foot, fastened a snap and did the same with the other foot.

Then he held the bird carefully in his hands and walked to a fenced-off place with it.

Someone else came over with a bird rigged up the same. They nodded at each other and a wave of excitement passed through the crowd of people. Some man Emma had never before seen came over and said ''You backing your uncle or what?'' When she gave him a cold look, he seemed to interpret it for himself. ''Bet?'' he said. Emma had three dollars in her pocket, her allowance for the entire month, and she didn't have any idea what in the world she was betting on, but something nudged her, and she pulled out her money. ''Jesus,'' he mocked, ''last of the bigtime spenders, ain't you?'' but she just cold-eyed him, and he shrugged.

They dropped the chickens over the fence and the feathers flew like hell. Then, suddenly, the other man's bird dropped, blood welling from its eye, and Jack was cheering and yelling. The man came over and handed Emma six dollars. ''Beginner's luck,'' he scorned.

''Eat shit,'' she said with a wide smile. He gaped. He knew and she knew and everyone who heard it knew if she had been five years older and male, he'd have cold-cocked her right then and there. But she wasn't five years older and she wasn't male. All he could do was laugh. Emma did, too, even though what she really felt like doing was puking because of the bird's eye and the looks on the faces of all the men watching.

When they went back home again, two of the birds were dead, but Emma had more money in her pocket than she'd ever seen at one time before. Flo was six sheets to the wind, but there was a pot of stew on the stove. Emma served it up, glad it was beef and not chicken.

A few weeks later, Jack started training the cougar hound pups. They'd been alone in a great big pen ever since they'd been weaned. Twice a day they saw Jack only as long as it took him to fill their feed bowl with raw fish and bits of unidentifiable meat, and replenish their water dishes. The rest of the time they were by themselves, squabbling, fighting and yapping. One day Jack deliberately did not feed them at supper. They yapped and yelled all night, and Flo got blind and fell asleep mumbling.

''Go get me six kittens,'' Jack said the next morning. ''Six small ones.'' Emma, with no idea of what was going on, went over to the cat shed and got half a dozen kittens, the cutest ones she could find. Maybe he was going to take them in to the GiveAway or the pet store or something.

He took them to the pups' pen and dropped them over the fence. Emma screamed. No words, no pleas, no accusations, just raw horror. He grinned at her while the hounds at first stared in puzzlement, then pawed curiously at the kittens. One pup tried to play and a kitten screamed, scratched and died. The hound pup, his nose clawed, yapped; a kitten skittered, and that was it, the pups chased the kittens. The pups were hungry. The kittens, bloody, smelled like supper. Emma screamed.

"Get tough, Emma," Jack said. "And don't you ever think I showed you this for no reason at all. Learn now and learn fast; everything stinks like shit."

For breakfast the pups got six more kittens. By the end of the week they knew the smell of cat was the smell of food. By that time Jack was heaving in full-grown cats who could fight, scratch and cause a lot of damage to an unwary pup.

"Jack's the best cougar hunter in the area," the neighbours said. "Maybe the best on the Island."

"He stinks," Emma said, and Jack laughed.

"Have a drink," Flo suggested with a twisted smile.

"No, thank you," Emma said politely. "I don't think I like the stuff."

"What's the difference," Jack asked, "between that and the bacon with your goddam breakfast? Got any idea how they kill pigs? They bleed 'em to death." He described the entire process graphically. "You like veal," he continued. "Well, that's even worse." His powers of description expanded. "Want to know about the geese and how they make liverwurst?" he dared, but Emma had had enough and knew it. She just shook her head and surrendered.

Stu was no taller than Emma, slender, fair-haired and good-enough-looking if you took the time to bother looking at him, although most people didn't take a second look; he had a face you could forget in a crowd of two. Emma could have told him to go away and he would have gone, but she didn't tell him that, and she didn't know why she didn't tell him. She was not what you'd call too impressed by it all, but thought it might be something like fly fishing, which you got better at the more you practised. Stu was impressed, though, and waited for her every afternoon that summer.

"Want to go to a movie?" he asked her afterward.

"No," she said each time.

"How come you never want to go out with me?" he asked finally.

"If you don't like the way things are," she said reasonably enough, "you don't have to meet me." But he knew a good thing, and everything continued on Emma's terms. Finally she got bored and said she wasn't going to meet him any more.

"Why?" he asked, deeply hurt.

"Listen, you're a nice guy, and I'm as homely as a slice of stale bread. You deserve a pretty girlfriend, and I like you too much to cheat you out of what you deserve." He went away feeling confused, but two weeks later he had a pretty girlfriend, and was so grateful to Emma for what he saw as her selfless sacrifice that he told everyone he knew that Emma Jonstone was the nicest person he'd ever known.

"Yeah," his friends said, "but homely as hell."

"What's so great about her?" his pretty girlfriend asked. "She's got a face you'd sooner forget than look at."

"Maybe so," he hedged, smart enough to know he'd better be careful of what he said, "but she'll help a guy with his English homework and never make him feel stupid for needing the help."

"English," the pretty girl friend scoffed, "who cares?"

Emma cared. Emma left them all behind in English class, and everyone knew it. If she wasn't sure how to spell a word, she closed her eyes and tried to picture the word as she had seen it when reading a book. Invariably the spelling would come to her, as if printed on the inside of her eyelids. Emma attributed it to her memory. She was very grateful that she had such a good memory. Whenever anyone lost something, or needed help finding something, they would eventually wind up asking, "Hey, Emma, have you seen. . . ." Emma would close her eyes, as she did when trying to envision the spelling of a word, and in just a few seconds there would be, on her eyelids, a picture, and she'd say, "I think I saw it over by the woodshed, behind a sack of feed," or "Do you think maybe you left it in the far front corner of the basement?"

"Jesus, Emma," they said, "how'd you know where it was?"

"Lucky, I guess," she shrugged.

"By God," they'd laugh, believing they were giving her a compliment of sorts. "By God, if your looks were as good as your memory, you'd be in the movies."

"On the other hand," she smiled widely, and with what seemed to be open friendliness, "if they were as bad as your brain, I'd be locked away for the protection of the public."

Emma's sense of humour was considered to be excellent. "Why she's damn near as funny as she is funny looking," they said.

Because she read so much, so fast, Emma was always running out of books, and if she couldn't make it into the library for another armload, she read the Bible.

"*Lady Chatterly's Lover,*" she said in English class, "is tame alongside the *Song of Solomon*. The difference is, most of the bigots can't lip-read well enough to realize Solomon was a pederast, a sodomite and a voyeur."

"Huh?" said her classmates.

"Emma. Stop," said the English teacher. Pretending innocence, Emma stopped. From that moment on, Emma's English teacher kept a very close eye on Emma.

Stu wanted, more than anything in the world, to go to university to study pharmacy. Math, chemistry, biology, physics, the skills a pharmacist would actually need, came easily to Stu. English killed him. It was boring. His attention wandered and down came his average.

"Jesus, Emma, if I can't bring up my English, I'm sunk" he mourned, hunched over his brown bag lunch in the cafeteria.

"That bad?" she asked.

"That bad." He dropped his half-eaten sandwich into the bag. "I'll wind up slingin' riggin' like my goddamned dad and all my gorilla uncles," he groaned.

So Emma did Stu's English homework for him. They met before school so he could copy it in his own handwriting, with just enough mistakes so that his mark would not skyrocket and his answers not coincide too completely with Emma's. She helped him with his compositions, while his pretty girlfriend sat at the kitchen table with them, frowning and listening to the radio, cracking her gum and driving Emma to an appreciation of axe murderers. Come the final exam, Emma chose a seat directly across the narrow aisle from Stu. She switched blank exam forms with him and he hunched over hers, frowning with concentration, while Emma quickly pencilled in his answers for him. He was on his own for the final composition, but they had half-memorized a formula-comp to cover almost any situation. When she knew there were enough correct answers on the test to get Stu a decent grade, Emma waited until the teacher's back was turned, then slipped the exam form to Stu, got her own back and settled down to get the very best mark she could manage. Emma had the grade eight English award, the grade nine English award, the grade ten English award and the grade eleven English award, but what Emma wanted was the special award that told the world that, for your entire junior and senior high school years, you had the best average.

Emma felt a little uneasy about the look the English teacher gave her as she handed in her exam, but as the Bible said, ''the wicked flee when no man pursueth,'' and there was no way the teacher could have seen. Unless she had eyes in the back of her head, which was, of course, physiologically impossible.

On awards day both Emma and Stu got hung on a fine golden hook. Everyone expected Emma to win the award, and nobody was more surprised than Emma when the English teacher took the stage to say that, for the first time in the history of the school, the Best Over-All Achievement Award had been altered to Most Improvement in a Semester, and the award went to Stu. He didn't think it was fair, Emma didn't think it was fair, but neither of them could say a word. They knew the teacher knew, and they knew the teacher knew they knew she knew, and they also knew they had cheated.

''She could have failed us both,'' Emma managed, choking on her disappointment.

''Jesus, Emma, I'm sorry.'' Stu was miserable.

''Oh well,'' Emma shrugged and tried to grin, ''que sera sera.'' But it stuck sideways in her throat all the same. She wanted to debate with the English teacher why a pharmacist had to know the first epic poem in the history of English literature; why Stu should be stuck up a Douglas fir because Wordsworth and Hardy lulled him to sleep. And just what does *cheat* mean, anyway? But there was nothing to be said; Stu's name went on the list in the main corridor, and both he and Emma lived with their knowledge for the rest of their lives.

If you're going to do it, Emma learned, do it in such a way nobody can do anything about it, even if they do catch on.

With that philosophy firmly centred, it is God's own mercy Emma didn't become a bureaucrat or, worse, a politician. But there was an unfortunate streak of basic honesty in Emma that made both of those choices impossible. She would have liked to have gone to university to become a veterinarian, but that was out, not only because of finances but because the daughters of drunks, nieces of drunks and sisters of drunks didn't break that kind of class barrier, and Emma was daughter, niece, sister and, by now, sister-in-law to some of the town's most dedicated drunks.

She almost went to work for the BC Telephone Company but was saved that hideous fate by walking into the only bookstore in town just as the owner prepared to put a Help Wanted sign in the window. She got her own place, two rooms on the second floor in what had once been a nice, large, old family home on Kennedy Street, bathroom shared, down the hall.

Emma quite enjoyed the bookstore. She got to read almost anything she wanted and most of the people she met also liked reading. She got two weeks vacation every year and took them at the end of January or middle of February, when the goddam endless rain was at its most lunatic-making. She went to Hawaii once, to Mexico, briefly, and dreamed of Australia.

By sheer chance, Emma embarked on an interesting sideline. She was minding her own business, tending the store, and overheard a customer say to a friend, ''and I can't find any trace of it.''

''Look under the fridge,'' Emma said unthinkingly.

''What?'' the woman stared.

''Under the fridge,'' Emma repeated, with no idea what she was talking about. The woman gave Emma a very odd look, paid for her book and left. The next day she was back, all smiles. ''How did you know?'' She held out her hand, her gold wedding band glittering. ''How did you know?''

''I don't know,'' Emma said. Because she was feeling foolish and mischievous and had always had a good sense of humour, she added humbly, ''I think it's a gift.''

That's all Emma said. She did not say it was a gift of God, she did not say she had the Power of Divination, she did not say any of the things everyone else immediately started to say about her.

''It's been stolen,'' Emma said, ''and sold. It's in a secondhand store on the main street in Ladysmith. Right next to the Chinese restaurant.''

''It's caught in the gooseneck of your bathroom sink.''

''No, she's not dead, nor has she run away with the circus. She and Teddy Singh ran off to Port Angeles to get married because Teddy's parents don't want him to marry a white girl, and they aren't telling anybody they're married. She's living in Duncan, and he comes to stay with her every night once it's dark.''

''Emma,'' the people said gratefully, ''you're a saint.''

''I am not the one who found it for you,'' Emma said firmly. ''Thank the Power.''

''The hand of God has touched you,'' they insisted.

"God works," Emma said straight-faced, "in mysterious ways, His mysteries to perform," Nobody even bothered to check if Emma had quoted correctly or not.

"How much do I owe you?" they asked.

"Oh, I don't charge," said Emma, who quite enjoyed the whole thing.

"Nonsense," the woman replied and gave Emma ten dollars. Emma sat in her room that night, staring at the ten-dollar bill, unable to stop remembering the English Award and Stu's name on the list and the English teacher who had cheated to teach Emma about the wages of sin. Emma tried to think of Kay, and how Kay had loved her, cuddled her, laughed with her but never at her, but all Emma could think about was pie-face, flat-face, homely-ugly and don't look at the clock, Emma, jesus, you'll break it. She realized she hated quite a few people. Like almost the entire population of Vancouver Island, save, perhaps, her Aunt Elaine, who had never once done Emma any harm and had always made sure Emma had money and new shoes and clothes. And Aunt Flo, who was maybe never sober, but never threw kittens in the cougar hound pen either. And Jack, an asshole of the first degree, but at least honest enough and caring enough to make sure that Emma knew it was all shit. "Pick it up, Emma," he had said, "and put it in a solid gold box, wrap it up with silk and satin and tie a great big ribbon around it, but if it was shit when you picked it up, it will still be shit when they unwrap it."

Surrounded as she was by good reading material, Emma had no problem finding books to inform, educate and uplift her, no trouble finding books to challenge and stretch her mind; what she had was trouble turning off her mind long enough to be able to fall asleep at night. She tried watching television, but that only made her angry. She wanted to soothe her brain, not insult it so badly it left home forever. In the supermarket, doing her sensible and economic shopping, without any forethought, she picked up a garish tabloid. Sprawled on her couch that evening, Emma amused herself by reading articles that teetered dangerously on the thin line between fanciful invention and outright libel. She learned, for example, that "Vampires Can Help Your Child Get An Education," "Lady Di Yearns For Freedom; Tells Royal Hubby She Wants A Divorce," "Pre-Schooler Murders Parents" and "Sex Causes Cancer." Emma snickered and chortled and shook her head in wonder, and when she had read every badly written article, she turned to the advertisements and cracked up completely. "Worried?

Poor Health? Subdue Evil Influences. World's Greatest Psychic Healer Guarantees Results. Phone Day Or Night. Guaranteed.'' ''Mama Grande, Indian Spiritualist, Results Guaranteed Within Ten Hours. Phone Or Write.'' ''Mme Sanglee Will Help On All Problems. Restore Nature. Reunite Loved Ones. Send $10.00 For Immediate Help. Overcome Enemies.'' ''Send Now, Immediate Results. Wealth. Revenge. Receive Millionaire Spells Plus Wealth-Attracting Potions, Personal Lucky Numbers, Lucky Charm Collection. Bonus For Immediate Reply, Candle-Burning Ritual And Chant Guaranteed To Restore Nature, Bring Wealth. Send $20.00 And Birth Date.'' ''Personal Ju-Ju, Hoodoo Doll Complete With Pins, Phonetic Chant, Full Instructions. Revenge, Satisfaction, Restore Nature, Win Your Loved One. Send $10.00 Plus Button From Your Favourite Shirt.'' ''Enjoy AAAA Credit Rating, Receive Credit Cards, Eliminate Debts, No Snoops, No Questions Asked. Driver's License Any Name, Send Photo.'' ''Become Ordained Minister, Legitimize Your Right to 'Reverend'.'' ''Become Bishop, Evangelist, Missionary, Chaplain, Disciple, Reverend.'' ''Serve Our Saviour, Become Priest, Nun, Cardinal.'' ''Become Ordained Minister, Legal, Certificate $3.00.''

Emma nearly fell off the sofa laughing and then, because she was bored and because the tabloid had successfully done what she had wanted it to do—turned off her mind—she went to her desk, got a sheet of paper, an envelope, a stamp, a pen and her cheque book, and before her brain could turn on again she wrote one of the addresses requesting to be ordained and sent a cheque for four dollars Canadian, because nobody ever knows how far the Canadian dollar will fall in the time it takes a letter to go from Vancouver Island to the US.

Emma almost forgot about her little personal joke. And then, there it was, waiting in her mail box, a letter addressed to Sister Emma, telling her she was now God's Agent. Telling her Christ had ordained her through his mercy, telling her Christ demanded nothing from her other than the will to HELP OTHERS. Telling her Christ had simply said ''Follow me,'' and made no scholastic demands of any kind on his disciples and teachers. Emma read the letter four times before looking at the other piece of paper in the big envelope, an 8½-by-11-inch embossed certificate suitable for framing, bearing a very large, very official-looking gold seal, an impressive and respectable piece of paper, proclaiming that Emma Jonstone was an Ordained Minister, fully qualified and legally empowered to perform marriages, baptisms and funerals, and to give aid and comfort to those in need, to council, advise and console. Emma burst out laughing.

On her lunch break the following day, she went into Woolworth's and paid two dollars and sixty-five cents plus tax for a framed picture of Elvis Presley. That night she took out Elvis' picture and tossed it in the trash, replaced it with her Ordination Certificate and, snickering and giggling to herself, hung the certificate on the wall of her apartment, just above her sound system. Then she opened the latest tabloid and began reading the articles. ''Cannibal Children Seized By Authorities,'' ''Alien Space Invaders Spy On Earth's Defences,'' ''Fountain of Youth Found Near Toronto.'' Emma made herself a pot of almond spice tea and turned back to her tabloid. ''University Degrees By Mail. Legal. Fast. Inexpensive.'' ''Accredited Bachelors, Masters, PhDs, Send For Details.'' ''Earn Your Degree By Mail. Graduate In Bible, Philosophy, Metaphysics, Or Doctor Of Divinity. Send For Catalogue.'' Emma moved to her desk, reaching for her pen, paper, envelope, and, of course, cheque book.

Every week Emma bought the tabloid, and any time a new diploma was offered Emma fired off three dollars or five dollars or ten dollars or whatever was being asked. By simply omitting ''Emma'' and putting ''E.M.'' in the space for her name, she even got a diploma that insisted, against all sane evidence to the contrary, that Emma was a fully ordained Catholic priest. As soon as she got that one, Emma stopped saying things like Thank you very much, and started saying things like Dominus Vobiscum and Et Cum Spiritum Tuum, although she hadn't the foggiest notion what they meant. Mea Culpa, Emma said, Mea Maxima Culpa.

Paying for three sets of flannelette sheets by cheque at a local department store, Emma was asked for identification. Without really thinking about it, she pulled out her Social Insurance card, her driver's licence, her medical insurance Card and her laminated, wallet-sized ordination certificate. The clerk, who had known Emma since grade one and ought not to have needed any identification at all, barely glanced at the official documents but stared long and hard at the ordination certificate. Then stared at Emma, then back at the ordination certificate. Smiling wider than she had ever smiled at Emma before, the clerk quickly accepted the cheque, wrapped the sheets, stuffed them in a free shopping bag and waited with obvious impatience for Emma to leave so she could reach for the phone, dial ''9'' for an out-line, then call her best friend to pass on the news that Puddin'-Face was a Reverend, a Messenger of God, an Ordained Preacher.

That very evening, for the first time in recent living memory, three former schoolmates climbed Emma's stairs, knocked on her door and beamed at her when she answered their summons. "Thought we'd drop by for a visit," they suggested. "Visit?" Emma gaped. "Sure, uh, come on in."

They sat in Emma's small living room, trying to find some subject of conversation, sipping cups of tea and devouring with their eyes the wall full of Emma's private little jokes. Reverend Emma Jonstone. Reverend Doctor Emma Jonstone, Doctor of Psychology With All the Rights And Privileges Thereunto Appertaining. "I guess," one of them hazarded, "working in a bookstore and all, I guess you get lots of chance to . . . learn, eh?"

"Oh, yes," Emma smiled, "to paraphrase a famous man, another chance every day."

"Well," another announced, "you always were kind of . . . deep." They finished their tea, fumblingly managed to get themselves back out of Emma's living room and walked off down the cracked sidewalk together, nattering and chattering intently. Emma shrugged, closed her front door, and began collecting the teacups.

Emma herself didn't have to say anything about her supposed credentials. Everyone else was very willing to do all the saying for her. People had felt uneasy referring to Emma's Power, but once they had either seen or heard about the diplomas, the touch was given, the touch of respectability, and uneasiness vanished. Of course, a few irreverent yahoos, like her father, her brothers and most of her uncles and their friends, made jokes like, "Power, well then, just plug'er in and see if she'll run a band saw, har har." "Emma's power, yuk yuk, maybe it will cut down on the light bill." But, as everyone knew, a prophet, or for that matter a prophetess, was without honour in her own country. And there was no doubt Emma could find things. Lost kids, lost letters, lost wedding rings, whatever you wanted to find.

Emma's growing crowd of converts became determined their prophet would not be without honour. The women were slower than the men to become convinced of Emma's near divinity, maybe because so much of a woman's own life is so close to the magical, what with her biology, and all too often her destiny, linked to the moon, and with virtual strangers growing inside her body for months on end, like tapeworms, only noisier when they emerged. The men, those who did not automatically risk hernia by laughing, believed immediately. "Flat-face Emma's got the gift," they agreed, stuffing Copenhagen behind their bottom lips and spitting. "No doubt about it." They reminded themselves and each other of how she had always been different. "I mean, you just got to look at her to know she ain't like the rest of us. Emma is . . . different."

Cousin Darryl showed up one day and hemmed and hawed and sucked his teeth and just about got his nerve up to apologize, but Emma just looked at him and smiled, very coldly. "I might have forgiven you for what you did as a sin-filled child," she said quietly, "but God might not have. I only know what you did. God," she grinned wolfishly, "knows what it was you wanted to do." Darryl paled and nodded and would have promised to repent if he'd known how, and left hurriedly. He worried and fretted and prayed, and if he had known about scourging or flagellation or making long barefoot trips carrying crosses made out of splintery unplaned planks and posts, he'd probably have set off for Victoria with two four-by-sixes nailed together and slung over his back, but Darryl didn't know Italy from India or Mexico from Mars, so he twisted and rolled in nightmares for the rest of his life.

Having decided and agreed Emma was not like the rest of them, they attributed to her all the things they knew damned well they were not. Witty, intelligent, compassionate, understanding, and decent.

"Em, I don't know what to do with my life. I'm just in a knot all the time. I get mad at my kids for no good reason, and honest to god, there's times I don't know if I want to sit down and cry or kill someone."

"Something in your life," Emma said wisely, "isn't what you want it to be," and it would pour out, the boring marriage, the husband who drank, the financial mess, the feeling of powerlessness.

"There are only two kinds of people in the world, the Chosen and the Ordinary. The Ordinary never question, never search, never aspire and never truly *feel*. The Chosen," Emma smiled encouragingly, "have an awful time of life."

A few minutes with Emma and the Chosen felt better. They had the answer for every occasion. When they echoed Job—"why me, oh Lord?"—Emma's voice would vibrate in their minds—"The Chosen The Chosen The Chosen"—which was a message one hell of a lot more comforting than the one they had previously imagined— "Because you piss me off, asshole."

"Will you be my Spiritual Healer?" they asked.

"You are the only one who can heal your spirit. The Power is there, you have to learn to trust it. It's not like bad coffee, you know,'' she scolded, ''it doesn't come in instant.''

''I know,'' they bargained, ''that if someone would just heal me, I, too, could become a healer and heal others.''

''Heal yourself first,'' Emma insisted.

''Will you help me, show me, teach me, make it easy for me?'' they begged.

Emma gave them what they wanted. She told them Everything is Everything, therefore it stands to reason Nothing is also Everything and, by inverse logic, it is also true that Everything is Nothing, which is what most people have in the way of quality in their lives. So they have it all, all there is to be had, all there will ever be to be had, so what in hell are they complaining about anyway? Don't they even know how to appreciate things?

The only person Emma didn't try to do a snow job on was Blackie Williams. He and Esther walked into the bookstore to buy a book on fish and sea mammals for their granddaughter. Emma looked at Blackie and suddenly the bookstore vanished in fog or mist or both. Suddenly she was somewhere between here and now, between then and there, hearing the whistle of a train and the sobbing of a heartbroken young man.

''Hey Blackie,'' she said softly, ''it's okay.''

Blackie stared at her, his face pale, his head spinning, the sound of the train whistle still echoing in his ears. He knew Emma knew what nobody in the world but him ought to have known. He almost panicked. And then something inside him relaxed, something he hadn't even known was tense and waiting for the other shoe to fall. ''Thanks Emma,'' he said quietly, ''I very much appreciate it.''

Esther asked no questions at all about the somewhat unusual exchange in the bookstore.

When Henry Pearson was finally, to everyone's relief, actually dying, he sent for Emma and asked her, ''What is the meaning of life?'' Emma looked at the old bastard and laughed. She fluffed his pillow, lit him a cigarette and poured him a glass of whiskey forbidden by his doctor. ''Henry,'' she said, ''the ultimate truth of all time is . . . there isn't one.''

''Hellfire,'' Henry laughed, ''I think I've been had.''

''Ah,'' Emma teased, ''but you don't go out of this world as ignorant as you were while you were still in it.'' Henry laughed again. ''You're a goddamned fraud,'' he guessed.

"I never claimed to be anything at all, Henry," Emma agreed. "But in view of the fact some people call *you* a gentleman, it's a real case of the pot calling the kettle black. You're a robber, a liar and a scoundrel of the worst sort."

"Oh that," Henry pooh-poohed. "Tell me more about the meaning of life."

"Well," Emma lit a cigarette too, because she knew Henry didn't have enough breath left to tell anyone even if he wanted to. "The Meaning of Life isn't any more important to you at the end of life than the Reality of Death was the day you were born. You're going to die, you crabby old bugger. And nobody will cry."

"Emma, you're a bitch," Henry sighed. "But you're an honest bitch." After he was dead and buried and out of everyone's hair forever, the lawyers told Emma she now owned it all.

The Chosen waited to see what Emma would do. Would she sell out, as so many others had, and fall victim to the wiles and temptations of wealth? Because what Henry had left her was wealth of the kind usually only associated with Americans from Florida, California or Texas.

Emma incorporated herself as a church. Not because she felt any sudden surge of sanctity, or felt particularly holy or righteous, but because Emma had worked long enough in that bookstore and kept her eyes and ears open, sucking in information like a first-class vacuum cleaner, that she knew about tax benefits and tax incentives, as well as write-offs and downright evasions. Emma did not give her inheritance to the church; Emma used her knowledge of words to donate her inheritance to the church Emma had declared herself to be. From right hand to left hand by way of devious phrases. Since nobody had thought it could be done, nobody had expected anybody to try it. And after it was done, nobody believed it, so nobody challenged. Emma got acres and acres of land, several hotels, motels, marinas and boatels, plus a large and very deluxe house, without paying inheritance tax. Nor did she ever have to pay income tax on the considerable earnings of her holdings because Emma, you see, was a church. As surely as St. Paul's Cathedral, or even the Vatican itself, Emma Jonstone was a church.

"You want something more substantial?" she asked the Chosen, who looked at her with awe and a degree of puzzlement. "You want me to build you a temple?" They nodded. "Then don't sit on your duffs waiting for old Henry Pearson to give you one; he never gave anyone anything but a pain in the face. You want a temple, you build a temple. Put your donations in the jam jars and your faith in the Power and DO something about what you want.''

''What should we do?'' they asked.

''Well,'' Emma said, straight-faced and serious, ''you could fix your eyes on the stars, plant both feet firmly on the ground, bend your shoulders to the wheel and grasp destiny with both hands. Stiff upper lip, straight-eyed gaze, backs straight, shoulders square, tummies tucked in, heads held high, chin up, chest out, nothing ventured, nothing gained, and remember these immortal words, 'Say nothing, do nothing, be nothing.' Work as though everything depended on you and pray as though everything depended on God, anything worth doing is worth doing well, faint heart never won the day, and if you can't say something nice, don't say anything at all. Hop to it, get a wiggle on, shoo, scoot, beat it.''

While the jam jars filled, Emma busied herself keeping Henry's ship of commerce afloat. She quit her job in the bookstore and spent her time overseeing the brewery and the string of hotels, beer parlours, pool halls and video arcades.

''Isn't the accumulation of wealth a sin?'' they asked.

''Says in the Bible 'Render unto Caesar that which is Caesar's'; I was given this accumulation of wealth, this Caesarian burden, and I'm rendering it. 'Hide not thy light under a bushel.' Remember the parable of the talents. What about the wise and foolish virgins? What about the parable of the faithful servant? And what about the unwritten commandment, 'Thou shalt not poke thy nose into thy neighbour's business'?''

''Does it really say that in the Bible?'' they gasped.

Emma fought her laughter. ''It might not be entirely untoward if you sat down and read it.'' This was something few had ever tried to do, depending most of their lives on the interpretations and quotations of others, virtually all of whom had a private axe to grind.

The jam jars filled, and Emma bought a piece of absolutely horrible land up Nanaimo Lakes Road. What heaving geography hadn't done, the coal mines and logging companies had managed; the place was a mess of rock, clay and bog. ''Anybody,'' Emma told her congregation, ''can find beauty down on the beach, which is, in case you've forgotten, hidden behind the oil tanks and six-storey apartment buildings. But up here, it's something else. Down there nobody ever appreciates anything. How many times have you ignored the sunset, or cast an unseeing eye on Protection Island? Ah, but if you work, and from the sweat of your brow create beauty, you will have something else. Something you *will* see.'' Emma worked their little asses to nubs.

''There's at least six first-class artesians under that territorial uproar,'' Blackie Williams said. ''I know where each one is, and I'd be quite willing to drill the well for you.''

Emma poured him a glass of huckleberry wine. ''Blackie, I would really appreciate it if you waited a little while. Now you know and I know and anybody who'd take the time to sit down and think about it would know that clear, clean, sweet water is the most precious thing in the world. But have you seen what the assholes are doing with it?'' Blackie nodded sadly. ''Well, let's us let 'em think the well has gone dry; remember, that's when you start to miss the water.'' Blackie grinned, his funnybone touched and his sense of humour responding to the appeal.

''When something has hold of you,'' Emma told her Chosen, ''and is twisting your soul, making life a misery and making you confused and sad, reach out with those two capable hands of yours, take hold of a piece of hard, physical work, and have the courage to allow the Power to manifest itself. And when it is time for you to realize the beauty that is inside you, your hard work will be finished. Look at me,'' she dared them. ''Look at this ugly face. I was born with this ugly face and I've lived my life with this ugly face, but I tell you, brothers and sisters, what's inside me is identical to what's inside you! And what's under the mess here, on this land bought with the jam jar money, is identical to the Garden of Eden!''

''Beauty,'' Emma lectured, ''is where you make it, not where you find it.''

''Never mind manicured lawns and marble fountains,'' she preached. ''You were born here, in bush country, and you're bush babies, babies who have got to learn to appreciate the beauty of bush. There is more here than overhang, undergrowth, slash and greenery. Stop looking at the trees and search for the forest.''

''Are we the Moral Majority?'' they asked.

''Are you what?'' Emma laughed.

''The Moral Majority?'' they replied hopefully.

''You are not,'' she said. She reminded them of how they had felt lost, misunderstood, frightened, confused and weird when they had first come to talk to her. ''If you were a majority,'' she reasoned, ''you would have felt safe, secure, and been able to expand your souls to have empathy with and feel friendship for the minority. No, you are not the

Moral Majority. And I would point out to you that the Moral Majority is not very moral as long as it feels holier than thou. Look at what they write, listen to what they say. Are they the smartest? Are they the brightest? Are they the nicest? Who do you think they really are? Assholes all,'' she answered her own question. ''And so how could you be part of them, working as hard as you are to overcome your own assholiness?''

They picked rocks, they hauled rocks, they stacked rocks and piled rocks, then tried to turn the rocks into rock gardens. They cleared slash, they stacked slash, they burned slash, then spread the ashes in the boggy areas to try to turn the acid-reek soil into something that would support life instead of killing it. Winter, summer, spring and fall they toiled. Their backs ached, their shoulders throbbed, their hands were often like swollen bags of flame and they fell asleep at night as soon as they lay down on their beds. No time for self-pity, no time for staring at the moss growing in their navels and convincing themselves it was important.

Emma dismissed any sign of invert preoccupation. ''You don't have time,'' she told them off-handedly. ''Angst is a luxury, and we're here for basics.''

''Emma?'' The woman was young, with tanned skin and clear gray eyes. ''Pardon me, but the folks have asked me to do the talking for them.''

''Talk away,''Emma invited.

''Emma, we've thought about it and talked it over and, well, we hope you aren't going to be too disappointed, but . . . we don't want to build a temple.''

''Too much work?'' Emma asked.

''No.'' The young woman gestured with her arm. ''Emma, look at this place. Look at the green trees, look at all the different colours in those piles of rocks. Look at the moss, the salal, the Oregon grape, smell the thimbleberries and the perfume from the over-ripe salmonberries where they've fallen on the ground.'' The young woman watched with pleasure the smile that grew on Emma's face, transforming her from a homely-ugly pie-face to a great-looking woman. ''Emma, this place *is* a temple.''

''Hey Blackie,'' Emma yelled. ''How'd you like to dowse this place? What we need here is some crystal-clear drinking water and a damn fine swimming pool. We've earned it.''

Blackie walked around the property, whistling softly, his heart as light as dandelion fluff, the soles of his feet itching, his hands in his pockets. Every time he stopped and did a little jig of joy, the Chosen yelled with glee, and started digging.

"I never knew a church before," Esther teased Emma.

"Well," Emma grinned, pouring the huckleberry wine, "you know how it is, with the Power all things are possible." Esther laughed.

"Keep laughing,"Emma said, "it makes me feel good."

DID'JA EVER HEAR OF
A GOOLIEGUY?

The final straw is so often nothing at all. You go through years of daily give-and-take, each trying to adapt to the moods of the other, making adjustments of minor or major proportions and then, there you are, part of you knowing it's no big deal and part of you numb with fatalistic horror, watching the third, external part of yourself, fiercely packing, stern, unyielding, stubborn as a terrier. And she is just as stern, unyielding, stubborn, getting ready for work as if nothing at all was happening, as if your life together wasn't in jeopardy.

And I knew nothing was going to make any difference. This wasn't happening for any of the reasons we might say. It had a life of its own, and we were both observers as well as players, caught in some damn thing for reasons we probably would never understand.

Carol left for work. I hauled out clothes from drawers and closets, stuffed them in black garbage bags, knotted the tops shut and hauled them, two at a time, to the pickup truck, heaved them in the back, under the canopy.

Then I whistled for Bess, opened the door of the pickup truck and patted the seat. She was there in an instant, wagging her stub tail, her tongue lolling in that spaniel grin that could usually make me laugh. I slammed the door, moved to the other side, got in and started the engine. Then I drove away from the place that had meant Home for those days, weeks, and years.

The angry part of me drove to the gas station, filled the tank, topped the oil, checked the tires, handed over the credit card and waited until the attendant fussed with the form. Then I signed my name, took my receipt, put it and my plastic card in my wallet, stuffed that in my pocket and drove to the bank. I got some cash and headed out, pretending I didn't know where I was going.

But we always run home, don't we? We always run back to that first place, that place where we got hurt worse than anywhere else, that place where we were so scarred by what they told us was love and family that any hurt afterward seems small in comparison.

Three days of steady driving, three nights in forgettable motels, a ride on the ferry and there I was, back where I hadn't been for more than half my lifetime.

I had memories of huge fir trees swaying gently in the summer breeze, of miles and miles and miles of road winding through forests of evergreen, dogwood and arbutus. I looked for the net racks and sheds full of crab traps, I looked for the small trollers with names like *Barbara Anne* and *Margaret Joyce*, and what I found were four-lane highways, golden arches, two-storey painted ice-cream cones and a foreshore lined with motels boasting ridiculous names.

The hotel the old man had built decades earlier looked the same on the outside, but any hint of individuality inside had been very carefully either painted over or covered with that ghastly red carpet they seem to think is compulsory.

It was easier just to check in like any other befuddled tourist than to bother with the phone calls and verifications. I signed the register and the clerk didn't even check my signature, let alone react to the name.

I went up to my room, had a shower, changed my clothes, then went down to the dining room for supper. It was strange sitting at a table by the window, looking out on the harbour, remembering other times, when the harbour wasn't a place for sea planes to land, wasn't constantly crisscrossed by one power boat or another. The meal was exactly what you would have had every right in the world to expect for what they were charging. Good, but not great.

In the morning I went to see the lawyer. I think the receptionist thought I was some country housewife wandering in to ask about divorce proceedings; she was aloof and a bit off-putting until I told her who I was and why I was there. Then she was polite, efficient and smiling so widely you'd have thought I was her long-lost cousin. Who knows, considering the way some of the men in the family had behaved, maybe I was.

The lawyer came from the same mold all lawyers on that Island seem to come from: the one with the very expensive suit, the shoes treated to look shined at all times, the expensive shirt and tie, the hair carefully combed over the growing bald patch, the flabby little pot belly already starting to spread and burgeon. This blond had been pulling in a good yearly retainer for most of his working life, ever since the old one had offed himself with too much alcohol, and this was the first time anyone had come to see him face to face. He wasn't quite sweating, but then, he hadn't known I was going to drop by his office.

He was burning with curiosity, but I wasn't interested in giving him any details. All I really wanted to know was if the old place was rented out to anyone or if it was, again, empty.

"There hasn't been anyone in it since, uh, the, uh, late spring of, uh, last, uhm, year," he managed, quickly moving pieces of paper around on his desk, checking the file as he spoke, trying to cover the fact he hadn't really been doing much about earning his money.

"Fine." I gave him the frosty smile they had taught me in private school, the one almost guaranteed to make anyone except the royal family suddenly feel diminished. "Please remove it from the listings; I'll be staying there myself for a while."

"Oh!" he blurted, blushed, fussed with the papers a bit. "Well, uh, if you could, uh, give me a day or two to, uh, have the place, uhm, well, prepared for your arrival . . . yard cleanup, housecleaning, the usual thing after a place has been empty for, uh, almost a year."

"That's okay." I gave him the cheerful, we're-just-folks grin I learned from my aunt who was, in fact, just-folks and not at all anyone the family could accept. But she'd been nice to me, and had given the grisly bastards a good run for their money until Uncle Tony caved in under the constant disapproval and patronizing and started to rot his brain and liver with the finest of Glenfiddich. That grin, learned from her, coming close on the heels of the private school frost-face smile, always throws the Philistines off balance. "I'll just contact the Blue-Collar Army." He probably wasn't going to be too happy about that; it would give me a chance to find out first-hand what those organized handymen really charged, and compare that with what this beagle had said they charged. I was willing to bet everything had been inflated and he had pocketed the difference himself. You have to expect that if you choose, as I did for so long, to pay as little attention as possible to any of the details.

I declined his offer to take me up there himself. I knew if he was given any control over anything, he'd find a way to delay the visit until someone had been up there and started doing what probably ought to have been done months ago.

When I was young, the mucketymucks had their summer cabins up Nanaimo Lakes Road, and the family had finally put in a gate to keep these upwardly aspiring trespassers from coming to the old place to visit as if we were all really neighbours in the accepted sense of the word. For the most part, those mucketymucks worked for the logging company, which had grown only after the mines had begun to decline. They seemed to think we would have things in common, although I can't imagine what they thought those things would be, and now that the trees were gone and the slopes ruined, the logging company had moved on, the mucketymucks were gone and the summer cabins and cottages they built were becoming derelict shacks, used by the locals for hunting shelters and fishing shacks.

The logging had scarred the hillsides. What had been a solid cover of stately evergreen was a stubby cover of trash wood; alder, wild cherry, several kinds of maple—what they call ''non-commercial deciduous''—and the lake was not what I remembered at all. I suppose someone must have signed whatever permission paper was necessary to allow the butchers onto the family land, but I knew it wasn't me, and I wasn't interested in finding out which of the idiot uncles was responsible.

My four-times great-grandfather came out from Scotland with nothing more than a change of clothes and a head full of schemes. He smiled and joked and made friends until he was trusted to the limit by everyone who knew him here, and then he went into partnership with someone who knew something about mining and between them they laid out claims and proved up a seam of rich anthracite coal. They started mining with three or four trusting men who worked for shares, and while those men worked digging coal, my four-times great-grandfather kept looking around, laying claims and then, suddenly, my great-great-great-great grandfather owned the whole thing, what the natives here call the whole shiterooni. His partner got a gravestone, a marble marker, after they brought his body up out of the cave-in which crushed him and two other men. The surviving men who had started working for shares with the old man had either gone back to Scotland, been given the title of supervisor or just somehow seemed to disappear off the face of the earth. The scheming heatherhopper wound up a millionaire so many times over that, even when the bottom fell out of coal, even when miners were out of work and starving, even when the shafts had been sealed shut, even when other fortunes were lost, none of us had to worry. Not even with those ridiculous uncles involved, not even with those lawyers the children of those ridiculous uncles hired and put in charge.

That old crook had three wives and buried each of them, he had a dozen children who married and had children, all of whom married and had children, but there is only me and my Uncle Tony left, and Tony has been living in a rubber room since he realized he lost more than his wife when he gave in to the pressure the family put on him.

It was my aunt had the old place fixed up. Maybe she hoped she could get Tony to live there with her, miles from the rest of them. The main part of the old place was built by my grandfather, when he was a young man and hadn't yet started to turn into what he eventually became. He took it into his head to return to the place the old crook had built when the first mine was in production up there in the hills. He tore down the rotting cabin and brought in a crew of Chinese to flatten a big section of hillside, and on that flat piece he had them build a rectangular house of peeled fir logs. By the time my aunt saw it, the big log house was a neglected mess. She had it all fixed up and had a porch added along the front and the south-facing wall. The old roof was replaced and extended out over the porch so you could sit out there, even on a rainy day, and look down to the lake.

She had a studio built there, too, separate from the house, a place where she would go by herself and write her poems and books, paint her pictures, make her figures carved from wood, her strange sculptures of rock and bone, even of feather and moss. All of which the family used to prove she just was not the kind of person Uncle Tony should have married.

Even after he'd caved in and she'd left him, she tried to help the sodden fool. She was the one got him out of the drunk tank and took him up to the old place, even moved a piano in for him in the hope he'd dry out and go back to the music she had once thought he would play for the world. He dried out all right, but sat on the porch and wept until the family smartened up enough to figure out where he might be and sent someone out to collect him. Six months later they took him off to the funny farm.

The peeled logs had been treated with some kind of preservative. It darkened the wood, made the place look more solid than I remembered it, more firmly entrenched in the landscape. A tin roof had been put on it, and that was a shock; I had expected cedar shakes, weathered to a dull silver. The small sheds were ramshackle and the chimney looked as if it badly needed attention—the mortar was missing and some of the bricks slipped to crazy angles or were absent completely. But no crisscross of fallen branches or rotting logs, no slash or mess, no English ivy gone mad and crowding out the grass. No trashy elderberry tangle or salmonberry thicket, and the meadow of knee-high grass was brightly spotted with foxglove, lupine, columbine and dahlias gone wild and escaped from what had once been flowerbeds. Small arbutus and maple, none of them more than twelve feet tall, had moved into the clearing, but not among the dozen large fruit trees.

Bess was whining nervously, trembling and sticking to me like adhesive tape, but I ignored her. She'd been too many days in a car, sitting so close as to almost be on my knee. She needed to get back to being a dog instead of my security blanket.

I looked at the studio first, because it had been my aunt's place, and a refuge for me at a time when I badly needed to be away from the family. For a minute I thought I'd gone crazy. Then I decided the former tenant was the one had gone goofy. The front door was open, and it was obvious birds of all kinds had been flying in and out at will, building their nests inside the studio, shitting over everything. The enormous front windows were filthy, smeared with mess, festooned with cobwebs. The beautiful big wood-and-glass built-in storage buffet was piled with old magazines; the expensive enameled woodstove from Ireland was covered with bits of metal, rusted heaps of nails, nuts, bolts; the built-in double bed was hidden by bits of broken board, lengths of damp warped plywood; and the floor was littered with stove wood, heaps of it, stacks of it, piles of it, all the way to the gigantic counter-weighted door, propped open by dropped wood.

And someone had nailed sheet metal all around the edge of the door and around the frame. It made no sense. The windowsills outside were sheeted with metal, nailed with big-headed nails every three inches, as if there was some reason the metal had to be put there and kept there until after the crack of Doomsday.

The big house was incredible. Not in the sense of crystal chandeliers or gold-leaf paint; just incredible in the sense of "who'd'a thunk it." Someone had left this place in exactly the same way I'd just left a place. Grab the clothes that come to hand and never come back for the other stuff.

Except for the thick layer of dust and cobwebs, you'd have thought someone was due home any minute.

Big windows looked out over the covered porch, over and past the studio, down the slope to the lake. From the north window, in the corner by the sink, you could look out and down to a year-round stream feeding into the shallow end of the copper-coloured water at the foot of the hill. A hint of what might once have been a fenced-in enclosure around one section of the stream and a small hoochie made of plywood, but no sign of the ducks which might have lived there, unless they had been turned loose to become part of the flock down on the lake.

A large combination kitchen-living room was the original part of the house, and behind that room there were two bedrooms, once accessible from the kitchen itself. But when the porch had been added, the old house had been extended, and now you stepped up two small stairs to the addition: a small room, barely big enough for a double bed, opening into a larger room so spectacular I knew that was where I was putting a sound system, a collection of books and comfortable chairs to sit in at twilight and watch the colours of the lake change as the sun slipped behind the mountains.

The hallway to the back rooms had an old sideboard in excellent condition and a large table, similar to the one in the studio, but this one, thank god, was unmarked by bird shit. Windows in this strange cross between a dining room and a hallway looked out over the porch to the south slope and the thicket of maple, alder and arbutus, past that to the blue-green mountains rising on the other side of the lake. I knew why my aunt had put the porch around this side, had the old wall removed, the addition put on, but I didn't know why whoever had left so suddenly had abandoned the furniture.

The back bedrooms were creepy. The windows were covered with plywood, the sills sheathed in sheet metal, like the metal around the door and on the sills of the studio. Metal like the metal laid on the threshold of the studio door, on the stairs leading up to the porch of the main house, even on the threshold of the door to the house.

The back bedrooms were dark. They were also damp, musty and faintly foul-smelling, that heavy, sick smell that means mould and fungi are moving into the corners and under the furniture.

Outside, the oddness continued. I knew the windowsills would be sheathed with metal; I hadn't expected to trip over a railroad spike driven into the path. It had heaved partway up in the winter freeze, otherwise I might never have noticed it. But having found it, I soon found others, and I almost giggled at the thought of some supreme lunatic trying to nail the topsoil to the earth. Maybe the former tenant hadn't gone away at all. Maybe he'd been taken away in a jacket that fastened his arms to his sides and closed at the back.

Some things I just don't bother thinking about until I absolutely have no choice. Carol used to tell me I needed to learn how to deal with things. I told her not dealing with them was my way of dealing with them. Things are either internal or external. Even problems and troubles are either caused by something inside yourself or by something outside. If it's something inside, there probably isn't much you can do about it; even clinical depression either wears off or doesn't. If it wears off, you don't have to do anything about it because it's gone; if it doesn't wear off, you still don't have to do anything because they'll put you away and feed you funny things to combat it. If your problems and troubles are caused by something outside yourself, what can you do about it? Force someone to love you? Stop the war? Insist the world run the way you want it to run? Demand everybody be nice to you so you can be happy?

The puzzles about the old house and the former tenant were things I wasn't ready to even try to think about, let alone solve. I knew that sooner or later they'd stop puzzling me, or I'd stumble over the reason and they wouldn't be puzzles anymore. I had other things to do.

I made arrangements for the Blue-Collar Army to come out and start fixing up the place so I could move into it. Three men in a pickup truck full of tool boxes, ladders, scaffolding boards and an assortment of brushes and chains put ladders up to the roof, climbed up, cleaned the chimney from top to bottom and started replacing bricks and mortar. They took the stove apart and scrubbed the inside of it, cleaned out all the years and years' accumulation of caked soot and baked creosote, then put the stove back together again. They hauled the plywood off the back windows, they put new stovepipe from the stove to the chimney, they chinked around the windows and doors, they winter-proofed the place as if we were living in the barren lands of the far north and they never spoke to me. They spoke messages to the left of my head and messages to the right of my head, they grunted responses and talked over my head, but their eyes slid away from mine and they seemed so uneasy I wondered if there was a big secret none of them wanted me to find out—like maybe none of them knew what they were doing.

The linoleum in the kitchen was awful, and I had them rip that up, but when I said I wanted the metal sheeting over the threshold of the door removed, they hesitated and looked at each other, then looked past me to the bush, then looked at each other again. They looked at the bush and the lake, they looked at the studio and the woodsheds, they looked everywhere and then looked away, but they wouldn't look at me.

"Is something wrong?" I asked, impatient and getting angry. "Is there something wrong? Like maybe a big hole in the floor or dry rot in the joists, or . . . ?"

"Foundation's solid," the young one blurted, "joists is fine. You want that taken up, I'll take it up, but . . ." he darted a shame-faced look at the other two, "what about the goolieguy?"

"I beg your pardon?" I said carefully.

"The goolieguy," he repeated stubbornly.

I didn't want to laugh, vowed to myself that, whatever else I did or said, I wouldn't laugh. It wasn't their fault. They're ignorant and under-educated to the point of being functionally illiterate, but they didn't ask to be born on an Island which has been abused, mistreated, exploited and ruined by companies exactly like the one started by my four-times great-grandfather. People with smooth-tongued skill talked of blue sky and free land, of the chance to own your own place, of brand new coal mines with the best of working conditions, of top wages working in seven- and eight-foot shafts, not the miserably low-roofed shafts where men had to work with their heads and shoulders bowed, their backs bent and aching. Clean streams, they were told, and nobody with the authority to refuse you the right to fish for free food.

And so they came. And found most of what they had been told they would find. But generations later their descendants were chronically under-employed or unemployed, and the land they had been promised was still controlled by people who lived elsewhere.

"Tell me about the goolieguy," I suggested. The poor, superstitious fool looked miserable, and the other two weren't about to do or say anything to let him off the hook. I just waited and finally he nodded and stuffed his hands in his pockets. "The guy who left here took off because of the goolieguy." He seemed to feel an incredible relief once he started to talk, and the other two, although they in no way relaxed their disapproval of his indiscretion, seemed glad the cat was out of the bag. "He was okay as long as his missus was alive, but after she died, well, he started to get . . . goofy." He took his hands out of his pockets, started to reach for the round can of snuff in his back pocket, then blushed and reached instead for the papers and tobacco in his shirt pocket and began to roll himself a cigarette. "He was just about on a par with your average outhouse rat inside of about a month of her dying. I guess he nailed up the metal before she died, but he got lots worse real fast.''

''What are we talking here?'' I probed.

''Goolieguy,'' he repeated. ''Lives in the bush most of the time. Or in old sheds and barns.''

''Are we talking roof rats?'' I asked carefully. ''Or pack rats or . . .''

''No, we ain't!'' he said stubbornly, insulted by my questions. ''We're talkin' goolieguy. I suppose,'' he said, as if excusing me for something I couldn't control, ''I suppose you're not Welsh.''

''No,'' I admitted.

''You related to that bunch as owns this place? Or did. They're pretty well all dead. Or locked in the bin, I suppose.''

''I am,'' I admitted, and then I laughed, and it didn't insult them because they knew, or at least intuited, why I was laughing. I wished with all my heart that the entire sanctimonious collection of them could hear themselves described as ''that bunch.'' Dismissed as a crackpot collection instead of being revered, as they had revered themselves, as some kind of superior form of life.

''Well, even so,'' he grumbled, ''you ought to know goolieguy. That bunch was Scots and so was my gran, and she knew goolieguy.''

''I'm sorry.'' I gave him the friendly grin. ''I've been off-Island most of my life. I'm not very . . . clued in.''

''Well, we all figured as much,'' he admitted, the corner of his mouth twitching in what could pass for a grin among this dour bunch. ''A goolieguy,''—he had his cigarette rolled and in his mouth, and lit it with a big wooden match he ignited by drawing it quickly across the rough denim of his jeans—''came from the old country with the first people who came here. They brought people to work the pits at White Rapids Coal and Coking Company, and the goolieguys hid.'' He was serious, as serious as any teacher in a classroom. ''They hid in the big wooden boxes they shipped the blankets and bedding in, and maybe some of them hid in with the sheep and cattle the people brought over with them. My gran's gran on my mother's side told my gran, and my gran told me, a goolieguy attaches herself to you or to your family, and they stick to you, no matter where you go. They'll die rather than . . . abandon you.''

''They're brown,'' the oldest worker said sternly, ''brown-skinned and brown-haired, brown-eyed and kinda hairy. Real long thin brown fingers'n'toes. Even their nails are brown. Live where they can, in the bush or in the hayloft of the barn or under the house.'' He looked at the place at the edge of the porch where the boards were splintered away and the ground flat and bare, the place were Bess wouldn't go but sat watching, whining softly. ''The only way to get rid of'em is to use iron on'em. It burns them,'' he finished, glaring at me and defying me to contradict him or deny what he was saying.

''My gran said,''—the young man rose, stubbing his cigarette out by pinching it between his fingers, then scuffing a small hole in the dirt, dropping in his butt and covering it with dirt—''the goolieguy used to live with us, but when we started using metal they had to back off from us. Couldn't stand bein' around the metal, you see. My gran says they never abandoned us, we abandoned them, and when they moved us off the crofts and moved on the machines, the goolieguys had to go further away. She says it was said that what had been the ruination of the goolieguys would be the ruination of us. Machines. Industry.'' He looked out at the clear-cut slopes, shook his head gently, and looked as if only good manners kept him from spitting.

''And what do they do that is . . . bad?'' I was careful about my tone of voice, the expression on my face. I didn't want these workmen taking insult and walking off the job before it was done. Poor ignorant bastards, I thought, reminded of my uncles and their lucky rings made from horseshoe nails, or their endless other superstitions.

''Nothing,'' the young man admitted, ''but most people go kind of . . . wingy.'' He was suddenly very uneasy again, looking over his shoulder at the bush, stuffing his hands in his pockets and removing them again hurriedly. ''Can't stand being watched by something they don't believe they can see. Goolieguy likes to look in your windows and such. You hear them on the roof, warming their hands at the chimney. Under the house at night. But if you want that metal sheeting taken offa the doorstep,'' he said quickly, obviously wanting to terminate the conversation, ''I'll take'er up. But without that metal . . . goolieguy could get into your kitchen. Pull the soft middle out of your bread, leave nothing but the crust. Drink your cream, you wake up in the morning and there's no cream for your coffee. Eat your cheese.''

The whole thing sounded more like mice to me than some kind of hairy brown spook smuggled in from Scotland. A good mouser cat would probably keep the goolieguy away a lot better than any amount of nails or sheet metal. Still, had I known any of this before I asked them to remove the metal, I wouldn't have decided to have it taken up, but I wasn't going to back down now in front of these three ignorant louts. "Well, I think we might as well take up the metal sheeting," I said, trying to sound casual. "After all, if the goolieguy doesn't really hurt anything..." All three of them looked at me as if I was absolutely insane. But the tension between us was gone and, who knows, maybe those people know they themselves are crazier than the proverbial outhouse rats and can afford to be relaxed and friendly with lunatics. The metal came up off the kitchen floor, and I drove into town to rent a sander for the boards exposed when the linoleum was removed.

While they were busy working on the main house, I busied myself in the smaller one, the one I had thought of as a studio. I heaved the stove wood outside, making no effort at all to stack it neatly, just heaving it out onto the grass. Then I wrestled the big square table to the doorway and got it outside in the light where I could have a good look at it. Even with chicken shit, bird shit and pigeon shit smeared on it, it was beautiful, and anyone would have been proud to have it in their home. I knew I could wash it clean, and if the dried droppings had stained or damaged it, a good refinisher could have it like new in only a couple of days.

The Blue-Collar Army worked on the main house for a week and I worked on the studio, sweeping, scrubbing and doing a lot of cursing. It just isn't right to treat a place like that, as if what you'd really rather do is just burn it down, but first you want it to suffer. I had the metal removed from the doorway and sanded the floor, then rented a propane heater and boiled linseed oil. Just before the oil was hot enough to burst into flame, I turned off the propane and started dippering out the boiling oil, spreading it on the boards liberally, literally frying the wood. It was something my grandfather had always done with his floors. He said you could use ordinary fir for the flooring, and by the time the boiling oil fried and hardened the fir, you had a floor better than the most expensive hardwood. What he didn't tell me was how much hard work it was, spreading it liberally but not unevenly, scrubbing it into cracks with a long-handled brush. While it was still wet, I took a big, rented, commercial floor-polisher to it. Why spend all that time getting blisters if there's a machine to do the worst of it?

And when the floor was finally dry, it didn't shine like it would if it had been varathaned or varnished, but it glowed rich golden and looked the way I remembered floors looking. By then I had the various kinds of guano off the table and the youngest workie had it sanded smooth,

Danish-oiled and polished. He helped me move it back into the studio and set it up in front of the big window at the front, and even if there weren't any matching chairs, it looked gorgeous. The stove was cleaned, the new stovepipes carefully and properly wired and metal-screwed in place, the chimney cleaned and the walls and cupboards scrubbed. Of course I had no need or use of the place, but all this tidying and elbow greasing kept my mind off all those things I knew I wasn't ready to try to sort out, explain or even decide.

The main house looked even more wonderful than the studio did. Nothing fancy, nothing your average millionaire would covet, but everything was clean, in good repair and all the cracks were chinked and sealed; it could turn winter tomorrow and the house wouldn't care. The junk and garbage was heaved into the two pickup trucks and driven off to the festering mess that is the local garbage dump, and none of us had made any mention at all of the supposed resident goolieguy. But that part of the skirting at the far end of the porch was left unrepaired, and I was the one that had to go under the house to check and repair the insulation.

They did as much as they could from outside, but not one of them would come under the house. I knew I could offer them ten times their hourly rate and they would just stand there, pretending they had suddenly been struck deaf, blind and mute. So I got them to explain what it was I was supposed to be doing and I went under the house with a trouble light.

They moved the big, lightweight, fibreglass batts where I could get them easily and called advice from outside, but I was the one had to lie on my back, push the fibreglass up between the joists and stuff it in place. I was the one had to run the heating tape along the pipes and drains and pass it out to them to finish off at the plug-in box. I was the one looking for chinks of light showing from outside, and I was the one stuffing wadding into them. I was also the one stapled polyfilm vapour barrier over the insulation. It took two days and let me tell you, I know of no other job so goddamned miserable.

And after all that insulating against winter draughts and winds, we all of us ignored the place where the skirting was fractured and the wind could blow in at will.

They left, finally, and by then the phone was installed and I had a new big woodshed. There was still enough work left to be done to keep me half occupied for the rest of the summer, but nothing pressing. I wrote them a cheque and we all shook hands and then they left, and not one of us had said a word about the stove wood I'd thrown out of the studio onto the grass. The stove wood was stacked in the old woodshed the next morning, when I woke up to find most of my coffee cream had vanished.

Once the workmen were gone, I went back under the house with the trouble light, back to that horrible thing I had found while I was under there with the insulation. Now that I didn't have to try to appear to be at least partways normal, I could admit to what I was seeing. The old bastard! Evil old bastard! No wonder the goolieguy had driven him off the place!

It was a big metal box, like a tool chest or a steamer trunk, about two feet long, a foot wide, and a foot high. Metal sides, metal top, metal snap-lock, metal handle for carrying it. I opened it, as I had the day I was under there swearing at the fibreglass.

It was hard to tell how big it had been; it was withered and dried like a little brown mummy. Curled up on its side with its tiny knees against its baby chest, its skeleton hands up by its face, and I was sure it had been crying and sucking its thumb when it died. A rotted piece of rope around its waist, like a lasso.

Just like the first time I opened the box and saw the goolieguy baby, I had a fantasy image of a little kid toddling in the field, picking foxglove flowers for momma, and then the Thing coming from the Place, whirling a rope, yelling, running faster than baby legs could run, and then something around the baby's waist, catching it, and big rough hands grabbing and stuffing the baby into this awful, burning thing, this metal monster, this burning, burning, burning, and the lid closing, and burning burning burning.

He hid the box with the baby in it, hid it under the house where his wife wouldn't see, she who had sat crippled by arthritis, watching from the window as the goolieguy moved with her baby, moved hidden in the bush when He was at home; moved openly around the clearing when He was away to town. Away to town to buy more nails to put where a goolieguy might get burned, to buy more metal to keep the goolieguy out of the buildings. Away to town to buy a metal box to hold a baby goolieguy until it died of burning and suffocation, its mother frantic enough to rip the skirting from the porch and try to get to her dying infant.

I could see her as if I had been there, sitting with her knees jack-knifed almost in front of her face, rocking and mourning, reaching out to try to open the box and release her baby, her fingers blistered and bleeding, unable to grasp the metal, unable to open the lid, unable to do anything but go nine-tenths mad knowing the goddamned metal held her child.

And the pain, the terrible pain, rising through the floorboards, flooding the back rooms of the house, poisoning everything until the woman moaned and the prescription was changed, the medicine made stronger and stronger, and still the goolieguy's pain mounted, until the woman's heart stopped.

I took the box out from under the house and carried it to the front yard, and then went into the house and got a clean, fluffy blanket. I lifted the desiccated little mummy-shape from the metal box and laid it on the blanket, and didn't know if I wanted to cry or swear. I didn't know if the goolieguys buried their dead or put them in trees the way Indians used to do or what, so I finally figured the best I could do was do what I'd have done if it had been Bess or even my own kid. I got a shovel and started to dig the hole.

I was crying and digging and sniffling, and then this skinny, long-fingered, brown hand reached from behind me and wrapped around the wooden handle of the shovel. I let go of the shovel and the goolieguy took it from me, walked a few steps and laid the shovel on the grass. Then she moved to the hole, knelt and started to dig with her bare hands. She winced at first, winced every time her hands touched soil that had been dug with the metal shovel, but once past that, everything happened very quickly. Goolieguys have amazing fingernails, about the same shade of brown as the shiny shell of a horse chestnut, about as wide as ours, but probably a hundred times tougher, and, just like a dog can dig up a rat hole quicker than a person can dig with a shovel, a goolieguy can get a two-foot-deep hole done in no time at all. Two feet deep, two feet long, about a foot wide.

She lifted the goolieguy baby, blanket and all, and put it in the grave, then covered its face with a corner of the blanket. I could understand that; it gives me the shivers to think of sleeping forever with dirt in your face. And she moaned a bit, her big, round, dark brown eyes flooded with tears, then she filled in the hole and patted the earth flat again.

The goolieguy is maybe five-foot-two or five-foot-three inches tall, and very slender. Most of her height is in her legs, and her arms hang down—her hands are below her knees when she's standing upright. Long, thin arms and long, thin fingers, nicely shaped, with fine, downy hair on her body and limbs. She's got a face just like you or me or anyone else—not as round, maybe, as most of us, but nothing you'd call animal-like. Little pug of a snub nose, high cheekbones, wide, delicately shaped mouth, and teeth like ours. I'm not a dentist, and I don't know any more about tooth and jaw structure than anyone else knows, but I'd bet you could look at a goolieguy skull and not really know for sure you weren't looking at a person's skull. You might know that person wasn't exactly caucasian, but you'd know you weren't looking at any animal. The goolieguy has lips like ours, except for the colour. Not exactly purple, not exactly blue, but if you've ever seen a kid who has just spent most of the past three hours pigging out on blackberries or blueberries, you've seen the colour of the goolieguy's lips. And when they cry, their bottom lip trembles, just like ours. And their eyes flood tears down their dark brown faces. When a goolieguy kisses you on the cheek, it's like being kissed by any gentle person, and I don't think they hug or cuddle the way we do. I think they pat gently, because that's what the goolieguy did to me; she patted my shoulder repeatedly. Then she left, running graceful as a deer across the clearing, disappearing into the alder and wild cherry scrub.

I took the goddamned metal box to the dump and heaved it in with all the other slime and mud, then stopped at the store on my way back and stocked up on different kinds of cheese and plenty of french bread, a couple of pints of whipping cream and two quarts of half-and-half coffee cream.

In the morning I wakened to the sound of hummingbirds zizzing at the feeder, quarreling with each other. A small rufous was so busy fighting with the others, so busy darting and threatening, she had no time to push her beak into the spigot and drink. She could wind up winning the power struggle and starving herself to death.

I put water on to boil for coffee, put the plastic cone on the porcelain coffee pot, put a paper filter in the cone, measured coffee and stared out the side window at the woodshed, at the clearing, at the brush beyond, and thought of her, swollen and cramped with the agony of arthritis, hurting even when he was being incredibly gentle, unable even to cuddle him without feeling pain, unable to be held and comforted, and I wondered at his frustration. What must he have felt when he discovered that the goolieguy could come into the house and sit quietly on the floor beside the aching woman, sit quietly and, for a while, take the pain and pass it on to some other place, so the woman could sleep without medication, could even hold in her contorted hands a cup of fragrant tea, sip its soothing warmth and relax. What must he have felt on realizing that the goolieguy could reach out with her abnormally long-fingered hands and touch lightly, so lightly that even the most inflamed tissue felt no pain, only comfort and love. What he could not give, the goolieguy gave, what he could not convey, the goolieguy could, and in his own house, to his own wife, until he couldn't stand it any more and went for the first lengths of sheet metal to protect what was his, to claim his own territory, to piss on all his own fence posts like a dog become vicious.

I sat on the front porch, looking down past the studio to the lake. The ducks were feeding in the shallows, bums up more often than their heads. Off beyond the peaks of the mountains, a small dark cloud was creeping eastward, towards the sea. It looked almost lonely in a pale blue sky, where high, thin, white, cirrus clouds streaked gracefully. One small storm looking for a place to happen, too far from here to cause even two seconds worry.

Families have storms too, some of them large, some of them small, most of them kept hidden from the sight and gossiping tongues of outsiders. My mother had been a tempest the crazy bunch had first tried to absorb, then tried to hide and eventually erased.

All the anger was gone, and most of the regret as well. I had no memories of her, no faded photographs, no souvenirs, no keepsakes. I didn't even have any stories given me by someone who had known her. I never learned who she was or where she came from before she met my father. They'd done a good job of erasing her. I had always felt they were trying to erase me too, so that all sign of her ever having drawn breath would be gone. I had no idea how tall or short she had been, whether she had been beautiful or merely pretty, whether she was quiet or bubbling with laughter. Nothing. Any question I had ever asked had been ignored. What I knew about my father you could have poked under your eyelid and not felt discomfort. The oldest son of the oldest son of the oldest son. All the best schools. His first sign of rebellion was his decision to go to university here instead of to a "good" one in Britain. Instinctive genius for business, he pulled the loose ends of a fraying fortune together, guaranteed everyone's continuing comfort, then met and married my mother, and the year after I was born, they both were gone. Died, I supposed.

The family used the money he had protected to hire nursemaids and what they insisted on calling nannies. As soon as I was old enough, they shipped me off to private school. Summer holidays in camps with names I always remembered as Wanna PeePee. Young women I did not know who suddenly appeared at my school to escort me on ten-day Easter holiday tours of the cathedrals of Europe.

And then one summer holiday, it wasn't some adenoidal companion who a few years earlier would have been called nanny; it was my aunt, in jeans and a loose shirt, cotton socks and sneakers, and before the headmistress had time to rally her wits, we were gone, heading off in an improperly racy bright green sports car.

"My god," my aunt said as soon as we were away from the ivy and brick, "we've got to get you some decent clothes!"

I'd lived in school tunics for so many years, it hadn't occurred to me I could wear anything else. I knew, of course, that other people wore other clothes. Somehow they had taught me that was fine for Other People, but not for me.

The first time I saw myself wearing jeans, cotton shirt, white tennis socks and leather sneakers, I felt as if the clothes were wearing me. The second look I took, I recognized myself for the first time in memory. When I sat on a rock on the shore of the lake and felt the sharp blades of my aunt's big paper shears slice off the heavy mane of hair they had taught me to wind in a thick, heavy bun at the nape of my neck, I felt as if my brain was being unwrapped, taken from a thick layer of shit and exposed for the first time in my life to sunshine and fresh breezes. I wept, but not because I felt sorry my hair was being cut.

Actually, I didn't weep at all. I bawled and howled, snoffled and sobbed, and didn't even want to look at my long hair, cut loose from my head. My aunt took it and I have no idea what she did with it. Nor do I care.

Uncle Tony was still functional then. Still laughing, still joking. He played the piano, thundering complex chords that rolled across the lake and came back to us from the opposite hills. He played the guitar, sitting on a stool on the porch, the individual notes almost visible in the air.

I didn't go back to school in Britain. Uncle Tony and my aunt forced them to enroll me in a school on the Island. I still had to wear a tunic, I still had to troop around wearing the school tie, I still didn't live a normal life with normal people, but how could I have done that with the anything-but-normal family I'd inherited? My uncles, in various states of debauchery, dressed to the nines, working overtime to develop cirrhosis. And each of them, for all their stuffy insistence on things of culture and class, wearing rings made out of bent horseshoe nails, for luck.

I would have liked to have known if my mother had ever seen this place, if there was one particular part of it she had liked, some place she went to when being alone was important. If I knew even that much about her, she would be real to me and I could mourn her death, celebrate her life and my own.

I asked my aunt about my parents. Not immediately, but later, when I felt we knew each other a bit. She shook her head, shrugged almost apologetically, and said she knew almost nothing. "Car crash, I heard."

"Nobody tells me anything," I confessed. "I ask and ask, but . . . ."

"Then you have every right to invent the mother you want." She patted my hand.

"No," I argued, "I can't invent her back alive, and that's what I want: a live mother!"

My aunt was like a mother—for a while. Then she disappeared, too. It made headlines for a day or two. Local Artist Vanishes, Police Lack Clues. The headlines withered, the articles got smaller, eventually the mystery diminished to a half-inch filler toward the back of the local rag. Search parties stopped going out into the bush, eventually the Reward For Information posters faded and were taken down in the bus, train and ferry depots, and the only one who seemed aware of the fact something had obviously happened was Uncle Tony, but nobody had listened to him for years. Every time one of his brothers went to visit him, Uncle Tony screamed and raged, and only his canvas restraint jacket held his arms at his sides, kept him from ripping out throats.

They disappeared in a hurry then. It took less than eight years and the whole lot of them went. A suspicious number of Death By Misadventure verdicts, a few Probable Suicide decisions, and some of them incredibly inventive and awful. One seems to have gone to the time and trouble to pry open the gelatin capsules containing his allergy medicine, replacing the medicinal compound with ordinary Drano which, of course, ate holes in his stomach. He'd had an ulcer for years, most drunks develop them, so nobody paid attention to his bellyache until he was bleeding internally so badly even waterglass doses of gin couldn't stop the pain. An ambulance was called, he was taken to hospital screaming and died before they could diagnose anything. The truly bizarre part was, nobody seemed to find it at all odd that the man had put Drano in more capsules than he swallowed. There were four others in the bottle, but nobody discovered that until months later, when another member of the family checked out the same way. That one was deemed an accident, however, because how could he have known how the other had done himself in?

Powerful automobiles wrapped around hydro poles; a speedboat hit a deadhead and five people drowned because they were too drunk to survive, had been too stupid to wear lifejackets. Mostly, though, it was suicide of one sort or another, the self-destructive impulses of generations of alcoholics bubbling suddenly to the surface, demanding something faster than genteel soddenness.

And now there was me and Uncle Tony, and he might as well have been dead. Tony, who went from music to money because the family demanded it, who went by way of the London School of Economics and the World Bank to a rubber room, where he sits reading the Dow Jones Index and muttering spells like some kind of sorcerer. The last coherent thing he said to me was that the International Monetary Fund is a game of Monopoly, and it only matters because so many people continue to pretend it matters.

I put my coffee cup in the house and walked down to the lake. A duck was swimming, with a flotilla of yellow ducklings accompanying her. She was like no wild duck I'd ever seen. She was a light chocolate colour, lighter than a Khaki Campbell domestic duck, bigger than one too, with dark bronze markings in the pattern of a mallard.

I heard something whispering in the bush. I didn't turn to look—you seldom get to see a goolieguy unless she wants to be seen—but the movie began to unroll behind my eyes again; tame ducks, virtually helpless on their own, left to survive or perish by a grief-crazed fool who did nothing more for them than grab the enclosure fencing and rip it open to allow them to wander. And they had; they had wandered down to the lake, propelled by hunger. Small-bodied, unable to fly, they copied what they saw the wild ducks doing, ate what they saw the wild ducks eating, and eventually mated with the mallard drakes, and their offspring, neither wild nor tame, stayed when the others left for the winter. They probably thought the lake was theirs, now.

I had a vision of millet seed, and didn't know it was millet seed until I remembered a canary my aunt had kept here, a stalk of millet hanging in its cage. It could be planted around the rim of the lake; the ducks would feed on it all winter.

I turned to go back to the house, and for a moment I thought I saw my Uncle Tony sitting on the porch, sobbing, unable to play music because he had betrayed his gift, betrayed it by dabbling in the cesspool of family approval, betrayed it by turning his genius to the gathering of money, betrayed it by letting those soulless bastards convince him their standards were the ones that mattered. She would have done better than merely forgiving him, she would have done better than merely understanding why he had done it. She would have loved him. He could have lived here with her, and if he had never again been able to play as well as he once had, well enough to fill concert halls and bring people to their feet crying and cheering, he would have been able to play, play for her, play for himself, play for the goolieguy. But they had taught him not to believe in or trust in love, and because he didn't believe, it wasn't there for him, and he wept, knowing he had thrown away the only salvation possible for any of us.

They did something to her, too. My aunt, I mean. She wasn't one to kill herself, or leave because they'd taken Tony to an asylum. She would have been getting ready to fight them, to bypass the hired beagles and get a decent lawyer, maybe storm into court with writs of habeas corpus or whatever, get Tony out of the quiet, aseptic place where they put coloured pills in your custard and jabbed needles into the slack flesh of your flaccid arm.

But she vanished. In rolling hills, honey-combed with mine shafts; in valleys where ventilation tunnels dropped straight down for two hundred feet, covered by heavy metal plates to keep half the world from falling in. It wouldn't take much. A bump on the head. One burly creep to pick her up and walk off with her, unconscious, until he got to the shaft, pulled aside the big metal plate and tossed her inside, into the dark and the air foul with rat shit and bat droppings. Then put the metal plate back in place and leave. Those shafts are full of gasses of one kind or another, most of them poisonous. And the poor goolieguy digging, digging, digging, unable to get past the crisscross of railroad tracks, the shafts with the metal coal cars still standing, waiting, the winches and machinery slowly rusting in the dripping dampness. A goolieguy whose fingers were seared to the bone, whose poor hands dripped blood as red as our own, trying to dig in a place throbbing with metal, digging and howling like the mad winds of autumn, trying to free the woman who had been kind, who had left bowls of cream, who had bought frozen yogurt and left it where a goolieguy would find it on a hot summer day.

She vanished because she knew something they didn't want anyone else in the family to know. She knew it wasn't necessary to worry about the big game of Monopoly, to turn yourself into something like my four-times great-grandfather, who was willing to bury people for stuff that doesn't really exist or matter. Maybe they'd done in my mother, too. Maybe they didn't trust a man who had the talent to accumulate the invisible and non-existent, but who preferred to turn his energy to other things. Maybe the only reason they hadn't done me in was they thought they could bring me up to be like them, and, after all, I was family, and crazy people get bent out of shape by little things like that.

There was no sense looking for the place the goolieguy had nearly killed herself fighting the metal. The rain forest can cover anything in three years, and it had been far more than three years since she had vanished into thin air. The sword fern, elderberry, salmonberry, alder and evergreen can cover the black scars of forest fire, the abomination of bad logging practices, the ripped-out and vile refuse of mining; they can cover sin, they can cover love. I knew what I knew and that's all I needed. It's all any of us need.

Back at the house again, I tidied up, thinking about gardens. About rows of peas held upright by small sticks, of tomatoes ripe and musty-smelling in the sunshine. Curly kale and swiss chard, collard greens and red leaf lettuce, broccoli and cabbage, cauliflower and eggplant and the magic of bright pumpkins in dark soil. Rows and rows of corn, beets, and beds of green onions and garlic. I'd never had a garden, not really. A few flowers if they wanted to grow, a lawn that needed cutting, but not a real garden.

I whistled to Bess. We went into town to the feed store and I got packages of seed at reduced price because it was several weeks past the time to plant. "Might not get a good crop," the clerk warned, "it's a bit late in the season."

"Better late than never," I quoted, and he grinned as if I'd come up with something original, amusing, and very intelligent. I almost bought a roto-tiller, too, but turned away from it. There was no rational reason why I turned away, but the goolieguy doesn't like machinery.

When we got home, the place where I'd envisioned the garden, the place which had been grass and clover when I left, was dug and ready, the clods of earth broken into fine soil. Instead of daring to intrude, I put the seed packets on the grass and left a small blue cardboard container of imported hothouse cherry tomatoes beside them.

Several miles from the flatland city where I had spent so many years of my life being a fool, there was a roadside stand where farmers had taken their produce and left it to be sold by sun-tanned and smiling teen-agers, out of school for the summer. We would go there on weekends and buy far more of whatever was in season than we needed, and Carol always got cherry tomatoes. She ate them one after the other, the way some people eat grapes. She never put them in the fridge, she left them out so they would be warm; she said chilling them took the sunshine taste out of them.

She had loved me so completely and unquestioningly. I moved to a flat, dry, yellow place, not because I loved her, but because I needed the love I knew she had for me. Every love affair, every relationship is uneven. There is always one person loves stronger, more, better, more completely, and the one who loves the most, gives the most, and gets less in return. And maybe that is what love is, the giving without thought of what might come back in return. It can't be easy to try to hold something with an open hand.

She loved me so much she did not get custody of her daughter, and saw her only at intervals, for part of Easter and summer holidays. And not at all at Christmas. When her daughter arrived, I always found a perfectly good reason to go somewhere else within a couple of days. Gwen would bring silly chatter and clattering feet, would get Bess wound up like a hysterical mutt; mealtimes became clattering of knives and forks and jokes like, "How do you know if there's an elephant sleeping in bed with you? Because he's got a big picture of a peanut on his pyjama shirt." Carol would laugh happily and I would try to smile as if I meant it, but it didn't seem funny to me, it seemed ridiculous. And so, within two or three days, I would absolutely have to go somewhere for some absolutely legitimate reason, and by the time I got back, Gwen would have returned to her father's apartment, three hundred miles away, where the "stepmother" figure changed every year or so.

We were supposed to take a vacation together, everything was planned, and then the phone call from the ex-husband and everything got changed. Instead of coming in August, Gwen would come as soon as school let out; instead of staying a month, Gwen would stay six weeks. My whole summer turned inside out because one unofficial stepmother was leaving to make room for another, and it would be best all round if the new one was given a period of time to adapt without having Gwen there because it seemed Gwen was showing signs of being upset and disturbed; the school marks had not been up to expectations; there had even been, perish the thought, arguments and visits to the school counselor.

And who had thought to ask me how I felt about it? Too many people had, for too long, had too much control over my life. And no more! Carol wouldn't argue about it, she wouldn't even talk about it, she just quietly made arrangements to have her holiday time rescheduled to accommodate the kid's arrival.

I left before the kid got there. Left, and discovered within minutes that what I had taken so lightly for so long had become such a part of me that just knowing it was over was pain. I'd been away from Carol before for days, even weeks, and not felt this cold, burning hole in my stomach. I knew she'd be there when I went back. But two blocks from the house, knowing I was not going to go back, never going to be held by her again, never going to hear her soft laughter in the lilac dusk of our bedroom, something started to burn and every day it took more and more of my energy to not confront what I had done, not look at what it was going to mean.

I heard a chittering, high-pitched, half melody, and turned to see the goolieguy standing by the corner of the house, beckoning with her long-fingered hand. I went to see what it was she wanted, and she was standing with the blue cardboard carton in one hand, picking little tomatoes one at a time with her other hand, putting them carefully in her mouth, and eating them slowly. The garden was planted, straight rows, spaced maybe eighteen inches apart, marked by little sticks at each end.

I would have sworn I could taste the slightly acid tang of tomato in my own mouth, and I understood why the goolieguy was trembling with joy. So many years without the taste of tomato. Think of it. An ordinary thing like that, but it had been denied her because, in the time she should have been tending a garden, she was insane with pain, trying to help a woman who had dared to show the family the power of love. And the garden died, and with it the seeds the goolieguy might have saved and planted for herself. Years and years without the tang of tomato, without the crunch of green onion or the delicate wonder of fresh green peas.

And Uncle Tony had let them do it. Hell, he had helped them do it! And he knew it. Knew it and sat blubbering when what he ought to have done was come down off the porch, run across the grass to the door of the studio, and yell I Love You! She would have stopped what she was doing, she would have put aside whatever it was and gone to him and taken his hand and laughed up and said I Know You Do, and they could have gone down to the lake together and had a life.

"Hi," I said into the phone, "is your mother there?"

"She's at work," Gwen said cheerfully. "Where are you?"

"When will she be home?" I avoided the kid's question. If you answer one, she's got six more waiting in the wings, and I wasn't up to it.

"She'll be back in about an hour. Where are you?" she repeated.

"When are you going back to your dad's place?" I countered.

"I asked first," she said, in that cheeky tone that means she isn't going to back off until she gets her answer.

"I've been busy," I evaded.

"Yeah? Doing what?"

"Insulating my new house, among other things. If it's any of your business."

"It's my business," she said angrily. "Of course it's my business! What new house?"

"When are you going back to your dad's place?" I repeated. "I answered, now it's your turn."

"You never answered. I asked where you were, you talk about a new house. You don't say where it is, so I don't know where you are!"

"That's a secret," I said. "Maybe a surprise. Stretch yourself, you brat, trust me."

There was a long silence. What reason did she have to trust me? She hardly knew me. I was a signature on birthday cards Carol bought.

"I don't want to go back to my dad's place," she said, her voice trembling. "I think I'll run away if they try to make me."

"They who?"

"You know. Them. Custody people, I guess."

"Fuck'em," I said, and was surprised at how much I meant it. "If I give you my phone number, will you make sure your mother calls me? Please?"

"Sure," she said easily. "What's your new house like?"

"Gorgeous," I said. "It's got a spook lives in the bush. Like an elf or a leprechaun, only taller."

"Oh, I just bet." She was laughing that high-pitched cackle that so often had annoyed me to the point of wanting to slap her. Now it sounded like the kind of laugh that makes it almost impossible not to join in and laugh along with her.

Carol phoned back two hours later, and I knew the kid was hanging around, trying to hear at least that half of the conversation. Ordinarily that would have enraged me, but it didn't seem to matter. The goolieguy was twittering around the side of the house, fussing with the rose bushes, and that didn't bother me; why should a human kid bother me? I told Carol where I was and I told her I was staying at the old place, wasted some time telling her about the repairs and such, and then asked, if I bought the plane tickets, would she come out for a visit. "Gwen is living with me now," she said, her voice carefully controlled, her tone neutral.

"I gathered as much from Gwen," I said, my tone as neutral as hers.

"She doesn't want to go back to her father's place."

"That's what she told me," I agreed stupidly. "Ask her how she feels about a lake and a creek and some hummingbirds." And I tried not to feel as if Carol's sigh of relief had knifed into my throat.

The goolieguy came to the window of the music room and stared in at the sound system, her eyes wide with longing. I watched her until she looked at me, twittered pleadingly, and then I beckoned for her to come inside. She isn't comfortable in the house, and has to watch where she's putting her long, thin, bare feet, because if she steps where there's a nail, even if the head of it is pounded down below the level of the surface of the board, it hurts her. She can't go near the stove, of course, and can only open the door of the fridge by using a stick to hook the handle on the door and pull it open, but I know she comes inside when she wants to, so there was no reason to think she wouldn't come in when invited.

I showed her how she could use a yardstick to push the button on the sound system and turn it on, how a second push could turn it off. I demonstrated several times, then handed her the yardstick and gestured. And then the music was playing and she was grinning happily. I opened the window to let the music outside, and the goolieguy jumped easily over the waist-high sill, onto the porch, then over the porch rail to the grass.

Some people laugh and say herons are ungainly, awkward, even clumsy, but I have always thought them graceful. And a goolieguy dancing in the sunlight reminds me of a heron walking slowly, proudly, in shallow water, lifting each leg deliberately, placing it exactly where she wants it to be, totally a part of her own world.

The music was playing when I drove Carol and Gwen up to the house, and neither of them asked why I had left the sound system on, or why it was turned up so loud. Of course Gwen fell in love with the studio and wanted to sleep there instead of in the main house, and things between Carol and I were such that it seemed a good idea when she put her sleeping bag on the built-in bed next to Gwen's blue one. But on the fourth day, Carol brought her suitcase into the house and put it down on the floor in my bedroom. I know for a fact Bess slept on the bed in the studio, curled up beside Gwen, breaking half the rules of existence that night—or, at least, those rules imposed by me for reasons which no longer seemed the least bit important.

"I guess you weren't kidding," Gwen said softly, sitting cross-legged on the grass between Carol and me. "I guess there really is a spook in the bush here, eh?"

"Does she scare you?" I asked, not looking at the kid because I'm still not sure what it is I feel when I look at her. Amazement, maybe.

"No. Not scared. But. . .I bet if I told people, they'd think I was nuts."

"I'm not sure," I admitted. "People don't admit that they believe she exists but. . .there are a lot of people here who will deny she doesn't!"

"But not a leprechaun," Gwen said firmly. And so I told her what the youngest workie had told me, and some, not much, but some of what I had experienced myself in the time I had been here. And all the time, Carol stared at us as if she wasn't sure we shouldn't both be put in a jar and the lid screwed on tightly.

"What does she want?" the kid asked uneasily.

"Nothing," I said. "Everything," I amended.

"I think she likes me," Gwen blushed.

"I'm sure she does," I agreed. And I told her about ice cream cones and about tropical fruit, about coffee cream and soft bread, and she nodded. "If you tell people," I laughed, "they'll tell you that I'm as crazy as everyone else in my family, and they'll insist it's raccoons or cats eat the food."

"Are you?" Gwen asked. "Crazy, I mean?"

"Sure I am," I said, and it didn't hurt to admit it. "I'm absolutely insane. In a world like this one, a person would have to be a fool to want to be sane and normal and like everyone else, " The kid began cackling wildly, and Carol was staring at me, laughing, but not at me. Never at me.

"The goolieguy," I said, tears pouring easily, "really believes in love, and all she wants is for some of us to be willing to defend love at least half as fiercely as we're wiling to defend stupid stuff like private property and money. To put as much effort into learning how to love as we're willing to put into learning how to balance a chequebook." I knew both of them could see me crying, but they didn't take it as a sign of weakness or stupidity or of anything other than that I was crying, and we ought to be able to do that as easily and unselfconsciously as we laugh. Or argue. "I guess I have a long way to go," I admitted. "It isn't as easy as it sounds."

Even pot-bellied legal beagles can come in handy. You treat them like shaman's rattles and wave them in the face of the ones pestering you, and the bothersome interference backs off, leaves you alone.

The kid is as noisy as a Stellar's jay and as undisciplined as any supposed savage. There is no school tunic, no highly polished oxford shoes, no boarding school; she lives here and every weekday morning Carol drives her down the Lakes Road to the highway to catch the bus to school.

There's a new building on the place now, out behind the orchard at the edge of the clearing. Brick and mortar and a fitted tile roof, with big windows for light and a stone fireplace where, on wet winter days, a bed of warm embers can keep the place warm. A thick, foam-stuffed mattress and some warm blankets, and the cheerful orange bowl in the middle of the table always has grapes or tangerines, apples, and even peaches in it. Cottage cheese and fresh fruit can make a goolieguy vibrate with pleasure.

The metal roof is gone from the main house, we leave the pickup parked halfway down the hill and all the metal pots and pans have been replaced with glass. The metal knives, forks and spoons are silver now, and Carol insisted on covering the floor with glazed pottery tiles, so that even an inexperienced baby goolieguy can come in the house without burning her toes on the fire from the nail heads in the flooring.

They aren't that different from us. All they want is a bit of room, a bit of acceptance, a chance to be what they are, to become what they are capable of becoming. A chance at a bit of love, and the freedom to love in return.